PRAISE FOR ME[...]

"With her wonderful characters and [...] Foster is a must-read author!"

—*New York Times* bestseller Julie Kenner

"Melissa Foster is syn[...]s with sexy, swoony, heartfelt romance!"

—*New York Times* bestseller Lauren Blakely

"You can always rely on Melissa Foster to deliver a story that's fresh, emotional, and entertaining."

—*New York Times* bestseller Brenda Novak

"Melissa Foster writes worlds that draw you in, with strong heroes and brave heroines surrounded by a community that makes you want to crawl right on through the page and live there."

—*New York Times* bestseller Julia Kent

"When it comes to contemporary romances with realistic characters, an emotional love story, and smokin'-hot sex, author Melissa Foster always delivers!"

—*The Romance Reviews*

"Foster writes characters that are complex and loyal, and each new story brings further depth and development to a redefined concept of family."

—*RT Book Reviews*

"Melissa Foster definitely knows how to spin a tale and keep you flipping the pages."

—*Book Loving Fairy*

BROADVIEW LIBRARY

NO LONGER PROPERTY OF SEATTLE PUBLIC LIBRARY

RECEIVED

DEC 08 2021

BROADVIEW LIBRARY

"You can never go wrong with the heroes that Melissa Foster creates. She hasn't made one yet that I haven't fallen in love with."

—*Natalie the Biblioholic*

"Melissa is a very talented author that tells fabulous stories that captivate you and keep your attention from the first page to the last page. Definitely an author that you will want to keep on your go-to list."

—*Between the Coverz*

"Melissa Foster writes the best contemporary romance I have ever read. She does it in bundles, tops it with great plots, hot guys, strong heroines, and sprinkles it with family dynamics—you got yourself an amazing read."

—*Reviews of a Book Maniac*

"[Melissa Foster] has a way with words that endears a family in our hearts, and watching each sibling and friend go on to meet their true love is such a joy!"

—*Thoughts of a Blonde*

Maybe We Should

MORE BOOKS BY MELISSA FOSTER

LOVE IN BLOOM ROMANCE SERIES

SNOW SISTERS

Sisters in Love
Sisters in Bloom
Sisters in White

THE BRADENS

Lovers at Heart, Reimagined
Destined for Love
Friendship on Fire
Sea of Love
Bursting with Love
Hearts at Play
Taken by Love
Fated for Love
Romancing My Love
Flirting with Love
Dreaming of Love
Crashing into Love
Healed by Love
Surrender My Love
River of Love
Crushing on Love
Whisper of Love
Thrill of Love

THE BRADENS & MONTGOMERYS

Embracing Her Heart
Anything for Love
Trails of Love

Wild, Crazy Hearts
Making You Mine
Searching for Love
Hot for Love
Sweet, Sexy Heart

BRADEN NOVELLAS

Promise My Love
Our New Love
Daring Her Love
Story of Love
Love at Last
A Very Braden Christmas

THE REMINGTONS

Game of Love
Stroke of Love
Flames of Love
Slope of Love
Read, Write, Love
Touched by Love

SEASIDE SUMMERS

Seaside Dreams
Seaside Hearts
Seaside Sunsets
Seaside Secrets
Seaside Nights
Seaside Embrace
Seaside Lovers

HARBORSIDE NIGHTS SERIES

Catching Cassidy
Discovering Delilah
Tempting Tristan

STAND-ALONE NOVELS

Chasing Amanda (mystery/suspense)
Come Back to Me (mystery/suspense)
Have No Shame (historical fiction/romance)
Love, Lies & Mystery (three-book bundle)
Megan's Way (literary fiction)
Traces of Kara (psychological thriller)
Where Petals Fall (suspense)

Maybe We Should

Silver Harbor, Book Two

MELISSA FOSTER

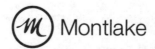 Montlake

This is a work of fiction. Names, characters, organizations, places, events, and incidents are either products of the author's imagination or are used fictitiously.

Text copyright © 2021 by Melissa Foster
All rights reserved.

No part of this book may be reproduced, or stored in a retrieval system, or transmitted in any form or by any means, electronic, mechanical, photocopying, recording, or otherwise, without express written permission of the publisher.

Published by Montlake, Seattle

www.apub.com

Amazon, the Amazon logo, and Montlake are trademarks of Amazon.com, Inc., or its affiliates.

ISBN-13: 9781542027663
ISBN-10: 1542027667

Cover design by Letitia Hasser

Cover photography by Regina Wamba of MaeIDesign.com

Printed in the United States of America

For everyone who has suffered at the hands of others

CHAPTER ONE

THE WARM SUMMER sun beat down on Cait Weatherby's shoulders as she came to Brighton Marsh at the end of her three-mile hike through the wildlife refuge on Silver Island. She dropped her backpack in the sand and gazed past the marshy inlet to the ocean in the distance, remembering when she was a little girl and had dreamed of walking into the sea and becoming a mermaid. She'd imagined basking in the freedom of the water and reveling in the beauty of the changing tides. She couldn't even swim, but she'd always felt a kinship with the sea, coming and going under the cover of night, guided by the light of the moon. It had been a long time since she'd needed that camouflage, but the ghosts of her past still hovered, ever-present reminders of how quickly things could change.

Those ghosts were a burden she was sick of carrying, but short of having her memory erased, she had no idea how to get out from under them. She planted her hands on her hips and focused on the beauty before her instead of getting lost in the past. Long lush grasses sprouted through the surface of the murky water like thick patches of spiky hair swishing in the late-afternoon breeze. The pungent aroma of sulfur hung in the air. It was a natural deterrent to most hikers, and since Cait treasured her privacy, this spot had quickly become one of her favorites.

She'd discovered the refuge when she'd overheard a customer talking about it at the beachfront restaurant she'd inherited a little more than three months ago from the birth mother she'd never known, Ava de Messiéres. Cait's life had been forever changed when she'd been summoned to the island by Shelley Steele, one of Ava's closest friends, to go over the details of Ava's will. In the span of one afternoon, Cait had discovered the identity of her birth mother, inherited one-third of the Bistro and one-third of Ava's cottage, and learned that she had two half sisters—Deirdra, a strong-willed, stressed-out attorney who lived in Boston, and Abby, a sweet, free-spirited chef who had returned to the island from New York for a fresh start. Abby had since fallen madly in love and gotten engaged to Aiden Aldridge, one of the nicest guys Cait had ever met. Abby had welcomed Cait into her life without hesitation, and together with Aiden, they'd revitalized the Bistro, while Deirdra had been less trusting of her at first. Cait knew all about distrust. Hell, she was the queen of it. But as she had learned to trust her newfound sisters, Deirdra had learned to trust her, and they'd become close, texting often to keep in touch.

Most days Cait still had a hard time wrapping her head around the impact of the last few months. She'd gone from wondering where she'd come from to having a blood-related family, a new group of friends, and a new life that she was trying to fit into her old one—the life she loved on Cape Cod, where she worked at Wicked Ink as a tattooist and body piercer. The owner, Tank Wicked, was the closest thing she'd ever had to a best friend. She loved the broody biker and his family. Now she traveled between Silver Island and the Cape, working at the Bistro and at Wicked Ink. As much as she loved the people and the jobs at both locations, traveling back and forth was exhausting. She knew she needed to figure out her future before she wore herself down, but how could she choose when one life offered the safety she'd come to count on and the other held the promise of a new beginning with her *real* family?

She knelt in the warm sand and opened her backpack, withdrawing one of her many sketchbooks and a water bottle. She sat down with the pad in her lap and took a drink, thinking about how blessed she was to have *two* families. Well, technically she had *three*, since she'd been adopted as a baby. Her adoptive mother had died when she was four, but her snake of an adoptive father was still alive and well in Connecticut. Not that she ever wanted to see him again.

As she'd done forever, she buried thoughts of the two-faced man who had raised her and opened her sketchbook, refusing to let memories of him ruin her afternoon. Her chest squeezed at the sight of the unopened letter Ava had left for her. Abby and Deirdra had also been given letters. Abby had read hers, and it had helped her move on with her life, but Deirdra had so much pent-up resentment for their alcoholic mother, Cait had doubts she'd ever read it.

She ran her fingers over Ava's loopy handwriting on the front of the envelope, feeling a sense of peace and apprehension. She'd always wondered if she'd been unwanted and forgotten. Now she knew neither was the case. Only seventeen at the time of Cait's birth, Ava had been forced by her overbearing parents to give her up. She'd turned to alcohol to numb her pain and had run away, eventually coming to Silver Island for a fresh start, where she'd met Olivier, the Frenchman who had owned the Bistro. He'd helped her get sober, and they'd married a year later. Soon after, they'd tracked down Cait's adoptive parents. After Ava's death, Cait and her sisters found letters and pictures of Cait that her adoptive mother had sent to Ava every month like clockwork. The letters—and life as Cait had known it—had stopped when Cait was four and her adoptive mother had passed away.

She'd never forget the flood of emotions she'd felt when Shelley handed her the letter, but she still couldn't bring herself to read it. She *wanted* to read it and had imagined all the lovely things Ava might have written. But if she'd learned one thing from her difficult upbringing, it was that there was always another shoe waiting to drop, as if they were as plentiful as rain. She wanted to pretend her life was beautiful for just a little while longer before diving into whatever her birth mother had wanted to get off her chest, *just in case.*

She went back to flipping the pages of her sketchbook, and her pulse quickened at a sketch of Brant Remington. Too hot and charming for his own good, the dimple-cheeked, flirtatious man had been hitting on her since the day they'd met, when she'd first come to the island. He made her feel things she'd never felt before, like the butterflies currently taking flight in her stomach at the mere thought of him. She quickly turned the pages to shut those buggers down, stopping on a drawing she'd been working on of Aiden proposing to Abby the day she and Cait had won the Best of the Island Restaurant Competition. He'd proposed in front of everyone *at* the award ceremony, like he couldn't hold back a second longer. Cait couldn't imagine being loved that much. Abby and Aiden were getting married in the fall, and she planned to give them the picture as a wedding present.

As she began working on the sketch of Abby, wide-eyed and teary, and Aiden down on one knee, looking at her like she was all he ever wanted, Cait filled with longing to be as openhearted as they were. She was anything *but* open, especially toward men.

A high-pitched *yelp* cut through the silence, bringing Cait to her feet. She brushed the sand from the backs of her legs, trying to figure out where the noise had come from. Splashing sounds and strangled cries sent chills down her spine. She hurried to the water's edge as more cries rang out, and her eyes caught on ripples coming from the right. She ran along the shore, searching the water with her heart in her throat, and spotted an animal's tiny snout poking through the surface. It *yelped* again and went under the water. *Oh no! What was that? A cat?* She couldn't let it drown.

"I'm coming!"

Scrambling to untie her boots as fast as she could, she looked around to be sure she was alone and pulled off her top and shorts. She hurried into the water, her feet sinking into the muck at the bottom. When the water hit her waist, she held her arms out to her sides, telling herself she was *fine, fine, fine.* The cold, murky water inched up her stomach, and the animal's head bobbed a few yards away, its tiny yelps tearing at her. Her next step met emptiness, and she sank, screaming as she went under and was swallowed by darkness. She fought her way back up toward the surface and gasped for air. Arms flailing, legs kicking, she lunged for the animal—and missed—sinking beneath the surface again. She'd only just found her sisters, and now she was going to drown in the marsh, and nobody would ever find her *or* the animal she was trying to save! She hadn't survived the horror of her father just to die in this muck. She fought her way up to the surface and grabbed the tiny beast with one hand, holding its frail body up above her head as she sank again despite her frantic efforts, taking the animal down with her.

Nononono!

She clutched the animal to her chest, holding her breath, one arm grasping for the surface, legs kicking frantically. Something thick and strong circled her waist, hauling her back against something hard. She fought to free herself, clutching the animal she was trying to save. Were there man-eating octopuses or maniacal anacondas on Silver Island? *Oh God!* Suddenly she was thrust to the surface, and she gasped a breath just as her foot connected with whatever held her, and a deep male voice shouted, "*Cait!* It's *me!*"

Clutching the tiny animal, she looked over her shoulder, catching a glimpse of electric-blue eyes as she sank beneath the surface again and was instantly hauled back up.

"Cait, it's me, *Brant!*"

Brant! She threw an arm around him, gasping and coughing.

"*Stop* kicking me!" he snapped. "*Jesus.* Are you *trying* to kill me?"

In her panic-stricken state, she hadn't realized she was still kicking. *I'mokayI'mokayI'mokay.* She tried to calm herself down, but her pulse was racing and her lungs hurt.

"I've got you, Cait," he said reassuringly.

She froze, having heard him say those exact words in her dreams. Their eyes collided, sparking the nerve-racking connection she'd spent

5

the last few months trying to deny. It wasn't just the heat blazing between them that had rattled her since she'd first set eyes on him. She was practiced at ignoring lust. It was the *way* he looked at her, as if he saw all the parts of her she tried to hide, making their connection feel deeper, even more intense than any other.

"*Cait!* Are you okay?"

His voice snapped her from her frenzied state, and she was suddenly hyperaware of his strong arms around her and their bodies touching *all* over. *God*, he felt good. *Too good*, setting off her warning bells. She pushed back, but he wouldn't let her go.

"What're you doing? You can't swim."

"I just . . ." *Pull yourself together.* The possibility of drowning was nothing compared to the thought of losing herself in those all-seeing eyes. She drew upon the trick she'd honed over the years to keep from showing fear, tears, or panic and conjured memories of the feel of her mother's hand holding hers, birds soaring, and mermaids swimming, locking down her emotions and forcing herself into a calmer state.

"Sorry." The confidence she'd also honed during those desperate years took hold, and she felt more in control. She narrowed her eyes. "Can you get your hand off my *butt* now?"

Brant grinned, revealing those panty-melting dimples. "Where would you *like* my hand?"

She rolled her eyes.

He moved his hand to her back and headed toward the shore with Cait pressed tight against him. "Whose dog is that?"

"Dog?"

He cocked his brow. "The one you're holding."

She looked down at the animal she'd forgotten she was holding, and sure enough, it was a tiny dog with a crooked mouth and two teeth sticking out. It looked like a wet rat, and it was trembling. Its tongue shot out and licked Cait's skin.

Brant's eyes drilled into hers. "Lucky dog."

"Brant!" Cait snapped, earning one of his lighthearted sexy laughs.

He kept his arm around her as her feet touched the mushy bottom of the marsh, and they made their way out of the water. Brant was a sought-after boatbuilder, and he owned the only marine equipment supply company on the island. He'd grown up there and seemed to know, and was loved by, everyone. But Cait had firsthand experience with guys who spun webs of kindness, luring in their prey to lower their defenses and then striking at precisely the right time to bring them to their knees. That was why she no longer attempted to have long-term relationships with men. If she needed to scratch a sexual itch, she did it with someone who didn't matter, when *she* was in control of who, where, and when, and she didn't do it often.

"Are you okay?" he asked as they stepped onto the shore. "What happened out there?"

She clung to the dog, Brant's voice turning to white noise as her eyes moved over his broad, muscular chest, down the treasure trail bisecting his abs, to his drenched shorts clinging to *everything*.

"Are you going to answer me or check me out?"

Her eyes darted up to his smirking face, and she felt her cheeks burn. What was wrong with her? She never checked out guys like that. It had officially been *way* too long since she'd scratched that particular itch. "Where am I supposed to look when you're strutting around like you're on *Baywatch*?"

He cocked a grin. "Maybe now you'll dream about me in lifeguard shorts."

"Shut up," she said with a laugh, trying *not* to think about how he appeared in her dreams, because she didn't understand them. She'd always had vivid dreams, but since she'd met Brant, he monopolized them. She'd had *three* recurring dreams about him, which was odd in and of itself and made her nervous. In one dream, she was in a dark tunnel and Brant was shrouded in moonlight at the other end, beckoning her toward him. In another, he was holding her in a room she didn't recognize, and she was trembling and staring at the word *paradise* hanging in the distance. The third dream was a scorcher. In it, they were tangled up in each other, lost in the throes of passion, and in all three dreams, he was whispering, *I've got you.*

"I'm serious, Cait," he said firmly. "What happened out there?"

She held the trembling dog tighter. "He was drowning, and I went in after him. I didn't expect the bottom to drop off the way it did."

He reached out to pet the dog, his eyes never leaving hers. "That's pretty brave for someone who can't swim."

She hated that he'd seen her in such a vulnerable state. "I'd call it *stupid*, considering I nearly killed both of us." She felt a pang in her chest and brushed her chin over the dog's head. *I'm sorry, buddy.*

Brant lifted his hand from the dog and ran the backs of his fingers down Cait's cheek, causing goose bumps to chase over her flesh. "Nobody's dying today. Not on my watch." His eyes trailed down the length of her, taking on a seductive glint. "I pegged you as having a thing for black lingerie. Pink is *much* hotter."

She'd forgotten she was in her underwear. "Don't gawk at me!"

She stalked toward her boots and clothes piled on the ground a few feet away and had a momentary bite of curiosity about what Brant thought of her many tattoos. He'd seen her in tank tops but never in shorts, much less with her stomach bared. She wasn't so heavily tattooed that her skin was totally covered, but she had several tattoos, and Brant didn't seem to have any reaction at all to the ink. Only to her body, and she could still feel him checking her out as he followed her.

"Where am I supposed to look when you're prancing around like a Victoria's Secret model?" He plucked his shirt off the ground.

He was ridiculous. There was nothing remarkable about her tall, thin body. She gave him a deadpan stare, having trouble tamping down her smile. He had that effect on her. He made her smile more than anyone ever had. "Now you're really grasping at straws. I have practically no boobs, and I'm built like a lanky guy."

"Not like any guy I've ever known."

She kissed the dog's head and held him out toward Brant. "Can you hold him for me and *turn around* while I get dressed?"

He took the dog, his eyes sweeping down her body again. "Definitely *not* like a guy." He tossed her the shirt he'd picked up. "Put this on."

"I have my own clothes." She clutched his shirt to cover herself, her clothes still piled at her feet.

He made kissing sounds, and Scrappy licked his lips. "Trust me, Cait, you don't want to have marsh muck all over your clothes."

Cait turned around to put on the shirt, and Brant said, "That's not a guy's ass, either."

She glowered over her shoulder as the shirt tumbled down to cover her butt, and she saw an athletic-looking sandy-haired guy coming up the trail behind him. "Who is that?" she asked, taking the dog from him.

Brant turned. "That's Robert Osten, the manager of the refuge. He went to school with my younger brothers. Mayor Osten is his father." He waved. "Hey, Robert. How's it going?"

"You tell me." Robert's brows knitted as he looked at Cait standing behind Brant. "Everything okay?"

"Yes, *fine*, thank you," Cait answered.

"Robert, this is Cait Weatherby, Abby and Deirdra's half sister. She had a little run-in with the marsh."

"I was *saving* this dog," she explained. "It nearly drowned."

Robert's kind eyes warmed. "It's nice to finally meet you, Cait. I've heard a lot about you."

Cait was still getting used to being part of such a small community. Things were different here than on the Cape, where she could exist in a comfortable bubble of anonymity. "It's nice to meet you, too."

"I'm sorry I missed the grand opening of the Bistro. I hear that you and Abby did a great job of fixing it up," Robert said.

The Bistro had gotten a tremendous amount of buzz before the grand opening last month, and they'd been packed ever since.

"Thanks. We had a lot of help." Aiden, Brant, and a few of Abby's other friends had pitched in to help paint and clean up the Bistro.

"I'll have to get over there and check it out sometime." Robert nodded toward the dog. "I'm glad you saved that little guy. I've been trying to catch him for weeks. I've already reported him to animal control. Do you want me to take him in?"

"No," Brant and Cait said in unison.

Robert smiled. "Okay, then. I'll just notify them that the dog has been found. Who should they call if the owner turns up?"

"Me," they said at the same time.

Cait looked at Brant incredulously. "I found him."

"And I rescued you both," Brant reminded her. "Since *you* won't come home with me, it's only fair that we share custody of the dog."

Robert stifled a laugh.

"Share custody of a dog?" *This guy . . .*

"Think about it. You can't bring him to the restaurant when you work, and I'm sure you don't want to leave him alone all day." He petted the dog again. "Look at him. He's terrified."

She looked at the dog's sad eyes staring up at her. "I hadn't thought about what to do while I'm at work." She handled the inventory and accounting at the Bistro, and when needed, she worked as a hostess or waitress.

"I'll take him to the marina with me during the day and bring him to you at the Bistro so you can have him in the evenings," Brant suggested. "I'm there all the time anyway." He came into the Bistro often to grab a meal or sit out front and listen to Jagger Jones, their musician and part-time cook, play his guitar—or, according to Abby, to flirt with Cait.

"What about when I go back to the Cape? I'm going tomorrow night and won't be back until Wednesday night." Cait's schedule varied from week to week, depending on her clientele at Wicked Ink and the needs of the Bistro.

"We'll figure that out." He winked and looked at Robert. "I guess you can get in touch with me."

Cait gathered her things and put on her boots as Robert and Brant finished talking.

When Robert left to complete his afternoon check of the property, Brant picked up Cait's backpack, studying her with a serious expression. "Now that you're okay, I can say this: You scared the shit out of me. I'm going to teach you to swim so the next time you have the urge to be Aquawoman, you won't get yourself in trouble."

"You don't need to teach me to swim."

"Yes, I do. It'll be much more fun than drowning. I promise." He slung her backpack over his shoulder. "What were you doing here anyway?"

"I hike here sometimes. What were you doing here?"

"I was out for a run." He raised his brows flirtatiously. "Come on, we'll rinse off in the shower at the marina. I'll wash your back."

"I'm *not* showering with you," she said as they headed down the sandy path. "My bike's in the parking lot. I can shower at home."

"I was only thinking of conserving water."

She rolled her eyes, smiling again.

"You can keep trying to deny the heat between us, but we both know that won't last."

It *had* to last, because getting together with Brant was not an option, even if he was doing his best to wear her down every chance he got. She felt too much toward him, and history told her not to trust her instincts. Besides, she didn't have room in her complicated life for a man who made her feel out of control, much less one of Abby's close friends. The last thing she needed was to get together with him, get hurt, and put her sisters in the uncomfortable position of having to choose between their newly discovered sibling and a friend they'd known forever.

"You barely know me," she said flatly.

"I know you do your best to avoid being alone with me, and you're careful, and witty when you want to be." His tone was dead serious. "I know you put your arm across your stomach when you're nervous, and you light up when you see Abby and Aiden together. And the thing I like most of all is that you're less wary around me now than you were three months ago."

She looked away, feeling *too* seen, and caught herself sliding her arm across her stomach. She quickly dropped it to her side and focused on the trail ahead.

"I'll tell you what else I know," he said in a less-serious tone. "You can't ride a bike with a scared dog, and we have to take him to the vet to get him checked out and buy him—or *her*—food and toys."

She was impressed that he'd already thought about all those things. She lifted the pooch over her head, eyeing his plumbing, and said, "*Him.*"

"How about that? We've got a son."

"You're so weird." She laughed softly.

"I'm taking that as a compliment." He whipped out his phone and poked around on it as they followed the trail up a hill. "We'll toss your bike in the back of my truck and swing by my place so I can change, since it's closer than yours. Then we'll stop by yours before heading out." He put his phone to his ear, and a second later, he said, "*Whitney*, how are you, beautiful?"

"Seriously?" Cait whispered.

He winked. "That's good to hear. Listen, I found a stray dog, and he's in pretty bad shape. Think you can get Doc Davis to fit us in?" He paused. "Great. You're the best. See you then."

"Do you flirt with every woman you know?" Cait asked as he pocketed his phone.

"That wasn't flirting. That was charming my way into a vet appointment for Scrappy. We have to be there in an hour. They close at seven."

She raised her brows. "Scrappy?"

"Scooby-Doo's nephew. Have you got a better name in mind?"

"I think Scrappy-Doo was Scooby's brother," she said as they walked around prickly bushes encroaching on the trail.

"Nope. He was his nephew."

"Are you sure?" She hadn't watched many cartoons as a kid, but she used to like drawing the characters.

"I'm positive." He draped an arm over her shoulder. "We're watching *Scooby-Doo* tonight, darlin'."

She shrugged him off. *What have I gotten myself into?*

A little while later they pulled into the Seaview cottage community, passing a large house at the entrance and several cute cedar-sided cottages lining the gravel road. Brant was so rugged, Cait had imagined him living in the woods or on a boat, not in a neighborhood with adorable cottages that all looked alike. She stole a glance at him as he pulled into a driveway. They'd driven home with the windows down, and his brown hair had partially dried in thick waves. He usually wore a bright blue baseball cap, and she liked seeing him without it. He had a nice face—kind and handsome—with a few days' worth of scruff, as if shaving were an afterthought he didn't have time for.

They climbed out of his truck, and Cait waited on the sidewalk with Scrappy as he headed up to the front door. "Don't you want to come in?"

She shook her head. "I'm fine out here."

"Okay. I'll grab a bowl of water and some food for Scrappy. We'll have to clean him up, too." He motioned to the side yard. "The back is fenced, if you want to take him out there."

As he headed inside, Cait walked around back, wondering how he had convinced her to go along with his plans. The backyard was buffered from the neighbors by trees and bushes. There was an outdoor shower and a nice-size patio with a wicker couch, two lounge chairs, and a large glass dining table for six, with a blue umbrella. She set Scrappy down, and he stared up at her, shaking. Now that his matted fur was drying, she saw that he was a Yorkie. His back was black and his head and legs were gold. He was all skin and bones, and the right side of his mouth was higher than the left. She crouched and loved him up. "It's okay, buddy. We're going to get you all checked out and fed."

The back door to the cottage opened, and Brant came out carrying two bowls and wearing a towel low on his hips, much lower than his shorts had ridden. Now that Cait wasn't frazzled, she got a better look at him, and *holy cow*, he was beautiful, with defined abs and those muscles by his hips that turned girls' brains to dust. Cait had never been one of those dusty-brained girls . . . *until now*. Her gaze slid lower, riveted to the bulge swinging against the towel between his legs. Her body heated, and her nipples pebbled with desire.

Brant whistled, pulling her from her stupor. "Come on, Scrap. I had a leftover hamburger and chopped it up for him."

He crouched to set the bowls in the grass, and the towel parted against his thick thighs. Cait forced her eyes away, but they drifted back, her loneliest parts hoping the towel might slip.

"You're right," he said in a low, sexy voice. "You don't feel the heat between us at *all*."

"I *wasn't* . . ." She felt her cheeks burn.

He chuckled as he pushed to his feet. "Sure you weren't, darlin'."

He went into the outdoor shower, and the half door clapped closed behind him. He draped the towel over the side and after turning on the water, he began singing "Livin' on a Prayer." Shampoo bubbles slid down his calves, pooling on the deck beneath his feet. Cait stared at his legs, imagining those bubbles dripping down his slick, naked body, and her mouth went dry.

A few minutes later the shower door opened, and those seductive blue eyes peered out from behind it, catching her in a lustful trance.

A sexy grin slid across his lips. "Ready?"

Shitshitshit. "I'm *not* showering with you."

Amusement rose in his eyes. "I was talking about handing me Scrappy so I can rinse him off."

Embarrassment heated her cheeks as she scooped up the pup and handed him through the narrow opening. "Be careful. Don't drop him. He's already terrified."

"Don't worry. I've got him." His lips quirked up. "But if you want to join us, Caity, I could use a hand."

She gave him a stern look at the invitation. She'd never liked the name Caity, but when Brant said it, it sounded nice and strangely familiar. It had been a long time since she'd wanted to be with a man. But there was no denying the way her body came alive at the thought of joining him in the shower.

"Last chance," he taunted.

Dragging air into her lungs, she reminded herself of where lust had led her in the past and the pain that had followed, which was enough to send a chill to her bones. It was just the reality slap she needed.

She tore her eyes away and said, "I doubt that."

CHAPTER TWO

BRANT HAD THOUGHT his heart was going to stop when he'd heard Cait scream and saw her flailing in the water. Thank God he'd been there. He didn't want to think about what could have happened if he hadn't been. He glanced at her in the passenger seat of his truck as they drove to her place and was hit with another wave of relief that she was safe. He'd damn well make sure she learned how to swim. She possessed a quiet strength that contrasted, and even rivaled, the caution in her mossy-green eyes, and he'd been drawn to the tall, tattooed, raven-haired beauty since the moment he'd seen her across the room at his buddy's restaurant, Rock Bottom Bar and Grill. For the first time in his life, he'd felt a magnetic pull toward a woman, as if they'd met in some other lifetime and were meant to find each other again. He wasn't a spiritual person, and he didn't believe in that kind of thing. But he trusted his gut, and the attraction was so strong, he couldn't fight it if he tried.

He pulled up to the quaint white bungalow overlooking the water where Abby and Aiden lived and parked in front of the garage, above which was the apartment where Cait stayed when she was in town. He'd known Abby and her older sister, Deirdra, their whole lives, and even though their mother hadn't always made things easy on them, Ava's death had been felt by everyone in the close-knit community. Discovering that Cait was their half sister had come as an even bigger shock. Brant couldn't stop thinking about how overwhelming it must have been for Cait, who he'd heard hadn't even known *who* her biological mother was until after Ava had passed away. She'd been as close-lipped about that as she was about the rest of her life. He'd learned little about her over the last three months, but he'd noticed that she *never* asked for help, and he was sure it pissed her off that she'd needed rescuing in the marsh. He should probably feel a little guilty for using Scrappy to get closer to her. But he'd take any opening he could get to peel back the layers of his gorgeous and mysterious new friend.

He climbed out of the truck and went around to help her out, but just as fiercely independent Cait had done at his place, she was already on the pavement with her backpack over her shoulder, closing the passenger door behind her.

As he lifted her bike out of the back of the truck, she said, "Thanks. You can leave it by the garage." She brushed her cheek over Scrappy's head, and her hair tumbled in front of her eyes.

She wore her hair short, just below her ears, reminding him of the actress from *Blindspot*. He had the urge to tuck it behind her ear so he could see her face. He'd never had urges like that before, but he liked looking at Cait and reading the emotions in her eyes. But he didn't want to scare her off when she was finally letting him get closer. Instead, he wheeled the bike to the garage and followed her up the steps that led to her apartment.

She was adorably sexy in her hiking boots and his T-shirt. He couldn't take his eyes off her ass as it shifted against the thin cotton. She was as *wrong* about her looks as she was untrusting of most people. She had the face of an angel, the most delicate, feminine curves he'd ever seen, and legs that went on forever. Her porcelain skin was decorated with an interesting mix of tattoos of buildings, trees, animals, shapes, webs, all in varying shades of muted colors. He wasn't usually a fan of so many tattoos on women, but they looked beautiful on her, and he wanted to know the story behind each and every one.

She stopped halfway up the steps. "You don't have to come in."

He hoped seeing where she lived might provide some clues to why she was so wary. "What kind of a dog daddy would I be if I didn't check out where Scrappy was going to be spending half his time?"

"Are you always this pushy?"

"I like to think of myself as caring, but you can call me pushy if you want."

She shook her head, a small smile curving her lips. *"Fine."*

"You've got a great smile, Cait." He followed her up to the landing. "You should do it more often."

She gave him a disbelieving glance as she unlocked the door. "You should know by now that flattery won't get you anywhere."

"I didn't think it would," he said as he stepped inside, catching a glimpse of her bedroom to their right, decorated in earth tones, the bed neatly made.

"You can wait in here."

He followed her in the opposite direction, into an impeccably clean kitchen/living room combination overlooking the front yard. Several sketchbooks and colored pencils littered countertops and a small kitchen table near a wall of appliances and oak cabinets. A beige love seat and couch created a cozy nook by the large windows, and a corner bookshelf sported mostly art titles and a few framed photographs.

"This is nice," he said as she pulled a bowl out of a cabinet.

"Thanks. I can't take credit for any of it. It was furnished when I moved in."

As she filled the bowl with water, he glanced at a sketchbook on the counter that was open to a page with a logo for Strings and Things, a music shop in Chaffee, an artsy town on the island.

"Did you design that logo?"

"Yeah. That's not the final design, but it was close. The final had thicker chords. Jagger asked me to help his friend who owns the music store."

"You're really talented."

She kept her eyes trained on the bowl. "Thanks."

Brant went to the side window, gazing out at the ocean. "You have an awesome view. Do you like living here?"

"Mm-hm. It's nice living near Abby and Aiden." She set the bowl on the floor, kissed the dog's head, and set him down, but he pawed at her leg, whimpering. She picked him up and rubbed her nose over his. "You can't shower with me."

She was so loving toward the dog, Brant wondered if she'd ever been that affectionate toward a human. "Don't feel bad, Scrap. She told me the same thing. You can hang with me while she gets naked." He went to her and reached for the dog, earning another eye roll from Cait.

"I'll be fast so we don't miss the vet appointment." She hurried into her bedroom, closing the door behind her.

"Let's see who Caity's got pictures of." He carried Scrappy to the bookshelf and picked up a picture of an adorable green-eyed little girl with long, light brown hair who had to be Cait at three or four years old. She was sitting in the grass with a young blond woman. Cait was looking up at her with stars in her eyes. He wondered who that woman was to have earned Cait's glorious smile.

He set down the picture and picked up another. Cait looked to be in her late teens, wearing a black T-shirt, jeans, and black Converse like the ones she often wore. She was rail thin, and her hair was cut short above her ears on the sides and longer on top. She stood with one arm across her stomach, her other elbow resting on it, her knuckles grazing her chin, as if she needed a barrier between herself and whoever was around her. Brant had witnessed that shield of protection a lot during the first month he'd known Cait. She still stood that way when she was uncomfortable, but it was less often these days. She had only a few tattoos on one arm in the picture, but the wariness in her eyes was as sharp as ever. He wondered what had changed in the years between the first picture and that one.

He set that one down and picked up another. In it, Cait was sitting at a table with three tattooed guys. The largest, a mountainous bearded man with several piercings and coal-dark eyes, sat with his arm around her, holding her so tight, despite her smile, Brant wondered if she was being held against her will. He knew that was a ridiculous thought. Why would she have put up the picture if that were the case? He didn't know anything about her life on the Cape other than that she was a tattooist and body piercer, but now he wondered if she'd gotten herself mixed up with rough people.

He mulled that over as he admired the last picture, taken at the grand opening of the Bistro. Cait was sandwiched between Deirdra and Abby. They were all smiling, but those ever-present shadows dimmed Cait's eyes.

"Snoop much?"

He turned with the picture in his hand as Cait strode toward him, looking hot as sin in a tight white tank top, skinny jeans with tears in the thighs—his favorite pair, the ones with a tear just below her left butt cheek—and red Converse. Her hair looked towel dried and finger combed, giving her a sultry appearance that made him want to bury his hands in it and kiss her.

She reached for Scrappy, eyeing Brant as she cuddled the dog.

"I was just checking out my competition." He set the picture he was holding down and pointed to the tatted-up guy with his arm around her in the other picture. "Is that your boyfriend? Is that why you won't go out with me?"

She headed for the door. "We'd better go so we don't miss the vet appointment."

"Way to avoid the question." He followed her out.

Aiden was climbing out of his car as they came down the steps. He was a dead ringer for David Beckham, minus the tattoos, and probably worth three times as much as the soccer phenom. "Hi. What are you guys up to?"

Brant couldn't resist teasing Cait. "We had an afternoon tryst."

"We did *not*." Cait shot him a death stare.

Brant crossed his arms and lowered his chin, speaking in as serious a tone as he could muster. "Did you, or did you not, have to come home to change your underwear?"

"Ohmygod." Her eyes darted to Aiden. "I went into the marsh to save this dog and nearly drowned. *Liar* over there rescued us."

Aiden's brows knitted. "You almost *drowned?* Are you all right?"

"Yes. I'm fine," Cait reassured him.

"Thank God. I'm glad Brant was there." Aiden reached out to pet Scrappy, and amusement rose in his eyes. "Better watch your comments, Brant. You're going to get yourself in trouble."

"I wouldn't mind getting into a little trouble with Cait." He winked at her.

Cait shook her head. "We're taking Scrappy to the vet."

"Scrappy? He's a cutie," Aiden said.

"Do you think Abby would mind if I keep him?" she asked.

"Abby's a sucker for animals," Aiden said. "I'm sure she'll be thrilled."

"Great. See you later," Cait said.

They headed to the vet's office, and as they walked up to the door, Cait said, "Maybe I should wait out here."

"Why?"

"So you can flirt with Whitney without me hanging around."

"I told you I was *charming* her, not flirting with her."

He pulled open the door and waved her in. He went to the reception desk, where Whitney, one of his mother's friends, who was probably in her late fifties, smiled up at him. Cait's brows furrowed.

"I'm glad you made it in time," Whitney said, coming around the desk to hug him. "How's your mama? I didn't see her at bunco the other night."

His mother played cards with a number of the women on the island. "She's doing well. I think my dad surprised her with a night out. You can take up the timing with him." He put a hand on Cait's lower back. "Whitney, this is my friend Cait Weatherby. She's the one who found the dog."

"Cait Weatherby," Whitney said warmly. "You're Ava's daughter. It is a pleasure to meet you, dear. I'm sorry for your loss."

"Thank you. It's nice to meet you, too," Cait said a little nervously.

"I'll just ring Davis and let him know you're here."

As Whitney went around to the other side of the desk and picked up the phone, Brant noticed Cait's arm sliding anxiously across her stomach. He took her by the elbow, guiding her away from Whitney, and lowered his voice. "What's wrong?"

"Nothing," Cait said.

He held her gaze. "I'm buying that about as much as you'll buy that I *don't* want to go out with you." He softened his tone. "What's going on?"

"It's just a little weird meeting people who knew Ava better than I did. I'm never sure if I should say I'd never met her or not."

"I can see how that would be uncomfortable." Everyone on the island was quick with kindness, whether it be condolences, congratulations, or simply saying hello on the sidewalk. "Maybe it'll help to know that there's a good chance everyone on this part of the island knew Ava, and given how fast gossip spreads, they probably already know you never met her."

"You think?" she asked with a hint of relief.

"Yeah, I do. In any case, you shouldn't worry too much about if they know or not. You're here now, and you're part of our community. That's what matters most. The people here just want to welcome you and let you know they care. That's a good thing."

Her eyes darted to Davis Barrington coming down the hall in his white lab coat. He was a year older than Brant, an avid outdoorsman, and looked more like a surfer than a veterinarian, with thick blond hair and perfect teeth that belonged in a Crest commercial.

"Thanks for fitting us in," Brant said, shaking his hand.

"No problem." Davis's expression brightened as he turned to Cait. "We have to stop meeting like this or we'll be the talk of the town."

She smiled confidently, so different from the way she smiled at Brant. "It's nice to see you again. How did it go with the anxious shepherd?"

What the hell? She knew about his work? Brant had never been a jealous guy, but there was no denying the claws climbing up the back of his neck.

"He did fine, but he was back again a few days ago. This time he swallowed a sock." Davis scratched Scrappy between his ears. "This is the dog you found in the marsh?"

"He's *ours*," Brant said, putting his hand possessively on Cait's back.

Davis ran his eyes between them. "*Got it.* Why don't we go check him out, scan him for an identification chip, and see what we're dealing with?"

Brant was stuck for far too long listening to Davis chat up Cait as he checked out Scrappy and ran tests. They learned that Scrappy had not been chipped, was probably five or six years old, and was undernourished but otherwise appeared to be in good shape. Brant was relieved about the dog and jealous as hell over Cait's ease with Davis. He'd give anything for her to talk that easily with him.

He stewed over that as they headed to Salty Paws for pet supplies. Brant didn't believe in stewing any more than he believed in hiding his feelings, and his curiosity magnified as they picked out crates, dog beds, brushes, bowls, and other paraphernalia for his cottage and Cait's apartment. By the time they began weeding through collars, he was ready to burst.

He needed answers and tried to sound casual when he said, "So, you and Davis seemed pretty tight."

She shrugged. "Not really. Why?"

"Just curious."

She arched a brow. *"Curious?"*

"Yeah, you know. We share Scrappy now. I figured I should know if some other guy's going to be hanging around him."

She laughed and shook her head, going back to leafing through the collars. "You're ridiculous."

He chuckled. "Yeah, I sound a little ridiculous to myself, too, but what can I say? It bugs me that you seem nervous when we're together, but you're an open book around Davis. What's up with that?" Sometimes he hated the way honesty flew from his lips, but his parents were open communicators and had raised all of their children to value honesty, loyalty, and hard work—but never so much work that they lost sight of the more important things in life, like family, friends, and their own need to decompress.

"*Pfft.* I'm not an open book around anyone. I know Davis from the Bistro." She held up a thin blue collar with a charm hanging from it. "Do you like this one?"

"It's kind of *too* perfect, don't you think? But I guess if you like pretty boys."

She tried to give him a deadpan look, but laughter bubbled out. "Are you talking about Davis or Scrappy?"

"You really do have Davis on the brain, don't you? *I* was talking about our pup."

"Yeah, right." She put the collar back, and without looking at him, she said, "Davis does come across a bit *pretty*, doesn't he?"

"Lots of girls dig him. He's a great guy, if you're into guys like that . . ."

Her eyes darted briefly to Brant. "I'm not looking for a guy."

"Good, because you've already got the best man on the island," he said cockily, pointing both thumbs at himself.

She rolled her eyes. "You're not my man, Remington."

"Yet." He picked up a spiked leather collar. "What do you think? This'll make our boy look tough."

"I think *you* need that more than Scrappy does, but the spikes need to go on the *inside* so I can tighten them when you say stupid things."

He laughed. "I'd gladly wear a spiked collar for you, baby. In fact, you can tattoo *Cait's property* across my abs if you'll go out with me."

She giggled. *Giggled!* It was the rarest and most joyful sound he'd ever heard.

"You might have trouble keeping dates after that," she said. "Once they see you without a shirt on, they'll *know* you're crazy."

He leaned closer and lowered his voice. "Crazy about you, darlin'."

"Why?" She drew out the word like it was painful, but she was smiling, and it was a whole different smile from the one she'd shown Davis. It was lighthearted and curious, and utterly beautiful.

Take that, Barrington.

"Because you intrigue me, Cait."

"Ah, you're a thrill-of-the-chase guy. That makes sense." She plucked a brown collar off the rack. "Too boring, right?"

"Definitely too boring for *our* little guy, and I'm *not* a thrill-of-the-chase guy. In fact, I've never chased a woman in my life until you came along. I never had to. Most women like nice guys who are easy on the eyes."

She laughed softly and put her mouth beside Scrappy's ear. "Hear that? Your human is full of himself."

"Just honest to a fault. You'll see." He snagged a forest-green collar off the rack and dangled it from his finger. "How about this? It goes with your eyes, and the color will remind us of where we found him."

Cait tilted her head, looking it over. "I like it, but not because of your flattery. I like the marsh connection."

"That's still a win in my book." He put a hand on her back. "Come on, Caity, we've got a lot to buy."

"Why do you call me that?"

"Because it fits you. It's feminine and beautiful, but it's also strong and unique."

She held his gaze for a heart-thrumming second before heading down the next aisle.

As they stocked up on dog food, toys, and leashes, Cait's guard came down. They joked around, laughing and teasing each other. He *loved* her laugh, and the way she wrinkled her nose when she didn't want to say she disliked something was adorably sexy. After they loaded up a cart, they picked out a silver bone-shaped dog tag from a machine and had their phone numbers etched into it.

"Let's put *Scrappy the Superdog* on it," Brant suggested.

"Do you want to buy him a cape, too? And we almost forgot puppy pads to use while we're housebreaking him."

"I'll get them, and I'll get the cape while I'm at it." He took Scrappy from her and went in search of housebreaking pads. He found a dog-gy-carrier sling along the way and put it on, settling Scrappy into it. He found the puppy pads, but no cape, and as he walked up behind Cait, he said, "Hey, angel face, check this out."

She turned with a *don't call me that* scowl, but her eyes went soft at the sight of them, and he *loved* it. Seeing her walls come down was even more fascinating than watching a boat take shape.

"It's a keeper," he said. He'd wear it daily if it got that reaction.

He dragged out their shopping for as long as he could, wanting to see more of her freer side. He didn't know what had changed, but *this* Cait didn't carry a shield, and when they left the store with four bags of goodies and two crates, he vowed to do everything within his power to keep things light.

Cait leaned against the side of the truck, cradling Scrappy, while Brant stowed their purchases behind the seat. She hadn't given Scrappy up for more than a few minutes since they'd found him. Brant knew she had become close to her sisters, and she was fairly close with their friends, but he had a feeling she needed Scrappy in her life as much as

Scrappy needed her. He was glad for both of them and a little jealous of the tiny dog getting all that honest affection from their girl.

"We bought *way* too much," Cait said, kissing Scrappy's head.

"I don't think so. We don't know how long this little guy has been alone, or if he even knows what it's like to have a home and people to care for him." As he righted the seat, he wondered about Cait's life. Was the big guy in the picture her boyfriend? What was her family like? He scratched Scrappy's back and said, "We're showing him that he can trust us to take care of him."

"By *spoiling* him?" she mused.

"By showing him that we care and we're committed to helping him have a great life. That's what caring about someone or something is all about, making sure they feel safe and happy."

She was looking at him like she was trying to figure him out, that magnetic pull drawing him closer. He knew he should keep things light, but there was no holding back the truth. "I'd like to spoil you, Cait."

Her cheeks pinked up, but she didn't look away, and it was the sweetest thing he'd ever seen. *Oh yeah*, she felt the thrum of desire cranking up the heat between them, and the curiosity of what it meant begging to be explored, too. Cait had so many sides, he never knew if she was going to give him sass or shut him down, but he hoped to learn everything there was to know about her, and that pink-cheeked confident stare encouraged him to do just that.

But in the next breath, a challenge arose in her eyes, and she lifted her chin in defiance—*To herself? Her feelings? To him?*—and said, "I don't need spoiling, thanks."

"Nobody *needs* spoiling, Cait. But it sure feels nice to relax and let someone else take care of us for a while." He touched her arm, and she tensed.

Realizing he'd struck a nerve, he stepped back. Cait slid her arm across her stomach, and his heart pitched. *What have you been through?* He wanted to tell her that she didn't need to shield herself from him, that he'd never hurt or take advantage of her. But he didn't want to make her more uncomfortable.

"We should go," she said anxiously, and climbed into the truck.

He closed her door before going around to the driver's side. When he climbed in, she looked out the passenger window.

Who the hell made you so scared?

As he drove out of the parking lot, he vowed to show her she could trust him on *every* level and to find out what bastard had made her feel that scared in the first place.

CHAPTER THREE

CAIT DREAMED ABOUT Brant *again*.

Of course it was the sexy dream this time, as if seeing him half-naked yesterday and feeling his hard body pressed against her hadn't been enough torture. In her dream, he'd perched above her in all his naked glory, his alluring blue eyes gazing at her so intently, she hadn't needed to speak for him to know *exactly* what she'd wanted. The dream was far more vivid than ever before. Not only had she seen him, but she'd *felt* every blessed inch of him as their bodies had come together and his deliciously kissable lips had covered hers. She'd felt his weight on her thighs and chest as they'd moved to an erotic rhythm, and it had driven her wild. She'd woken up moaning his name, wet, wanting, and beyond irritated at herself for even *thinking* about him.

But *wow* . . .

That dream.

She'd spent the morning focusing on Scrappy and refusing to think about the dream, which was now playing in her mind like a perfectly choreographed water ballet. *Ugh!* She was determined *not* to get all hot and bothered again and lowered her gaze to the perfect distraction, her new furry friend happily walking beside her as they made their way down the hill toward the Bistro. She already loved the little dog, even though he'd peed on her floor, refused to be crated, and snorted all night as he'd slept curled up beside her. He was a great mood enhancer.

He'd pulled her out of her drunk-on-dreamy-Brant stupor earlier, and an ice-cold shower had taken the edge off her far-too-lonely lady parts.

If only there were a shower available now . . .

She *really* needed to stop thinking about Brant. She focused on the colorful awnings and displays in the shop windows on her way to the Sweet Barista, her favorite coffee shop and bakery. It was just up the street from the Bistro and owned by one of her new friends, Keira Silver, whose parents owned the Silver House resort. Cait stopped in nearly every day on her way to work to get coffee and a blueberry Danish. She'd seen other people bring their dogs inside, so she picked up Scrappy to take him with her, and her attention caught on the funky little building that stood alone just beyond the shops. There was a DAILY NEWS sign on the building, but it hadn't been open since she'd first come to the island, and the building was different from the other shops, which intrigued her. It had a slanted roof, higher in the front than the back, and a wide door made of horizontal wooden slats that appeared to open like a garage door, with rectangular windows above it. The sides of the building were half glass, but newspapers were taped to the inside of the glass.

A young couple came out of the coffee shop and held the door for Cait.

"Thank you," she said as she walked in.

Keira looked up from where she was wiping a table, her light brown hair spilling over the shoulders of her pink SWEET BARISTA shirt. "You got a puppy!" She hurried over and took Scrappy from Cait, burying her face in his fur.

Scrappy looked a little anxious, but Cait knew Keira would win him over. "He's not really a puppy. We think he's five or six years old. I found him by the marsh."

"He is the cutest! I love his name, too. Can I give him a puppy treat?" Keira asked. "They're organic. I make them myself."

Scrappy licked Keira's cheek, putting Cait at ease. "Of course. Thank you."

Keira nuzzled Scrappy as she went around the counter. "Do you want a yummy treat, cutie pie?"

"Hey, Keira, do you know what's up with the Daily News stand? It's never open."

"It's been closed for a couple of years. The Barringtons own it. They run the island newspaper, and they used to sell newspapers and magazines out of it. But everyone other than Aiden reads on their phones now." Aiden read a physical newspaper every morning. She gave Scrappy a treat as another customer came in. Keira passed Scrappy over the counter to Cait. "You'd better take him. He's adorable. Do you want your usual?"

"Yes, please."

A few minutes later Cait was on her way down the hill toward the Bistro. She'd always loved walking. It cleared her mind and gave her a sense of freedom and control. No matter where she was, on the Cape or on the island, her surroundings were usually enough to distract her from her thoughts, which sometimes took her back to places she'd rather forget. As her thoughts turned to Brant again, she knew nothing could distract her from remembering how safe she'd felt in his arms. She'd spent hours picking apart those feelings, and she'd decided that she only felt that way because she'd been terrified of drowning.

At least that's what she'd been telling herself since he'd dropped her off last night. He'd wanted to come by her apartment this morning to get Scrappy and had offered to drive her to work, but she'd nixed that idea. He'd gotten to her effortlessly when they were shopping yesterday, and she'd completely let her guard down. She knew better than to let that happen again and had asked him to pick up Scrappy at the Bistro instead.

She walked past the Silver House resort, which sat majestically on a bluff overlooking Silver Harbor, and the Bistro sign came into view at the bottom of the hill. A sense of calm washed over her at the sight of the renovated-boathouse-turned-restaurant. She'd helped turn the Bistro into something special. She'd never had that sense of accomplishment before, and she'd done it with her *sister*. It was still unbelievable to her. She'd spent years imagining what it would be like to have siblings, and she hadn't even come close to the way it made her feel or the ways her relationships with Abby and Deirdra were changing her.

The Bistro was built on the edge of Sunset Beach. There was a deck along the side and a patio across the front, which faced the water. As she made her way across the pavement, a salty breeze wrapped around her. She pulled open the heavy back door to the kitchen, and Abby looked up from where she was chopping vegetables.

Abby's excitement lit up her pretty face. "You're early! *Faye!* Cait's here, and she's got the puppy!" She took off her chef coat and hurried out the door in her shorts and tank top. Her thick brownish-blond hair was pulled up in a high ponytail. She crouched beside Scrappy and held out her hand. "Hello, cutie." Scrappy licked her, and she scooped him up and rose to her feet.

"Hi, Cait! Let me see that little muffin," Faye Steele said as she came out the door waving her hands, her layered blond hair bouncing around her rosy cheeks. She was as voluptuous and maternal as her ex-sister-in-law and bestie, Shelley Steele. Shelley had recommended Faye for the job with them, and Faye had moved to the island from Trusty, Colorado, just a few weeks ago.

Abby gave Scrappy one last kiss and handed him to Faye. "Isn't he adorable?" She looked at Cait. "I've been dying to meet him. Aiden told me about him last night, but your lights were out when we got home."

"I had a long day. Sorry about that."

"I heard you and Brant had an *interesting* day," Abby said with a knowing grin. "Aiden said Brant rescued you? You told me and Dee that you love the water. Did you *really* almost drown, or didn't you want Aiden to know that you and Brant hooked up?"

Abby was always nudging her toward giving Brant a chance in a fun, sisterly way. "Ohmygod. I did *not* hook up with Brant, and I do love the water. But I don't know how to swim, and I really did almost drown."

"Oh, *Cait*, sweetheart. Are you okay?" Faye asked.

"Yeah. I'm fine."

Abby hugged her. "I'm sorry I joked about it. How did it happen?"

"I was hiking at the refuge, and I sat down to sketch by the marsh and heard Scrappy crying. I went in after him, and suddenly I was underwater. I was frantically trying to get up to the surface to save him, but I kept going under. I thought we were both going to die, and suddenly Brant was there, lifting me to the surface. It was like a miracle. He saved us both."

"You must have been terrified." Faye squeezed Cait's hand, nestling Scrappy against her chest.

"I was really scared. I kept thinking that I'd *just* found Abby and Dee and that was going to be the end of it." Three months ago Cait wouldn't have admitted being scared to anyone other than Tank. But Abby and Faye were easy to talk to. They made her want to open up about everything, but while she was glad to have people to share this type of fear with, she wasn't about to bring the ugliness she'd suffered into this beautiful new life she'd been blessed with.

"Thank goodness for Brant," Abby said. "And I'm signing you up for swim lessons."

"According to Brant, *he's* going to teach me to swim, but I don't plan on going in the water anytime soon."

Abby and Faye exchanged a secret look, and Faye said, "That boy is sweet on you, honey."

"So he says every chance he gets, *and* he's staked a claim on Scrappy. *Joint custody.* Can you believe that?" Cait rolled her eyes, but she knew he'd been as instantly attached to the dog as she was.

"Smart man," Faye said. "He knows how to stay on your radar."

"I guess it makes sense, since I have to go back to the Cape tonight, and I'm working too many hours at Wicked Ink for this little guy to be alone." She was going to miss Scrappy while she was gone. The truth was, lately, when she went back to the Cape, she missed Abby, Faye, and Aiden, and though she'd never admit it, she missed Brant, too. She'd never met anyone like him. He wasn't arrogant and obnoxious like some guys. He somehow knew when to push and when to back off, which underscored his ability to see her more clearly than most people ever did, and he did it with humor and charm.

Needing a reminder of why those were dangerous thoughts, she glanced at the tattooed spiderweb on her elbow.

"Brant's clever like that," Abby said, bringing Cait's mind back to the conversation. "Leni said she's never seen him turn on the charm like he does with you." Leni Steele, Shelley's daughter, was Abby's best friend. They had grown up together, and now Leni lived in New York, but she visited often.

"Well, he's wasting his time," Cait said. "He got the only thrill he's going to get from me when he rescued me. I was in my bra and underwear, clinging to him like a lifeline."

Abby laughed. "You know he *loved* that."

"He loved it, all right. The problem is"—she lowered her voice—"I did, too. *Way* too much. I don't need a man in my life, and he is Trouble with a capital *T* for me. He's going to be here any minute to get Scrappy."

"*Trouble*, she says," Faye said in a high-pitched voice to Scrappy. "If that gorgeous man were twenty years older, I'd become the biggest troublemaker around."

They all laughed.

"You could go for it in full-on cougar mode," Cait teased.

Faye raised her brows as she handed Scrappy to Abby. "I have kids older than Brant. I can just see my oldest, Reggie, looking down his nose at me. I don't need *that* headache in my life."

Abby laughed. "Cait, you know how I feel about Brant. I've known him forever. He's a great guy and a loyal friend. I've heard you guys bantering back and forth, and you just said you like him. Maybe you should give him a chance."

"I *do* like him. We had a great time buying supplies for Scrappy, and you should see him love up that dog. He can melt an iceberg with a single smile. Imagine the puddle of goo I turned into when he walked up carrying Scrappy in a doggy sling."

"Oh my gosh," Abby said dreamily.

Faye said, "I've known Brant since he was knee-high. Those blue eyes and dimples have melted hearts of all ages forever, but like I said, that's trouble I'd run *toward*, not away from."

"I've had more than my fair share of trouble," Cait admitted. "And Brant got jealous of Davis Barrington when we took Scrappy to get checked out. *Davis!* He's in here *all* the time. The last thing I need is an overly possessive guy questioning everyone I come into contact with."

"I can't see Brant getting jealous. Everything rolls off his back," Abby said. "He must be really far gone for you."

"Did you tell him you're not interested in Davis?" Faye asked.

Cait planted her hand on her hip. "I can't tell him the *truth*. You know how he is with me. If I told him that Davis is like drinking milk, and he's a double shot of tequila with a whiskey chaser, he'd *never* leave me alone."

Abby and Faye laughed.

"Speaking of Hottie McDimples . . ." Faye nodded in the direction of the street.

Cait turned to see Brant driving into the parking lot, and butterflies took flight in her stomach. She was *not* a butterflies-in-the-stomach girl!

He parked and climbed out of his truck in khaki cargo shorts and a gray T-shirt, his bright blue baseball cap on backward, flashing that dimple-baring smile. He didn't even have to speak to be too damn charming for his own good.

Abby nudged Cait, whispering, "How can you resist him?"

It was getting harder by the minute. If only she could learn to turn off her feelings for him and they could just be friends.

"Hello, ladies." Brant took Scrappy from Abby and kissed the pup's head. "How's our little boy? Did you sleep with Mama last night?" He held the dog up to his ear, pretending to listen, eyes trained on Cait. "What? Mama was chanting my name all night?"

Abby laughed.

Cait felt her eyes widen and quickly narrowed them. Did he have a freaking camera in her bedroom? She crossed her arms and lifted her chin. *Operation Stop the Butterflies, here we come.* "He must have misheard me. I was saying *Davis*'s name. Or maybe he heard me say *Wells* or *Fitz*." Wells and Fitz Silver were two of Keira's brothers, both of whom were single.

Brant's jaw clenched at the mention of his good-looking friends.

Cait shrugged nonchalantly. "It was a busy night."

Brant held Cait's gaze as Abby and Faye tried to stifle their laughter. He knew she was just messing with him. He'd seen arrogant Wells in action, flirting with Cait in all the wrong ways, and now that he knew Davis wasn't her type, he was pretty sure Fitz, who ran the Silver House resort with his parents, wasn't, either. But if Cait wanted to play, he was going to *win*. "You might as well play the field in your dreams *now*, Caity, because once you go out with me, I'll ruin you for all other men. I'll be *all* you see in those dirty dreams."

"You were right, Cait." Faye raised her brows. "This one *is* trouble."

"No wonder my ears were burning." Brant stepped closer to Cait, loving that she'd been talking about him. Her eyes narrowed further, and it made her even sexier.

"Come on, Abby," Faye said. "Let's give these two some privacy."

"But it's just getting good," Abby said.

Brant smirked. "And it's only going to get better."

Cait planted her hand on her hip, those enchanting green eyes locked on him. She never wore much makeup, only eyeliner, as far as he could tell, and she didn't even need that. She was uniquely beautiful with a slightly upturned nose and high cheekbones. She probably thought she could scare him off with that scowl and no-bullshit stance, but she was too damn adorable with her bright orange tank top hugging her curves, torn jeans rolled up at the ankles, and black Converse. Alluring hints of tattoos peeked out from the tears in her jeans above her right knee and left thigh.

As soon as Abby and Faye were out of earshot, he said, "Wells and Fitz? Surely you can do better."

"They're good-looking men."

"True, and they're good guys, but they're wrong for *you*." He stepped closer. "Neither of them is rugged enough for you, and Wells is too arrogant."

She lifted her chin. "Maybe I like arrogant."

"Don't fool yourself, darlin'. You like *confidence*, and you have no patience for arrogance."

She swallowed hard.

That's right, baby. I see you.

"Maybe I like *brothers*," she challenged.

"We both know you're not a sharer, Cait. If you're going to let a guy in, he's got to be everything you could ever want and *more*. You're a nature girl, which means you need a guy who can keep up. You're creative, and you need a guy who gets that, because we creative types think differently than others. And I don't think you give a damn about looks, because if you did, you'd be on my arm already." That earned him a soft laugh. "You're all about who the person is on the inside. You want loyalty, honesty, and patience." The flinch of her brows told him he'd nailed it. "I haven't figured out what the *more* is that you're looking for yet, but I will."

"You think you have me all figured out."

"I thought I just admitted that I *don't*." He could take the conversation deeper, but he knew she'd shut down, so he eased up. "Actually, I was wrong about you not being a sharer, since we share our baby boy, which makes me a lucky guy. How did Scrap do last night?"

Her lips quirked up, and she reached for Scrappy. Brant handed him to her, and the tension in her body visibly eased. She cradled Scrappy against her chest, petting him. "He was great. He had a couple of accidents, but that's to be expected. He's eating, which is a good sign. I think he trusts me, and he did great on the leash walking here. But he hates his crate." Empathy rose in her eyes. "He cried when I put him in it, so I let him sleep with me, which I know isn't great for training, but you said he could use a little spoiling, and I think he needs to feel safe."

Brant had a feeling Cait needed that, too. "I get it. I'm glad he wasn't too much trouble."

"He wasn't. But fair warning, he snorts when he sleeps."

"I can handle a little snorting."

She kissed the pup's head. "I hate leaving him tonight."

"I wanted to ask you about that. What time do you have to be back at the Cape?"

"I'm working until six. Then I'll race home, shower, get my stuff, and hopefully make the late ferry."

"I have a better idea. Since you want more time with Scrappy, why don't you let us take you back to the Cape? We can have dinner on the way."

Wariness rose in her eyes. "I don't know."

"Come on, Cait. What's more fun, sitting on a ferry packed full of strangers or time with me and our boy?"

"What would I owe you for the ride?" she asked carefully.

"*Owe* me?"

"Beyond gas. I'll pay for gas."

He scoffed. "You're not paying for gas. This is what friends do, and if you're worried that I'll try something, then you don't know me very well. You can tell Abby you're going back with us. You know if I do anything inappropriate, she'll kick my ass when I get back."

"If you do anything inappropriate, you won't make it back," she threatened.

He loved her tough side. "Does that mean you'll let us take you?"

"I guess."

"Awesome." It took everything he had not to pump his fist. "We'll pick you up at your place at seven. Does that give you enough time?"

She nodded, kissed the dog again, hugged him, and handed him to Brant. "I have to get to work. Thank you for offering to take me so I can spend more time with him."

With us. "It'll be fun."

"As long as you really don't mind. It's a long trip, about an hour each way."

"I *know* how far we are from the Cape, Cait. Now get into work before Scrappy and I abscond with you and get you fired."

She started walking toward the restaurant but turned back, hesitation written all over her face. Before she could say a word, he said, "Tell Abby you're coming with us, because if *you* try anything, I'm going to report back to her!"

Cait laughed and shook her head. "Don't make me regret this!"

"I wouldn't dream of it." With a wave, he climbed into his truck, mentally making plans for their first boat trip.

CHAPTER FOUR

"*THIS* IS YOUR boat?" Cait asked as they boarded Brant's motor yacht.

It was a perfectly clear evening, and Cait looked like a million bucks in a black tank top, torn jeans, which Brant was convinced was all she owned, and a flannel shirt tied around her waist.

"It's one of them." Brant put her duffel and backpack in a storage compartment beneath the seats.

She raised her brows. "One?"

"Boats are my life. Everyone has tools of the trade. How many tattoo guns do you own?"

"Good point. Is this one of the boats you rent out to people?"

"No. I have a handful of personal boats. Some I made, and some I bought—like this little gal. She's a motor yacht."

"A *yacht*?" Her eyes swept over the interior. "Of course. No wonder it's so fancy."

"I didn't choose this one for tonight's trip to impress you. I'd rather take you out on one of the boats I built, but they're smaller, and I wanted you to be comfortable and feel safe." He patted the side of the boat. "There's no falling out of this baby. You'd have to climb on the seats and jump to get over the side."

Her eyes moved slowly over his face, as if she were studying him. "Thank you for thinking of me."

I think about you all the time. "I can't have you worrying for an hour." He grabbed the Deckvests and handed her one. "Just in case."

She wrinkled her nose. "I'll feel silly wearing a vest."

"But you'll look *hot* and you'll be safe, which is what matters— the safety part. The hotness is just a bonus." He began putting on his Deckvest.

"You're not really going to wear that, are you? You've probably been swimming since you could walk."

"That's true, but I'd never ask you to do anything I wouldn't do myself." He winced. "Actually, that's not *exactly* true, and I can't lie to you. If we ever get together as a couple, like *really* together, I can think of a few things I might ask you to do that I can't do myself."

Her eyes widened, but she laughed. "You should have lied to me."

"Sorry, no can do." He picked up the vest he'd bought for Scrappy. "Hold our boy so I can put this on him."

"You've got to be kidding. He can't even get over the sides of the boat."

"Family solidarity. We practiced wearing it several times today." He put the vest on Scrappy. "He likes it, and where we go, he goes. When I *do* take you out on one of my smaller boats, he'll be with us and he'll need to wear it." He picked up Scrappy by the handle on the back of the vest, his tiny legs dangling.

"He's too cute." She laughed and pulled out her phone. "Let me get a picture."

"Sure, but then I get one of the three of us."

She gave him a sideways look. "You always want *more*."

"Only with you, baby," he said as she took Scrappy's picture.

"Your turn. Get in here." He tugged her to his side, ignoring her groan as she took the picture of the three of them. "I want a copy of that."

He helped her put on her Deckvest and adjusted the fit. The high-performance jacket and harness combination had two slim shoulder straps that connected to another thin strap worn just below the chest. "There you go. As I thought, you look wicked hot."

She laughed softly and wiggled her shoulders and torso. "This isn't bad at all. It's light. I'm used to the life vests that cover my whole chest. They bother my arms, but this is like wearing nothing. How can it keep me up in the water?"

"This is a Deckvest. There are bladders in the straps, and it auto inflates. But if you decide to jump off the side of the boat and for some reason it doesn't inflate, just pull this strap to inflate it manually." He pointed to the manual-inflation strap. "Let me untie us from the dock, and we'll get going." He climbed off the yacht and went to work untying the ropes. When he returned, he said, "Come on, babe, you can drive us out of here."

"You mean *you* can drive us out."

He shook his head. "You're driving, Caity."

"I can't drive a *boat*." She took a step backward.

"I'm going to teach you."

"*Brant!* You've lost your mind. I'm *not* driving this expensive boat. *Yacht!* Oh my gosh. It's a freaking *yacht*. I am definitely *not* driving it."

He took her hand, leading her to the helm. "I told you I want you to be comfortable, and that starts with feeling in control of your surroundings. It'll be fun."

"I'll crash."

"You won't. I'm going to be right here next to you."

"*Brant.*" Her beautiful eyes pleaded with him.

"Save your breath, babe. You're learning to drive this vessel."

Before she could complain any more, he began going over the controls, explaining the functions and proper use of each. Cait's brows knitted in concentration, and after each explanation, she nodded in understanding.

"It's as easy as driving a car. You *can* drive a car, can't you?" He realized he'd never actually seen her drive.

"Yes. I don't bring my car to the island because Abby and I have Ava's old car, and I prefer walking or riding my bike." Her eyes swept over the controls. "What if I blow an engine or something?"

"You won't," he reassured her. "But if anything were to happen, I know this guy who builds boats. I'm pretty sure he could handle fixing it."

"I'm not kidding, Brant. I could screw everything up."

"Relax. You're going to do great." He motioned to Scrappy lying in one of the extra dog beds he'd bought earlier in the day. "Even Scrappy trusts you to pilot the boat."

"Then you're *both* off your rockers."

"Maybe, but you only live once. Ready to start this baby up?"

"No." She looked at the controls again.

He guided her hand to the key. "Let's do this."

She took a deep breath and started the engine. The tiny blue lights he'd strung around the railings bloomed to life, and Cait gasped, her happy eyes flicking to his.

"I figured our first evening on the water should be special."

"This isn't a *date*." She pressed her lips together like she was trying to tamp down her delight, but it wafted off her like the wind.

"I know. It's just one friend taking another to her destination, but I still wanted it to be special."

She was looking at him with hedged appreciation.

Don't worry, Caity, you can trust me. "Go ahead and turn on the navigation lights I showed you." He waited while she did that. "Awesome. Now you're going to ease slowly away from the dock. Watch your speed. We're in a no-wake zone. Do you remember how to go forward?"

She nodded, putting one hand on the wheel, the other on the throttle, and glanced anxiously at him. "How will I know how hard to push it? I can't do this. I'm too nervous."

"We'll do it together until you can get the feel of it." He moved behind her and put his hand over hers on the throttle. She smelled like peppermint and sunshine, and he wondered if she tasted just as sweet.

They piloted the boat away from the dock, and Cait bounced on her toes. "We did it!"

He laughed. "You're too damn cute. Now we can go a little faster." His hand rested lightly on hers, giving her control of the equipment as she increased their speed. "Perfect. Keep her there until we're farther away from the marina."

"This is fun!"

He'd never seen her so enthusiastic. "Just wait until we're out of the harbor and you can really open her up." The urge to slip his other arm around her middle and press a kiss to her neck was too strong. He moved to her side to keep from doing just that. He had a feeling this was going to be a gloriously torturous trip.

"*Brant!* Where are you going? Get back here!" she said anxiously. The wind blew her hair away from her face, and she stood strong and tall, her eyes fixed on the water ahead of them.

"You've got this, Cait, and you look *good* at the helm."

"You have no idea how nervous I am."

"You're doing great. I have a feeling there's nothing you can't do, given the chance."

She was smiling, but she said, "What'd I say about flattery?"

"It's only flattery if it's not true."

He guided her out of the harbor and set her on their course.

"Do you let all your ladies drive your boats?" She stole a quick glance at him, happiness illuminating her beautiful face.

Christ, she was incredible. "No, but I make them call me Captain."

She shook her head, laughing softly. "You're awful."

"I'm kidding. I've never let a woman I was seeing pilot any of my boats, and I definitely don't want women calling me Captain."

"Because you prefer *Big Daddy* or something?" she teased.

"I guess the secret's out."

They made small talk and joked around as the sun set over the water, leaving gorgeous ribbons of oranges, yellows, and grays in its wake. The lights on the island glittered like diamonds against the darkening sky.

Cait sighed. "Isn't this gorgeous?"

Brant couldn't take his eyes off *her*. "Stunning." She glanced over, and he didn't want to make her nervous, so he said, "This is my favorite time to be on the water. I love dawn, too, and dusk. Okay, I just love being on the water, but watching the sun rise or set is pretty damn magical." *Almost as magical as your smile.*

They rounded the northeast side of the island, and his favorite secluded cove came into view, cradled between rocky cliffs and a sandy beach.

"Let's slow her down," he said, and as Cait reduced their speed, he pointed to the entrance of the cove. "That's Mermaid Cove. Steer us a little closer, but stay parallel to the land. We're going to cut the engine when we're outside the entrance."

"Did you say *Mermaid* Cove? Why are we stopping?"

A flicker of apprehension flashed in her eyes, and it cut him to his core. He was going to hunt down whoever had hurt her and tear him to shreds.

"Yes, and I promised you dinner. You can't eat and steer at the same time. Don't worry, Cait. I promised you I wouldn't try any funny stuff, and I always keep my promises."

"I'm sorry. I know everyone trusts you," she said regretfully. "I'm just weird."

"You're cautious, and that's good, but hopefully one day you'll learn that I'm a man of my word and that *you* can trust me, too."

She cut the engine. "If I didn't trust you, I wouldn't have come on your boat."

"Good point. Then hopefully one day you'll *fully* trust me and realize I'm not the kind of guy who would ever hurt anyone unless they were hurting someone I cared about."

He felt her studying him again as he anchored outside the cove. "I'm just going belowdecks to get our dinner. I'll be right back."

"Okay." Cait picked up Scrappy, and she seemed more relaxed.

When he came back up with place settings and the insulated bag from Rock Bottom Bar and Grill, she was gazing out at the cove with a peaceful expression.

"I can't get over how pretty it is here. I love the way the blue lights on the boat reflect off the water, and the moonlight hitting the rocks around the cove gives it an ethereal feel," she said as he set everything on the table. "I wish I could sketch it."

"There's no better sight." At least that's what he'd always thought, but the look on Cait's face surpassed even his favorite cove. He opened the storage compartment where he'd put her bags and said, "I'm sure you have a sketchbook in there somewhere. Go for it." He took Scrappy from her.

Her eyes widened. "You don't mind?"

"Why would I mind? Life is meant to be enjoyed, not missed. You can sketch and eat or sketch, then eat."

She snagged her backpack, and when she unzipped it, he spied at least four sketchbooks inside. She fingered through them and plucked one out, sending an envelope sailing down to the deck.

He picked it up and saw her name written across the front. "An unopened letter. *Very mysterious.* Secret admirer?"

"Hardly." She snagged the envelope and put it in her backpack.

He was curious about the letter, but her tight-lipped expression had him holding his tongue as he set out the containers for their dinner.

"What is all that?" she asked in a less annoyed tone.

"Chips, guacamole, and the makings for shrimp tacos on pita bread. I worried it might get soggy if they put it together. I figured we could assemble them ourselves. Is that okay? You ordered this the night we met, when we had dinner with Abby and Aiden and everyone else."

Her eyes widened with disbelief again. "You remembered what I ordered three months ago?"

"I remember everything about that night, including the moment I first saw you across the room, when everything else failed to exist. You wore a peach sweater, and I couldn't take my eyes off you during dinner. I wondered all night about the tattoos on your neck, which disappeared beneath your collar. And you kept sneaking glances at me and then looking away."

She bit her lip and looked down, absently touching her neck.

"You did *that* a lot, too." He gently lifted her chin, heat billowing between them. "What I felt that night has only gotten stronger, but I don't have to tell you that any more than you have to tell me you feel it, too."

She swallowed hard. He fought the urge to press his lips to hers and reluctantly lowered his hand, putting space between them.

"I know talking like this makes you nervous. For that reason, we're going to pretend that whatever this is between us doesn't exist and get on with our evening." He waved to the seats. "Get comfy, and sketch your little heart out."

Get comfy? How the heck was Cait supposed to get comfortable when he'd just recounted their initial meeting with pinpoint accuracy? She'd been captivated by him, and Abby had caught her staring as he'd approached the table. It was ridiculous. Almost as ridiculous as the jitters she felt now.

Except that they were at *Mermaid* Cove.

It was like he knew *all* her secrets, which was impossible. This was just a coincidence, wasn't it? She was bound to overthink that unless she could turn her thoughts off. She knew how to close herself off from the rest of the world. She had become a master at it out of necessity when she was just a little girl. So *why* was it impossible to do around Brant?

"You okay?" he asked.

"Mm-hm." She sat on the cushions with her sketchbook and focused on the cove, hoping the beauty of the sight before her would work its magic. She studied the angles of the rocks, the motion of the water, and the reflection of the moon, welcoming the serenity of each sight, letting them lull her in. Before long, she was lost in them. Her pencil moved swiftly across the paper, adding depth and texture, until she was one with the drawing, her movements as fluid as water, her thoughts as clear as the night sky.

A tap on her shoulder startled her. She looked up at Brant standing beside her holding Scrappy, and it took a moment for her brain to function enough to remember she was on his boat.

"Sorry to interrupt, but you've been at it for a little more than an hour, and I thought you might be hungry. I made you a taco." He lifted a plate into view.

An hour? "Sorry," she mumbled. "I can stop. I sometimes get lost when I'm sketching."

"You don't have to stop. I love watching you draw, and *look* at that picture." He shook his head. "I can feel the water moving around the rocks. I thought the mural you painted at the Bistro was phenomenal, but this drawing is even better. You're incredibly talented. Your work should be shown in galleries and sold in stores."

She scoffed, uncomfortable with such high praise, and glanced at the sketchbook, feeling she was seeing the drawing for the first time. That happened often when she was in the zone. She quickly closed it and set it aside to take the plate from him. "Thank you. I'm sorry to screw up your schedule."

"I have nothing on my schedule but getting you safely to the Cape tonight." He sat with Scrappy on his lap as she ate. "Where did you learn to draw?"

"I've been drawing since I was a kid. I've read up on techniques, but I've never taken classes or anything. When I first came to the Cape, we found some old sketches Ava had done when she was young. I guess I inherited her artistic genes." She held up her taco. "This is really good. Thank you."

"My pleasure. That's where I'm going to teach you to swim, in the cove."

"I don't plan on going in the water anytime soon, so you don't need to teach me."

"You didn't plan on saving Scrappy, either. You can't live on an island and not know how to swim. It's too dangerous. Mark my words—you're swimming in Mermaid Cove."

She knew he was right about needing to learn to swim, but the thought of his hands on her as he gave her lessons set off those butterflies she was constantly trying to squash. "Why in *this* cove?" she asked, curious about their mermaid connection.

"Because you're a private person, and I have a feeling getting you to swim in the pool where I live would be like pulling teeth. Only islanders know about this cove, but it's hard to get to. The only people willing to trek through the woods to get there are the Bra Brigaders."

Shelley's mother, Lenore, headed up the Bra Brigade, a group of women who gathered in remote places on the island to sunbathe in their bras. Lenore was in her seventies, but she'd started the group as a teenager, and it had grown to include many of the women on the island. Cait had heard that Ava had taken part in it, and Abby had told Cait that she and her friends had joined them on occasion, too. Deirdra wanted nothing to do with sunbathing in her bra, and Cait was definitely on Team Deirdra.

"Besides," he said with a coy grin, "it's my favorite spot on the island."

She was floored, and pleased, that he had thought of how private she was. He was full of surprises, and they were slowly chipping away at her resolve to keep her distance. She also liked knowing that he had a favorite spot *and* that he'd shared it with her. "Why is it your favorite?"

"Because when I was ten, I went there with my friends and we were all horsing around. I went under and couldn't find my way back up. I don't remember much, but I remember swallowing water and being scared shitless, and then a mermaid came out of nowhere and saved me." His expression brightened. "She brought me right up to the surface."

Cait felt her jaw go slack. She wasn't sure if he was kidding, but even if he was, the story and the cove made their connection feel that much deeper. "You don't really believe in that stuff, do you?"

"Sure do. Don't you?"

"Um . . . *yeah*." A little thrill scampered through her at his belief in mermaids. She didn't want to admit that she used to believe her mother had turned into a mermaid after she'd died—or the crazy notion that was currently going through her mind. That her mother had been the one that had saved him.

"I knew we had things in common. Let me make you another taco." He reached for her plate as if he talked about mermaids every day.

"It's okay. I can do it." Her mind reeled. "Did your friends see the mermaid?"

"No. I was with Jock, Archer, and Grant, and they were busy messing around. They didn't even realize I was in trouble until I broke the surface, gagging and coughing, and then they didn't believe me about the mermaid. No one believes me, but that's okay. I know what I saw." Jock and Archer Steele were twins and the oldest of Shelley's six kids. Grant Silver was Keira's oldest brother, and he was engaged to Shelley's youngest daughter, Jules.

As she made another taco, her pulse quickened. She liked how he owned his beliefs, even if everyone else laughed them off, and she wanted to know more about him. "How did you get into boatbuilding? Have you always liked boats?"

"Yes, but it borders on more of an obsession. My mother will tell you that *boat* was my first word. I've been around boats my whole life. You know my family owns the marina and my father runs it. But you probably don't know that my grandfather was a boatbuilder before he retired. I remember as a little boy wanting to figure out how something so big and heavy could stay afloat. By the time I was six, I spent every free minute I could with my grandfather, following him around as he built and refitted boats."

He looked out at the water with a thoughtful expression, then turned that soft, sexy gaze on her. "I worked at the marina with my dad as a teenager, but in the evenings I'd hang out with my grandfather to learn from him. The two of them taught me almost everything I know. My grandfather pulled some strings with his friends who taught engineering, and by the time I was in high school, I was learning from them, too. I started designing and building boats in my senior year of high school, and within a few years, I'd made a pretty penny. By the time I was in my midtwenties, I had developed a solid business. When the marine equipment supply company came up for sale, I wanted it in the worst way. I wanted people to think of us for all their marine needs. I had saved up some money by then, but of course not nearly enough, so I asked my father and grandfather to go in on it with me. They put me through the wringer, making me come up with a prospectus with projected earnings and expenses, the whole nine yards. They approved, and we went in on it together. I've never looked back." He laughed softly. "*And* I've just given you way more of an answer than you asked for. Sorry."

She envied his openness and wished for the millionth time she'd grown up differently. She couldn't imagine growing up with that kind of love and support. "I like hearing about your life. You're lucky to have such a great family. Did you ever want to move away?" If she had a family like his, she sure wouldn't have.

"No. Family is everything to me. I wouldn't be who I am without them. What about you? Where did you grow up? Do you have other sisters or brothers?"

"I was adopted as a baby, but I was an only child." She could stop there, but Brant was so open with her, she wanted to give him something back. "We lived in Rhode Island until I was four, when my adoptive mom passed away. Then my father moved us to Connecticut."

Empathy rose in his eyes. "Oh, Cait, I'm sorry. I didn't know you lost your other mom, too. That must have been difficult, especially at such a young age."

"It was. I have very few memories of her, but I have a sense of her. Or maybe of the emptiness she left behind, because I still miss her every day." She had no idea why she admitted that, but it was easy to be honest with him.

"I bet you do." He put his hand over hers, giving it a reassuring squeeze, then moved it away, as if he knew keeping it there might make her nervous. "Do you have a favorite memory of her?"

Nobody had ever asked her that before, and she wanted to share her favorites with him. Maybe because he had such great memories of his family, she wanted to cling to hers, too, or maybe it was just because she enjoyed talking to him. She had a feeling it was the latter and went with it. "I have two, actually. She wore a mermaid-tail necklace. It was blue and silver, and she never took it off. I have flashes of memories of reaching up and touching it as she leaned over me to kiss me good night. Her name was Karen, and it was engraved on the back."

"A mermaid tail?" He leaned close and lowered his voice. "I think we were fated to meet, Caity."

She was starting to wonder about that, too.

"I hope your father saved that necklace for you."

"He gave away all of her possessions." The ache in her chest softened her tone.

"Aw, babe. I'm sorry."

"That's okay. I have another favorite memory," she said, wanting to get away from the ugly subject of her father. "My mom used to walk a lot. I remember holding her hand and walking fast to keep up. I feel like we went on a lot of walks, but I could have made that up in my head, you know, wanting special memories."

"Is that why you prefer to walk?"

"Maybe," she said. "Probably."

"Are you close to your father?"

"No." She answered too fast, instantly regretting it as questions rose in Brant's eyes, and his brows knitted.

"What about your extended family? Are your grandparents still around?"

Relieved he hadn't pushed about her father, she said, "I never saw my mother's parents after we moved, and my father's parents are gone." She was careful not to say they'd passed away. She didn't like to lie any more than he did, and technically it was the truth. The mean-spirited couple *was* gone from her life.

"I'm sorry to hear that." His brow furrowed again. "You said you moved after your mom died. Was it hard moving away from your friends and the place where you lived with her?"

"I don't remember much about it except that it wasn't easy."

"I can only imagine. My younger brother Rowan lost his girlfriend, Carlotta, when their little girl, Joni, was an infant. He still drives the food truck he and Carlotta ran together, and he bought the café where they met just so he would always have that memory to share with Joni."

"Rowan is your *brother*? I know him and Joni, but I didn't know their last name was Remington. I met them through some friends on the Cape a couple of years ago." Cait had met them through the Wickeds. Joni was a sweet little girl with a big personality, and Rowan was a nice guy and a bit of a hippie, which made sense given that Brant's parents, Roddy and Gail, had always reminded her of seventies throwbacks with Gail's earthy style and their laid-back attitudes.

"Really? I'll have to ask him for all your secrets."

"You already know more than he does. Joni's lucky to have such a thoughtful father. My father never talked about my mother. After she died, it was like she never existed." The hair on the back of her neck prickled. She'd never forget the empty feeling of walking into a house where her mother had never lived, or the changes in her father after her mother died.

"Jesus, you poor thing. I would have done anything to take away Rowan's pain when he was grieving. I can't imagine expecting a little girl to shut down those feelings."

Cait needed to escape the memories and pushed to her feet. "Why are we even talking about my boring life? We should clean up and get going."

She started closing the food containers, and Brant gently touched her hand, drawing her eyes to his.

"We're talking because I'd like to get to know you better."

"Trust me, you don't," she said firmly, her pulse quickening with the sincerity in his voice.

His expression turned serious again. "You're wrong, Cait. I like who you are, and not just because you're more beautiful than the sun on a cold winter's day."

A smile tugged at her lips. Why did he have to be so damn nice? "I'm *not* that pretty. Why do you even want to go out with me? Shouldn't you be going after a free spirit with a personality more like yours or Abby's?"

"I happen to like your spirit. We had fun shopping and out here tonight, didn't we?"

"Yeah, but still . . ." *Fun can turn ugly fast.*

"You have no idea how great you are, do you?"

He was looking at her *that* way again, like he wanted to kiss her, and *boy*, did she want to kiss him. She rolled her eyes, a nervous habit she didn't love but couldn't kick.

"Get this through your gorgeous head, angel. I like you because you are sharp, strong, and creative. You're not afraid to challenge anyone. I've never met anyone like you. Everything you do either turns me on or makes me want to know more about you. You're unique, and your air of mystery intrigues me. But I'm not an oblivious twentysomething kid just looking to get laid. I see the wariness in your eyes, and I feel the walls you've built around yourself. But I want to understand what's behind them, not run from them. This inescapable connection we share isn't going away, and all of it—all of *you*—makes me want to try harder to show you that you *can* trust me, because I know that once you do, we'll be phenomenal together."

She could barely breathe for the desire building inside her with the intensity of his stare and the honesty in his voice. But it wasn't just sexual. Something much bigger and all-consuming was urging her to let him into the safe little bubble in which she'd lived for so long—a prospect that was as scary as it was comforting and tantalizing.

His gaze softened. "You're a woman who should be adored, and I have a feeling you might have trusted the wrong people in the past."

She inhaled a ragged breath. He really did see *all* of her.

"I'd like to make sure that never happens again."

The hope in his eyes was palpable. Every iota of her wanted to believe him, to step into the safety of his strong arms as she had yesterday. To block the rest of the world out and pretend she could be the open, carefree woman he deserved. But history held her back, and she regretfully forced her attention away, reaching for the containers.

"We should go. I have a friend picking me up at the dock." She didn't want to ruin their night. She'd had a wonderful time, and as scary as it was to admit the little bit she had, it felt good knowing someone other than her knew about the necklace and how much she'd loved walking with her mother and that her father had basically erased her from their lives. She hadn't even told her sisters about those things. But she needed room to breathe, because *whoa*, that was a lot of herself to share.

"I'll get this." He took the containers from her, holding her gaze. "Is it the tatted-up guy who had his arm around you in the picture?"

She nodded. "Tank." She'd texted him to say she was going to be late when Brant had gone belowdecks to get their dinner.

"That's an ominous name. Is he your boyfriend?"

The thought made her laugh. Tank was more like a guard dog or a protective brother she'd wished she'd had growing up. She put her hand on her hip, going for a playful vibe to break the tension. "If I say yes will you stop hitting on me?"

Those all-seeing eyes bored into her. "Do you *want* me to stop hitting on you?"

Yes. No. I don't know.

A slow grin spread across his handsome face. "I'm going to take that as a *no*."

"I didn't say *no*."

"You didn't say *yes*, either. Which is it, Cait? Yes or no?"

Oh God. She mustered all of her courage and said, "Sometimes I want you to stop, and sometimes I don't."

"*Fifty-fifty*," he said with an even bigger grin. "I'll take those odds. Let me clean this up and we'll get out of here."

He went belowdecks, and she groaned. *Sometimes I want you to stop, and sometimes I don't? What is wrong with me?*

She texted Tank to let him know they were on their way. Thankfully, Brant let the topic go after that, and the rest of their trip was light-hearted and fun. She had no idea how he could make her feel like her entire body was on fire one minute and have her laughing until her sides hurt the next. He'd even coaxed her into piloting the yacht for a little while, but then she loved up Scrappy, hating that she wouldn't see him for a couple of days.

When they reached the Cape, she gave Scrappy several *last* kisses and finally handed him over to Brant and gathered her things. "Promise me you'll let him sleep with you if he gets scared?"

"I promise." Brant scratched Scrappy's head. "He'll be fine. Say goodbye to Mommy." He waved the pup's paw.

She was going to miss them. *Him. Scrappy!*

Yeah, right.

"Thanks again for the ride, and for letting me sketch the cove, and for dinner, and for teaching me to drive the boat." She sighed. "Thanks for a great night. It was fun."

"Anytime, angel. Tell your tatted friend I said, *Game on. Prepare to lose.*"

She laughed and stepped off the yacht, the endearment—*angel*—growing on her just like her dimple-cheeked charmer was. As she headed down to the end of the docks, where she saw her burly friend waiting, she knew she should probably tell Brant that Tank wasn't her boyfriend, that he was madly in love with his pregnant wife, Leah Yates, and their two little girls, Junie and Rosie. But as she'd told Abby and Faye, Brant was hard enough to resist when he had competition. She couldn't imagine how he'd turn up the heat if he knew he had none.

She glanced over her shoulder and saw him standing at the front of the boat, watching her. He waved, and her stomach flipped. *Operation Stop the Butterflies* was now *Operation Keep Him from Seeing Me So Clearly*, which was something she wasn't even sure she wanted to do.

In other words, she was screwed.

Tank lifted his bearded chin in greeting as he took her bag and embraced her. "Hey, sweetheart."

At six four, with a body built for a fight, inked and pierced to the hilt, and donning his ever-present black leather Dark Knights motorcycle club vest, Tank had an intimidating presence, softened only by his heart of gold. After the death of his younger sister several years ago, he'd become a volunteer firefighter and had been on a mission to rescue everyone in his path, until meeting Leah, who had helped him deal with those demons. Cait had never been more thankful than the day she'd met him, when he must have added her to that list. He was the best friend a girl could ask for.

"Thanks for coming. Sorry I'm late."

"It's all good. Your ride go okay?" Tank asked as they headed to his truck. "You look a little funny."

That's because I liked opening up to Brant way too much. "Yeah. It was fun. I'm just a little tired."

"Uh-huh. I believe you're beat, and to be honest, I'm worried about you going back and forth so much. It's got to wear you out." He looked at her out of the corner of his eye. "But I'm feeling something else. Want to tell me what's up?"

His ability to read people was on par with all-seeing Brant's. "It's nothing, really. I guess I'm just not used to having fun with guys, except you and your motley crew of brothers and cousins, but that's different."

"You really *like* this guy, don't you?" He sounded as surprised as she felt.

She shrugged one shoulder, feeling his eyes on her, but she stared straight ahead as they crossed the parking lot. "He's nice."

"I checked him out," he said, bringing her eyes to his.

"You checked out Brant?" That shouldn't surprise her. Tank was the most protective man she'd ever met, and not just of her, but of everyone he called a friend. The Dark Knights helped to keep the community safe, and they had members in every walk of life and more connections than one could imagine.

He cocked a grin. "'Course I did. Did you know he's Rowan's brother?"

"I didn't until tonight when Brant told me." She thought about them for a moment, searching for similarities. Rowan was taller than Brant but not as muscular as his boatbuilding brother. They had the same wavy brown hair and similar blue eyes, though Brant wore his hair shorter, and his eyes were electric and full of energy, while Rowan's were midnight blue and contemplative, but she could see the similarities now.

When did I start picking apart men?

"Well, I can't find any dirt on Brant or his family." Tank stopped walking beside his truck. "Near as I can tell, he's clean as a Boy Scout."

"I told you that everyone on the island loves him. He's an open book. He can't even lie." *So why am I worried that he could be like Jekyll and Hyde?* Wouldn't her sisters know that by now and have warned her? All it took was one thought of her father to find the answer. The pillar of society everyone saw in her father was in complete contrast to the man he was behind closed doors. But *still.* Her sisters and their friends seemed to know everything about the people they'd grown up with. It was different from living in Connecticut, where most of the students in her own school hadn't even known her name.

Tank studied her eyes the way she caught Brant doing sometimes. "Do you trust him?"

"That's just it, Tank. I feel like I *can* trust him, but . . ."

"But you're afraid to trust your instincts."

"Bingo." As she climbed into the truck, she realized that with Brant, Jekyll and Hyde *wasn't* her biggest fear after all, which came as a shock because it had been her biggest fear about men since she was a little girl. But she knew that the more she let him in, the more he'd want to know about her, and *that* was all the reason she needed to try to keep her distance. Once he knew about her past, he'd probably bolt before she even had a chance to discover his flaws—leaving her even more broken than she'd been before she met him.

CHAPTER FIVE

THE BUZZ OF tattoo guns and murmurs of hushed conversations rose around Cait as she cleaned her work space before her last client Tuesday evening at Wicked Ink. She'd worked twelve hours yesterday, and by the time she left tonight she'd have racked up another twelve hours. She pulled out her phone and saw she'd missed a text from Deirdra and one from Brant, sparking a flutter in her chest. The butterflies in her stomach had migrated with every picture and text he'd sent since Sunday night, starting with an impossibly cute picture of him and Scrappy sitting on his front porch when they'd gotten home that evening. Cait had woken up to a good-morning text yesterday—*He slept like a champ in my bed*—immediately followed by, *We'd both sleep better if you were here with us,* and a winking emoji. Another text had rolled in seconds later. *I can't lie. If you were in my bed, we would get very little sleep.* Brant was so freaking honest, she didn't know if she should commend him or slap him. She'd never gotten texts like that, and they should probably cause her red flags to fly, but somehow Brant managed to come across sweet and funny instead of threatening, not to mention how that combination conjured very *enticing* images. He'd also sent less flirtatious texts like, *We're out for a boat ride and miss our captain.* He'd made her not only think about him constantly but *miss* him incessantly.

She opened Deirdra's message first, since they hadn't touched base for a few days. *You almost DROWNED? WTH? Why didn't you tell me?*

Deirdra was two years younger than Cait and two years older than Abby. She was used to being an older sister, and it showed in her take-charge attitude. Cait didn't mind. It was nice having sisters who cared about her. She thumbed out a response, eager to get to Brant's message. *Because I'm fine and you're busy. Sorry. Next time I almost die, I'll let you know.* She added a kissing emoji and opened Brant's text.

A picture popped up of Brant sitting on a boat with Scrappy standing on his lap. He captioned the photo *Our boy's first haircut!* Scrappy looked like a whole new dog, his fur neatly trimmed. They'd left the fur on his head longer, which made it look too big for his tiny body, making him even more adorable. Brant was leaning forward with his face close to Scrappy's. He wore his baseball cap backward, and the deep-dimpled smile that had been setting her body aflame sent those flurries into a wild frenzy.

"I've never seen you so attached to your phone." Gia, another tattooist and a close friend, leaned over the half wall separating their work-stations. She had more tattoos than Cait decorating her light brown skin and enough sass for a city of women. Her mass of corkscrew curls stuck out in all directions, and her pink-painted lips were set in a wide grin as she craned her neck to see what Cait was looking at. "*Mm-mm.* Who is *that* fine piece?"

"Just the friend that I told you about who's watching Scrappy." Cait started to put her phone away.

"Do not even *think* about putting that away." Gia strutted into her workstation, all legs in a skintight gray minidress, and snagged her phone. "*Girl*, now I see why you like spending time on that rinky-dink island."

"Yeah, it has nothing to do with my sisters," Cait said sarcastically.

Aria, another tattooist and friend, walked past with a customer, and Gia said, "Hey, A. You've got to see this." She motioned for the petite and shy tattooed blonde to join them.

Aria sent her customer on his way and hurried into Cait's work area. "What are we looking at?"

Aria had social anxieties, which made them all protective of her, and she was the most soft-spoken person Cait had ever met, rarely speaking louder than just above a whisper.

Gia showed her Cait's phone.

Aria's eyes widened. "*Who* is that with your dog?"

"The guy she *failed* to tell us about." Gia handed Cait her phone and crossed her arms. "I thought we were friends."

"We *are*." Cait put her phone away.

"Friends don't keep hot guys from each other," Gia pointed out.

"She's only been back a day," Aria reminded her. "Maybe she was going to tell us about him."

"There's *nothing* to tell. Brant is just a friend I met through Abby, and he's watching the dog. It's not a big deal." She hadn't told any of them about almost drowning, either. If Tank got wind of that, he'd probably send a Dark Knight to watch her twenty-four-seven, and that was the last thing she needed.

"You're doing that twitchy thing you do when you're not telling the truth." Gia nudged Aria. "You see that? Our girl Cait has secrets."

Tank eyed them from his workstation across from Cait's, where he was finishing a tattoo on a customer's leg. He turned off his tattoo gun, reaching for a paper towel, his dark eyes trained on Cait as he lifted his chin. He was a man of few words, and Cait had learned to read his silent messages. The narrowing of his eyes and the serious set of his jaw told her he wanted to know if there was any truth to what Gia had said.

Cait shook her head, knowing he'd see through her half-hearted denial. Sure enough, his eyes narrowed further, and his nostrils flared.

Damn it. Cait pushed to her feet, shooing the girls out of her space. "Get out of here and clean your stations. I don't have time for this. I have a client at seven."

"We're not done with this conversation," Gia said as she headed back to her area. "You and I are going to have a long talk tonight at the Salty Hog. And don't even think about ghosting me."

Tank's parents owned the Salty Hog restaurant and bar in Harwich Port, not far from the tattoo shop, and they hung out there pretty often after work. She'd agreed to meet Gia there for a drink after work. As per usual, Aria had already turned them down, and Tank couldn't wait to get home to Leah and the girls.

"Fine. *Whatever.* Just let me get through my last client and I'll meet you there." Cait could use a little downtime. She'd been working nonstop, and she had to do it all over again tomorrow. She began preparing for her next client, and a few minutes later she heard Tank saying goodbye to his client, and then she felt him watching her.

She didn't turn around as she said, "*What?*"

She heard him walk behind her, and his heavy arm circled her shoulder. She looked up at his serious face. His pitch-black beard and hair rivaled his dark eyes, making the silver jewelry he wore in his nose, ear, and around his neck seem even brighter.

"Is there something you're not telling me?"

His deep, gruff voice used to frighten Cait, but now she found it reassuring. "Not really."

"That sounds like a *yes.* Want to talk?"

She shook her head.

He arched a brow.

"How can I talk about something I haven't figured out yet?" she said sharply.

"That means there's something *to* figure out. It's a good thing I ran a check on that guy. I think I'd better make a visit to the island."

She rolled her eyes. "You *don't* need to do that."

"This is the first time since I've known you that you've shown interest in any man. I know you can handle yourself, and Rowan assured me that Brant is a great guy, but I'd feel better if I met him and let him know *who's* got your back."

Cait sighed. "How about you *don't*? Things are different on the island, Tank. They're like one big happy family, and I don't want to screw that up. What will they think if you show up and start threatening people?"

"Who said anything about threatening? Besides, they know how Dark Knights work. Did you forget that your friend Shelley's son Levi is in the Harborside chapter?"

"Yes, as a matter of fact, I *did* forget that. But I still don't want you going all Neanderthal on—" The door to the shop opened, and they both turned as Brant strode in wearing the doggy sling with Scrappy's little face peering over the top. She got all melty inside, but in the next second, her chest constricted. What the heck was he doing there? This was supposed to be her time *away* from butterflies and Brant's all-seeing blue eyes, which were now locked on her. Her body ignited, and *"Brant"* came out strangled.

Tank rolled his shoulders back, standing up to his full height, and Cait grabbed his shirt, speaking through gritted teeth. "Be *nice*."

Cait hurried to the front, her nerves prickling. Brant flashed a smile, and her knees buckled. *Damn him.* She took his arm and led him back to the door. "*What* are you doing here?"

"We missed you, too, angel."

Her stomach fluttered. *No fluttering!* "Don't call me that." She shot a glance at Tank, who was closing the distance between them. "I'm *working*. Why are you on the Cape?"

"I came to get a tattoo. Don't worry. I've got an appointment for seven o'clock." His eyes shifted to Tank, and he offered him a hand. "Hi. I'm Brant Remington, a *close* friend of Cait's."

"Tank Wicked." He shook Brant's hand. "A *closer* friend of Cait's." *Ohmygod . . .*

"And I'm *Gia*." Gia said her name seductively as she hurried into the lobby, hips and boobs swaying. She pushed between Cait and Tank, fluttering her long lashes, openly checking out Brant. "Aren't you *sweet*."

Brant looked at Scrappy. "He is, isn't he?"

"Oh, yes, the dog is too, honey." Gia winked.

Cait glowered at her.

"It's nice to meet all of you." Brant looked past them, and Cait followed his gaze to Aria, who was standing at the entrance to the lobby watching them, fidgeting with the hem of her sleeveless shirt. "Hey there. I'm Brant, Caity's friend."

Tank and Gia turned wide eyes to Cait and said, "*Caity?*"

Cait gritted her teeth. *This cannot be happening.*

"You give Zander hell when he calls you that." Tank gave her a scrutinizing glare.

"Zan calls me *Caity Cat*. Now, can we move on from whatever this is?"

"Who's this Zander guy?" Brant asked gruffly.

"*Ugh!* He's Tank's cousin." Cait pulled Brant away from the others. "What are you really doing here?"

"I told you. I have an appointment for a tattoo." Brant pulled out his phone and showed her a picture of an anchor with a mermaid's tail wrapped around it.

A knot formed in her stomach.

"Um, *Cait?*" Aria said from behind the reception desk. "There's a *BR* down for seven o'clock with you."

Brant grinned. "That's me."

Gia sauntered over and put a hand on Brant's shoulder. "I can *do* him if you don't want to, *Caity*."

"I've got him, thanks."

"Okay, chickadee." Gia ran her hand down Brant's arm and said, "You should come party with me and Cait tonight at the Salty Hog. It's a bar and restaurant a few minutes from here. We'll have a few drinks, get to know each other better, and get our groove on."

Cait shot Gia a death stare. Her worlds were *not* supposed to collide like this. She saw Tank's eyes narrowing and knew he was chomping at the bit to insert himself into the conversation.

"I'd love to, but I've got our boy," Brant said, petting Scrappy. "I really can't leave him alone."

Cait breathed a little easier.

Gia waved her hand. "Bring him along. Tank's parents own the bar, and they bring their dogs all the time."

That slow, sexy grin appeared as Brant's gaze returned to Cait. "Sounds fun. I'd love to."

Are you freaking kidding me? The Salty Hog was her safe space, where she could let her guard down and relax. Now she'd be a nervous wreck all night.

Gia wiggled her shoulders. "Awesome, sugar. You *won't* regret it."

But will I?

"Let's go, *BR*. Looks like I've got some tattooing to do." She grabbed Brant's sleeve, dragging him toward her workstation, wondering how she was supposed to give him a tattoo when her nerves were fried. She pointed to the chair, said, "*Sit,*" and turned her back to Brant, taking a deep breath. *I can do this. He's just a customer.* When she turned around, Tank was handing Brant a clipboard with the paperwork for the tattoo and a pen. *Way to go, Cait.* Brant had her so frazzled, she'd totally forgotten their procedures.

As Brant completed the paperwork, Tank walked into his work area, talking on his phone. "Hey, babe. I'm going to be late tonight," he said in the soft tone he used only with Leah. "I've got to run over to the Hog for a bit . . ."

Of course you're coming.

Okay. She could deal with this. Maybe Tank would be a good distraction from Brant and his dangerous dimples.

Brant was watching her, petting Scrappy.

Why did you really come all this way?

66

He set the clipboard on the counter, stepping so close to Cait she could barely breathe. "I thought you'd be a little happier to see us."

The disappointment in his voice tugged at her, but his proximity had her rambling thoughts falling from her lips too fast to stop them. "I *am* happy to see you and I'm glad you brought Scrappy, but you could have told me you were coming. I could have done a tattoo for you on the island. My life here is different from my life there. It feels weird to have them cross like this, and it makes me *flustered*. I hate to be flustered."

He gazed deeply into her eyes, casting some sort of spell on her that made her want to press her lips to his. "I'm sorry, Cait. I didn't mean to make you uncomfortable. Maybe this will help."

He took Scrappy out of the sling and handed him to her. Scrappy licked her face, wriggling excitedly, easing some of her tension. *How did you know?* "Hello, baby. I missed you." Her eyes flicked to Brant. "How did you get an appointment with me so fast?"

"I booked it almost a month ago because I didn't like not seeing you for two or three days at a time when you came back here. This was the first appointment you had available." He leaned closer again, his warm, minty breath whispering over her skin as he said, "But if you really want me to leave, I will."

Lord. A month ago? She tore her eyes away and looked at Scrappy, trying to process what that meant.

"So you're not here just because of the last few days?"

"No, but if I didn't have the appointment, I *definitely* would have shown up anyway." His lips quirked up. "What can I say? I missed seeing you yesterday."

She inhaled shakily. *You missed me.* She should tell him she'd missed him, too, but she couldn't. Wouldn't.

"We're out of here," Gia said loudly, bringing the sexual tension between them down a notch. Unfortunately, the difference between *combustible* and *blazing* wasn't enough to calm Cait's nerves. Gia waved as she and Aria headed for the door. "See you at the Hog, Blue Eyes!"

Brant's gaze never left Cait's. "What do you want me to do, Cait? Stay or leave?"

Tank glanced over, making her even more nervous, but no part of her wanted Brant to leave, even if she was frazzled. Scrappy licked her chin, reminding her to answer. "You're here. You might as well stay."

"Now, that's more like it," he said in a low, enticing voice.

Tank cleared his throat.

Brant turned his attention to Tank. "Sorry, man. I don't mean to step on your toes over here." He glanced briefly at Cait, threw his shoulders back, and puffed out his chest. "Actually, I *do* mean to step on your toes."

Tank arched a brow.

Cait stifled a laugh. "Um . . . *Brant*, Tank and I aren't going out."

"You're *not*? Why didn't you tell me that when I asked about him?" Before she could respond, he looked at Tank, completely unruffled, and said, "Do you have any idea how long I've been trying to get a date with this woman?"

"No, but I'll know everything there is to know about you two in a few hours." Tank leaned back in his chair, kicked one booted foot up on the table, and crossed his other over his ankle, watching them.

Cait stalked over to him and handed him the dog. "Can you *please* take Scrap for a walk or something?"

Tank pushed to his feet. "You sure?"

"Positive. Thank you."

With a nod, he headed out the front door, and Cait went back to Brant. "Where do you want your tattoo?"

Brant cocked a grin. "Wherever you want to put it."

Her mind immediately ran down a laundry list of parts she'd like to touch, taste, and tattoo. *Down, girl.* She should have bought herself a shock collar at the pet supply store. She narrowed her eyes, trying to regain control of her runaway hormones. "You sure? I've tattooed some pretty sensitive body parts."

His brows slanted. "How about my chest?" He pulled off the sling and set it on the counter, then tugged his shirt off, tossing it on top of the sling, and rolled his shoulders back.

Cait's mouth went dry, her fingers itching to touch the dusting of hair on his chest.

"Where do you want me, angel?" he asked huskily.

Everywhere . . .

He brushed his fingers over his pecs and across one nipple, causing *both* of their nipples to pebble. His hand slid down his stomach and his muscles flexed.

Yesss. Keep going . . .

He cleared his throat, and his grin turned cocky, snapping her from her stupor. She waved her hand, laughing at having been caught for the billionth time gawking at him.

"Get all of that away from me." She pointed to the table. "On your back."

He chuckled as he climbed onto the table, and she turned to wash her hands. When she turned back, her eyes locked on the beefy buffet before her—thick thighs straining against his shorts, the impressive bulge behind his zipper, and planes of rough, rugged *man*. She needed to pull herself together or she'd drool on him, which he'd probably enjoy.

So would I.

Ohmygod.

What was wrong with her? She'd tattooed plenty of hot guys and never had reactions like that. She grabbed a paper towel and rubbing alcohol, reminding herself she was a professional.

He raised his brows. "Want to see my anchor?"

She gave him a deadpan look. "An anchor is a pretty common tattoo around here, and I know how to draw a mermaid's tail. I'm going to do it freehand on your skin rather than drawing it on the computer and then printing a stencil, if that's okay."

"That's fine, but you might want to take a good hard look at it. My *anchor* is heftier than others."

She shook her head, stifling a laugh. "Where do you want it?"

"*Well . . .*" That slow, sexy grin appeared again.

She rolled her eyes. "Which *side*?"

He patted his left pec. "This way you'll always be anchored to my heart."

She felt a tug in her chest at Brant connecting *her* to the mermaid tail, but she told herself that he loved Mermaid Cove, and she was overthinking it. "How long did it take you to think that line up?"

"About seven seconds, which is about six seconds longer than it took for me to be attracted to you."

His charm was sucking her right in. She tried to focus on cleaning his chest, which was torture in and of itself. She didn't dare look at his face. If she didn't see it, maybe she could pretend he was just another customer. After cleaning the area, she grabbed a new plastic razor and unwrapped it.

When it touched his skin, he flinched and snapped, "What're you doing?"

Why are you so nervous? "I have to shave the area."

"Oh, *right*. Go ahead."

He lay rigid as a board as she shaved that side of his chest. His skin was warm, his muscles hard, and he smelled fresh and manly. She had never noticed those types of things when she worked. She was usually too focused on the design. She set the razor aside and grabbed a pen. "How big do you want it?"

His eyes held hers. "You decide. I trust you."

Why did those words touch her so deeply? She leaned over him and began drawing the anchor.

"Do you freehand all of your work?" he asked.

"Mostly. Sometimes the smallest changes can make it a thousand times better. I didn't become a tattooist to follow other people's lines."

"Why did you?"

She felt his fingertips on her back, making it even more difficult to concentrate. "A lot of reasons."

"Like?"

"I like to draw."

He ran his fingers up and down her back as she drew. "That's it?" he asked softly. "You like to draw?"

She lifted her eyes to his, and the genuine interest in them drew the truth. "I feel good when I'm drawing. I can disappear into it and tune out the rest of the world."

"And you do piercings, right? Does that mean you like to inflict pain?"

"Everyone asks me that, and the answer is no. I like how body jewelry looks, and the money is good. I can make my own hours doing this type of work, and I don't have to deal with awful bosses or crowds."

He seemed to think about that as she finished the drawing and handed him a mirror.

He waved it off. "I don't need to see it."

"Brant, this is permanent. You should make sure it's exactly what you want."

"I don't need to," he said, holding her gaze. "I *know* what I want, and so do you. I trust you to do right by me, the same way you can trust me to do right by you."

His words sank in, and *I do trust you* was on the tip of her tongue. But she held it back. "Okay. It's your body. What colors do you want?" She began gathering her tools.

"Black for the anchor. Pink for the banner."

She froze, his voice whispering through her mind. *I pegged you as having a thing for black lingerie. Pink is much hotter.* She looked over her shoulder at him. *"Pink?"*

"It's a new favorite of mine."

She couldn't look away, and there was no suppressing her smile. "You're too much."

"Don't be silly, angel. I'm exactly enough."

Oh boy. There went her nerves again.

She got the tattoo gun ready, put on gloves, and scooted her tool tray into position beside him. When she leaned over his chest with the tattoo gun, his entire body flexed, hands fisted. "Nervous?"

"Why do you say that?" he asked.

"Because you're wound tighter than a top."

"*Nah*, I'm good." His jaw clenched.

"Okay, here we go." She turned on the tattoo gun.

He sucked in air between gritted teeth and closed his eyes. When she touched the needle to his skin, his entire body jerked. She lifted the needle as Tank came in the front door, and Brant bolted upright, gritting out, "*Holy mother of Christ.* Is it supposed to feel like you're tearing a hole in my chest?"

Tank chuckled as he headed into his work area with Scrappy.

Cait shot him a narrow-eyed stare to shut him up. Brant was rubbing his chest. She'd never seen him like this. He was always overly confident. "The night we met, didn't you say you had tattoos below your waist?"

"Yeah." Brant's gaze softened. "That wasn't exactly true."

"Looks like we got back just in time for the good stuff," Tank said.

Cait glared at him, then turned a kinder expression to Brant. "You lied to me?"

"I *embellished.*"

She raised her brows.

"*What?* I wanted to impress you. Is that a crime? You have tattoos, so I figured I'd say I did, too."

"What if we had gotten together? I'd see that you didn't have any tattoos and know that you lied."

"*Embellished.* Come on, Cait, cut me a little slack. I'm not as edgy and cool as you are, but I've got a lot of other great qualities." He flashed a dimpled grin. "Besides, I would have gotten temporary tattoos."

She and Tank laughed.

"So what Grant said the night we met was true? You're afraid of needles?"

"*Afraid* is a little strong. I don't love them," Brant admitted. "But trust is a two-way street, and I figured if I want you to trust me enough to go out with me, then I need to show you I trust you, too."

Cait's chest constricted. "You would get a tattoo just to show me that?"

"*Damn,* man." Tank gave Cait a look that either said Brant was nuts or that he was impressed—she couldn't tell which. He turned away, giving them a modicum of privacy.

She didn't care what the look Tank had given her meant, because she knew how she felt about what Brant was prepared to do for her. He'd come all that way thinking he'd get a tattoo and then go back to the island just so he could see her and earn her trust, *and* he'd brought Scrappy when he could have left him with someone on the Cape. She knew Brant well enough to know he didn't shirk his responsibilities, and that meant as much to her as his efforts to gain her trust did.

"Brant, do you *want* a tattoo of an anchor and a mermaid tail?"

He shrugged one shoulder. "Maybe."

She set down her gun. "I don't tattoo *maybes.*"

"Come on, Cait. It's not like I'll pass out or anything." He leaned closer with a playful expression and lowered his voice. "But you can revive me, right? Just in case? Mouth-to-mouth?"

She laughed. He was too frigging charming; it made him *almost* irresistible. "You don't have to get a permanent mark on your body to earn my trust."

His gaze turned serious. "Then tell me how to earn it."

Her pulse quickened. Nobody had ever done *half* the things he'd done for her or spent even a fraction of the time he'd spent patiently trying to get her to go out with him. She *wanted* to trust her instincts, but she wasn't there yet. She wished she had a crystal ball that could see into the future and tell her if Brant was truly the man everyone thought he was. She glanced at Tank and realized the answer was right there in front of her. Nobody read people like the Wickeds. She might not trust her own instincts, but she trusted Tank and his family with her life.

"What do you say, Caity?" Brant's gaze warmed. "Tell me how to earn your trust, and I'll make the effort."

She believed he would, and she really *did* like the way that too-girly nickname sounded when he said it, all warm and welcoming and special. "You've already done a lot. Why don't we go have some fun and see how tonight goes?"

"Now you're talkin'." He looked down at his chest. "How does that look?"

"Like you nicked yourself shaving." She wet a paper towel and held it out for him.

"I like it better when you do it."

"That's what all the guys say." She pressed the wet paper towel into his hand. "You can't always get what you want."

As she turned to clean up, he said, "We'll see about that. I'm a very patient man."

CHAPTER SIX

BRANT FOLLOWED CAIT to the Salty Hog in the truck he'd rented, thinking about how tempted he'd been to kiss her at the tattoo shop. When he'd first seen her, drop-dead gorgeous in faded jeans with holes in the knees riding low on her hips, her blue tank top stopped just above her belly button, giving him a delectable view of her taut stomach, the shock in her eyes had been as palpable at his surprise of her belly-baring top. He'd never seen her wearing one on the island, which told him she was much more comfortable on the Cape and made him even more curious about her relationship with Tank.

He parked beside her car, taking in the two-story rustic restaurant overlooking the harbor, thinking about how he'd felt Cait giving herself a little more freedom to dip her toes into the sea of desire between them, like when he'd touched her back as she was drawing on his chest. He'd thought she might push him away, and when she hadn't, the moment had taken on a hum of intimacy. He wondered which Cait would show up in the bar. Nervous, watchful Cait? Flirtatious, snarky Cait? Or maybe easygoing Cait, the woman he'd gone shopping with and who had piloted his yacht. He admired all of those aspects of her personality, and the last few days had proven that he was right about their connection. It was utterly unstoppable.

He climbed from the truck into the cool night air, greeted by the faint beat of music. As he closed his door, Cait stepped out of her car.

He shook his head. "One day you're going to let me open your car door for you."

He put Scrappy's leash on and grabbed the puppy sling.

"I'm not one of those girls who needs a guy to do everything for her." She reached for Scrappy, loving him up.

"I know you're not. But you're a beautiful woman, and you deserve to be treated special." He motioned toward the restaurant. "This is a great location. You sure we can bring him in there?"

"Yeah. Tank's parents and his brothers Gunner and Baz bring their dogs sometimes. Do you want me to wear the sling? The guys might give you a hard time."

Brant scoffed. "I don't give a damn if they do. This is our boy, and I'll wear this thing proudly."

"Okay, it's your razz fest."

"I think I can handle it, but I want to take him in the grass in case he has to pee before we go in." They headed over to the grass at the edge of the lot. "What's up with your friends' names? Tank and Gunner?"

"Those are their road names. Tank and his brothers and cousins are members of the Bayside chapter of the Dark Knights. Their father, Conroy, and their uncle, Preacher, founded the chapter when they were younger."

"Really? Rowan knows most of the Dark Knights around here. He usually helps out at their suicide prevention rally. I wonder if they know Levi."

"They do." She pointed to the stairs leading up to the second floor. "We're going up there to the bar. I know Rowan and your sisters, but do you have any more siblings?"

Brant's sisters lived on the island. Tessa was a pilot, and Randi was a marine archaeologist working on an expedition with famed treasure hunter Zev Braden off the coast of Silver Island, where they'd discovered the wreckage of the *Pride*, a pirate ship that sank in 1716. "We have one more brother, Jamison. He's an astrophysicist and lives in DC. He's wicked smart, and I can't understand half the things he goes on about, but he's a great guy."

"That's impressive," she said as they climbed the stairs. "Where do you fall in the lineup?"

He was loving this new, relaxed Cait. He'd have to visit her on the Cape more often. "I'm the oldest. Rowan is three years younger than me, and a year older than Jamison. Randi is two years younger than Jamison, and Tessa is the youngest at twenty-six."

"Wow. You guys must have kept your parents busy when you were young."

As they stepped onto the deck, he said, "I'm sorry for catching you off guard at your work."

"It's probably better that you did. If you'd asked if you could swing by, I probably would have told you not to." She smiled more easily, as she had when they were shopping. "I'm actually kind of looking forward to seeing how tonight goes. You're different than I thought you'd be."

"Yeah? In what way?" He pulled open the door.

A tease rose in her eyes. "I can't tell you all my secrets."

He followed her into the crowded bar. The place had a rough vibe. There was a mix of tough-looking guys wearing black leather vests with Dark Knights patches, professionally dressed men in slacks and short-sleeved button-downs, guys wearing shorts and jeans, and women decked out in all sorts of sexy and cute summer outfits.

A couple of older men glanced over from the bar. One had longish silver hair and movie-star good looks; the other was tatted up, bearded, and giving Brant a once-over. Brant put a hand on Cait's back as the men waved to her.

"Boyfriends of yours?" Brant asked.

"Hardly. That's Conroy and Preacher."

She waved to them, and he followed her toward a table in the corner, where Tank was sitting with Gia and a guy with longish blond hair and a trim beard who had his arm around—*holy shit*—Evie Lawrence.

Brant had briefly dated Evie's sister, Brandy, a voluptuous redheaded caterer who lived on the Cape.

Before they reached the table, a stocky guy in a tank top, tattooed from neck to wrist, with military-short blond hair intercepted Cait, hauling her into an embrace. "Good to see you, Weatherby. Where's the new dog?"

"*Our* dog is right here." Brant stepped beside Cait and extended his hand. "Brant Remington, and you are?"

"Gunner Wicked. Nice to meet you." He eyed Cait as he shook Brant's hand. "*Our* dog?"

"We sort of share custody of Scrappy," Cait explained.

Gunner looked between them. "Shared custody. I'm going to need more information on that, but first . . ." He pointed at Brant. "Cool sling, dude. Can I hold the pooch?"

"Sure. He's not used to being passed around. He might get nervous." Brant handed him Scrappy.

"I get it. I run Wicked Animal Rescue. I'm used to this." He rubbed noses with Scrappy, speaking in a playful voice. "Hello, little guy. We're going to be good buddies, aren't we?"

Brant liked him already. They headed for the table, and Evie jumped to her feet. "Brant?" Her long brown hair flew over her shoulders as she hurried around the table to greet him. The guy with longish blond hair who'd had his arm around Evie followed her.

"You know Evie?" Cait asked.

"I dated her sister a while back," Brant said as Evie opened her arms to hug him. "Hey, Evie. Good to see you. How's Brandy?"

"She's fantastic." Evie turned an incredulous look at Cait. "I didn't know you knew *Brant*. Are you two going out?"

"No. We're just friends," Cait said. "Abby introduced us."

"Hi. I'm Baz. Tank's brother." The shaggy-haired blond guy held out his hand, and Brant shook it.

"*Brant.* Nice to meet you," he said, trying to catch what Evie was saying to Cait, but he couldn't hear her.

"Hands off, Evie," Gia shouted across the table. "I've got dibs on Cait's island man."

"Don't let Cait kid you, Gia," Brant called over to her. "I'm not on the market. Cait and I are in a committed relationship, co-parenting that little guy." He nodded to Scrappy and set his eyes on Cait. "I'm a loyal guy. I take my commitments very seriously."

Tank chuckled, and Baz raised a brow curiously at Cait.

"Gotta love a guy who respects commitment," Evie said, nudging Cait.

Gunner clapped Brant on the back. "If Tank hadn't already checked you out, I'd tell you to back the fuck off our Cait. But since you're Rowan's brother and you're willing to wear a dog purse, you get a free pass. That is, unless Cait tells us to push back. Then the only thing you'll get is buried six feet under."

Brant splayed his hands. "Hey, we're on the same side, man. We're both looking out for Cait."

"Good to hear it," Gunner said.

"Take a seat," Baz said. "We'll pour you a beer."

As Gunner went to the bar to get more glasses, Baz tugged on the back of Evie's shirt, and they went to sit down. Brant pulled out a chair for Cait and sat beside her. He leaned closer and said, "Your friends seem nice."

"They are, unless you do wrong by them. Then they're your worst nightmare. So . . . you and *Brandy*?"

Did he detect a hint of jealousy? "We went out a few times last year, but there was no spark between us."

"Really? She's beautiful and outgoing—that's hard to believe," Cait said.

"She's also a hell of a cook, and we're still friends." He put his hand on Cait's under the table, giving it a quick squeeze. "But I've never felt even remotely close to the chemistry you and I have, with her or anyone else."

She held his gaze for three hot seconds, before looking away and sliding her hand out from under his.

Damn . . .

Gunner returned with a pitcher of beer in one hand and two glasses tucked under his arm and Scrappy in the other. Clearly he was used to juggling pups and other things. Brant pushed to his feet and took the glasses and pitcher, pouring their drinks.

Baz took Scrappy from Gunner, and as Gunner sat down, he said, "Scrappy's in good hands. Baz is a vet. So tell me, Remington, I've heard you're a good guy, but I didn't get all the details. What do you do for a living?"

"I'm a boatbuilder, and I own a marine equipment supply company." Brant took the sling off and put it on the back of the chair.

"A boat guy. Awesome." Gunner rubbed his hands together. "I feel a fishing trip coming up. Now, tell me about this co-parenting madness."

Brant started to tell them about Cait almost drowning, but Cait bumped his knee with hers, shaking her head slightly, her eyes imploring him not to tell the story. He quickly turned the near-drowning story into a tale about chasing the dog along the shore and made a mental note to find out what that redirect was all about. Her friends asked him dozens of questions, both personal and about the island, and before he knew it, they were taking turns loving up Scrappy, joking around, and talking about getting together to hang out in the future. Brant was captivated by Cait's carefree persona. She laughed loudly and was right in the thick of every conversation. He'd gotten a glimpse of this side of her on the boat and when they were shopping, but she was so easygoing with this group of friends, he longed to be part of her inner circle and was even more determined to earn her trust.

As the night wore on, Cait got more comfortable with him, too. She didn't move away when he put his leg against hers, and when he told Tank that he helped with search and rescue on the island, Tank told him that he had been a volunteer firefighter and shared a heartbreaking story about rescuing Leah and her children from an accident that had killed her brother. The reality of how quickly life could change had him reaching for Cait's hand. She didn't pull away, and as the conversations turned lighter, they traded whispers. She teased him about this and that and clued him in with background information on some of the things her friends were talking about.

When Tank got up to leave, he asked Cait to walk him out, and when she returned to the table, Brant noticed Baz and Gunner giving her approving looks. He took that as a good sign.

A little while later, Gia and Evie dragged Cait off to the ladies' room. They came back twenty minutes later giggling and looking at Brant. He had sisters. He knew what that meant, and he was proud to have their approval.

That was twenty minutes ago. Now, as Cait loved up Scrappy, Brant caught her stealing another glance at him. She quickly looked away, and he draped an arm over the back of her chair, pulling her closer, and said, for her ears only, "Your friends like me. You know what that means?"

"That they're drunk?" she whispered.

"Nice try. It means I *passed* your test."

Cait felt like she'd swallowed her tongue. Were she and her friends *that* obvious? By the look on Brant's face, the answer was *yes*.

"In your dreams, boat boy. Why don't you just sit there and drink your beer." She tried to play it off casually, but there was nothing casual about tonight. He made her colliding worlds feel more like they were shifting and molding seamlessly into one, as if they had always coexisted.

He hooked his arm tighter around her, his lips grazing her ear as he said, "I'd much rather tell you how beautiful you look tonight."

Her body whooped and cheered, urging her to flirt, flirt, *flirt!* But while Cait was excellent at deflecting, she pretty much sucked at flirting.

She glanced across the table at Gia, who flirted shamelessly with all the good-looking guys, and Evie, Baz's best friend and assistant at his veterinary practice, who enjoyed a constant stream of flirting and deflecting with Baz that had gone on for years. They'd both encouraged her to go out with Brant. Actually, if Gia had it her way, Cait would *drag Brant's fine ass out to his truck and have raunchy, wild sex with him.* Cait would give anything to be a normal woman for once in her life, to feel okay throwing caution to the wind and give in to her desires. But she'd done that before, and it had bitten her in the ass. It had taken years before she'd even wanted to flirt again, and the few times she had tried, the ghosts of her past had peered out, shutting her down.

"Dance with me," Brant said, drawing her from her thoughts.

The adoration in his eyes enveloped her like an embrace. How could he make her feel so much with nothing more than a look? She wasn't drunk. She'd had only two drinks over the span of almost three hours. Oh, how she *wanted* to dance! But that was another thing she sucked at. "I don't dance."

"It's time to change that." Brant stood and took Scrappy from her. "Gunner, would you mind snuggling our pooch so I can dance with Cait?"

Gunner chuckled. "You think you're going to get Cait on the dance floor?"

"Cait doesn't dance." Baz looked encouragingly at her and said, "But I think she should. Give me Scrappy."

Brant handed Scrappy to Baz and took Cait's hand, lifting her to her feet.

Why was she standing? *Traitorous legs!* "Brant, I really *don't* dance. I'll embarrass you."

"You couldn't embarrass me if you tried." He slid his arm around her waist.

"I don't know how to dance," she whispered, trying to pry his arm off her. "I'll embarrass *myself*."

He wrapped his arms around her, calm as could be, and transfixed her with his gaze as he looked into her eyes. "I'm not going to let that happen. Can't you trust me enough for *one* dance?"

"*Girl*, the hottest guy in here is asking you to dance," Gia said loudly. "Get your skinny ass on that dance floor before I kick you in it."

Cait glared at her. Gia *knew* she didn't dance. She turned pleading eyes to Evie and said, "Evie, tell him I really don't dance."

"Sorry, Cait, but I think you should give it a try," Evie said sweetly. "Thousands of middle school boys make it through dances every year. I'm pretty sure you can do this."

"Let's go, my tattooed princess." Brant led her toward the dance floor.

"Traitors!" she called over her shoulder to her friends, who waved her off. "You're going to regret this, Brant. I have two left feet. I'm not even sure they're left feet. They're more like *middle* feet."

He laughed and swept her into his arms, guiding her hands over his shoulders.

"*Brant*," she pleaded, looking around at the other couples dancing like they were born knowing how.

"Trust me, babe. I've got you."

Her heart raced as he slid one hand to her lower back, moving the other up her back and curling his fingers over her shoulder, holding their bodies together from thighs to chest. He began moving his hips, guiding hers to the same rhythm, and *boy* did he feel good.

"That's it, baby. Let your body move with me," he said huskily, gazing deeply into her eyes. She felt like she was floating. He kept her close and pressed his cheek to hers. "Sometimes all you need in life is the right partner."

His voice, and his words, sent heat slithering beneath her skin. She was actually dancing, and she wasn't tripping or making a fool of herself.

She felt herself smiling, her heart opening to the beautiful man she'd been lusting over for weeks. He was helping her do something she'd wanted to do forever and hadn't been brave enough to try. She wanted to stay right there in his arms, feeling his body moving against hers. She wondered if her friends would mind if they just danced hour after hour, until their legs could no longer hold them upright.

Brant's eyes found hers. "What are you thinking right now?"

She shook her head, embarrassed to tell him the truth. "Nothing."

"I'll tell you what I'm thinking." He paused just long enough for her nerves to *ping* again. "That *this*—you and me together—feels right."

God yes . . .

"And that I'm really glad I came to see you and that you let me meet your friends. I know they're important to you, and I can tell they always have your back."

He was so sweet and caring, she melted against him, and he must have felt it, because he tightened his hold on her, and those devastating dimples came out to play.

"I wondered why you hadn't moved to the island full-time yet," he said softly. "I understand now. You have a family here and a new family on Silver Island. It must be hard wanting to be in two places at once. But I get that. Family is everything to me, so if you're worried that if you go out with me, I'll become one of those possessive guys who tries to get you to stop seeing your friends, I promise I won't ever do that."

Her heart was beating so fast, she could barely hear past the blood rushing through her ears. He really *did* see her and understand her, and Tank and the rest of her friends liked him, all of which made her want to throw caution to the wind even more.

"Let me in, Caity," he whispered. "I won't let you down."

Yes, yes, yes. I can do this. I am doing this! She went up on her toes and pressed her lips to his. The first touch was electrifying. His hand moved into her hair as he slowly deepened the kiss, their tongues dancing to the same exquisite beat as their bodies. He didn't rush, didn't push, but kissed her with the same robust confidence as he did everything else. How did he know that this sweet, sensual, *intoxicating* kiss was exactly what she needed? He made a low, appreciative sound, and she cupped the back of his neck to counter her weakening knees. She'd never been kissed like this before, had never *wanted* so viscerally. She felt so good in his arms, she gave herself over to her desires, losing herself in a sea of pleasure. He tasted familiar and addicting, as if she'd been there before in some other time or some other life. She couldn't get enough, and pressed her hips harder against his, pushing her hands into his hair as she thrust her tongue hungrily into his mouth. She was swept up in the white-hot passion coursing through her and lost all sense of time and place. When their lips finally parted, she was breathless and lightheaded, her mouth burning for more.

Brant brushed a kiss to her forehead, and reality slowly filtered in. They were in the middle of the dance floor. Everyone had seen them, had seen *her* losing herself in him. He made her feel too much too fast. She'd been so consumed with desire, she'd been *this close* to dragging him off the dance floor and home to her bed. Her legs began to shake as ghosts flew out the darkest recesses of her mind, whipping their evil tails, slamming her with degrading slurs and hurtful reminders of her past. *What was I thinking?* This wouldn't last, and when everything fell apart, it could ruin her relationship with her sisters.

"Cait? *Cait.* Look at me, babe." Brant touched her face, bringing his into focus. "Are you okay?"

"I . . ." Her throat constricted, and the room started to spin. Anxiety prickled her limbs, exploding like a bomb in her chest. "I need air." She ran through the crowd and out the door. Brant was right behind her as she gulped air into her lungs and ran down the steps and under the deck.

"Cait!" He grabbed her wrist gently, not aggressively. "Caity, what's wrong? Was it the kiss? I'm sorry. I didn't mean to freak you out."

"You didn't." She paced, her thoughts in tatters. "It's not you, Brant. It's *me*. I'm messed up."

"I don't believe that, babe." He pulled her closer, but she pushed out of his arms. He held up his hands, his face a mask of concern. "Sorry. Talk to me, Cait, please."

"I shouldn't have kissed you. You make me feel too much." *So much it scared the shit out of me.* Tears of embarrassment burned her eyes. She crossed her arms, choking out, "I don't lose control like that. I can't afford to. I told you I'm a head case."

He stepped closer, hands out to his sides. "You're *not*. You're a smart, strong woman who has obviously been hurt. I don't know what you've been through, but maybe I can help you sort it out."

"You can't." She was trembling, wanting desperately to slay the dragons that were breathing fire between them. "I'm sorry. I *hate* this."

"Caity," he said softly, anguish swimming in his eyes. "Whatever *this* is, you don't have to try to figure it out alone."

Her thoughts spun with embarrassment, old hurt, and self-loathing for being stuck in a hellish cycle she couldn't break. "I fucking . . . *Ugh!*" She threw her hands up. "Trust me, Brant, that kiss was a mistake."

"Why don't we talk about it? I can't just watch you suffer. We're too connected." He walked slowly toward her, one hand over his heart. "When you're upset, I feel it, too."

"*Brant,*" she said softly, wanting him to hold her and wanting to run away at the same time.

"I won't leave you like this, Cait."

"*Please.*" She turned away with the half-hearted plea.

He put his arms around her from behind, holding her gently. "Friends don't leave friends to suffer alone. I've got you."

A lump lodged in her throat.

He moved around to her front, gathering her in his arms, and guided her cheek to his shoulder. He stroked her back and kissed the top of her head, sending gratitude and disbelief rumbling through her, taking the edge off. "I'm right here, and whatever you've gone through, whoever hurt you, is never going to get the chance again."

She soaked in his comfort but knew she couldn't drag him into her nightmare. "Don't you have alarm bells going off in your head? Red flags telling you to run? Why are you doing this?"

"Because I care about you."

Voices of her past slammed into her, reminding her that she'd heard those empty words before. Those voices warred with her heart, which was telling her that Brant wasn't like the men who had hurt her. The conflicting emotions made it all worse and more confusing. Her anxiety mounted until she felt like she might scream.

She pushed out of his arms, hating *and* appreciating the worry in his eyes. "I'm sorry. I need to go home."

"I'll drive you. You shouldn't drive when you're this upset."

"Thanks, but I'll be *fine*."

He held his hands up, as if to remind her that he wasn't going to manhandle her, and she hated that he felt the need to do that.

"Cait, if you won't let me drive you home, then I'm following you to make sure you get there safely. I'll leave right after I know you're safe. I promise. I just need to get Scrappy. Will you wait here for me? Give me three minutes to get the dog?"

"You don't need three minutes," Gunner said, and they both turned to see him walking toward them with Scrappy in his hands.

Embarrassment engulfed Cait. "How long have you been standing there?"

"Since about ten seconds after I saw Brant run after you." He handed Scrappy to Brant, his eyes on Cait. "Are you okay?"

"*Fine*," she said too sharply, but she couldn't help it.

"Brant's right. You shouldn't drive."

"I'm driving myself home, Gunner."

"I've got her," Brant said with a nod.

"I know you do, man." Gunner looked at Cait. "You good with him following you? Or do you want me to follow you?"

"He's *fine*. He's great." *I'm the messed-up one.*

Gunner pulled out his wallet and handed Brant a card. "My number is on there. Call me if . . ."

If I fall apart?

"I will." Brant pocketed the card. "She'll be okay."

As Brant walked her to her car, she saw her other friends standing on the deck, watching them. They didn't know about the abuse she'd suffered, which meant they probably thought she and Brant were fighting. She was going to screw up his life if she didn't get away from him.

"We'll be right behind you." Brant held up Scrappy. "Want to give him a snuggle before you get in?"

She took the pup, burying her face in his fur, and a mild sense of calm washed over her.

"Do you want to take him with you?"

Cait shook her head and handed him the dog. "I shouldn't."

On the way home, she tried to pull herself together, putting distance between herself and her thoughts. It was more difficult than ever, because she wanted to relive their kiss, but she was afraid to. She felt like a battered tree in an ongoing storm, but at least she'd stopped her tears by the time they arrived at her cottage.

Brant parked at the curb, and when he climbed from the truck with Scrappy in his arms, her heart ached. She never should have kissed him.

He met her on the front walk. "Listen, Cait, I'm going to sleep on my boat at the marina tonight in case you need anything."

"You don't have to do that. Don't you have to work in the morning?"

"I'm tight with the boss," he said with a troubled attempt at a smile. "I think he'll forgive me. Do you want to keep Scrappy and I'll come get him in the morning?"

She did, more than anything in the world, but she couldn't because she needed to cut Brant free from the noose of her past. She shook her head. "Let me just hold him for a minute." She gave Scrappy one last kiss and cuddle and handed him to Brant. Her throat felt like it was closing as she choked out, "I'm sorry about tonight."

"It's my fault. I showed up here, and—"

"*No.* You're perfect. I'm glad you came. I had a great time until I freaked out."

"You must have really hated kissing me," he teased.

She knew he was just lightening the mood, but it still made her want to cry. "I'm pretty sure that was the kiss of a lifetime." She lowered her eyes, unable to look at him as she said, "But I need some space."

"Cait—"

"Please don't try to talk me out of this," she interrupted. Before she could chicken out, she forced herself to look him in the eyes. "My life is crazy, going back and forth from here to there, and I'm pretty messed up when it comes to relationships. You're an amazing guy, and you deserve to be with someone who's equally wonderful."

"I hear what you're saying, but I'm *not* okay with this, Cait."

"I'm not sure I am, either, but it's what I need, and trust me, it's what you need, too."

He shook his head, those blue eyes filling with sadness. "What about Scrap?"

She lowered her eyes. "He doesn't need this chaos, either. He deserves a stable life, and he'll have that with you."

Brant stepped closer and gently lifted her chin. "Whatever it is that you're dealing with, it doesn't scare me, Cait. I *want* to be here for you and help you navigate whatever's got you so shaken up. Do you *hear* what I'm saying?"

"Yes, I hear you." Tears threatened, and it took everything she had to hold them back. "But *please* give me space."

He stared at her for so long, her lower lip began trembling. She gritted her teeth.

He finally relented. "If this is what you need, then I'll back off. But it doesn't change how I feel about you, so when you're ready to let me in, or if you just need someone to lean on, I'll be there. If you change your mind tonight or you don't want to be alone, I'm ten minutes away until morning." He leaned in and kissed her cheek. "We'll miss you, angel. I'll call you tomorrow."

"Please don't," she said regretfully. "It's too hard."

His shoulders sank and his jaw tightened, but he headed to his rental truck, his every step slicing through her chest until she felt like she couldn't breathe. "*Brant!*" flew from her lips without any thought.

He turned with hope in his eyes.

She wanted to run to him, to tell him she'd made a mistake, that she wanted his help more than she'd ever wanted anything. But she couldn't do it, wouldn't put him through that, and instead she asked what she desperately wanted to know. "Why me?"

A thoughtful smile lifted his lips, and he patted his hand over his heart. "Because when you know, you *know*."

Tears slid down her cheeks as he climbed into his truck. She hurried inside before she could run after him and leaned her back against the door, her body aching like she'd run a marathon. She heard him drive away and slid down to the floor engulfed by sobs, the skeletons of her past breaking her heart into a million jagged pieces.

Leaving Cait went against every fiber of Brant's being, but he knew to earn her trust he had to respect her wishes. He called Gunner on his way back to the marina to let him know that she was home safe, and then he paced on his yacht for half an hour before finally giving in to the urge to drive back to her place. He didn't have a plan. He just wanted to be nearby in case she needed him.

As he drove down her street, he saw a truck in front of her house. He slowed as he drove past it, and Tank looked over from behind the wheel. *Fuck.* Had she called him? He parked in front of Tank's truck, certain her monstrous boss was going to give him hell. But there was no way he was going to back down or leave. He left Scrappy in the truck and went to face Tank.

Tank watched him intently as he approached. Before Brant could get a word out, Tank said, "Did Cait ask you to come back?"

"No. I just wanted to be nearby in case she needed anything. Did she call you?"

Tank shook his head, eyes serious. "Gunner told me what went down. I'm here for the same reason you are. You want to climb in? Looks like it's going to be a long night."

As much as Brant wanted to be the guy Cait went to when she was in trouble, he wasn't sure she'd ever let him, and he was glad she had someone she trusted watching out for her. He and Scrappy sat with Tank all night. Brant didn't ask about Cait's demons, and Tank gave nothing away. They made small talk about non-Cait-related topics.

Brant was thankful for the distraction, because every minute that passed was another minute Cait hadn't changed her mind. When morning came, he didn't want Cait to feel pressured by finding him there. He headed back to the marina at five and caught a few hours of sleep. For the first time since he was a boy, he dreamed of being saved by the mermaid, only this time it was Cait's face he saw on the nautical beauty as she pushed him to the surface. He took a breath and dove in again, searching for her, but she disappeared into the depths of the deep blue sea.

CHAPTER SEVEN

BRANT STOOD AT the helm of his yacht at the Harwich Port marina at nine o'clock the next morning with the engines running, fighting the urge to go see Cait. He pulled out of the harbor and started the long journey home. But the farther he went from shore, the more he felt like he'd left a big part of himself behind.

He thought about texting her a hundred times on the way home, each time recalling the sadness in her eyes when she'd asked him not to reach out. Respecting her wishes fucking sucked.

Back on the island, he walked Scrappy and headed into the boathouse. His buddy Grant Silver was sanding the bow of a boat. Grant was an artist and ex–covert operations specialist. He'd lost his left leg from the knee down during a mission about two years ago and had returned to the island last summer. He'd been as angry as a snared bear before their friend Jules Steele, who was now Grant's fiancée, found her way into his heart and helped him find his way out of the darkness. Last winter, Grant founded the Silver Lining Foundation, Resources for Amputees, and he helped Brant when he needed a break from his real work.

Grant saw him approaching and turned off the sander. He pushed his mask below his beard, flicking his chin to get his collar-length brown hair out of his eyes, and gave Brant a scrutinizing once-over. "You don't look like a guy who just got laid. You okay?"

"Stayin' alive, man. Just stayin' alive." When they were younger, their friends had called them the Bee Gees, and Brant couldn't resist referencing one of their songs to try to lighten his own mood.

"Oh yeah? You want to do some *jive talkin*?"

Loving that Grant was playing along, he said, "Only if you know how to mend a broken heart."

Grant chuckled at the song reference he'd gotten wrong. "That depends. How deep is your love?" He laughed, but Brant was all out of levity. Grant set the sander down and scooped up Scrappy. "That bad, huh?"

"Pretty damn bad." Brant unhooked Scrappy's leash and set it on a workbench. "She sent me away."

"*What?* She sent the prince of Silver Island packing? That's gotta hurt." Grant nuzzled Scrappy. "Did your papa cry the whole way home?"

"Don't be an asshole," Brant said as his father walked in.

"That's like asking a bear not to shit in the woods," his father said.

Roderick "Roddy" Remington wore his thick gray-brown hair too long and sported a short, scruffy beard. He favored loud Hawaiian shirts opened three buttons deep, ancient shorts with frayed hems, and sneakers he'd had forever—and as far as Brant was concerned, he was the coolest father on the island. Roddy had grown up with Grant's father, and they'd gone to college together, which was where they'd met Steve Steele. Steve had moved to the island with them after college and married Jules's mother, Shelley, and the three families had done everything together ever since.

Grant laughed. "How are you doing, old man? I haven't seen you around this morning."

"I'm friggin' fantastic. I went for a morning sail with my gorgeous wife and watched the sunrise, did a little smooching." He petted Scrappy's head. "*Mm-mm.* I am one lucky devil."

"Yes, you are," Grant agreed.

"Sounds like a perfect morning, Dad." Brant wished he could have done the same thing with Cait.

"And it just got better, son. Jamison called a few minutes ago. He's got a meeting in Boston tomorrow and he's coming for dinner tonight. Tessa's picking him up, then stopping in P-town to get Rowan and Joni, and flying them all in around six o'clock. Randi's hosting a barbecue. Think you can make it?"

"I'll be there." As Brant said it, he realized that if Cait needed him, he'd head back to the Cape without hesitation. "Unless Cait needs something."

His father arched a brow. "You finally stopped pussyfooting around and told that pretty little lady how you feel?"

"I've *been* telling her, but she's going through some shit, and she wants to weather the storm alone."

"And how do you feel about that?" his father asked.

"Like I want to take her in my arms, help her deal with whatever she's battling, and never let her go. But she won't tell me what's going on, which means I'm left guessing, and my thoughts are pretty dark."

His father's expression turned serious. "Do you think she's in imminent danger? I've got friends on the Cape police force if we need to intervene."

"I'm not sure, but I get the sense it's something she's gone through and is still dealing with rather than something that's happening to her now. I could be wrong, but she's got friends watching out for her. I met them. They're good guys. Dark Knights, like Levi. I just wish she'd talk to me." He couldn't shake the image of her going from clear-eyed and happy to lustful to shaking uncontrollably.

"I know a little something about not wanting to burden others with your shit." Grant set Scrappy on the floor, and the pup padded over to his doggy bed by the workbench.

"I'd love to hear your thoughts," Brant said.

"I don't know if they'll be much help," Grant said. "But if it's something from her past, then she probably doesn't want to make her problem your problem. There's all sorts of guilt and shit wrapped up in that. At least there was for me. So once you open that can of worms, be ready for a shitload of other things to come crawling out."

"That's good advice for any bad situation, current or past," his father agreed. "There's always more going on than you think. You sure you want to get involved, son?"

"I want to do whatever it takes to help Cait through this. It killed me to see her so upset, and when she sent me away, she said she wasn't sure she really wanted to do it. But honestly, Dad, there's no choice to be made. From the moment we met, I felt connected to her. Grant was there." He looked at his buddy. "Do you remember what you said to me at the end of that night?"

Grant nodded. "I said I'd never seen you look at a woman the way you looked at Cait, and that hasn't changed. For what it's worth, Pix thinks you two are meant for each other, brought together by the universe and all that starry-eyed stuff she believes in." Pixie was his nickname for Jules.

"In that case, what can I do to help?" his father asked.

"Tell me I did the right thing by giving her the space she asked for, because I've been questioning it every second since I left."

"I can't tell you that, son, because I didn't look into her eyes when she said it, and women and men speak different languages. We're visceral. Unless we're testing the waters or something, we say exactly what we mean. But when women speak, *nothing* can mean *everything*, and *go away* can mean *if you leave, we're done*—or it can mean exactly what they said. Hell, I've been married to your mother forever, and I still get it wrong half the time."

Grant laughed. "He's right about the languages."

"Yeah, I get it," Brant said.

"But here's the thing," his father said. "It sounds like you two are already tethered together. Whether that's by the universe or by the powers of lust or love, I have no idea. But I believe if you two are meant to be, there ain't no storm powerful enough to tear an anchor as strong and stable as you out of the ground. And if that's the case, then once the storm passes, she won't be able to help but find her way back to you."

Brant held his gaze. "And if I want to battle that storm *with* her instead of letting her flap out there in the wind and rain by herself?"

"Then bring a raincoat, son." His father cocked a grin. "Because going against a woman's wishes just might bring on a shitstorm, and that's a *whole* other problem."

A nest of bees had been swarming in Cait's stomach since last night. She hated that she'd fallen apart and sent Brant away. By midday she'd been snappy and too irritated to concentrate. She'd canceled her evening clients and caught the five o'clock ferry to the island early to apologize to him. She needed to return the doggy sling Brant had left at the bar anyway. But the thought of seeing him made her ache almost as much as not seeing him did, and as she coasted down the hill on her bicycle toward the cottage community where he lived, she was still talking herself *into* and *out of* seeing him in rapid succession.

She veered right at the bottom of the hill, pedaling toward the yellow-and-blue SEAVIEW COTTAGES sign. She was so nervous, she'd probably babble like a moron when she saw him, but she wasn't sure she'd get through another night without making things right. Brant was incredibly good to her, so patient and caring, he deserved a better explanation than the discombobulated one she'd given him outside the bar. She'd been spinning the truth all day, trying to come up with the best version to tell him so he understood enough to realize he was better off without her without revealing all of the ugliness she'd been through.

She turned into the community and stopped by the main house, a cute two-story cedar-sided home with a wide front porch and an Office sign hanging from a post out front. She looked down the street at the nearly identical cedar-sided cottages with colored doors and shutters, but for the life of her she couldn't remember which one was Brant's. She climbed off her bike and pushed it along the sidewalk, trying to find something that called out to her. She spotted his truck in a driveway up ahead. The butterflies in her belly had turned to bees last night, and now, as she made her way to the cottage, they morphed into swarming hornets.

She parked her bike in the driveway and grabbed the doggy sling from the basket, staring at the cottage. His front door and shutters were blue, reminding her of the umbrella in the backyard. She remembered him peering out of the shower, and her heart stumbled. Tank had told her that Brant had sat in front of her house all night, and that had done her in. She knew Tank did things like that, but she'd never met anyone else who would.

As she climbed the porch, Tank's voice ran through her mind. *I like him, Cait. I trust him.* Tank didn't trust easily, and his respect for Brant validated that cutting ties was the right thing to do, no matter how much it hurt. Brant deserved to be with someone easier, with less freak-out potential. Someone who knew how to be in a relationship.

I can do this. I have to do this.

She took a deep breath, clutching the sling to her stomach, and knocked. The door flew open, and Rowan's daughter, Joni, stood before her wearing a scuba mask that covered her eyes and nose, a pink bathing suit, a rainbow tutu, and red rain boots decorated with yellow flowers, throwing Cait totally off-kilter.

"Mermaid!" Joni threw her arms around Cait's waist, hugging her tight. She'd been calling Cait *Mermaid* since the day they'd met. Joni's flair for creative nicknames and funky clothes was as wild as the imaginative stories she told. Rowan claimed that Joni had been making up

stories since she'd learned to talk. Joni tilted her pretty little face up, her fine brown hair brushing her chin, and said, "You're just in time for our under-the-sea dinner at Aunt Pickle's house!"

"Cait? What're you doing here?" Brant's sister Randi, a petite brunette, came to the door dressed in a bikini top and shorts and wearing a scuba mask like Joni.

"I found her feeding the giraffes in the zoo," Joni exclaimed.

"Did you?" Randi grinned at her niece.

Cait wondered if she had the wrong cottage. "I was . . . *um* . . . I came to return something to Brant, but I must have the wrong cottage. I saw his truck and—"

"No you don't. This is Uncle Doodle's house!" Joni exclaimed. "Come on. I'll take you to him." She grabbed Cait's hand and tugged her toward the street.

Cait's brain finally kicked into gear, and she stopped walking. "It's okay. I'll just leave this on his porch."

Randi closed the door behind her, carrying a canvas bag over her shoulder, and looped her arm with Cait's. "Don't be silly. You're here. You might as well join us for a barbecue at my place. But you need a mask."

"A mask?" Cait was confused. "I don't need—"

"We're going *underwater*. See?" Joni pointed to the street.

She realized this was one of Joni's elaborate stories.

"I have an extra one. Here you go." Randi pretended to hand Cait a mask.

"Wait! We're so silly! Mermaid doesn't need a mask. She has gills," Joni said, and they dragged Cait across the street, Joni and Randi pretending to do a one-armed breaststroke while holding Cait hostage between them. "Wiggle your tail, Mermaid!"

As they neared the cottage across the street, a cacophony of voices and music came into focus. Cait needed to get out of this crazy mixed-up situation, *stat*! "My tail is broken. I should go."

"Don't worry. Uncle Tootsie will fix it! He can fix anything," Joni said as Randi opened the gate to the backyard.

"*Uncle Tootsie?*" Cait repeated.

"My brother Jamison," Randi said as they entered the backyard.

Scrappy ran over barking loudly as several sets of eyes locked on them. In the space of a second, Cait realized she'd interrupted a family gathering. Brant's parents, Roddy and Gail, were standing across the yard talking with an older couple. Roddy wore a snorkeling mask, and the older woman he was with had a purple inflatable ring around her stomach with a dolphin head in the front and a tail in the back, and the white-haired man wore a Hawaiian shirt and several leis around his neck. Rowan stood by the grill with Tessa, who was wearing yellow water wings. Cait's eyes swept over an enormous table set for dinner and another table littered with refreshments. But she didn't see Brant anywhere.

She *had* to get out of there. "I should be go—"

"Uncle *Doodle*!" Joni hollered. "*Mermaid* is here to see you, and she needs Uncle Tootsie to fix her tail!" She ran toward the open patio doors just as Brant and a tall, handsome guy with glasses and wavy hair walked out.

Brant's eyes locked on Cait, sending her already rampant pulse into a frenzy and turning those nasty hornets back into butterflies. How was it possible to feel so much for a man she wasn't even going out with? She was vaguely aware of Gail and Tessa calling out to her. But Cait had tunnel vision, seeing only the confused happiness in Brant's eyes as he closed the distance between them. Their connection was more intense than ever, buzzing with electricity, making her want to run to him. But she couldn't. She was there to apologize, explain, and put an end to whatever this was between them.

"What a great surprise!" Tessa said.

"Right? I'm glad she's here, too," Randi added.

"It's lovely to see you. Jamison, come meet Cait!" Gail hollered. "Those are Roddy's parents over there, Freddy and Millie."

Rowan shouted, "How's it going, Cait?"

I can't breathe, but I'm still standing. She lifted her hand to wave, or at least she thought she did. She still couldn't take her eyes off Brant.

Joni stepped between Cait and Brant, holding Scrappy, who was wearing an orange bikini, and beamed up at Cait. "Look! Scrappy fit in my doll's bathing suit. And guess what? Daddy's grilling whale dogs, crab burgers, eel kabobs, and shark meat for dinner!"

"Uh-huh," Cait managed, unable to get a word out for the emotions stacking up inside her. Seeing Brant was torture, and the thought of losing Scrappy, too, nearly sent her over the edge.

"What are you doing here?" Brant's eyes remained trained on her, as if he couldn't look away, either. "I thought you weren't coming back until later tonight."

"We found her at the zoo!" Joni exclaimed. "She's having dinner with us."

"Jojo, I could use your help over here," Rowan shouted, and Joni scampered off.

Gail pulled Jamison closer and said, "Cait, this is our son Jamison. He's in for the evening. I'm glad you'll have a chance to get to know him."

Cait glanced at Brant's serious-looking brother, who was wearing a Deckvest like the one she'd worn on Brant's yacht, but as she said, "Hi," her eyes were drawn back to the man she wished she'd never sent away.

"It's nice to meet you. How do you know Brant?" Jamison asked.

"Abby introduced them," Tessa answered.

Brant tore his eyes from Cait, as if he'd only just noticed they were surrounded by his family. "Would you mind if I talked with Cait for a second before you scare her off?"

"Where are our manners?" Gail said kindly. "Of course, honey. Why don't you get our guest a drink?"

"A drink. Good idea." Brant took Cait by the arm, leading her to the other side of the yard. He stood close, and she realized he was wearing his bathing suit, an open Hawaiian shirt like Roddy wore, and two leis around his neck. "I've wanted to reach out to you every minute since last night. I'm happy to see you, but you're back early. Is everything okay?"

"Yes. I didn't mean to interrupt your dinner. I just came to give you this." She handed him the sling.

Disappointment rose in his eyes. "*That's* why you came?"

"I also wanted to apologize, but we can talk another time. I should go."

He put his hand on her hip. "We'll both go. We can talk at my place."

"I'm *not* making you leave your family."

"Then stay. Please?" The plea in his eyes burrowed deep inside her. "We'll eat quickly and then go back to my place and talk."

She looked around them. His father had one arm around Randi, the other around Gail, who was wearing a bathing suit and grass skirt, her thick, curly mane hanging loose around her shoulders. His grandparents and Tessa were laughing with his brothers, and Joni was pretending to swim around the yard in her tutu and mask. Cait had never met a family like this, and they were a little intimidating.

"Brant . . ."

"Dinner in two minutes!" Rowan hollered, and Cait saw that he had flippers on his feet.

Joni squealed and ran to the table. "I'm sitting next to Papa French Fry and Mermaid!"

Brant nudged Cait. "Joni calls you *Mermaid*?"

"She has ever since we first met."

"That's a sign." He squeezed her hip, his sexy smile tugging at her. "Say you'll stay so I can call sitting on your other side."

She laughed softly. "Seriously?"

He leaned closer, and her entire body flamed. "Say *yes*, Cait."

"Come on, you two!" Randi waved them over.

Brant cocked a brow.

"*Fine*," Cait relented.

"Thank you." He never took his eyes off her as he hollered, "I'm sitting next to Mermaid, too!"

What have I gotten myself into?

CHAPTER EIGHT

BRANT'S FAMILY WAS a boisterous crew, and as platters were passed and plates were filled, laughter and chatter rose around them. Cait tried to keep up as Brant and his siblings bantered back and forth and his family peppered her with questions and shared funny stories about one another. Brant's more serious siblings, Jamison and Tessa, sat at one end of the table, and Randi, who was as feisty as ever, sat at the other end, while their parents and grandparents sat across from Cait, Brant, Joni, and Rowan. His parents held hands, kissed often, and had no shortage of praise and teasing for their children. His grandparents shared glances that told of a secret language Cait imagined only decades of couple-dom could provide. Brant held Scrappy on his lap, feeding him bits of burger. When Cait questioned the dog being allowed at the dinner table, he'd said Scrappy was family and therefore he was welcome to join them. His mother had nodded her approval.

There was so much love around that table, it was easy to see why Brant was so open and genuine with his feelings—and how different Cait was from all of them.

Rowan leaned forward, catching Cait's attention, and mouthed, *Are they driving you crazy yet?*

She shook her head, smiling as she'd been doing for most of dinner. She might be different from them, but she really enjoyed being in their company.

"Some of my favorite memories are of storms when you kids were little." Gail looked thoughtfully around the table and set her loving eyes on Brant. "You were always watching out for the others. You used to make tents out of sheets in your bedroom and cover the floor with pillows and sleeping bags, and all the kids would sleep in there during storms. Do you remember?"

"I do," Brant said.

"You read us stories and watched movies with us," Rowan said.

"And *that's* only one reason why Brant, the lifeguard, search and rescue volunteer, and savior of drowning girls and pups is *the good one*," Randi said with a dose of sarcasm.

"That's lucky for you, young lady," their grandmother Millie said. She had short, layered gray hair with a hint of light brown throughout and a friendly face. "Brant came to your rescue more than once. Remember how scared you were to start middle school?"

Randi covered her face. "Gram! Don't tell Cait that story."

"What happened?" Cait whispered to Brant.

"It was nothing," Brant said so casually, she had a feeling it was *something*.

"Randi was nervous about changing schools, so Brant went with her to her classes for the first two days," Rowan explained. "He got approval from the principal and everything."

"That's the sweetest thing I've ever heard." Cait looked at Brant, and he shrugged humbly, which made her like him even more.

"It was sweet, but *also* embarrassing," Randi complained.

"It was better than you missing school, which is what you wanted to do," Roddy said. "You kids have always leaned on each other. That's what family's for. Brant taught Rowan how to sail, and Jamison took Tessa on her first plane ride and explained how planes work. From that moment on, she wanted to be a pilot."

"That's really nice," Cait said, wishing she had grown up in a big, caring family like theirs.

"It could be, but it wasn't always rosy. Rowan once tried to pee on Randi when she got stung by a jellyfish," Tessa said, making everyone laugh.

"*Ew!*" Joni wrinkled her nose.

"Don't remind me." Randi made a disgusted face. "That doesn't even work, you know."

"Hey, I was just trying to help." Rowan chuckled. "I saw it in a movie."

Their grandfather looked at Brant with an infectious grin, revealing the source of Brant's and Roddy's dimples. His hair was white as snow, and his skin was mapped with wrinkles that Cait imagined were from working on boats in the hot sun. He arched a thick white brow and said, "Do you kids remember the time your brother was saved by a mermaid?"

"It was Cait!" Joni exclaimed. "Cait saved him!"

Everyone laughed.

"Maybe *that's* where you learned to tell stories, Jojo," Rowan said. "From your Uncle Doodle."

"Hey, that really happened," Brant insisted, and his siblings talked over one another, telling him he was full of it. "You're just jealous that you've never been saved by a mermaid."

"I almost forgot! Uncle Tootsie, can you fix Mermaid's tail?" Joni asked.

Jamison took a drink and looked at Cait. "That depends. How did you hurt your tail?"

Thinking quickly, Cait said, "I hit it on a rock."

"Don't be embarrassed to tell them the truth, Caity." Brant bumped her leg under the table. "She got it wrapped around an anchor."

His entire family said, "*Ah*," as if that made total sense, and she remembered what Brant had said about his tattoo. *This way you'll always be anchored to my heart.* Goose bumps rose on her arms.

"Shark!" Joni yelled, startling Cait.

Brant and his family began making swimming motions with their arms. "Faster!" his grandmother said.

"There's a cave!" Roddy shouted.

"Wait!" Randi held up her hands, eyes wide, her long dark hair framing her face. "Stay very still and it'll pass by us."

Everyone froze. Cait held her breath, eyeing Brant, who winked. She was captivated by his family, who went along with Joni's shenanigans and had welcomed *her* with open arms.

Brant's grandfather said, "*Whew!* That was a close one," and everyone exhaled loudly. "Thanks for the warning, Jelly Belly."

Joni giggled, and they all went back to eating their dinner as if they had close calls with sharks every day. And for all she knew, they did.

"Tell me, Cait," Gail said. "Are you going to move to the island permanently at some point? It must be hard going back and forth."

Brant's siblings gave him curious looks.

"I'm trying to figure that out," Cait said. "I really like what I do on the Cape, and I have friends there."

"Cait's one of the best tattooists and body piercers around," Rowan said. "She's got quite a loyal following."

"Have you thought about doing that kind of work here on the island?" his father asked.

"Maybe she wants to work at the Bistro full-time," Tessa added.

"Do you?" Gail asked.

"I'm not sure what I want," Cait said honestly. "I love working with Abby, but the Bistro is her dream. I do mostly administrative and accounting work, and I help out on the floor sometimes, but my heart lies in art. I have been thinking about doing tattoos and body piercing here. But actually moving to the island and setting up a business of my own is a big decision."

"Cait's friends on the Cape are like her family, which makes it hard to just pick up and move," Brant explained, putting his hand over hers beneath the table.

Jamison nodded in Cait's and Brant's direction and said, "How does that work with you two going out?"

Silence fell around them, and Brant's entire family turned curious gazes their way. Cait's pulse quickened, knowing she had to clarify that they weren't a couple, and hating it. But it was better for Brant, no matter how much fun she was having with his family.

Before she could get a word out, Rowan said, "You two are going out?"

"No," Cait said too quickly, immediately regretting it. "We're not like that." *We just kissed like we were.*

God, that kiss . . .

"*Yet*," Brant added, squeezing her hand again. "We've got a lot to figure out."

Cait trained her eyes on her plate, trying to silence the ongoing battle between hope and uncertainty in her head.

"Way to put them on the spot, Jamison." Randi glowered at him.

"I'm sorry. That wasn't my intent," Jamison said. "I just assumed they were together. They *seem* like a couple. Brant lit up like the sun when he saw Cait walk in, and the heat between them is palpable. What's the issue? Is it just logistics? Because I think we could look at your schedules and the projected times that Cait anticipates spending on the Cape and here and come up with an algorithm that could—"

"Hold on, Jay," Brant said. "I appreciate your interest in helping, but the things we're dealing with can't be sorted out with algorithms."

Jamison's brows knitted. "Most everything comes down to mathematical equations."

"Not matters of the heart," Rowan said.

"I think I'd better start spending more time with you, Jamison," Randi said. "I bet you're missing all sorts of cues from hot women who are interested in you."

"Like *you* miss all of Ford's cues?" Tessa asked with a smirk.

Cait had met Randi's coworker Ford Kincaid when they'd come into the Bistro together. He'd introduced himself as Alex Pettyfer and had even used a British accent. She hadn't believed he was Alex, although he looked a lot like him, but she *had* thought they were a couple until Abby had set her straight.

Randi glowered at Tessa. "We're not talking about *me*. Can we get back to Jamison, please?"

Their siblings chuckled, and Tessa said, "Oh, right, *Jamison*. Every time I visit him, he's more interested in work than the women who are vying for his attention."

Jamison picked up his glass and said, "You find me a woman who can intellectually stimulate me, and maybe that'll change."

"See? That's your problem, Jay," Randi said. "For a smart guy, you're pretty clueless. Books are for your brain. Women are for your body."

"What kind of comment is that?" Brant snapped. "You've just set women back a hundred years."

Randi rolled her eyes. "You know what I mean."

"Okay, kids, let's not fight." Their mother patted Jamison's hand and said, "When the right woman piques my boy's interest, he won't be able to ignore her."

"Ain't that the truth," Rowan said.

Brant looked at Cait and said, "It sure is."

A shiver of heat ran through her.

"Your mother's right. When that Cupid's arrow hits, there's no getting away from it," Roddy said, putting his arm around Gail and kissing her cheek. "We've been together since high school, right, darlin'?"

"I have the gray hair to prove it." Gail shook her curls.

"Your grandfather and I were childhood best friends," his grandmother said, gazing lovingly at her husband. "I swear I fell in love with him before I knew what love was."

That sparked a loud conversation about friendship, dating, and how to know when someone was *the one*. Brant leaned closer to Cait and whispered, "You're the only one who's ever made me feel that way."

She wanted to say, *So are you*, but she couldn't have managed a word if she'd tried.

While they enjoyed dinner, Randi filled them in on the latest findings with her diving expedition, Jamison told them about a project he was working on, and everyone seemed to have something to update their family about. By the time they'd finished eating, Cait was no longer nervous. She really liked that feeling, and she knew that while his family had a lot to do with her comfort, it was Brant's tender glances, the touch of his hand when he silently checked in with her, and his sweet, funny whispers that settled her nerves and had her reconsidering the reasons for her visit.

Everyone helped clean up except his grandparents, who were playing with Scrappy and Joni. Cait picked up a platter from the table to carry it inside.

"Give me that, sweetheart," Gail said, taking the platter from her and handing it to Brant as he came out of the house. "Would you please take that inside for me? I'd like to take a walk with Cait."

Brant gave Cait an *Are you okay?* look, and she nodded even though she was getting a little nervous again.

They had a large backyard and gorgeous wildflower gardens along the back of the hill where they were walking. "I'm glad you stayed for dinner," Gail said sweetly. "I enjoyed getting to know you better."

"Thank you. I didn't mean to crash your family time."

"Don't ever worry about that, honey. Around here, the more the merrier." Gail stopped walking and gazed out at the lights of the island for a moment before turning a warm smile on Cait. "I just wanted to take a moment to tell you that I know our family can be a little overwhelming. We say what we feel. Some of us more than others, and I hope we didn't scare you off."

"You didn't. I had a great time. I love how your family goes along with Joni's extravagant stories."

"She's a firecracker, isn't she? She's got a lot of her mama in her. Did you know Carlotta?"

"No. I only met Rowan a few years ago."

"Well, you missed out on meeting a very special woman. Carlotta didn't believe in marriage, but she loved my son and Joni deeply. Losing her was a painful reminder that we must live for today. It's a shame Joni will never know her."

A pang of sadness moved through Cait. "Not knowing a parent definitely leaves you with a sense of emptiness."

"I know, sweetheart. I'm sorry that you never had a chance to meet Ava. I know you've heard stories about her alcoholism and how difficult that was for everyone who knew and loved her. But I want you to know that before she lost her way, she was a wonderful, loving mother and wife. I remember when she came to the island. She was *troubled*, drinking too much. At the time, none of us knew she'd been forced to give you up. But we could see that she had a big empty spot inside her. We girls swooped her into our nest, and she became one of us. But it was Olivier who made her heart sing. It was love at first sight, and their relationship was truly beautiful. She was devastated when he passed away. We all were." Olivier had died when Deirdra was eleven and Abby was nine. "That's when she turned back to alcohol. But in my heart, I still see her in that better place, and *you* remind me of the woman she was back then, when your sisters were little. I really miss her."

"Thank you for remembering her so fondly." It made Cait happy knowing that despite her alcoholism, Ava had been loved by so many people.

"If you'd known her, you'd understand why we all do. Ava was special. She saw everything so clearly back then. She had the ability to see things none of us looked deep enough to find, like my Brant does. I'm sure you know he sees the very heart of everything, not just people.

I swear he thinks boats are living beings. He takes the ones others have taken for granted and showers them with love, bringing them back to life. But I'm getting off track." She laughed softly. "That's easy to do when I talk about my kids. I get the sense that like Ava, you also see things others don't, and I guess I want you to know that I see Ava in you. The very best parts of her."

"Thank you. I like knowing that." She thought about her unopened letter, wondering if it held more about the best parts of her mother.

"Good. And please don't think I'm trying to push you toward Brant or to get on your good side or anything like that. I just wanted to share those things, woman to woman, because life can be scary, and we women need to look out for each other. I hope you know that if you ever need anything, I'm here. Even if you never go out with my son."

Cait's heart squeezed. "That means a lot to me. Thank you." It was no wonder Ava had settled on that island. It was easy to imagine Gail and Shelley and the other women their age that Cait had met welcoming a troubled teenage Ava into their close-knit circle.

Gail took Cait by the arm in the maternal way Faye and Shelley often did, and they headed back toward the cottage. "For what it's worth, I've never seen my son look at any woman the way he looks at you. Again, I'm not pushing, just sharing an observation."

The sincerity in her voice touched Cait, but she still had that nagging worry about Brant being better off without her. She looked across the lawn at him holding Scrappy, ruing her history once again. "I don't think you're pushing. But Brant and I are different. I don't even know how to be the way your family is."

Gail looked confused. "Why would you want to be like us?"

"Are you kidding?" Cait could think of a hundred reasons why. "Your family is warm and open, and you're all so carefree."

"Oh, honey, we have more cares than you could fit on this island."

"You don't seem to. You're always happy, and Brant is like a beacon of positivity."

Gail looked thoughtfully at her family talking and goofing around in the yard. "I guess we do come across that way most of the time, don't we? And we are happy, but we have our issues, like every family. I worry incessantly about all of my children, and my granddaughter. I worry that Rowan lives too much in Carlotta's shadow and that Tessa will never give a man a chance to love her. And don't get me started on my Jamison. The girls are right—he needs someone to clue him in on love. And then there are our businesses and parents. Life is generous. It gives us a series of worries, but you can't let those worries steal the joy that life lays out before you."

"Sometimes that's easier said than done," Cait admitted.

"Oh yes, it can be. Let me share the secret we've found. We surround ourselves with people we love and trust, and we talk about everything ad nauseam. A person can drown in their worries or they can set them free. We always go for setting them free. Some worries linger and take a while to scramble up to shore; others are carried away with the wind, and *yes*, some try to wrap around our ankles and drag us under. But *that's* where those trusting friends come in. When our concerns get to be too much, we lean on each other."

Cait thought about their conversation over dinner and said, "Like Brant going to class with Randi."

"Exactly. Sometimes you have to be open to being vulnerable in order to find your trusted tribe, or as I call them, my lifelines."

"But what if you trust the wrong person?"

"We all do at some point." Gail took her hand, holding it up between them. "That's when you grab hold of those good friends with both hands and let that bad one float down the river all by its lonesome. Your friends on the Cape sound like they've got you with both hands."

Cait nodded. "They do. Always."

"That's good, sweetheart, and from what I've heard, you're finding that here, too. If you're open to it, you'll find your lifelines, and you'll know in your heart who they are." She nodded to Brant striding toward them with Scrappy in his arms. "Here comes someone who I believe wants to be one of them."

Brant had spent the last twenty minutes fielding questions from his siblings about Cait. She had loosened up over dinner, gracing them with her good humor and those radiant smiles he adored. His brothers and sisters loved her and were rooting for them, just as he was. But Cait had said enough last night to let him know that her wounds ran deep, and he could only hope she'd open up to him. As he closed the distance between them, Cait lowered her eyes, nodding. He wondered what his overcommunicative mother had said to her. His mother was wonderful, but she acted as if everyone was as open about their lives as she was, and he worried about how that might affect Cait. He scooped up Scrappy, in case Cait needed a little extra comfort.

Cait lifted her gaze, and the light in her eyes brought relief that maybe his mother hadn't pried too much after all.

"Are you done telling Cait all of my secrets?" Brant teased.

"I haven't even *started* spilling your secrets yet." His mother patted his cheek. "I almost forgot to ask, have you invited Cait to movie night?"

"Not yet." Their family hosted dune-side movies, but with everything Cait was going through, he wasn't sure if she would be up for it.

"*Oops.* Sorry, honey. But now that the cat's out of the bag, Cait, I hope you'll join us Friday night for a dune-side movie on Rock Harbor Beach." His mother said it so eagerly, he was pretty sure she wasn't sorry. She was matchmaking. "It's a community event, and it'll be a lot of fun."

"I'm working until six," Cait said.

"Perfect! It doesn't start until dark," his mother exclaimed. "Brant, you're handling the movie announcements this time, right?"

"Absolutely. Looking forward to it."

"Wonderful. Then I'll leave you two kids alone." She gave him an approving look and went to join the others.

Cait reached for Scrappy. "Your mom is really nice."

"I guess that means she didn't scare you off?"

"I don't need anyone else to scare me off. I'm pretty good at doing that myself."

"Not from me, I hope." He closed the small gap between them, feeling too far away. "Can we go back to my place and talk?"

"Yeah. I'd like that."

He grabbed the doggy sling, and they started their goodbyes to his family. Joni chatted on about Tessa flying them and Jamison back to the Cape and Boston later tonight, and half an hour later, they finally got out of there.

"You have an amazing family," Cait said, looking back over her shoulder.

"I have a loud, intrusive family, but I love them." He put his hand on her lower back as they crossed the road. "Thank you for sticking around and putting up with us."

"I really enjoyed it. Do you get together often?"

"Pretty often. My grandparents own this community. They inherited it from my great-grandparents, and they live in the big house at the entrance. My parents' cottage is behind Randi's, which is where we had dinner, and Tessa's is around the corner." He pointed to the end of the street as they climbed the porch steps.

"You *all* live here? Is this where you grew up?"

"No. We grew up in Silver Haven, by the Steeles and the Silvers. My parents moved here to help my grandparents after we all moved out. I was already renting my cottage, which I've since bought. Randi and Tessa used to share Tessa's cottage, but Randi moved to her own a couple of years ago."

He pushed open the front door. "After you. Excuse the mess."

He followed her in, watching her eyes sweep over the wide-planked hardwood floors and open living area. The walls and ceilings were white with wood trim, and the rafters were stained to match the trim. The couches were blue and comfortable, the tables rustic and wooden. Built-in bookshelves separated the entrance to two bedrooms that shared a Jack-and-Jill bathroom at one end of the living room, and a fireplace anchored the other end by the entrance to the master suite. There was a small bar with a bay window in the dining nook just outside the kitchen and a laundry room and half bath on the other side of the kitchen. A plethora of family photos and nautical paintings, pictures, and gadgets decorated the walls. There was a blanket bunched up on the couch beside an open magazine, a half-full cup of juice on the coffee table, sneakers in the middle of the floor, flip-flops near the patio doors, and a wet towel hanging over a dining room chair.

"This is nice," she said.

"Thanks. I live a pretty simple life, but I would have cleaned up if I'd known you'd be here. Can I get you something to drink? Beer? Soda? Water?" he asked as they made their way into the living room.

"Sure. Water is fine."

"Water it is. Make yourself comfortable. I'll be right back." He went into the kitchen to get their drinks, and when he came out, Cait was standing in the nook by the bar, staring up at the surfboard hanging on the wall above it. Her face was white as a sheet. He set the glasses down. "What's the matter?"

Her gaze remained trained on the dark blue board that had PARADISE written across the length of it in bold colorful letters. "If I tell you, I'll sound crazy, and you already think I'm crazy enough."

"How can you say that after meeting my crazy family?" He slid his arms loosely around her waist, drawing her eyes to his. "I do *not* think you're crazy, but you look like you've seen a ghost, and I'd like to know why."

She had a pained expression. "I feel like I've been here before."

"Why would that make me think you're crazy? Lots of cottages look alike around here."

"Because I *have* been here before, but not in real life. Just in my dreams."

He couldn't stop the grin tugging at his lips. "You dream about me, huh?"

"Yes. A *lot*. Brant, this is *too* weird. I've seen these floors, and your couches, and that surfboard in my dreams. How can that be? It doesn't make any sense."

"That is strange, but does it have to make sense?"

"Yes. *No?* I don't know. That's the problem." She paced, fidgeting with her hands. "I'll just tell you what I came to say and then I'll leave."

He stepped into her path, and when she looked up, he swore the world stood still. She was so damn beautiful, it made her troubled expression even more heartbreaking. A lock of hair fell in front of one eye, and this time he didn't hold back. He reached over and tucked it behind her ear. He had a feeling it was now or never to tell her how he felt. "When I saw you in Randi's yard, gorgeous in that green knit top that brings out your eyes and the torn jeans I love, I was sure I was seeing things, and I'm glad I wasn't. I don't want you to leave, Cait. I want you to talk to me and trust me enough to explain what's going on. We can sit outside if that would be easier."

Her eyes flicked up to the surfboard, and he didn't wait for an answer. He took her hand, picked up her glass of water, and headed out the patio doors, leaving them open for Scrappy. They sat on the wicker couch, and he said, "Is this better?"

"Yes, but . . ." Her shoulders sank, embarrassment rising in her eyes.

"Cait, we all have shit that makes us feel different than everyone else. You and I obviously have a strong connection, and the fact that you feel like you've been here before is part of it. I can't explain it, but it doesn't scare me. It makes me want to know more about you. Do you feel that way at all? Or am I alone in this?"

"Sometimes I want to know more about you, and other times our connection scares the crap out of me," she said sort of jokingly, but he knew she was serious. "I'm sorry about last night. I feel horrible about how I acted."

"It's okay, but I would like to understand why you took off and why you sent me away, if you're willing to tell me."

She nodded, inhaling deeply and exhaling loudly. "I don't mean to be uptight. Part of it *is* our connection because it's so real, like the whole mermaid thing. You think you were saved by a mermaid. I told you about my mom's necklace, but what I didn't tell you was that after she died, I told myself she'd become a mermaid, and I fantasized about walking into the ocean and becoming one, too, so I could swim away and never look back."

His stomach knotted. "Never look back at what?"

"I haven't had the best luck with the men in my life."

He had assumed that, but he hated knowing he was right.

"The last guy I went out with led me to believe things about him that weren't true, and I ended up hurting people without meaning to because of it. But that's not all his fault. I was so wrapped up in being happy that I missed the signs."

"I can't imagine you hurting anyone. What do you mean by that?"

Her arm slid across her stomach, and she leaned the elbow of her other hand on it, nervously touching her chin with her fingers. "I went out with him for three months before I found out that he was married." She closed her eyes briefly and shook her head. "I *didn't* know. I would never go out with a married guy. I was working at a tattoo shop in New York at the time, and one day I was sitting on the curb out front eating lunch and he came out of the shop next door. We got to talking and hit it off. After that he'd show up and bring me flowers, take me to lunch. One thing led to another, and we started going out. We saw each other a few times a week because he said he traveled a lot. He treated me well, and I *thought* I was being careful, asking all the right questions to figure out if he was safe to go out with. It wasn't until I came to the Cape a few years later and I met Tank and he showed me what it *really* meant to check someone out that I realized I hadn't done nearly enough."

He'd like to get his hands on that asshole. "How did you find out he was married?"

"His wife came into the shop carrying their baby girl and went off on me. I honestly thought she had me confused with someone else, because he said his name was Frank, but apparently that was his middle name, and I wasn't the first woman he'd cheated with."

"The bastard took advantage of you, Cait. You can't blame yourself because he was a liar and a cheat."

"No, but I can blame myself for not checking him out more thoroughly before getting involved. I was twenty-six, and I'd been through hell with a guy before him. It had been years since I'd even given a guy the time of day. I should have known better. But I learned from that experience. I no longer try to have romantic relationships with men. If I have the urge to . . . *you know* . . . I'll go out with a guy once or twice on my terms, but that's it. Over and done. No chance for emotions. And I *don't* do that often. In fact, it's been a really long time."

"That explains a lot. What happened with the guy before Frank?"

Her jaw clenched, and she looked away.

Her reaction told him it was worse. "You don't have to tell me, but I'd like to know so I can understand what you're dealing with."

"He got rough with me," she said just above a whisper.

His gut seized. "Jesus, Cait. He hurt you?"

She nodded almost imperceptibly.

"Badly?"

"Bad enough that it took me years to get up the courage to get close to another guy."

Motherfucker. He took her hand between both of his, wishing he could track the asshole down and pound him into the ground. "Did you report him to the police?"

"No. I was twenty and I'd been moving from town to town, living in shelters and group houses. I didn't think they'd take me seriously."

He gritted his teeth, hating that she'd been abused *and* that she'd had such a hard life. He wanted to know why, but first things first. "What *did* you do?"

"I did what I could. I hitched a ride to another town, found a job, and moved on."

"*Christ*, Caity." It sickened him to think of her running scared from some prick who deserved to be in jail. "I'm sorry you went through that. I wish I'd been there. I never would have let that happen." He lifted his hands with hers between them and pressed a kiss to her knuckles. "How about you tell me who this guy is so I can make him pay for what he did?"

She shook her head. "Violence won't change anything, and it's been twelve years."

Twelve years, and she was still affected by it. The fucker must have messed her up pretty bad. Violence might not be the answer, but at least that guy would get his due and think twice about hurting anyone else. But Brant wouldn't push. He hadn't gone through anything even remotely like that, but he understood the need to move on.

"Do you mind if I ask why you were living in shelters? Did you have a falling-out with your father?"

She looked away again. "You could say that."

The hair on the back of his neck prickled. "What *else* could you say?"

She looked up at the sky, blinking repetitively, her jaw clenched tight.

Anger roiled inside him. "Did your father hurt you?"

She inhaled shakily, and he had his answer.

He moved closer, holding her hands in one of his and putting his other arm around her, speaking just above a whisper. "My sweet Caity. What kind of hell have you been through?"

"The kind where I consider myself lucky to have only been physically and emotionally abused and not sexually abused." She turned her face farther away, but not before he saw tears in her eyes. "I don't want to talk about my father. That's not what I came here to do."

Anger and sadness consumed him, but he forced that ire down deep because Cait was letting him in, and the last thing she needed was another angry guy in her life. He had to believe that she'd tell him more when she was ready. For now, he needed her to know that she was safe with him.

"No wonder you got scared by our connection and my flirting. You didn't know me from Adam when you first came here. Jesus, you had just learned about Ava and your sisters, and you had all of that in your past. I wish I had known. I wouldn't have come on so strong."

"I deal with guys flirting every day. It's not that." She was still looking away, tears slipping down her cheeks.

He waited for her to say more, and when she didn't, he said, "Cait, I won't push you, but I need you to know that I will *never* lift a hand to you. That's a promise. I'm not that guy. I can't even lie with a straight face."

"Except about tattoos." She swiped at her tears.

He didn't know if she was trying to be funny or showing him that he did lie, even if it was about something silly.

"Caity, please look at me," he said softly, and she wiped her eyes and turned with a regretful expression that cut him to his core. "Sweetheart, you met my family. You know my friends, the families I grew up with. I'm thirty-three years old. If I was that type of guy, people around here would know. You don't have to believe me, but one day I hope you will."

"I don't think you're like that. Abby wouldn't encourage me to go out with you if you were, and Tank checked you out the *right* way. He says you're as clean as a Boy Scout."

"Well, I am *the good one*," he said to lighten the mood, earning a small smile. "But if Tank checked me out and you knew I was a good guy, then why did you run?"

"Because I don't make out in public. Or at all, really, and I got so lost in you, it terrified me that I gave up control so easily. You literally kissed me senseless." She shrugged, tears brimming. "I forgot we were even on the dance floor, and as it all came back into focus, I wasn't thinking about Tank having checked you out or Abby telling me how great you are for the last three months. I was thrown right back into protective mode. I needed to regain control of myself and put my walls back up."

"It kills me that you've gone through so much that you need to do that, but I get it, and I'm sorry. Not for kissing you senseless, but that it made you feel that way."

She took his hand and said, "The thing is, kissing you was the *best* feeling in the world. I felt happy and safe and I *wanted* to kiss you. I still do. That's why I asked you to leave." Her voice softened. "Because you *are* good, and you deserve to be with someone who isn't broken, someone who knows how to have a relationship without freaking out."

He brushed her tears away, his hand lingering on her cheek for a moment. "That doesn't work for me, Cait. I've never felt what I feel for you for anyone else. I don't know where we'll end up, or if we'll last a month or fifty years. But I know I don't want to walk away from you, and if that means we deal with freak-outs, then it does. We'll get through them and hopefully come out stronger on the other side. Because you're *not* broken, Cait. Your trust has been abused by broken people. There's a big difference."

More tears spilled from her eyes, and she swiped at them. "I'm pretty messed up. I mean, look at me." She held out her arms. "I tattoo reminders of the things I've been through on my body—webs of deceit, rooms I've been locked in, pains I've suffered—so I never forget to look beyond what people want me to see."

"The people who hurt you are messed up, not you. Your tattoos show me that you're smart enough to know you need those reminders and strong enough to heed them. But you're not messed up, babe. You're *scared*. You've learned that men lie and they hurt you. But I saw you with Tank and his brothers, and I've seen you with your sisters. You know *how* to trust. It seems to me it's trusting someone as more than a friend that scares you, and after what you've gone through, it should scare you."

She lowered her teary eyes.

"Please look at me, angel." When she did, he said, "Your fear is a reflection of the people who hurt you, *not* a weakness or a defect. It's pure survival instinct. It means you're *strong*, Cait. A weaker person would never try to break the cycle."

"I *want* to break it more than anything," she said almost angrily. "I've been trying, doing all the right things. Tank hooked me up with a therapist a few months after we met, and I saw her for a little more than two years. I've been in a really great place. But I haven't had a romantic relationship with a man to test it all out, and then I saw you and something—*everything*—inside me lit up. Suddenly I wanted to spend time with you and do a lot more, which was terrifying, and I guess, along with meeting my sisters and finding out about Ava, it dredged up all those old memories."

She pushed to her feet and paced. "I *hate* living with this crap in my head. I hate that my father and those two jerks had the power to take away my chance at having a normal life. I'm tired of trying to figure out who to trust, so I stay in this little bubble of safety on the Cape with Tank and our friends there. But these last three months have changed everything. I miss Abby and Aiden when I'm at the Cape, and I miss Dee because she's far away. And you have to understand that I've *never* missed people like that before. Then there's you, and *everything* is different with you, more intense. I don't even know what to do with all the feelings I have for you, and we're not even dating."

She looked him in the eye and said, "I *want* what Abby and Aiden have and what Jules and Grant have. I want to be able to kiss you without losing my freaking mind. But I didn't grow up like you did." Her voice escalated. "While you were out at bonfires and barbecues, I was walking on eggshells, wondering if I'd get pushed into a wall or have my arm squeezed so hard, I'd have bruises for a week. I didn't have friends or birthday parties, or go swimming, or anything like that because someone might see my bruises."

Her every word broke his heart. He wanted to hunt down her father and tear him apart, along with the other cretins who had hurt her. "You've been hiding one way or another for your whole life. It's no wonder you looked like you'd woken up in a foreign land when you came here three months ago. You walked into the most open and communicative community around, where all the parents love and practically raise each other's kids. I can see how it would all be overwhelming."

"It is, and I'm sick of feeling that way. I *want* to trust you," she said sharply. "But it's not just you. I haven't even told my sisters about my past, and I *know* it holds me back from getting close to them. It's really hard keeping these kinds of secrets. They're like villains that only I can see standing between me and the rest of the world. You know that letter that fell out of my backpack on the boat? It's from Ava, and I can't even open it yet, because I don't want to know if there are any more secrets. We found out that she and my adoptive mother were in touch until my mom died. My father cut off all communication, and who knows, maybe if my mom had lived, I could have met Ava while she was still alive."

She huffed out a breath, still pacing. "I want to move forward. I *want* to tell my sisters about my past. They've been nothing but open and honest with me. But it's scary talking about it. Just like the prospect of being with you is scary. I have so *much* at stake. If I give in to my feelings for you and then I blow it, where does that leave my sisters? I don't want them to have to choose between you and me. And as I'm saying all of this, I realize it's even bigger than that. This whole community has welcomed me with open arms. All of my sisters' friends, your friends, your family, Shelley and Faye. There's *all* this love out there, and as much as I want it, I'm not sure how to accept it or love them back."

She wiped her eyes and sank down beside him on the couch. "I'm sorry for dumping all my crap on you." She leaned her elbows on her knees and covered her face with her hands. "This is why you should be with someone who isn't drowning in bad memories." She dropped her hands and looked at him. "I don't want to bring you down with me."

"You're not going down, and you're not going to push me away. Caity, you *deserve* to be with a man who understands everything you just shared *and* all the things you haven't. A man who will be patient when you're struggling and help you find your way to the other side of the abuse you've suffered. You deserve to be adored." She lowered her eyes, and he lifted her chin, brushing away her tears. "I *want* to be that guy, babe, and I think you want me to be him, too, or you wouldn't trust me enough to share what you have with me."

She curled her fingers around his, her eyes tearing up again. "I can't believe you still want to be with me."

"I see *you*, Cait, and I want to be with *you*. I like who you are whether you're wearing full-body armor or you let it slip and your heart leads you. If you let me in, I believe we'll find the person you're meant to be. But here's the other thing you need to know. Whether you choose to be with me or not, I will *never* let anyone hurt you again. I know you have Tank and his brothers at the Cape, but now you've got me, too. Okay?"

She nodded, breathing harder, holding his hand tighter. She opened her mouth, but no words came.

"What is it? Don't worry. I'm not going to share any of this with anyone."

"It's not that." She blinked several times, her eyes moving nervously over his face, and then, as if a veil of courage came down over her, she lifted her chin and sat up straighter, holding his gaze with renewed confidence. "I came here to give you an explanation and to end whatever this is between us, but that's the *last* thing I want to do. I don't want to fight my feelings for you. I *do* want you to be that guy, but if things don't work out, I don't want my sisters to feel like they have to choose between us."

Relief barreled through him. "That's not going to happen, but if you're worried, we can talk to them and get things out in the open to take the pressure off. And for now, we'll take it slow, go at whatever pace you're comfortable with."

"It took me three months to give in to a kiss. Slow kind of stinks." She laughed softly and licked her lips. She looked down at their joined hands, then out at the yard, at the cottage, and finally back at him. "I know I just laid a lot of scary stuff on you, but will you kiss me?"

Good God, yes. "The last time I kissed you, it didn't go very well. Are you sure? There's no rush."

"I know, but I feel better and much clearer now that you know what I've been through." She let out a long sigh. "I can't believe how much better it feels to have it off my chest. Knowing you're not afraid to be with me and that you're willing to try to deal with it together makes me feel safe, and that's no small feat. Even saying that I feel safe is huge for me, because that word usually makes me think of how I can't trust my instincts. But I want to with you. I can't promise I won't get scared, but I want to try."

"I want to try, too, but can you do one thing for me? If you get scared when we kiss, instead of running away, will you stay with me? I won't kiss you or even hold you if you don't want me to. I just don't want you to run off and be scared alone."

"I think I can do that." A genuine smile appeared. "You really are the *good one.*"

He put his arms around her. "I've never been so nervous about a kiss in all my life."

A soft laugh escaped her lips as his mouth came tenderly down over hers, hard enough to let her know he wanted this and soft enough to let her set their pace. Her tongue swept tentatively over his at first, gradually turning sensual, until they were as in sync as they'd been last night. Was it possible to miss kissing her after only one kiss? Because her mouth was sweet and hot, her lips were soft and perfect, and he felt like he'd been craving them for a lifetime.

Her arms circled his neck, and he gently pulled her closer, deepening the kiss in stages, like a leaf falling from a tree, slowly taking them where they were meant to be. She moaned softly, and the trusting sound wound through him, drawing him deeper into her. He slid his hand into her hair, still allowing *her* to give and take as she pleased—and she gave and took with fervor. She kissed him hard and deep, then slow and tender, driving him out of his ever-loving mind. It took everything he had to keep from claiming control, but he felt her losing herself in them just as he was, and last night told him how quickly their kisses could turn into a feast of desires.

In an effort to lessen the chance of her feeling out of control or scared, he forced himself to draw back and brushed his lips over hers, whispering, "Okay?"

"Perfect."

She pulled his mouth back to hers. Their kisses went on and on, in the sweetest devouring he'd ever experienced. Cait went soft in his arms, and he held her tighter, hoping she felt safe and respected on this special night, which he hoped was the beginning of so much more.

CHAPTER NINE

CAIT SAT ON her knees sketching on the wall, trying to ignore her growling stomach. Sunlight streamed in through the curtains, and she knew that soon she'd have to leave for school. She hoped to get breakfast first, but after last night, she wasn't sure what to expect. She brushed her hand over her ribs, flinching in pain, and heard the creak of the stairs. She stilled, holding her breath, listening to her father's footsteps coming down the hall. She scrambled out from where she'd moved her dresser away from the wall and quickly pushed it back into place, covering her secret drawings—her rebellion—and quickly smoothed her blanket, fixed her pillow just right, and sat on the edge of her bed facing the door, hands folded in her lap, heart slamming against her ribs. She smelled his cigarette as he opened the door and kept her eyes trained on the floor in front of her. She didn't have to look to know he was scrutinizing her readiness for school, from her freshly combed hair and tidy private-school uniform all the way down to the bows of her shoelaces. Next he'd visually inspect her bed and the rest of the room. She began her mental countdown. Ten Mississippi. Nine Mississippi. Eight . . . She'd learned his routines down to the second. It helped knowing when the pain would come.

"Teeth brushed?" he asked gruffly.

"Yes, sir."

"Get your backpack and let's go."

"Yes, sir." She stood with her heart in her throat, back pin straight, knowing better than to follow her instinct and run from the room. She'd made that mistake before. She bent at the knees to pick up her backpack, keeping her eyes low as she walked out the door and into the hall. Yes! She made it without being yanked back.

"Catherine."

She froze—and startled awake, eyes wide, heart racing. It took her a second to remember she wasn't ten years old and back in Connecticut, but thirty-two, lying safe and warm in Brant's strong arms on his couch. She must have dozed off. They'd kissed and talked well into the night before moving inside.

"You're okay, Caity. I've got you." Brant ran his hand down her back, pressing a kiss to her forehead. His body was warm. He'd changed into a T-shirt and sweatpants last night. "Did you have a nightmare?"

She nodded, lifting her eyes over his shoulder to the surfboard hanging in the nook beside the kitchen, PARADISE staring boldly back at her, and her racing heart started to calm. Her puzzling dreams were finally making sense, and the immense relief that brought was almost as intense as the relief she'd felt after she'd told Brant about her horrid past. "Sorry. What time is it?" She felt something move on the sliver of couch behind her legs as Brant pulled his phone from his pocket, and saw Scrappy curled up there.

"Just after two in the morning." He pocketed his phone and continued stroking her back. "What were you dreaming about?"

"My childhood. I had gotten a C on a test. It came with a side of bruises on my ribs and going to bed without dinner."

"Jesus, babe. I'm sorry." He kissed her again, holding her tighter. "Do you think your mom knew when she was alive?"

"I don't think he started hurting me until after she died. I think he hated that I was alive when she wasn't."

"That's horrible. Did you ever tell anyone that he hurt you?"

"I tried, but I quickly learned to keep my mouth shut. When we first moved to Connecticut, my father hired a housekeeper to watch me before and after school while he was at work. I'm pretty sure a few months went by before I made the mistake of confiding in her. That night I heard her confronting him. I sat at the top of the stairs listening to him calmly talking his way out of it. I don't remember what he said, but when the housekeeper left, she looked at me like I had been lying. She never came back, and I was punished for making her quit. After that my grandparents—his parents—watched me. They lived close by. But they were always cold, and they could be mean. Not physically, but I always felt like an imposition to them, which I'm sure I was. I think I tried to tell them once, and they got mad at me for telling stories. But I can't be sure if I actually told them, or if I just wanted to badly enough but expected that to be their reaction and didn't do it. They treated my father like he walked on water. Everyone did. He was an attorney—still is. As I got older, people made comments about how he was a *pillar of society* and *such a nice man* because he gave a lot of money to different organizations and sent me to expensive private schools. To everyone else he came across as the perfect father. He always made sure I looked and acted proper and happy around others."

"Did you go to the police when you got older?"

"*No.* It would have been my word against his, and he's got a lot of money and resources. But I like to think about how angry he probably got when he discovered my secret drawings after I ran away."

"What do you mean?"

"He was always banishing me to my room without meals, and I wanted to get back at him, but I knew he'd hurt me. So I rebelled by moving my dresser away from the wall and drawing on the wall behind it. I have a tattoo on my back of a little girl climbing through a tunnel behind her dresser. The escape route I'd always wished I'd had. By the time I ran away at sixteen, I had drawn on the walls behind every piece of furniture in my room that I was able to move and on the backs of the furniture, too. I wish I could have been there to see him find those drawings. Maybe he never did, but I like to think he did and that they made him lose his mind. He was *such* a perfectionist. Everything always had to be in its place. Just now, I was dreaming that I was drawing behind the dresser when he came to get me for school the next morning. I pushed the furniture back against the wall and sat on the edge of my bed the way he required that I wait for him every morning. I was counting, *one Mississippi, two Mississippi*, as he inspected the room. I knew exactly how long it took. If one thing was out of place in my bedroom or if I looked the littlest bit disheveled, I'd get hurt or told how worthless I was."

"Is that why your place is so neat?"

She nodded. "I tried to mess it up, but it gave me anxiety."

"Does my mess give you anxiety?"

"No, actually, it makes me feel even better about you. Most girls probably want a guy who puts everything in its place. But not me." She sighed, feeling good about sharing these things with him. "Growing up, it was always *yes, sir, no, sir*. I was made to look him in the eye when we were in public, but never in private because that could piss him off. That morning I was dreaming about, when I walked out of the bedroom, I thought I was safe, but then he said my name. *Catherine.* That's what he called me, and that's when I woke up from the dream. But I remember that morning as clearly as if it were yesterday. He'd grabbed a handful of my hair and yanked me back to the doorway, pointing to my pencil on the floor. I must have dropped it in my panic to put the dresser in place. I got lucky that morning. He only scolded me, told me it was no wonder my mother didn't love me, and sent me to school without breakfast. Some days were good like that."

"It makes me sick to think about you being treated that way, especially by someone you should have been able to trust to *protect* you. And for him to try to take away your mother's love? He's a fucking coward, a goddamn bully, hurting a little girl like that. I'd like to teach that asshole a lesson."

"You can't think like that. It took me years to get the courage to run away, and once I did, I fought tooth and nail to keep him from finding me. I went from being Catherine to Cait, which is what my adoptive mother had called me, but I spelled it K-A-T-E and used fake last names. If you went to see him, I'd be thrown right back into that nightmare."

"But you're still living it, babe," he said gently. "You deserve closure, and he needs to pay for what he's done."

She touched her forehead to his chest, feeling the steady beat of his kind heart, and she didn't fight the urge to press a kiss there. It felt good not to be afraid to lie with him and to kiss him like that. She scooted higher so they were face-to-face. "Tank wanted to do the same thing and I wouldn't let him, either. But he did track my father down to see if he was still looking for me. I don't know how Tank found out that he wasn't without talking to him, but the Wickeds have connections everywhere. He's still working at the same practice in Connecticut he'd worked at when I was a kid, only now he's a partner. Tank has Dark Knights in the area keeping tabs on him. If they get wind of him hurting anyone else, they'll have him arrested. But according to Tank, he has no one in his life outside of work."

"That's good, but I still don't like it. A guy like that shouldn't be out there walking around."

"I know, and I feel guilty about that, but I was just a kid when I ran away, and I was focused on surviving. And now it's been sixteen years, and it would still be my word against his. There are no medical records showing abuse, and I'm sure if his parents are still around, they'd deny anything I said. He's not looking for me, Brant. I don't know if he ever did, or if he just said I ran away and let it go at that. I'd imagine he looked for me if for no other reason than to keep up appearances, but I'm sure he was glad I was gone, and I don't want to open that door again. It took a long time for me to settle down in any one place, and despite the stuff that sometimes messes with my head, I'm happy with my life. I just found my sisters and *you*, and I've got the Wickeds, and I love my work. And now that I've told you everything, I realize that I don't want my past to define my future anymore. I want to make a concerted effort to move forward, and if that makes me a bad person for not trying to fight a bitter battle that won't end in my favor, then it does, and I'll understand if you don't want to be with me."

"Cait, that's not at all how I feel. I want to be with you, and nothing is going to change that. I just wish you had the closure you deserve." He kissed her softly. "You are one brave girl, Cait Weatherby." He cocked his head. "Is Weatherby your real last name?"

"Yes. I worked for cash wherever I could find jobs, so I didn't have to give my real last name, until I started working for Tank. Believe it or not, I've done everything from scrubbing toilets to construction. That's how I got into tattooing. I was drawing tattoos for some of the guys I worked with, and one of them introduced me to his tattooist. He hired me as his apprentice, and the rest is history."

"From what Aiden said, you're a whiz at math and computers, too."

"Aiden and I are both math geeks." A smile lifted her lips. "I have no idea where I get that from, but I worked on a housekeeping crew for a while, and one of the girls was taking an accounting class. She showed me a few things on her computer. I picked them up quickly, and she started showing me different accounting programs and procedures. When I realized how easy they were for me, I went to the library and used the computers to find online tutorials. That's how I taught myself accounting and website development. I help Tank with the website, social media, and marketing, and I also help his parents with accounting at the Salty Hog when they need it. I updated their accounting and staff software a while ago. Anyway, after Tank found out my father wasn't looking for me, he said I should either formally change my last name or use it, because he didn't want to keep paying me under the table, and he didn't want his parents to get in trouble, either. I didn't want to change my name because it was my only link to my adoptive mother, so I took the leap and went back to Cait Weatherby. I was terrified that my father would show up, but I knew Tank would watch out for me, and my father never did come after me. Do you know what's crazy?"

"Everything you've been through."

"Yeah, but also, Ava ran away at seventeen after her parents made her give me up for adoption, so we have the running away thing in common."

"Sounds like you come by your courage honestly. Maybe her letter will tell you there's even more that you have in common."

"I'm not ready to read it."

"Okay." He kissed her forehead, and she was thankful he didn't push for more. "Do you have nightmares often?"

"No. I haven't had a nightmare like that in years." She was surprised he'd circled back to that and didn't get lost in everything she'd said. But she was learning that Brant really did see more than most people, and he homed in on the important things. "Most of my dreams these days are about a blue-eyed guy. I think I had a nightmare because we've been talking about my past."

"I'm sorry for dredging it all up, but I'm glad you told me." He brushed a kiss over her lips. "I had a feeling you'd been through something, but I hadn't realized how bad it was."

"I don't know how you did it, but thanks for getting me to open up. Once I got past the embarrassment, it was freeing to tell you what I've been through. Holding in those secrets made it feel like they could swallow me up at any moment if someone found out. Now they don't feel quite so threatening. I don't think there's a worse feeling than being afraid."

"Sure there is. Being afraid and alone."

Her heart filled up, and she snuggled closer. "How do you always know what to say to make me feel better?"

"You can thank Randi for that one. My sisters were both afraid of the dark when they were young, but Randi used to wake up in the middle of the night and charge into my room and dive under my covers. She'd fall asleep in sixty seconds flat. Sometimes she'd go into my brothers' rooms, but most of the time it was me she woke up. That went on for a few months. She just needed to know someone else was there, and once she realized we would always be there, she was okay."

"You're such a good big brother. What did Tessa do when she was scared?"

"She'd lie in her bed bawling until one of us went in there. But the minute the lights were on, she was totally fine. She'd tell us to turn off the lights and she'd go back to sleep. It only took a couple of days for her to get past her fear of the dark."

"Why didn't your parents just give them night-lights? Wouldn't that have been easier?"

"I asked the same thing, especially since Randi was waking me up all the time. My dad said they needed to realize it wasn't the dark they were afraid of but the thoughts in their heads. He said once they learned that, they could try to find ways to get over their fears."

"It sounds like he was always teaching you guys."

"Both of our parents were. They still do. But that wasn't all there was to it. Years later my parents told me that they were also teaching our sisters that they could rely on me and my brothers and teaching me and my brothers to put the needs of others ahead of ourselves. It was a good lesson, but we went to school tired for six months."

She sighed. "Your family is incredible."

"So are yours—the de Messiéres *and* the Wickeds."

"Not a day passes that I don't think about how lucky I am."

He slid his leg over hers. "Not quite as lucky as I am that you're here with me right now."

"I don't know about that. I've kept you up most of the night, and you have to work in the morning. Do you want to take me home so you can sleep?"

"Have you gone mad? I've waited months to have you in my arms." His brows slanted, and he drew back. "Unless you *want* to go home."

"I'd much rather stay. I have lots of past-due kisses to collect." She couldn't believe those words had come out of her mouth without leaving a tinge of fear behind. But as his lips came down over hers, she felt like she was exactly where she was meant to be.

CHAPTER TEN

WHEN CAIT AWOKE, she was lying on her side fully dressed, with Brant's warm body pressed against her and Scrappy nestled in the slim space between their chests. She closed her eyes, soaking in the feel of one of Brant's legs resting over hers, his enticing erection against her stomach, and no anxiety in sight. Opening up to him had changed her, unleashing a part of her that had been locked down for too long. She'd taken his mother's advice and had grabbed hold with both hands and gone along for the ride, enjoying every delicious kiss, every sensual caress, and wanting so much more.

Brant's hand spread across her lower back and his hips rocked forward. He made a low, appreciative sound, setting off a five-alarm fire inside her. *Lord have mercy.* Three months was a long time to hold back. She felt like a racehorse waiting for the starting gate to open. She waited for anxiety to follow that thought, or awkwardness to spike between them, but when his sleepy eyes found hers, all she felt were butterflies— and this time she welcomed them.

"Morning, beautiful." He brushed his scruff along her cheek, sending tingles all the way down to her toes, and pressed a kiss beside her ear. "Hi."

He lowered his chin toward Scrappy. "Is our boy trying to get closer to my woman?"

"I thought you weren't possessive," she teased.

"So did I." He kissed her softly. "Did you sleep okay?"

"Mm-hm. Better than usual. I think telling you everything helped," she said as his hand traveled over her hip and up her side, stopping short of her breasts, making it hard to think about anything other than how much she wanted him to touch her.

"Either that or my kisses wore you out." His expression turned serious. "Are you okay this morning?"

"Better than okay. I feel really good, clear-headed."

"No more bad dreams?"

"Nope." That serious look morphed into a seductive, heavy-lidded one that made her want to pull him on top of her and make out again.

"Maybe you should sleep with me every night and they'll stop for good."

He was like a snake charmer, and she felt like his cobra. "You think that would solve the problem?"

"It's worth a shot. I'm used to sleeping alone, but I'm a generous guy. I can give it a whirl for the greater good."

She could think of several *generous* things she'd like him to take a whirl at. *Holy cow.* Her mind and body were on a race from zero to one hundred. She told herself to get a grip but couldn't resist teasing him right back. "Just how *generous* are you?"

His big body shifted over her, making her feel all kinds of good and drawing a needy sigh from her lungs. She clamped her mouth shut, barely recognizing herself. He was *not* helping her greedy thoughts, but she *liked* not being afraid, and she went with it.

His lips curved up. "Stay over tonight after your swim lesson, and I'll show you just how generous I can be."

Her overactive hormones came to a screeching halt. "After my *what?*"

She said it so loud, Scrappy jumped to his feet and barked.

Brant dipped his head beside hers, chuckling. "So much for my stealth moves. I have to take him out before he pees on the couch." He gave her a quick kiss and climbed off. As he picked up Scrappy, he said, "Little man, did you pee on the floor by the chair or was that Cait?"

"Oh *no*. I'll clean it up." She pushed to her feet.

Brant reached for her hand, pulling her closer. "Leave it, babe. It's just puppy pee. It's not a big deal." He studied her face for a moment, and she knew he saw her past peeking its ugly head out.

"Sorry. Knee-jerk reaction. Old habits die hard." *Am I ever going to get over this?*

"It's okay. It's going to take time. Come outside with us. I'll clean it after we put him out." He led her outside and put Scrappy down in the grass. "*Out*, Scrap. This is where you pee, little man." He drew her into his arms, looking unfairly handsome. "How late do you work tonight?"

Squinting against the bright sun, she said, "Six."

"Can I see you after you're off?"

"To swim?" The idea of learning to swim might not be that appealing, but seeing Brant in a bathing suit sure was.

"If you're up for it. If not, we can grab dinner or go out for drinks, take a walk, or go on a boat ride. Whatever you want. But I vote for swimming, because I don't like you being vulnerable."

She liked the way he cared about her safety and happiness. "How can I say no to that?"

"No argument?"

"Maybe I need to reconsider my answer." She twisted playfully out of his grip, and he hauled her back into his arms.

"Should I pick you up at the Bistro, or at your place?"

She didn't know what was going on with this new sense of freedom, but she had a feeling if he picked her up at her place, she wouldn't want him to leave. "The Bistro. I'll ride into work with Abby and bring my suit. I can change there."

Scrappy trotted over, and she scooped him up, nuzzling against his fur. "What will we do with Scrappy while I flail in the water and you rescue me?"

He laughed. "Good question." They went inside, and he cleaned up Scrappy's accident. "We can leash him to a stake on the beach. It's not like we're going far, and nobody's ever there."

Brant started the coffee maker and fed Scrappy. She was glad to see the pooch eating.

"I should get a move on. I have a boat coming into the marina this morning." He pulled off his shirt as he stalked toward her, sending her body into overdrive again as he gathered her in his arms and kissed her neck. "Want to join me in the shower this time, beautiful?"

God yes . . .

No, no, *no.* "What happened to going slow?"

"Didn't you say *slow* kind of sucked?" He cocked a grin. "I have no trouble going slow, and I'll never pressure you. But that doesn't mean I'm not going to let you know I want you."

She looked up at his dimples and dazzling blue eyes and wondered how many other women he'd invited into his shower. "Do you do this often?"

"Ask you to join me in the shower? That's twice this week, so I guess I do."

"Not *me.* Other women. I just realized that I don't know anything about your dating history."

"I'm not one of those guys who sleeps with every woman I meet, if that's what you're asking. It's a small island, and I'm not going anywhere, which is why I've always been careful with my reputation."

"Have you been with anyone long term? You're an affectionate guy, and you know you're hot."

"Who, me?" He chuckled. "I dated a girl named Teri when I was twenty-one for almost a year, but she was in school in Boston, and I was here. It wasn't serious, just comfortable, fun. I've dated tourists here and there, and a few women on the Cape, like Brandy, but there's never been anyone particularly special. Until *you.*" He pressed his lips to hers in a slow, sweet kiss. "I don't make a habit of asking women to shower with me, and I don't know why you bring that out in me, but you do."

There it was again, the honesty that was so hard to resist.

"I really do need to get going. Are you going to be okay?"

"I'll be fine. If you're running late, I can ride my bike home."

"The hell you will." He kissed her and patted her ass. "There are mugs in the cabinet above the dishwasher. I'll be ready in a few minutes."

She watched him saunter toward the bedroom in his low-slung sweatpants and bare feet, remembering something Tank had once told her. They'd been talking about men who hurt women and how many women rationalized abusive behavior and stayed in bad relationships, and he'd said, *When a man shows you who he is, believe him.*

For the first time since, she wondered if he'd say the same thing about good men, because the more Brant showed of himself, the more she believed that he'd never pose a threat—except maybe to her heart.

A short while later, they threw her bike in the back of the truck and headed for her apartment. Scrappy sat on her lap, and Brant held her hand as he drove, like he'd been doing it for years. It made their evolving relationship feel even more real, stirring those butterflies again. It felt good to welcome the fluttery sensations instead of running from them.

He brushed his thumb over the back of her hand and said, "I thought we'd stop at the Sweet Barista to grab breakfast to go."

"Sure. That sounds great."

He parked out front, and when she reached for the door handle, he said, "Do me a favor and don't open that door." He hopped out of the truck and came around to help her out. He picked up Scrappy and took Cait's hand as she stepped onto the sidewalk. "*That's* how a gentleman treats a lady."

"Brant, you don't have to try to impress me. You've already done it in all the ways that matter."

He stepped closer with his dimples playing on his cheeks and Scrappy tucked under his arm like a football. "It's not about impressing you. The minute a guy stops treating his girl like she's special, everything goes to shit. I haven't even had a chance to start treating you special yet. I know you're capable of opening your own doors, and you're used to being autonomous, but can you just give me this? I promise to go at your pace with everything else."

She didn't want to fight it, even if it was a bit scary. "Okay, you can open my doors, but is that what I am to you now, Mr. I'm Not Possessive? Your *girl*? Should I be worried that this is the start of an overbearing relationship?" She was only half teasing. But she was a quick learner, and taking a page out of Brant's open-communication book seemed to be a better approach than worrying herself into knots about it.

"Not at all. I'll never tell you what to do or who to hang out with. But I *finally* got you to give us a chance, and I'd like to do it right. So yes, I'd like you to be my girl. Hell, if it were up to me, I'd tell everyone on the whole damn island we're together. Not because I want to own you, but because I'm *proud* to be with you. If that's too possessive, just tell me, and I won't hold your hand, kiss you, or claim you in any other way in public."

Her nerves came alive at the thought of letting him call her his girl, but she was determined to try to be a normal woman going out with a guy she liked, without feeling like she needed to shield herself with walls of steel, and this was a good first step. "I like holding your hand and kissing you."

His dimples deepened. "Does that mean I can buy a license plate that says *Cait's Guy*?"

"*No*, you cannot," she said with a laugh.

"But I can do this?" He kissed her tenderly. "And I can do this?" He slung his arm around her.

"You're such a charmer. Yes, you can do those things."

"But this might cross a line in public?" He squeezed her butt.

She glowered at him.

"Okay, okay. I've got it." He laughed. "I was just making sure I knew the parameters."

He took her hand, and they headed inside. Keira was behind the register watching them curiously as they approached, and Cait's nerves caught fire.

"Good morning, *hand holders*, and hello there, Scrappy." Keira reached under the counter and handed Brant a puppy treat.

Cait felt her cheeks burn. "Hi, Keira."

Brant gave the treat to Scrappy and reclaimed her hand, giving it a squeeze. "Can you believe this gorgeous woman finally agreed to go out with me?"

"Yes, I can. You're one of the good guys." Keira looked at Cait. "But if he gives you any trouble, let me know and I'll get Grant to take care of him. Would you like your usual this morning?"

"Sure," Cait said, glad Keira hadn't made a bigger deal about them.

"And what can I get for you, Dimples?" Keira said lightly. "A *smitten* scone or maybe an *I've got a crush* coffee?"

"I'll take one of each of those *and* a blueberry croissant, please," he said without missing a beat.

"Coming right up."

As Keira went to fill their orders, Brant pulled Cait closer, grinning like a fool. "Sorry about that."

"No you're not. You loved it."

"I'm not gonna lie. I did. But are you all right? Our friends are definitely going to razz us. Can you handle that, or should we ease into exposing our relationship?"

"*What* is going on here?"

Cait startled, jerking out of Brant's arms at the sound of her friend's voice, and found Jules, a petite bundle of energy with golden-brown hair, and Jules's sister-in-law, Daphne, a curvy, careful blonde, standing in line behind them, grinning. *What is wrong with me?* She hated her knee-jerk reaction and felt silly for jumping out of Brant's arms, especially since she'd become good friends with both Jules and Daphne. They'd brainstormed marketing ideas for the Bistro before it opened, had gone to dinner on occasion, and had gotten together for bonfires a few times.

Before Cait could form a sentence, Jules exclaimed, "Oh my gosh, you brought Scrappy!"

"We bring him everywhere," Brant said as Jules and Daphne lavished Scrappy with love.

"Thank goodness I didn't bring Hadley." Daphne was married to Jock Steele, and Hadley was their three-year-old daughter. "She wants a puppy, and Jock keeps trying to wear me down."

Jules waved a finger between Cait and Brant, all bright-eyed with half of her hair pulled up in a ponytail in the center of her head, the rest cascading over her shoulders and down her back. "*Please* tell me you two are a couple. I've been pulling for you to get together."

"We all have," Daphne added.

"I guess there's no hiding it now," Brant said, giving Cait an apologetic look.

Cait fought her need to stay in the shadows and reached for his hand. "I guess not, but that's okay."

Jules squealed. "I'm so happy for you guys." She hugged them as Keira returned with their order.

"I guess you're island official now," Keira said.

As Brant paid, Jules talked about getting together for a couples' night, but Cait was busy fretting about suddenly being in the freaking island-couple spotlight. Jules was the queen of group texts, which meant that within the hour, all their friends would have heard that she and

Brant were together. She'd known going out with Brant would mean she'd have to come out of her shell, but she hadn't expected it to happen so soon, or all at once. She'd worn that shell for so long, it wouldn't be easy, but given how much freer she felt from opening up to Brant, maybe this would make her feel even more secure.

When they got back into Brant's truck, she was still feeling bad about startling when their friends had arrived. "I'm sorry for stepping away like I did. I'm not used to being half of a couple."

"Babe, that's okay. I shouldn't have pulled you into my arms."

"*Yes*, you should have," she said adamantly. "You are who you are, Brant. You're an expressive person. Unfortunately, I am who I am, too, and it might take me a minute to get used to being squealed over and talked about. But I *wanted* to be in your arms. I'm just as proud to be with you as you are to be with me. I've just lived in the background my whole life, and I've had my walls up for so long, sometimes I can take a leap, like I did last night, and sometimes I might stumble, like I did in there. I'm sorry about that. I know it's not easy to be with me."

He took her hand, his gaze soft and sexy. "I think we need to get your hearing tested, because I'm pretty sure I already told you that I'm *all in*. I know how shy you were when you first came to the island, and I've watched you open up and let all of our pushy, loud friends into your life. But I know that what I'm asking of you now, opening up to a man and being part of a couple, is a whole different ball game. I don't expect you to be okay with it overnight. Just do us both a favor, and when something like this happens, hear my voice in your head telling you that if you stumble, I'll still be there to help you find your footing."

"I'll try." She felt like the luckiest girl on earth, and at the same time, she wondered if he could really be that patient and understanding, or if she was getting tangled up in a web of deceit. But as they drove to her place, she refused to let her past diminish this beautiful present she was being given, and by the time they arrived, she was trying to wear that lucky-girl crown proudly.

They parked her bike by the garage, and Brant reached for her again. She had a feeling he couldn't stop if he tried. His open affection was as much a part of him as those dimples. "It means a lot to me that you trusted me last night."

"Yeah, well, I got tired of fending you off," she teased. "Seriously, though, thank you for not giving up on me. I feel like I can breathe better than ever before."

"I should have shown up on the Cape a month ago." His lips came coaxingly down over hers in a deliciously passionate, sensual kiss.

"Well, this is *new*," Abby said as she came up behind them.

Cait jerked out of Brant's arms and threw up her hands. "What is with everyone on this island sneaking up on people? You all need to wear cowbells around your necks."

Abby laughed, her eyes darting between the two of them.

"Don't give Cait too hard a time. I don't want her running for the hills," Brant said. "Jules and Daphne just gave us the full-squeal treatment at Keira's."

"Oh boy, poor Cait. But I'm sure if she runs, you'd find a way to catch her."

"You know me well," Brant said. "Are you and Aiden coming to the movie tomorrow night?"

"We hope to," Abby answered.

"Good. Let's make it a double date. We can grab dinner there and bring some wine," Brant said.

"What movie?" Cait looked between them, surprised that the idea of a double date actually sounded fun.

"The dune-side movie. My mom invited you," Brant reminded her. "You said you were working until six."

Oh, right. "I never said I was going."

He took her hand and said, "Cait Weatherby, would you be my date for the dune-side movie tomorrow night?"

She laughed. "You're a goof. *Yes.*"

"Ah, but I'm *your* goof." He kissed her cheek. "I'll see you at six." As he walked to his truck, he said, "Don't forget your string bikini."

"I think I'm busy tonight after all," Cait called after him.

"Damn right you are. Busy with *me*." He blew her a kiss and climbed into his truck.

Abby sidled up to Cait as he drove away. "Okay, sis. That was *too* cute. What is going on? When you didn't come home last night, I thought you decided to stay at the Cape for an extra night. Were you with Brant?"

Cait looked at the sister who had welcomed her into her home and her heart from the very first moment they'd met and knew she didn't want to hide anymore. "How much time do you have?"

"As much as you need." Abby raised her brows. "Was last night *that* good?"

"Yes, but not in the way you're thinking. Let's go up to my apartment."

As they went upstairs, Abby chatted about how happy she was that Cait and Brant were together. They sat at the table, and Cait split her Danish from Keira's with her, trying to figure out where to start. And the best place seemed to be with correcting Abby's assumption. "We didn't sleep together."

"Oh. Okay." Abby looked confused.

"I'll tell you everything, but would you mind if I called Dee so she can hear it, too?"

"Of course not."

"Good, because I have a lot to say, and I don't want her to feel like I chose to tell you first." She pulled out her phone, getting more nervous by the second, and made the call.

Deirdra answered on the second ring. "Hey, Cait. What's up?"

"I'm with Abby, and I have something to talk with you guys about. But if you're busy, it can wait until tonight."

"I'm always busy, but I'll make time. Give me a sec." She heard Deirdra telling someone to hold her calls and close her door. "Okay, I'm here."

"Can we FaceTime?" Cait asked.

A minute later Deirdra's beautiful face appeared on the screen. She had the same brownish-blond hair as Abby, but while Abby's was coarse and always a bit tousled, Deirdra's was silky and fell in perfect waves just past her shoulders. She wore a white blouse under a navy blazer, her makeup perfectly applied. As always, Deirdra looked ready to take on the world, while Cait and Abby were in comfortable clothes, their faces makeup-free.

"What's going on? Is something wrong?" Deirdra asked.

"No. I'm not sure where to start, but I stayed at Brant's last night, and—"

"*Whoa.* You and Brant?" Deirdra exclaimed. "He finally got you into bed? He must be on top of the world. He's a great guy, but if he hurts you, I'll kill him."

"He'd *never* hurt her," Abby added.

"And he didn't get me into bed," Cait added.

"*Okay . . . ?*" Deirdra said curiously. "So you christened the kitchen table? His boat?"

"We didn't have sex." Cait fidgeted with her hands beneath the table. "We talked most of the night, and we made out, but the talking is the important part."

"Cait, you making out with a guy is pretty damn important," Deirdra said. "Just last month you were doing everything you could to not be alone with Brant."

"I know. When you hear what I have to say, you'll understand why. When I went back to the Cape this week, he came to see me." She told them about Brant's tattoo fiasco, which they cracked up about. "He hung out with me and my friends and we kissed, and I freaked out."

"Why?" her sisters asked in unison.

"That's what I want to explain." She dove right into telling them about her past before she could chicken out, revealing everything she'd told Brant. Abby cried and must have hugged her a dozen times. Deirdra kept a firm upper lip, asking painful questions, but Cait understood how her attorney's brain worked. She needed to understand everything, including why Cait hadn't gone to a teacher or the police.

"I'm sorry I kept it from you for so long," Cait said.

"Don't be. We understand why you did," Abby reassured her. "I'm sorry you went through all of that, and I'm glad you feel comfortable telling us now."

"I'm sorry I joked when we first started talking. What can we do to help you through this?" Deirdra asked.

"Just sharing the truth with you helps. I've been thinking about this since I told Brant. In a sense, hiding that part of my past allowed the emotional abuse to continue. The therapist I told you about had warned me that even though I got to a great place, when I made close friends or got involved with a man, it would probably bring all this stuff up again."

"This summer brought big changes for all of us." Abby reached for her hand. "It makes me sad that you've been suffering alone for all this time."

"It's my own fault. I could have told you earlier, but I was afraid. You guys had gone through so much with Ava. I didn't want to add to that."

"We're *sisters*," Deirdra said. "We need to support each other through the good times and the bad."

"You were here for me when Aiden and I had trouble, and I want to be there for you," Abby said.

"I appreciate that." Cait felt like another weight had been lifted from her shoulders.

"Do you think you'll see the therapist again?" Deirdra asked.

Cait had been thinking about that, too. "I want to try to deal with this on my own, using the coping mechanisms she taught me, and talking with Brant if need be, or you guys. If I run into trouble, then I'll go back to see her. But I already feel like I've come out from under a dark cloud. I hadn't realized how stressful it was holding in my secrets until I told Brant. It's like I've shed old skin that was holding me back and making me sick."

"That's because you did shed something that was holding you back and making you sick," Deirdra said. "I talked with a therapist when I was in college—"

"You *did?*" Abby asked, wide-eyed.

"I had to. Guilt was eating away at me for leaving you to deal with Mom," Deirdra said. "That's why I never hold anything back. The therapist I saw told me that the longer I held it in, the longer it would take to heal. She said not talking about what we were going through with Ava was protecting her, and that I needed to protect myself."

"Don't you think you should have clued me in?" Abby asked.

"I should have, and I'm sorry I didn't," Deirdra said. "But I was nineteen and trying to hold my shit together. The point I'm getting at is that we suffered neglect. Dealing with an alcoholic mother is very different from what Cait went through. But I think the shame that goes along with it is probably similar. I had a hard time opening up about our mom with my college friends because of that. I thought it reflected poorly on me. But once I took the plunge and started to tell my friends, it got easier, and eventually the urge to hide it went away completely. That was a huge turning point for me. Cait, as hard as this will sound, my advice is to try not to hide it from anyone. You went through something horrible, but that's not *who* you are; it's what you endured."

"Thanks, Dee. That's what Brant said, too, about it not being who I am. And the therapist told me I should get it out in the open. I'm glad I'm starting to."

"And Brant is being understanding?" Abby asked.

"He's been wonderful. But it's going to take some getting used to being with him in public. Everyone around here is so in your face about things, and you know me. I like to blend into the background. But Brant is super affectionate, *and* he's a talker. He says and does exactly what he feels all the time, which is way better than not knowing what he's thinking, but I'm not real comfortable with PDAs. I want to be okay with them. It's just hard. He told me if it were up to him, he'd tell the entire island we're together."

"In all fairness, he has been trying to get you to go out with him for a long time. He probably feels like he won the America's Cup," Deirdra said.

"He said you saw Jules and Daphne this morning, which means everyone probably knows by now," Abby said. "But if you explain how you feel about PDAs, I'm sure he'll understand."

"I did and he does. The thing is, I *really* like him. I feel good when we're together. *Hopeful* even, and I hope I don't drive him away."

"Have you seen the way he looks at you?" Abby asked.

"Yes. It's hard to miss." Cait found herself smiling. She really did feel better. "It's funny, before meeting you guys and Brant, I never let myself think about the things I missed out on when I was growing up. But since getting to know you and the people you grew up with, and hearing stories about dates and breakups, bonfires and weekend parties, and other things that most teenagers experience, I've been thinking about it a lot. When I lived with my father, I was focused on doing and saying all the right things and hiding the abuse, and after I ran away, I was all about surviving without getting caught. I never had a first crush, a first love, or even that first great college-aged relationship when you have wild sex and eat pizza out of a box on the floor naked, you know?"

"I never did that. I'm putting that on my bucket list," Deirdra said.

"You were too focused on school for naked pizza eating," Abby reminded her. "I hate that you never experienced those things, Cait."

"Me too, but being with Brant feels like what I imagine all those things would have felt like, only better, because we're not kids. He gives me *butterflies*. I'm *thirty-two*. Do women my age even get butterflies?

150

How can I have butterflies and want to rip his clothes off and make up for all those lost years?"

"Aiden still gives me butterflies, and I always want to rip his clothes off and devour him," Abby said.

"We *know*," Deirdra teased. "Cait, you totally deserve butterflies and great sex. Are you worried about getting down and dirty with Brant?"

"Maybe I should be, but I'm not." Her cheeks burned as she said, "I think the fact that I've been having dirty dreams about Brant for three months has got me chomping at the bit."

"Let's hope he has more than a *bit*," Deirdra said, making them both laugh.

"He does," Cait said. "A lot more. He was wearing sweatpants this morning, and . . ." She mouthed, *Wow*.

They all laughed.

"We should let you get back to work, Dee. Thanks for taking the time to talk with me. I feel so much better having told you guys the truth," Cait said, feeling even more thankful for her sisters.

Abby pulled her into a hug. "We love you."

Cait held her a little tighter, wishing she could say those three words back. But she was still wrapping her head around being *loved* so quickly and easily. She loved them, but the words didn't come as freely for her as they did for her sisters.

"Sending you both virtual hugs," Deirdra said.

Now, that was more Cait's speed. "I'm lucky to have you guys in my life. I've never had anyone I could talk to like this before."

"What about Tank? You guys are close," Abby asked.

"Tank knows about my past, but I meant talking about Brant."

"I'm impressed that Tank had Brant checked out," Deirdra said. "If he wasn't with Leah, I might have gone over and checked *him* out for myself."

Abby snort-laughed. "You barely make time for anything outside of work, and you only date clean-cut guys who have ten-year goals and 401K plans."

"On that note, I need to run," Deirdra said. "Cait, call or text if you need anything, and I think you should enjoy naked pizza with Brant. Abby, give Aiden a smooch on his handsome face for me. I love you guys."

"Love you, too," Abby said.

Cait ended the call and drew in a deep breath.

Abby looked at her thoughtfully. "I was hoping your life had been easier than ours, not harder."

"I wish it were. I'm just glad I didn't change my last name for good, or Shelley might never have found me."

Abby finished her Danish and pushed to her feet. "I should go get ready for work. Do you want me to share this with Aiden, or would you rather I didn't?"

"You can tell him. He's going to be your husband. I don't want you to have to keep secrets from him. Besides, I think it's about time I try to figure out how to separate my fears about my past so I can start fully living my present, and as Dee said, that starts with learning not to hide it."

"Okay. I'm really proud of you. I know this wasn't easy, and I know everyone is in your face, but I'm going to hug you again." Abby embraced her. "I'm glad you opened up to us. That's what family is for."

Family. That word had brought such bad feelings for so many years, Cait had thought the Wickeds were unique in the way they'd welcomed her into their lives. But her sisters, Brant, and the other friends she'd made on Silver Island were showing her just how wrong she was.

CHAPTER ELEVEN

SCRAPPY SCAMPERED HAPPILY beside Brant as they followed the sound of guitar music and the din of diners toward the entrance of the Bistro Thursday evening to pick up Cait for their swimming date. He couldn't stop thinking about her. He wanted to take away her past and give her a clean slate, to make up for all the shit she'd gone through and the fun she'd missed out on as much as he wanted to take her in his arms and protect her from everything bad in the world.

A gentle breeze swept up the beach as they stepped onto the patio. Nearly every table was taken, and a group of young couples chatted around the conversation pit, while Jagger Jones played his guitar from a stool at the far end of the patio. His dalmatian, Dolly, lay sleeping at his feet. Brant peered into the restaurant and saw Cait, gorgeous as ever in black jeans and a white tank top with the Bistro logo she'd designed emblazoned across her chest. She was talking with a family as she seated them, smiling like she hadn't a care in the world. He'd known she was strong, but *strong* wasn't a big enough word for the incredible woman who lived with so much hurt and fear so deeply ingrained. It was no wonder she was relaxed and chatty with customers—and Davis Barrington—while it had taken her some time to get that comfortable with their friends. Talking with customers and guys like Davis wasn't threatening to her in the way that being peppered with personal questions by people who wanted to get to know her better was.

More pieces of the Cait Weatherby puzzle were falling into place.

Someone called his name, and he saw Aiden waving him over to the portable wooden table where he'd been sitting when he'd first met Abby. They'd set the table up for the two of them on the nights Abby worked late. Aiden had been a workaholic and on the island for a forced vacation set up by his sister when he'd met Abby. He was adjusting well to island life, and Brant had never seen Abby look happier. He made his way over to Aiden.

"Having dinner with Abby tonight?"

Aiden closed his laptop and stood to shake Brant's hand. "At some point. I was just catching up on a few investment reports while I waited. Have a seat." He gave Scrappy a quick pet and said, "I hear you're going to teach Cait to swim."

"Yeah. She scared the bejesus out of me the other day. I think she'll catch on quickly."

Aiden arched a brow. "I also heard she stayed at your place last night."

"I wondered if you'd heard about that." Brant had texted with Cait earlier, but he hadn't asked if she'd talked with Abby about her past. He was careful not to breach her confidence or let Aiden think they'd hooked up. "We talked for most of the night and fell asleep on the couch."

"Cait told Abby and Dee what she's been through." He shook his head with a pained expression. "I can't imagine growing up with such a monster and turning out as great as Cait is." Aiden knew about heartache. He'd lost his parents when he was in his early twenties and had taken over his father's business and raised his twelve-years-younger sister, Remi, from that day forward.

"She's a remarkable woman, and I'm glad she has Abby and Dee. I'd really like to get my hands on her father and everyone else who has ever hurt her."

"I can understand that, but from what Abby said, Cait just wants to move forward."

"That's the plan." Brant was going along with it, but he worried about her not getting closure to such a traumatic part of her life, and the more he thought about it, the more upset he became. In an effort to distract himself from those harsh feelings, he changed the subject. "In the spirit of moving forward, did Abby tell you we're double-dating tomorrow night?"

"Yes. We're looking forward to it."

Brant looked around at the waitstaff coming and going. "This place is really hopping."

"The girls have done a great job. It's hard to believe they've been open for just over a month."

Just over a month might not be a date most people would consider worthy of a celebration. But with all that Cait was going through and how exhausting it must be going back and forth to the Cape, celebrating her and Abby's success might be exactly what she needed. It would be a great reminder that she'd grabbed hold of her future three months ago and had been doing a spectacular job of moving forward, and Brant knew just how to make it special. "How would you feel about putting together a little surprise for the girls?"

Aiden sat back with a mischievous grin. "What do you have in mind?"

Brant shared his thoughts, getting more excited by the second. Just as Aiden agreed, Cait walked out of the restaurant, and like metal to magnet, her eyes found Brant's. That lustful look he adored came over her, making his temperature rise. He stood to greet her, dying to sweep her into his arms and kiss her breathless, but doing so in front of everyone at the restaurant would be a mistake. Instead he reached for her hand.

"Hey, beautiful." He squeezed her hand and sat back down.

Melissa Foster

She gave Scrappy a quick pet. "I just have to wrap up a few things in the office; then I'll change and we can go."

"No worries. My night is yours."

She turned her attention to Aiden. "Abby said she was sorry, but she'll be a little longer than expected. Would you like to order something while you wait?"

Aiden shook his head. "No thanks. I'm okay."

"I would like something," Brant said. If he couldn't kiss her, he could at least let her know he wanted to.

She started to pull a menu from her apron, and he touched her hand, stopping her.

"No need for that. I know exactly what I want." He dragged his eyes down her body. "One raven-haired beauty with a side of snark."

"Get *over* yourself," she said with a laugh. "Think you can behave for a few minutes?"

"Absolutely. But no promises after that." Brant winked, and she rolled her eyes. He loved that she could still be her sassy self with him. He watched her walk away and said, "She digs me."

"You're definitely getting under her skin." Aiden chuckled. "I think you're good for her."

"She's gotten under my skin, too. But that's enough about me and Cait. How's the wedding planning coming? Is Abby still trying to get the details about your honeymoon out of you?" Aiden was keeping their honeymoon a secret to surprise Abby, and she pumped him for information all the time.

Aiden's face brightened. "She asks about the honeymoon on a daily basis, but I have a built-in excuse not to tell her. I can't plan a honeymoon without a wedding date. We're meeting with Daphne and Shelley next week to nail down the date and make the rest of the arrangements."

They were getting married at Top of the Island Vineyard, which was owned by Steve and Shelley Steele, and Daphne was their event planner.

"I guess you'd better come up with a better excuse after that."

"I'm working on it, but I think the planning will take a while. Abby's going back and forth about colors, the time of day for the wedding, and everything else you can imagine. She's hoping to get Dee and the girls to go wedding dress shopping with her sometime soon . . ."

Brant was happy for Aiden and Abby, but as he listened to Aiden talk about their wedding, his thoughts returned to Cait. He remembered his sisters and their friends talking about white weddings and Prince Charmings when they were younger, and he wondered if Cait had ever had those types of dreams, or if her father had ruined that for her, too.

A little while later Cait got off work, and they said goodbye to Aiden and headed to the parking lot.

"Where's your truck?" she asked.

"I drove my grandfather's truck." He motioned to the 1952 red Chevy pickup parked at the far end of the lot.

"Wow. That's gorgeous. He lets you just borrow it whenever you want?"

"Yeah. The truck's pretty, but as he says, it's just a people mover and built to be used." He opened the passenger door and put Scrappy on the bench, then slid his arms around Cait, tugging her against him. She glanced over her shoulder, and he said, "Don't worry. I parked far enough away that nobody can see us." He lowered his lips to hers, kissing her deeply and devouringly, as he'd been longing to do all day, and she was right there with him, putting her arms around him and going up on her toes for more, as if she'd been just as starved for him.

When their lips finally parted, she sighed dreamily. "Your lips are lethal."

"Wait until you see what my other body parts can do." He opened the door and patted her ass. "Climb in, babe. We need to make a quick run through town on the way to the cove."

They drove out of the lot, and as they passed the old newsstand, she craned her neck to take a second look.

"That place has been closed for a while," Brant said. "Davis's parents own it."

"Keira told me. I don't know why it intrigues me. I guess because it's unique."

"Like you." He stopped at the light at Main Street and reached behind the seat for the megaphone.

"What are you doing with that?" Cait asked, wide-eyed.

He grinned and turned onto Main Street, slowing the truck to a crawl as he lifted the megaphone to his mouth and announced, "It's that time of year again, folks! Join us for a family-friendly dune-side movie on Rock Harbor Beach Friday night at eight!"

People stopped on the sidewalks, waving and pointing at the truck, and Cait sank lower in her seat, holding Scrappy tighter. "*What* are you doing?"

"Announcing the movie. You heard my mom say it was my turn."

"I thought she meant handing out flyers!"

"What fun is that?" He raised the megaphone again. "Join us for a dune-side movie Friday night at eight o'clock on Rock Harbor Beach. And don't forget to stop by the hottest restaurant on this side of the island, the Bistro on Sunset Beach, co-owned by this lovely lady beside me, Cait Weatherby, and her sisters."

Cait shielded her face with one hand. "You're *crazy!*"

"Crazy about you, darlin'." He offered her the megaphone. "Want to take a shot?"

"No!" She shook her head vehemently, holding her hands up like shields.

"Suit yourself." He announced the movie up and down the commercial streets, then tucked the megaphone behind his seat and headed for the cove.

Cait gaped at him.

"What? You just got great free advertising."

"Thank you, crazy man, but a little warning would have been nice." She sat up with a wide smile. "How often do you do that?"

"Whenever my parents decide to have a movie night. They don't do anything on a schedule." As they wound through the residential streets, he said, "When we were little, they'd pile us in the back of this truck on a whim, and we'd wave to everyone and take turns doing the announcements. Sometimes my dad would claim the megaphone because he missed doing it. He used to say he couldn't give up all the fun just because he was a grown-up."

"It sounds like you had such a fun childhood."

"Yeah, I'm lucky, and I realize that now more than ever. But I'm on a mission to get you swimming and make up for all the things you missed out on." He reached over to pet Scrappy. "Right, Scrap?"

A little while later he pulled down the gravel road and parked at the dead end by the woods that led to Mermaid Cove.

"This looks like the beginning of a bad horror movie. Should I fear for my life?"

He laughed. "The cove is through the woods. The pines are prickly, and there's no trail, which is why no one ever goes there." He got out and went around the truck to open Cait's door, but she climbed out with Scrappy before he reached her. "I need to get faster at that."

She wrinkled her nose. "I don't know if I'll ever get used to you opening a car door for me."

"There you go, robbing me of the small pleasures in life." He leaned in for a kiss, grabbed the bag of beach supplies he'd brought, tossed Cait's backpack over his shoulder, and reached for her hand. "Let's go, swimmer gal."

Brant held branches out of the way for Cait to walk by and pointed out logs and holes in the ground as they made their way through the woods. When they cleared the trees and hit the sandy beach, it was just as magical as Brant remembered. The cove was big enough for boats and small enough to feel like they were miles away from civilization, nestled between enormous boulders and cliffs and the beach.

He put a hand on Cait's back. "What do you think?"

"I can't believe we have this gorgeous beach to ourselves. It's even more beautiful than it was from the water." She looked at him with a wide grin.

"I bet you want to come back one day and sketch it from this side."

She whispered, "It's like you read my mind. It's weird how you can do that."

"I think it's pretty great." He kissed her cheek. "I haven't been here in a hundred years."

"In that case, you might be too old for me."

"I'll give you *old*." He swatted her ass.

She made a surprised *squeak* and took off running across the sand. He dropped everything and sprinted after her, catching her around her waist, careful not to hurt Scrappy as he hauled her closer, kissing her laughing lips. "That sassy mouth of yours is going to get you in trouble."

"If this is what you consider *trouble*, then I look forward to it."

"Not half as much as I do." He nipped at her lower lip, giving it a gentle tug. He wanted to lower her to the sand and love every inch of her until she couldn't remember ever having been hurt, but he'd promised to go at her pace, and he was not going to screw that up. "How about you strip down to your suit while I take care of Scrappy."

He took the pooch and went to get the bags. When he turned around, Cait was pulling her shirt over her head. He whistled, and she gave him a deadpan look, but her lips tipped up at the edges. She unbuttoned her jeans, and he hollered, "That's it, baby. Take it off."

Her cheeks flamed. "Would you stop?"

"And miss those blushing cheeks? Not a chance."

She turned around. Her bathing suit was backless, with one string around her neck and another tied across her back. Brant pounded a stake into the sand and tied Scrappy's leash to it as Cait shimmied out of her jeans. He looked at Cait, and *holy hell*, his body flamed. Her suit rode between her butt cheeks and high on her hips, revealing most of her gorgeous heart-shaped ass. "Damn, baby. Now, *that's* a million-dollar view."

She looked over her shoulder, killing him with her sexiness, and twisted her torso, pushing out her butt so she could see it. *"Ohmygod!"* Her hands flew behind her, spreading across her butt cheeks as she spun around. The front of her suit was just as revealing, with a plunging neckline that dipped to her sternum and intricate cutouts in the shape of a flower that went almost all the way down to her promised land.

"I had no idea it was like this!" she said anxiously. "I didn't have a bathing suit, so I ran out on my break and picked one up. I threw it on so fast before leaving work, I didn't even look in the mirror. The girl who sold it to me said this was *full coverage!*" She looked down at her barely covered breasts and began tugging at the string around her neck, trying to pull it higher. "Full coverage for a *child* maybe."

He went to her, trying to tamp down the heat in his loins. "You are absolutely stunning, and nobody will see you besides me."

"*I* see me. I don't wear *thong* bathing suits."

He drew her into his arms and tried to put her at ease another way. "I'm totally cool with you taking it off. Do you want me to skinny-dip, too?"

She buried her face in his chest, laughing.

When she tipped her face up, he kissed her. "I know you're not a thong girl, Cait. I saw your pink panties, remember?"

She groaned, and he kissed her again. He couldn't fight the urge to spread his hands over her ass, which felt incredible. "Want me to stand like this, just in case anyone comes by?" Her eyes darkened, and he was *this close* to blowing off her swimming lesson and blowing her mind instead.

"You're such a *guy*."

"Exactly, and you're my gorgeous half-naked girl. If we keep this up, you're liable to wake my *very* male sea monster."

She took a step back, but the hunger in her eyes told him she was just as close to giving in to the inferno between them as he was. But he didn't want to do anything that might set her back, so he tried to ignore his half-hard cock and said, "*Mm-mm*, angel. You look delicious." *And I'm in the mood for a feast.* "We'd better get in the water before I forget my manners."

As Cait headed down to the shore, he poured a bottle of water into a bowl for Scrappy, kicked off his flip-flops, and stripped off his shirt.

Cait dipped her toes in. "It's cold."

"Exactly. Let's go, baby." He scooped her into his arms, and she screamed as he strode into the water.

"*Brant!*" She clung to him. "Don't drop me!"

"I would never put you in danger, which is why *I'm* waist deep in cold water right now."

She giggled. "That's very chivalrous of you." Her butt touched the water, and she shrieked, scrambling up his body. She wrapped her legs around his waist, squeezing with her knees and using his shoulders to pull herself higher.

Laughter bubbled out before he could stop it. "Jesus, woman. You're like a freaking monkey."

"That water is freezing!"

"And you're making me too damn *hot*. Now it's *my* turn." He put his mouth over the cutouts on her stomach, slicking his tongue along her skin, and gave it a nice hard suck.

"Oh *God*," she said in one long breath, and slid down his body, wrapping her arms around his neck. "Your mouth is wicked."

"And you're testing every ounce of my control. On your feet, woman. It's time to learn to float."

Her eyes widened. "I can't *float*. You saw me go under."

"I promise I won't let that happen."

She looked at the water, tightening her hold around his neck. "I don't think I need to learn to swim. I can just stay on the beach."

"Unless you see a helpless animal or a small child drowning. Then that big heart of yours is going to take you in. How about I sweeten the pot?"

She narrowed her eyes. "What do you have in mind?"

"Well, you like my mouth, and I like your *everything*, so for every skill you learn, a kiss you shall earn."

Heat shimmered in her eyes. "I might need one for good luck."

"Get over here." He pulled her mouth to his, taking her in a slow, drugging kiss. "You don't need luck," he whispered against her lips. "You have me, and I've *always* got you."

His words were as lethal as his lips.

"I'm going to lower you into the water, but I'm right here and I won't let go."

Cait clung to his arms as he lowered her onto her tiptoes in the almost chest-deep water. There were no waves in the cove, but the water swished with their movements. *I can do this. I can do this.*

Brant had a solid grip on her torso, and his eyes remained trained on her. "You okay?"

"I think so."

"Good. Now let's take a little walk."

"A walk?" She tightened her grip on his arms. "That's how I got in trouble last time."

"Cait, this cove doesn't drop off until you get farther out. I'll stay on this side of you." He was standing between her and the deeper water. "Do you trust me?"

She nodded. She did trust him, but she was still nervous.

He put his arm around her, bracing her against his side. "All we're doing is walking and getting comfortable."

She repeated that in her head like a mantra as they walked about ten feet one way and turned around and walked back. He didn't rush her but let her walk at her own pace.

"Feel pretty good?"

"Yeah. I'm okay," She was surprised to find that her nerves were settling. "This isn't bad."

"I'm just going to teach you the basics today, so you'll know what to do if you find yourself in deep water."

She leaned against him. "Like pray you're nearby?"

"*No*, like remember how to tread water, float on your back, and doggy paddle to shore. If you know you can do those things, you'll be more confident."

"You make it sound easy." She hadn't even realized he'd turned them around and they were walking the other way again.

"After today, it *will* be easy. I promise. Just push past the initial fear. If you tell yourself you can do it, you'll learn quicker."

"Don't I need to know how to actually swim?"

"Eventually. I'll teach you freestyle in the pool by my cottage."

"Why aren't we using the pool now?"

"Because the more comfortable you are in the ocean, the more confident you'll be. If you learn in the pool, you might still be intimidated in the ocean. But if you're confident in the ocean, the pool is a piece of cake."

"Then I want to learn to swim here," she said insistently.

"Attagirl, but we don't have enough daylight left to do it all today. Let's get the basics down." He pulled goggles out of the pocket of his bathing suit. They were dark green, the kind that covered only her eyes, not ones that went over her nose like Joni and Randi had worn. "Put these on."

"Do I really need them?"

"No, but it might make it less scary when you learn how to hold your breath under the water. I'd rather you were concentrating on breathing than how much the salt water stings your eyes."

"Good point." She put on the goggles.

"And for that you get this." He pressed his lips to hers.

It was just a simple touch of his lips, but he was being so patient with her, it made the kiss feel even more special. "I like this game."

He chuckled. "Me too. Are you ready to learn to float on your back?"

"Not really, but I'll try."

"We'll stay here where it's not too deep. The great thing about floating on your back is that you can see everything around you. Once you master it, you can pull yourself across the water using your arms."

"Or sink to the bottom and flail like a maniac."

"That's *not* going to happen. If Scrappy gets into the water again, you need to be able to save him."

She looked over her shoulder and saw Scrappy sitting on the sand watching them and knew he was right. "Okay, I'm ready."

"You're going to lie back and try to keep your body parallel to the surface. I'll keep my hands under you. All you have to do is breathe, relax, and let the water carry you."

"Right, uh-huh, okay. And what do I do about the woodpecker hammering in my chest?"

He laughed. "You're too cute." He pulled her close, kissing her again. "I promise he'll go away soon. You're safe with me, angel. I'm not going to let anything happen to you."

"Right. I know. Okay. *Please don't let me drown.*"

"You've got this, Cait." His expression turned serious. "You said you used to believe that your mom turned into a mermaid. Think about how this will bring you one step closer to her."

God, this man . . .

He listened, he saw, and he cared. With that one sentiment, he'd filled her with a renewed sense of purpose.

"Thank you for that. I'm ready now."

"I told you I've always got you. Now lean back, feel my hands under you, and lift your feet."

She closed her eyes, silently praying she could do it.

As she leaned back, he said, "Open your eyes, Cait. You need to be aware of your surroundings."

She felt his hands on her back, lifting her.

"I've got you. Lift your legs." As she did, he said, "Good. Now tilt your pelvis up and put your head back. Perfect. Remember to breathe."

"I'm busy trying not to freak out, and you want me to breathe, too?"

He moved his handsome face into view. "Yes. Breathe."

She stared up at the clear evening sky. *Breathe. Don't freak out. Breathe. Don't freak out.* "What do I do with my hands?"

"Put them wherever they feel comfortable, but try to keep your body level with the surface."

She grabbed his arm.

"Cait . . ."

"You said wherever it felt comfortable!"

He laughed. "As much as I like that, it's not going to help you learn."

"Buzzkill," she said under her breath, and realized she was smiling, *not* freaking out. *Yay, me!*

"Trust me, baby. I'll let your hands explore every inch of me when we're done."

That thought sent heat pooling in her lower belly, and her butt sank.

"Hey, hey, *hey.*" He lifted her up. *"Concentrate,* Cait."

"How am I supposed to concentrate when you wave the *touch-me* flag?"

He moved his wolfish grin into view. "Because if you don't learn to float, you won't get to touch me at all."

"That's cruel."

"That's *bribery*. Now focus, woman. You've got a lot of things to learn tonight."

She closed her eyes for only a second, and when she opened them, she picked a spot in the sky and concentrated on it. She imagined herself as a buoy, feeling the cool water swish along her sides. She focused on that to keep her body parallel, adjusting her hips, legs, and head until she became the buoy floating along the surface.

"That's it! Good job, Cait. You've got it. Keep your chin up. Attagirl!" He held his hands up. "That's all you, baby."

She wiggled her fingers. "I'm *floating*!"

"And floating has never looked so good. Keep it up." A few seconds passed. "Excellent! I knew you could do it!"

She lowered her legs to stand, and he swept her into his arms, lifting her feet off the ocean floor as he kissed her.

"Look at my amazing girl. There's nothing you can't do!"

She laughed, feeling giddy for the first time in her life, and he kissed her again.

"Is it against the rules to have a crush on my teacher?" she asked as he set her on her feet.

"It's against the rules for you to have a crush on anyone *else*." His arms circled her, and he took her in another heat-inducing kiss. "Ready to hold your breath underwater?"

"First I need to catch my breath after that." She fanned her face, and they both laughed. "I know how to hold my breath. I just panicked the other day."

"Great. Show me, and we'll practice enough so you don't panic if it ever happens again."

She gulped air into her lungs and sank beneath the surface. He went under with her, giving her a thumbs-up, his hair waving in the water, those blue eyes dancing with joy for *her*. They broke the surface and took a breath, and then he was kissing her again, sweet and slow and oh so good.

Brant was patient and funny as he put her through the paces, teaching her to tread water, doggy paddle, and do the breaststroke with a flutter kick and her face out of the water, all while filling her up with laughter and kisses. They practiced holding her breath underwater between each lesson, and Brant made funny faces and swam around her like a shark. She was having so much fun, she forgot all about being nervous as she stood in waist-deep water watching him swim out deep one last time. His strong arms sliced through the surface, his thick legs propelling him like motors. He swam too far out, went under, and circled back, stopping about fifteen feet away.

He scrubbed his hand down his face and raked his hair back. Good Lord he was handsome, and he wanted to be *hers*. That blew her away.

"Okay, babe. Breaststroke."

She glanced at Scrappy, sleeping on the blanket, and then she set her eyes on Brant. It was his voice she heard guiding her motions as she stretched her arms out in front of her and kicked off the bottom—*Outsweep, insweep, glide. Outsweep, insweep, glide*—until she was safely in his arms.

"You're amazing, baby."

He was the amazing one. "Pay up, Coach."

His mouth came eagerly down over hers, firm and insistent. He broke the kiss long enough to take off her goggles. Then those magnificent lips were on hers again. She felt his legs kicking, one arm pulling them through the water, the other securely around her as they made out like they'd waited their whole lives to do it—and she felt like she had. He planted his feet on the ocean floor, guiding her legs around his waist as he deepened the kiss. He moaned, and it amped up her arousal. Their kisses were firestorms of pleasure. He felt so good and *right*, she didn't want to stop. She had a fleeting thought about trying not to lose control as she had at the bar, but *she* was making this decision rather than her body making it for her. Brant made her feel cared for and special, and she wanted him more than she wanted her next breath, making it easier to push her worries away and allow her desires to take over. And take over they did.

Their kisses turned feverish, and everything else faded away, leaving them in a bubble of lust and happiness. His rough hands spread over her ass, and she rocked against him, earning a greedy growl that made her go a little wild. She moaned, thrusting her tongue hungrily over his. She had no idea how he was still standing and holding her up, because her body was a bundle of live wires. He tightened his hold on her bottom, sending lightning searing through her, and she squeezed her legs around him, aching for more. But he slowed their kisses to luxurious slides of their tongues. Just when she was about ready to lose her mind, he drew back with a series of tender kisses, leaving them both breathless, as he touched his forehead to hers.

"Jesus, Caity," he panted out. "Do you have any idea what you do to me?"

She could feel it in every inch of his body, in every kiss, and hear it in the hungry sounds he made. But more importantly, at that very moment she felt it in her heart, because he was giving her the control he'd promised, letting her set their pace.

"I know because you're doing it to me, too. *Touch me,*" she whispered.

She didn't have to ask twice. He claimed her in a punishingly intense kiss that lit her up from the inside out as he carried her into shallow water and sat on the ocean floor with her straddling his lap, the water lapping at their chests. They kissed urgently and frenzied as he untied her bathing suit and pulled the top down, palming one breast. Electricity arced through her at the feel of his rough hand on her. He tangled his fingers in her hair, drawing her head back, and tore his mouth away, sealing it over her neck, sucking and licking until she was desperate and writhing for more.

"Oh *God*, don't stop." Every suck, every lick, made her body clench with need.

She rocked along his hard length, feeling every inch of it as he pushed his fingers into the bottom of her bathing suit, teasing between her legs. She arched back, lifting her breasts out of the water. He lowered his mouth, teased her nipple with his teeth and tongue, sending titillating sensations skittering through her. His fingers entered her at the same time as he sucked her nipple against the roof of his mouth, and the overwhelming pleasure drew a long surrendering moan from her lungs.

"You're dangerously sexy," he said against her breast.

She'd never felt sexy before, but when she was in his arms, he made her feel that way. She rocked her hips, riding his fingers. His thumb moved over the sensitive bundle of nerves, sending heat spiking through her. He sucked and licked and grazed his teeth over one nipple, then lavished the other with the same beautifully torturous attention. Her skin tingled, her blood burned, and she could barely breathe as he took her right up to the verge of madness—and kept her there. Her body trembled and shook, clenching greedily, as his fingers stroked over the hidden spot inside time and time again with laser precision, teasing and taunting, slow and sensual, then fast and urgent. She dug her nails into his shoulders, trying to keep up with the emotions whipping through her, but it was like being tossed in a storm of pleasure.

"*Brant*," she pleaded, riding his fingers faster.

"Let go for me, baby."

He tugged her mouth down to his, feasting on her, working her body like he knew it by heart. Every exquisite stroke caused a gasp, a quickening of her pulse, taking her closer to release. Need stacked up inside her, until she felt like she was going to burst. His tongue plunged deeper into her mouth, and his fingers fucked her faster. He pressed harder with his thumb in a mind-numbing circular rhythm, and spirals of ecstasy tore through her with savage intensity. Her hips bucked, her sex clenched, and she cried out. He swallowed her sounds, cupping the back of her head, keeping their mouths fused. Her climax went on and on, deeper than the thrill of an orgasm, more powerful and all-consuming than anything she'd ever imagined. Her entire body flexed and tingled. Her toes curled into the ocean floor, and all at once, lights bloomed behind her closed lids as a magnificent explosion of heat and cold burst inside her. And then she was floating down from the most exquisite peak, and Brant was holding her, kissing her, whispering between each tender press of his lips. *"So beautiful . . . Feel so good . . . Waited so long for you . . ."*

She collapsed against him, closing her eyes in sweet relief. He showered her in kisses, running his hands up her back and through her hair. Neither said a word, their hearts beating to the same frantic rhythm. Brant kissed her temple, wrapping his arms tightly around her, and for the second time in twenty-four hours, she didn't want to rush away. She braced herself for anxiety to hit, for the need to flee to consume her as it had at the bar. But as the minutes ticked by, she felt safe and happy, *high* on the beautiful thing blossoming between them. She stopped waiting for the fear to hit and reveled in the goodness of them.

He held her as the sky darkened around them, until they began shivering with cold, and then he tied her bathing suit, and they made their way up to the blanket. Brant wrapped her in a towel and kissed her softly, looking at her with longing, passion, and affection. She could tell he was struggling to find words, just as she was.

He pulled two sweatshirts out of his bag and helped her put one on. It was warm and cozy, and tumbled nearly to her knees. As he put on his sweatshirt, she lifted her sleeve, breathing in his familiar scent. He'd thought of this, of her needing a sweatshirt when the sun went down. How could something so little mean so much?

He took her hand and gazed deeply into her eyes. "I'm not ready to go yet. Are you?"

She shook her head, feeling more at peace than she ever had. He sat on the blanket, guiding her down to sit with her back to his chest, and wrapped his arms around her. Then he draped a towel over their legs and patted the blanket beside them, calling Scrappy over from where he lay on the sand, still tethered to his leash. Scrappy curled up next to them. They sat for a long time, barely talking above a whisper, listening to the sounds of the water kissing at the rocks and Scrappy snoring.

There was comfort in the quiet. Cait could almost feel his thoughts, and she had a feeling he could feel hers.

Brant kissed her cheek, whispering, "Stay with me tonight?"

She wanted to. *Desperately.* But this was perfect. She wanted to savor it, and she didn't want to take a chance that she might freak out later and ruin their night. She turned her face so she could see him. "*Tomorrow*, okay?"

"Everything's okay, babe."

He kissed her softly, and there beneath the stars, with the moon shining down on them and a cool breeze kissing their cheeks, Cait felt her walls coming down and Brant tiptoeing in.

CHAPTER TWELVE

CAIT HAD NEVER seen so much commotion at Rock Harbor Beach. It was Friday evening, and she stood at the top of the dunes taking off her sandals with Brant, Abby, and Aiden. All around them, people were chatting excitedly and carrying supplies down from the parking lot in preparation for movie night. They were playing *E.T.*, which Cait had never seen. She was as excited to spend downtime with Abby and Aiden as she was to be on a real date with Brant. Double dates were new to her, but then again, so was just about everything she'd been through these last few months. She picked up her sandals and Scrappy, taking in the activity on the beach below, where an enormous movie screen and massive speakers had been erected. People were milling about, setting up blankets and chairs, racing in and out of the water, and kids darted across the sand. It was a good thing Brant and Aiden had claimed a spot for them earlier in the afternoon because the beach was packed as far as the eye could see.

"Are you sure your stuff will still be there?" Cait asked.

"Yeah," Brant said. "Nobody steals stuff around here."

"This is going to be fun!" Abby shoved her flip-flops in her bag and took Aiden's arm. "I love dates with my man, but a double date with my sister and *her* man makes it even better."

"This is my first double date," Cait admitted.

"And it'll be your best." Brant winked, his eyes twinkling with heat. "Until our next one, that is."

As they headed down to the beach, he brushed his fingers over hers and blew her a kiss. When he'd picked her up at her apartment, they'd devoured each other until she'd been weak-kneed, but he hadn't even held her hand since they'd met up with Aiden and Abby in the parking lot half an hour ago. She kept waiting for him to reach for her, longing for that connection, but she knew he was trying to do the right thing by being careful about PDA. As much as she appreciated that, she missed the closeness they'd shared last night.

"I love beaches in the evening. Don't you guys?" Abby didn't wait for an answer. She fluttered her lashes at Aiden and said, "Is there a beach where we're going on our honeymoon?"

"Nice try, sweetheart." Aiden leaned down and kissed her.

Cait tried to ignore another pang of longing.

They walked past a row of vendors with long tables set up by the dunes selling everything from popcorn and candy to salads and burgers. Cait had never seen anything like this pulled together so quickly. "Your parents really know how to put on a show."

"They should. They've been doing it for more than thirty years." Brant pointed up ahead. "Our stuff is just past the three red umbrellas."

As they made their way down the beach, people waved and shouted greetings. Cait was surprised to be called out by name by customers she recognized from the Bistro. She was becoming more aware of her feelings and the things going on around her. With the burden of the past out in the open to those closest to her, she no longer felt the need to hide in the shadows.

Brant led them to an area covered in blankets, with a firepit already shoveled out and stocked with wood. "I told you our stuff would still be here."

"You already dug the firepit?" Abby looked at Aiden. "You guys went to a lot of trouble."

"That was all Brant. It's like he's been doing this forever," Aiden teased, putting down the cooler he was carrying.

"There's nothing better than beach life. I'm going to be the ninety-year-old man digging bonfire pits and kicking back with all of you." Brant glanced at Cait, nodding confidently, and then he dug a stake out of his backpack and began pounding it into the sand for Scrappy's leash. "I can't wait to teach Cait to surf."

"In your dreams." Cait laughed.

He tied the leash to the stake and sidled up to her, lowering his voice for her ears only. "Baby, my dreams are already full of you, and I can assure you, in them we're *not* surfing."

Their eyes held, bringing a rush of memories of last night's intimacy, and her body ignited.

"You picked a great spot," Abby said, breaking the moment.

Cait dropped her bag on the blanket and looked out over the water, wondering how she was going to make it through an entire movie when everything Brant did made her want him more. Maybe it wasn't the PDA but the secrets that had made them feel uncomfortable.

He put a hand on her lower back, his eyes flickering with another seductive tease. "Why don't we get *wet* before it gets too cold?"

She swallowed hard. He knew just how to get to her.

"Yes!" Abby exclaimed. She and Aiden dropped to the blankets and began rolling up their pants. "It's been too long since I've had my feet in the water."

"Are you going to slay me with double entendres all night?" Cait whispered.

"Are you going to look that sexy all night?" Brant stepped closer, and her breasts grazed his body, her nipples pebbling with the memory of his mouth on them. "Better roll up your jeans, beautiful."

Jeans. Right. She crouched to roll them up, her head swimming with lustful thoughts. Brant stood beside her in his shorts and Henley. His hips were *right there* as he talked with Aiden over Cait's head, bringing more thoughts of last night, when she'd felt every hard inch of him.

"Let's go, sis!" Abby took Cait's hand the second she stood up, and they ran down to the water. They got ankle deep, shrieked from the cold, and scrambled back up toward dry sand.

"Oh no, you don't!" Brant chased after Cait, and Aiden ran after Abby, driving the girls right back into the icy water.

They shrieked and laughed, splashing the guys and chasing after them. Brant turned on Cait, and she screamed, bolting in the opposite direction. He ran after her as Abby's voice rang out, "Cait! *Help!*"

Cait turned, catching sight of Aiden lunging for Abby just as Brant caught *her* around the waist and lifted her off her feet, both of them laughing hysterically. "If you toss me in, you're in big trouble!" she hollered, kicking as he carried her into the water.

"I think we both know I *like* being in trouble with you."

He put her down in almost calf-deep water. She squealed and tried to climb him like a tree, laughter flying from their lips. He lifted her into his arms, and her legs circled his waist. Overcome with happiness, she grabbed his handsome face between both hands and lowered her lips to his, turning their laughter into steamy kisses.

As their lips parted, she became aware of catcalls and cheers. She looked toward the beach, and their friends came into view, cheering and whooping. Jules and Grant were holding tiki lights on long poles with a CONGRATULATIONS sign strung between them, and Jock and Daphne were carrying several pizza boxes. Randi and Ford were waving champagne bottles, and Tessa was holding a gigantic sheet cake.

"Congratulations!" their friends hollered in unison.

"About damn time, you two," Jock said, looking right at Cait and Brant.

Cait looked at Brant in total confusion.

"Surprise, angel! You missed out on so many celebrations, we're going to make up for every one of them, starting with celebrating your and Abby's first month in business."

"It was all Brant's idea!" Aiden hollered from a few feet down the beach, prompting more cheers.

Cait's heart filled to near bursting as she looked down at the man holding her in his arms, looking at her like she was everything he'd ever wanted. She'd never been this happy, this cared for, and she wanted to hold on to that joyous feeling, to hold on to *Brant*. A trickle of trepidation moved through her, but on its heels came Brant's voice whispering through her mind. *After today, it will be easy. I promise. Just push past the initial fear.* With a deep breath, Cait threw her worries to the wind and grabbed his face between both hands, kissing him hard, deep, and *very* possessively, earning more whoops and cheers.

When their lips parted, she smiled down at him, laughing. "What have you done to me, Remington?"

"Not nearly as much as you've just done to me, Weatherby. Kiss me again."

"You greedy little bugger," she teased, and lowered her lips to his, because he was setting her free, and with *him*, she was becoming a greedy bugger, too.

Cait was on cloud nine as they sat barefoot and bundled up in sweatshirts on blankets around the fire, drinking champagne and eating pizza with their friends. Scrappy begged for tastes, and everyone spoiled him with pieces of cheese and crust. The CONGRATULATIONS banner fluttered in the breeze above the card table Grant and Jules had brought, which now held the cake and various chips and snacks. The cake had CONGRATULATIONS, ABBY AND CAIT (AND DEIRDRA!) written across it in blue icing. Cait loved that they'd thought to include Deirdra's name on the cake. Deirdra was a silent partner, having invested her inheritance in the Bistro. Cait wished she were there to celebrate with them. But she had taken lots of pictures and texted them to Deirdra.

Cait plucked another pepperoni off her slice of pizza, adding it to the stack on the side of her paper plate.

"What's going on with all that pepperoni?" Randi asked.

"I don't like them."

Brant's jaw dropped, and he made an incredulous sound. "You're a pepperoni hater?" He looked at Abby. "Did you know this about her?"

Abby laughed. "Yes. I'm surprised you didn't."

"Then you don't mind if I eat them?" Randi reached for a pepperoni, and Brant swatted her hand.

"She's *my* girlfriend, so those are *my* pepperonis." Brant popped a pepperoni into his mouth.

Everyone laughed, and Ford said, "Randi, you can have my *pepperoni* anytime you want."

Randi rolled her eyes at her tall, handsome friend. Ford had short brown hair, a great personality, and a penchant for flirting with Randi, who must be used to it, because he'd been doing it since they'd arrived, and his comments just rolled off her back.

"My grandmother Lenore would *love* you, Ford," Jules called from the other side of the blanket, where she was sitting with Grant.

"I've seen your grandmother *topless*," Ford said.

"Half the island has," Jock said. "If you've seen Lenore topless, you've probably seen all of our mothers topless, too. They're all part of the Brigade. So be careful about what you say."

Ford joked about getting an invitation to their next meeting, and as Randi gave him a hard time, Brant nudged Cait and said, "So, pepperoni hater, what else should I know about you?"

"That I won't be sunbathing topless."

"Unless you're with me." He leaned in and kissed her. "I sure like being able to do that when I feel like it."

She pressed her lips to his. "I like that you can, too."

He pulled her closer, bringing them nose to nose. "You shocked the hell out of me, baby. I can't think of a time I've been happier than right at this moment." He kissed her again. "No pepperonis and no topless sunbathing. Is there anything else I should know?"

As he plucked another pepperoni off her plate, she said, "I'm not usually a big food sharer."

"Oh *man*. I should've given you a questionnaire to fill out before we started seeing each other. I can forgive the pepperonis, but we'll have to work on the food-sharing thing." He eyed her pepperonis, and she handed them to him. "You just got even cooler. What else should I know about you?"

"She's a nightmare on roller skates," Aiden chimed in.

"Don't remind me," Cait said. "I had a bruised butt for a week after Aiden tried to teach me and Abby to skate."

Brant put his arm around her. "You should have told me. I could've kissed your bruises better."

"You're as bad as Ford." Tessa tossed a piece of sausage at him, and Scrappy caught it, making them all laugh.

"Don't feel bad, Cait," Daphne said. "I can't roller skate, either. My sister tried to teach me once, but I couldn't do it. Jules promised to show Hadley how to skate when she's six." Hadley was spending tonight with Shelley and Steve.

"Hadley is lucky. Nobody ever tried to teach me until I came here." Cait could have just as easily been talking about public displays of affection. She looked at Brant and said, "I may not be able to skate, but I can sketch you a pretty picture or tattoo a mermaid on your chest."

"You sure as hell could. *If* he wasn't afraid of needles," Grant said.

"I guess Brant didn't show you his tattoo," Cait said.

All eyes turned to Brant.

"*Christ*," Brant uttered, shaking his head, and he went on to tell them the story of the tiny line on his chest, leaving them in hysterics.

They finished the pizza and devoured the delicious cake. After cleaning up, they settled in for the movie. Their coupled-off friends snuggled together, and Ford squeezed between Randi and Tessa, putting an arm around each of them. Cait sat between Brant's legs with Scrappy curled up beside them, as she had last night.

Brant whispered, "This is quickly becoming one of my favorite positions," and pressed a tender kiss to her neck.

Abby buried her feet in the sand, tucked against Aiden's side, and said, "I needed this tonight. Thanks, you guys. Being here brings back good memories. My parents used to bring me and Dee to movie nights, and we'd run around the entire time. I don't think we ever watched a whole movie."

"None of us did," Brant said, looking over at Grant and Jock. "Our parents would have to track us down and drag us home."

"I've always loved all of the island events," Jules said. "I remember running around at the Christmas tree lighting with Bellamy and Tara when I was just a little girl." Bellamy was Grant's youngest sister, and Tara Osten was the mayor's daughter.

Cait listened to them telling stories of their youth, wishing she had stories to share. She looked over her shoulder at Brant and said, "I would have given anything to have even *one* night like this when I was young."

"I know, babe. We're going to make sure you have only good memories from now on. Memories of movie nights, holiday celebrations, and moonlight kisses in the cove." As the movie screen lit up and the din of the crowd hushed, he whispered, "Years from now we'll be sitting on this beach with even more friends, and you'll have so many memories to choose from, you won't remember a time when you had none."

She had no idea how he could be so sure, but she trusted him, and in the safety of his arms, surrounded by her sister and friends that *he'd* rallied for them, she borrowed Brant's surety to bolster her own, hoping he was right. As the movie began, she was glad for the darkness to hide her tears, because for the first time in her life, she wanted to slow down and enjoy her present instead of trying to outrun her past.

CHAPTER THIRTEEN

BRANT WAS TOO drunk on Cait to watch the movie. He hadn't even known that was possible. He looked around them at their friends and family cuddling and whispering as the movie ended and realized how they—and *he*, in his pre-Cait days—took intimacy for granted. The magnitude of courage Cait had exuded the night she'd shared her past with him was immense, and being close to her last night had left him feeling so much, he'd been speechless. But tonight, the way Cait gave of herself so freely in front of not just their friends but everyone on the whole damn beach had blown him away.

As the credits rolled, he kissed her cheek, reveling in all that she was. "Did you like it?" he asked, and heard her sniffle. "Caity?"

She turned on her knees, wiping her eye. "I just have sand in my eye."

He pulled her into his arms. "Hey, my girl has a mushy side."

"I have sand in my eyes, too," Jules said, swiping at tears.

"Come here, Pix." Grant lifted her into his lap.

"I have sandy eyes, too," Daphne said, and Abby nodded in agreement, burying her face in Aiden's chest.

"Not me!" Randi popped to her feet, and then her eyes widened at Ford. "Oh my God, *Ford*, are you *crying*?"

Ford pushed to his feet, glowering at her. "Shut up. It was sad when E.T. left."

Tessa laughed. "Softy."

"You two have hearts of *stone*," Ford said, and Brant's sisters cracked up.

They gathered their things, and the group made their way up to the parking lot. After many hugs, thank-yous, and an *I'm happy for you, man*, from Grant, Brant and Cait headed to his truck.

"I had so much fun tonight," Cait said as Brant put their things in the back. She put Scrappy in the truck. "Thank you for putting together such a great night."

"I think you're the one who's owed a thank-you." There were people all around them in the busy parking lot, but Cait was looking at him with desire and something new and different, so he didn't hesitate to gather her in his arms. "I assume this is okay now?"

"Yeah." She draped her arms around him, her soft hands touching the back of his neck. "Ever since I told you and my sisters about my past, things keep changing for the better. I feel like I'm seeing the world clearly for the first time. Even how I see *you* has changed. That veil of fear is lifting. It's strange and a little scary, which sounds backward. But it made me realize that you've said and done some of the sweetest things for me, and I was too afraid to embrace them. I don't know what's around the corner, or when this evolution I'm going through will stop, but I like it, and I like going through it with you. I'm realizing that the great place I *thought* I was in was only a stepping-stone. When we're together, I feel different, *happier*. And when we were close last night . . ." She shook her head, looking at him wondrously. "I felt fully alive for the first time in my life."

"God, babe. I did, too." He brushed his lips over hers, wrapping his head around all that she'd said. "I'm crazy about you." He thought he saw a hint of trepidation in her eyes, but it was so much less than before, he let the truth come out in hopes of easing it. "I'm with you, Cait, no matter what it takes. Two steps forward, one step back." He kissed her jaw. "One step forward, twelve steps back." He pressed his lips against hers again. "Or a race to the finish line." He gazed deeply into her eyes, the longing in them palpable. "I'm in this for the long haul."

"*Brant*," she whispered.

She pressed her fingers against his neck and went up on her toes, meeting him in a smoldering kiss. He tangled his fingers in her hair as he deepened the kiss, and she leaned forward, pressing her soft body against him. She felt like heaven, and like last night, she met his efforts with fervor. He wrapped one arm around her, keeping their bodies flush as they devoured each other, hips grinding, teeth gnashing. She made the sexiest noises, moaning and whimpering like she couldn't get enough of him, and he definitely couldn't get enough of her. Her knees buckled. He fucking loved that. He lowered her to the seat without breaking their kisses and heard Scrappy scamper to the far side of the bench, bringing reality slamming home.

They were still in the parking lot.

Fuck.

She was clawing at his back, feasting on his mouth, and grinding against him. He selfishly allowed himself one more mind-numbing minute of ecstasy before tearing his mouth away and gritting out, "Sorry, baby."

She stared at him, lips glistening enticingly, skin flushed, eyes flaming with desire. She grabbed his shirt, tugging him closer, and whispered, "Take me home."

Fuck yes.

"Scoot over to the middle. I want you next to me." He closed her door, mulling over *home* as he went around the truck and settled into the driver's seat. All his blood must have gone south, because his brain was too hazy to figure out if she meant his home or hers. He started up the truck. "Your place or mine?"

"Mine. No, *yours*. *Wait*." She put her hand on his leg, smiling at him.

Damn she was sexy. What was she thinking with that eager smile? He hoped to hell it was how much she wanted him. "No pressure, Caity. Take your time."

"Your place. I like it there."

Done.

They stumbled into his cottage in a tangle of greedy kisses and urgent gropes, slowing only to close the door and unhook Scrappy's leash. Then their mouths came together, and they stripped off their clothes between passionate kisses, leaving a trail to the bedroom. His eyes raced down her sleek curves as he tore back his blankets. She was waxed bare, tattooed down to her pubic bone. "Jesus, Caity, you're the most beautiful work of art to walk this earth."

Sparks glimmered in her eyes as he reclaimed her mouth, their naked bodies colliding as they tumbled onto the bed. His entire being flooded with desire and emotions too deep to name as he moved over her, and they devoured each other. Her skin was soft and hot, her kisses ravenous, and he ached to be buried deep inside her. But his heart spoke louder than his desire, and he forced himself to slow their kisses. He cradled her beautiful face between his hands, brushing his thumbs over her cheeks, and her eyes fluttered open. The tenderness gazing back at him took him by surprise and told him she had no hesitations. That sent his emotions soaring, but then he remembered what she'd said about sex.

Over and done. No chance for emotions.

"I don't want 'over and done,' Caity. I want to obliterate all the heartache that came before us."

Her eyes dampened, but her lips curved into a sweet smile. "That's a tall order."

It pained him knowing she was using humor to deflect her true feelings, but that was okay. What she felt toward him was inescapable, written in her mossy-green eyes and in her every kiss and hungry touch. But he wanted her to be free from all of her tethers and vowed to love her so thoroughly, one day her need to hide those feelings would go away, too.

"Trust me, Caity," he whispered. "I've got you."

Cait gazed into Brant's honest eyes, and her heart felt full. Coming together with a man she felt so much for was as terrifying as it was exhilarating. But Brant put all the men of her past to shame, emotionally and physically. If ever there was a man she trusted to live up to his promises, it was him. She'd already taken several leaps of faith, but tonight was the biggest one yet. She hadn't let a man take control in bed for years, but she wanted to bathe in Brant's adoration, to let him show her how he felt in the ways *he* wanted. As he lowered his lips to hers, taking her in a deep, sensual kiss, she clung to that exhilaration, to that *trust*, with everything she had, hoping to keep old fears at bay. She wanted to memorize everything about these moments. The feel of him lying on top of her, of his muscles flexing, his breath becoming hers. But as always, their kisses consumed her, fracturing her thoughts until she couldn't think at all.

"I want to learn everything about you." He kissed a path down her neck, every press of his lips sending a pulse of heat to her core. "What turns you on." He sank his teeth into her skin, sucking perfectly. She bowed off the bed as pleasure gripped her.

"*That*," she said breathlessly. "Definitely that."

He kissed the tender spot he'd sucked and said, "I want to know your dreams, Caity." He kissed her shoulder and dragged his tongue along her skin, sending tingles down her limbs. He traced her tattoos with his fingers and tongue, kissing, sucking, and caressing her breasts, rib cage, and every inch of her stomach and hips, rousing passions she never knew existed. Desire raged through her with every graze of his teeth as he explored her body, murmuring sweet sentiments about how he felt, how beautiful she was, and how much he wanted to pleasure her. His words were as powerful as his touch. His hands were rough but tender, his kisses tantalizing persuasions, and the feel of his hard length rubbing against her was excruciatingly alluring. She felt him savoring every spot he touched, lingering, memorizing, *claiming* it as his own, and there was no fear in sight. There was only *want* and *need* flowing through her like a glorious river.

"*Brant*," she pleaded, writhing beneath him.

"Soon, baby."

He kissed her lower belly and inner thighs, anticipation pounding inside her. Her body was on fire, throbbing with desire. She held her breath with every touch of his lips. He kissed the apex of her sex, his hot breath coasting over her wetness. She fisted her hands in the sheets, spreading her legs wider, and lifted her hips, *craving* him like a drug. The first slick of his tongue sent sparks searing through her core, and her eyes slammed shut. Every stroke of his tongue brought a rock of her hips. He feasted on her, working her clit to mind-numbing perfection with his hands and mouth, sending her soaring, spinning, *exploding* into ecstasy. Her head thrashed. She clawed at his shoulders, crying out in sweet agony as her body bucked and quivered. She fisted her hands in his hair, holding on for dear life as he sent her soaring again. When she finally floated down from the peak, she almost caught her breath, but then his mouth moved to her clit, and his fingers entered her, zeroing in on the pleasure points that made her toes curl and tore more pleasure-filled cries from her lungs. He stayed with her, stroking and kissing until she collapsed blissfully to the mattress.

She lay panting as he kissed his way up her oversensitive body. Every touch drew a gasp or a quiver, until she was hanging on to her sanity by a fast-fraying thread. His mouth came down over hers, the broad head of his cock nestled against her entrance, sending her heart thundering anew. When their lips parted, his eyes searched hers, silently seeking approval. Did he know the extra care he took with her was everything? She rose off the pillow and kissed him, whispering, "I want *all* of you."

The way he was looking at her made her insides go soft. He leaned across the bed and grabbed a box of condoms from his nightstand, then rose on his knees and tore it open. She had a fleeting moment of gratitude that it was a brand-new box and not a half-empty one, but on its heels came a strange and wonderful thought. It wouldn't matter if it had been half-empty. With everything he'd said, she knew this wasn't just *her* new beginning. It was *theirs*.

His eyes locked on hers as he gave his long, thick cock one slow stroke. Lust surged through her. *Holy cow.* That was the hottest thing she'd ever seen. He sheathed himself and eased down over her, cradling her beneath him like she was precious. His mouth covered hers as their bodies came together slowly and carefully. She held him tighter, feeling every blessed inch of him as he lifted her knees, opening her wider to accommodate him, until he was buried to the hilt.

They both inhaled sharply. She could barely breathe for the emotions whirling and skidding inside her. His eyes found hers, and it was all right there, everything he felt, every word he didn't have to say.

His forehead touched hers, and "Caity" slipped incredulously from his lips. She felt like she could cry at the intensity of what they had. Her eyes fluttered closed at the fullness in her heart *and* her body, but a ripple of fear tiptoed in, darkening her elation.

As if he'd felt the change in her, Brant lifted his face, gazing deeply into her eyes, and said, "I've got you" with such warmth and surety, he obliterated that fear. Their mouths came together in another soul-searing kiss, and they found their rhythm. Every pump of his hips sent scintillating sensations racing through her.

"*God*, baby," he gritted out, driving in deeper.

Lost in the heat spreading through her chest like wildfire, she pulled his mouth down to hers. He pushed his hands beneath her bottom, lifting her hips, taking her deliciously deeper. They both went a little wild, thrusting harder, holding tighter, and breathing air into each other's lungs. Heat blazed through her core, and her inner muscles clenched tight. She dug her fingernails into the backs of his arms as her orgasm crashed over her. Lightning seared through her, exploding in a downpour of fiery lights behind her closed lids. Brant tore his mouth away, growling her name as they spiraled into ecstasy, bound together in a world of passion far more exquisite than anything she'd ever known.

When they collapsed, spent and sated, to the mattress, Brant rained kisses over her face and shoulders, whispering, "*So good . . . Special . . . Incredible*," holding her so tight, she couldn't have rolled away if she'd wanted to. But moving out of his strong arms was the last thing she wanted. She'd never felt so cherished in all her life, and she knew in her heart that *this* was what dreams were made of.

A long while later, he took care of the condom and gathered her in his arms again, gazing deeply into her eyes. "Stay with me?"

"There's no place I'd rather be."

CHAPTER FOURTEEN

BRANT AWOKE SATURDAY morning in the same position he'd fallen asleep in, spooning Cait. His hips cradled her butt, her legs were tucked against his, and her dark hair tickled his chin. Scrappy was fast asleep on her other side, snorting softly. Everything he wanted was right there in that room. He knew that was crazy, since he and Cait had only just gotten together. But she'd been in his thoughts, and in his heart, for more than three months, and it felt like they'd been building their relationship for all that time, nurturing their friendship and establishing trust, proving that the initial attraction wasn't just a flash in the pan. He knew it was risky to put his heart on the line, given that Cait might wake up with regrets and take off. But he didn't believe that would happen after the way they'd come together last night. They'd made love twice, and the second time had been even more astounding than the first. There was no faking the way she'd looked at him, touched him, and most importantly, trusted him.

He kissed her shoulder, and she startled, flipping around to face him, eyes wide with surprise. She looked down at her naked body and yanked the sheet up to her neck. *So fucking cute.*

"Good morning, angel. Did you forget you'd spent the night?"

"Maybe." A sweet smile lifted her lips. "I was trying to figure out why there was a steel rod against my butt."

He chuckled, pulling her closer. "My *rod* likes your butt—and all your other parts. Do you really need that sheet after all we shared? I'm pretty sure I've memorized, tasted, and worshipped every dip and curve of your beautiful body." He kissed her pink cheeks, rocking his arousal against her and loving the way her breathing hitched. "I can still hear the sounds you made when I was buried deep inside you."

She lifted her chin defiantly. "Now you're just *trying* to make me blush."

"I do love to see you blush, but I'm just being honest, so you realize you don't need to hide from me. Last night was the most incredible night I've ever had. Am I alone in that? It sure didn't feel like I was."

A spark of mischief rose in her eyes. "It was *all right*."

"All right?" He grabbed her ribs, and she squealed, trying to wriggle away, both of them laughing. Scrappy barked and jumped off the bed, darting out of the room as Brant continued tickling Cait, ignoring her pleas to stop. "Care to change your answer?"

She broke free and rolled away. "It was . . . *fair*."

"I'll give you *fair*." He grabbed her by the waist and hauled her back, straddling her body and pinning her hands beside her head, both of them laughing. "Want to change your answer yet?"

Her eyes dropped to his cock, and as her smile grew, so did her laughter.

"That's not exactly the reaction I was hoping for."

"I can't help it." She giggled. "It's just so . . . big and *ready*."

"Now, that's more like it." He gathered her in his arms, kissing her smiling lips. "Any regrets, Weatherby?"

"Just one." She gazed at him with new light in her eyes. "After last night, I kind of wish I'd fallen in the marsh two months ago."

His heart stumbled. "Maybe we should make up for lost time."

"I don't have to be at work until one, which gives us lots of time for you to earn a higher mark than *fair*—*if* you're up for the challenge."

"Get ready to have your world shattered."

Her hips rose beneath him. "You shattered it perfectly last night. I'm not sure there's any earth left outside this room."

"Maybe we'll never leave."

He lowered his lips to hers and spent the next hour proving just how phenomenal they were together. Three orgasms later, they lay breathless and spent on their backs, gazing into each other's eyes and holding hands between them. The fitted sheet was off one corner of the bed, and the blanket and pillows were on the floor.

"Better?" He cocked a grin, knowing she was going to give him sass.

"Moderately." She giggled and rolled toward him, draping her arm and leg over him and resting her cheek on his chest. "But maybe with practice you'll get better."

He laughed and kissed her forehead. "When do I take you back to the Cape?"

"I can take the ferry. I leave Monday evening and come back early Thursday."

"I'd rather take you over so we can spend that time together."

"I'd like that."

"What are you doing tonight? Tomorrow night? Hell, what are you doing for the rest of your life?"

She laughed. "I thought you said you weren't possessive."

"You call it possessive. I call it knowing what I want."

"I'm used to spending every night alone, remember?" She gave him a coy look. "I'll have to let you know."

He skimmed his hand down her back, wanting to push for more and knowing she needed to set their pace. "Promise me tonight, and we can negotiate the rest."

"Okay, but only because you need to practice all the good stuff."

He chuckled and kissed her again. A knock sounded at the front door, and Scrappy barked. He heard the door open, and a second later his mother's voice rang out.

"Brant? I made muffins and thought I'd bring some over for you."

Cait dove for the blanket and scrambled to wrap herself up in it, whispering, "She has a *key?*"

"Honey, you left laundry all over . . . *Oh goodness,*" his mother said. "You have company!"

Brant whispered, "I must have left the door unlocked last night." He pulled on his briefs and called out, "Hi, Mom. I'm with Cait."

"*Oh!* Hi, Cait!" his mother exclaimed from the other room.

"Hello," Cait said nervously, shooting Brant a death stare as he gathered her in his arms.

"You kids go back to whatever you were doing," his mother said. "I'll just leave the muffins on the counter and let Scrappy out. He piddled on the floor."

"We are *such* bad parents," Cait whispered, frowning.

Brant called out, "Thanks, Mom," then lowered his voice. "I'm sorry I forgot to lock the door, and we're not bad parents. We were a little busy."

Cait buried her face in his chest. When they heard his mother leave, Cait said, "Talk about *awkward!*"

Brant laughed. "Why? We're adults. She knows how I feel about you."

"Our clothes are all over your living room! She knows I'm *naked.*"

"I'm sorry you're embarrassed. But like I said, she knows how I feel about you." He kissed the tip of her nose. "Please don't let that keep you from wanting to spend the night with me again. I'll remember to lock the door next time."

She stared at him, and laughter bubbled out. "The first time I sleep over at a guy's house and I get caught by his *mother*. I feel like that's something that should happen when you're a teenager."

"It did."

"*What?*" Her entire face lit up. "No way!"

"Yeah, I don't know what I was thinking. I was seventeen and horny, and this chick was here for a summer vacation. I snuck her into my bedroom, and my mom must have heard us. She walked in as we were getting it on."

Cait laughed. "So, this is normal for you?"

"Nothing about our relationship is normal for me, including my insatiable need to shower with you." He lifted her and threw her over his shoulder like a sack of potatoes, carrying her into the bathroom.

"Brant!" She laughed. "I might have to reconsider the whole spend-the-night thing."

CHAPTER FIFTEEN

CAIT SAT IN the Bistro's office early Monday morning, tattooing musical notes and WHERE WORDS FAIL, MUSIC SPEAKS on Jagger's rib cage. He lay on his back in hemp shorts, his flip-flops dangling from his feet, and his trusty dalmatian, Dolly, lying on the floor beside them. He was so relaxed, Cait wondered if he was sleeping. She liked the silence. It allowed her to relive the sunrise breakfast she'd enjoyed with Brant and his family on his grandfather's boat, which had been the perfect way to start the week after a magical weekend that had passed in a blur of steamy mornings, busy workdays, and sizzling nights. Cait had always treasured her alone time, and she liked her space. But lately she felt like a caterpillar who had morphed into a butterfly, and she was excited to explore the world, and her relationship with Brant, from her new vantage point.

Saturday evening they had taken out one of the beautiful boats he'd built and had stayed on the water for hours. She'd been as in awe of the boat as she was of the man who had built it. He had spoken so passionately, she thought his mother was right that to Brant, boats were like beings, and that made her like him even more. They'd talked, she'd sketched, and they'd made love beneath the stars. She'd wondered if she'd feel off-balance spending so much time with him and sharing so much of herself, but the more time they spent together, the happier she was and the more she wanted to share. Yesterday morning before work, he'd tried to give her a swimming lesson at the pool in his community, but with her newfound freedom came an insatiable desire to show Brant how she felt about him. They'd ended up practically ripping their bathing suits off at the pool and had run back to his cottage like a couple of horny teenagers. Cait had gotten the idea in her head that she *should* spend Sunday night at her place and tamp down her newfound sexual wickedness. But she and Brant had taken Scrappy for a walk on the beach and stopped at Rock Bottom for a drink, and they'd had such a good time, and she'd felt so close to him, she didn't want a forced night apart. He was a generous and masterful lover, but it was the emotions between them that had her heart drumming to a different beat. She wasn't looking forward to going without seeing him at the Cape.

She lifted the tattoo gun and wiped the excess ink from Jagger's rib cage. His eyes remained closed, so she took a minute to look at the twenty-five-year-old shaggy-haired guitarist and chef who had surprised them when he'd shown up one evening in a Baja hoodie with a guitar strapped to his back, looking for Ava. Apparently they'd been close friends, although Abby and Deirdra hadn't ever heard of Josiah "Jagger" Jones. They'd learned that he was a bit of a vagabond and had worked for Ava on and off when he'd come to the island. He'd even stayed in the apartment above the garage where Cait was now living. He and Ava had been so close, Ava had known his brother Gabriel, who had nonverbal autism, and she knew Gabriel well enough to have sung to him on a video call the Christmas before she'd died. That had shocked Abby and Deirdra, as they hadn't heard their mother sing in years. Cait knew how hard life with Ava had been for her sisters, but she liked knowing that even though their mother had battled demons, she'd still had the ability to make new friends and had brought joy to them.

"How are you holding up, Jag?" she asked.

Jagger opened his eyes and blinked several times. "*Whoa.* That was wild. You sounded just like Ava."

"I did?" Cait's pulse quickened. "Did she sound different at times? Or do I?"

He tucked his hand behind his head lazily. "Both. When she sang, she sounded angelic. You had that soft tone just then."

Goose bumps rose on Cait's arms, and she wondered if he'd ever heard Brant call her *angel*. "I like knowing that."

As she leaned over to start tattooing again, he said, "She would be glad you're here."

Cait stilled, her eyes meeting his. She'd met Jagger shortly after she'd met her sisters, and while they'd become friends, they hadn't really talked about Ava much. "Did she mention me to you?"

"Not really. Not by name or anything specific. Sometimes we'd sit on the hill by the house looking out at the water late at night, and she'd talk about forgiveness and leaving someone special behind but it being better for them. I always thought she was talking about an old lover, but I think she was talking about you."

"Maybe so. I wish I could have met her." She began tattooing again, and Jagger closed his eyes.

A few minutes later the office door opened, and Abby breezed in, looking cute in a short colorful sundress. "How's the secret tattooing going?" Dolly popped up to greet her, tail wagging, and Abby gave her some love.

The Bistro wasn't an approved tattooing facility, but Cait had sworn Jagger to secrecy. She finished the letter she was working on and lifted her tattoo gun. "You tell me."

Abby peered over her shoulder. "Lookin' good. You must really trust her, Jagger. She could write whatever she wants on you with that thing."

"It's cool. I trust her," Jagger said.

"Good. Can I trust you to close your ears for a minute?" Abby asked. "I want to ask my sister about something."

"No worries. I can totally zone out." He lay back and closed his eyes.

Abby sat on the edge of the desk, eyes dancing with curiosity. "So? Are you going to dish about your very long weekend with Brant?"

"I thought she was smiling an awful lot," Jagger said.

"I thought *you* were zoning out," Cait snapped.

He flashed a grin. "Girl, you're glowing brighter than the North Star. I felt your vibes before I even came into this room."

Abby laughed. "I felt them from the other side of the island."

Cait didn't even try to dispute it. She'd been grinning like a fool for days. "Let's just say I think I understand why you're happy all the time." She set down the tattoo gun. "It's pretty wonderful being with someone who gets me and likes being with me as much as I like being with him."

"Yay! I'm so glad." Abby hugged her. "I knew it was a good sign that you'd stayed with him over the weekend."

"Yeah, it was. I thought I'd hate sharing a bed because I've slept alone my whole life, but I'm kind of wondering how I'll get through the next three nights at the Cape."

"Take him with you," Jagger suggested.

"He has a job, and I'm not dependent on him." Cait wasn't surprised by his response. Jagger was the kind of guy who preferred to keep things *loose* rather than follow a consistent schedule. He'd been a reliable employee, and Cait liked his laid-back attitude, but she had a feeling if the wind blew a certain way and caught his attention, he would follow it.

Jagger leaned up on one elbow. "It's not about being dependent. You only live once, and we don't know when our number is going to come up. If you two are vibing, go with it."

"I understand where you're coming from." *All too well, unfortunately.* "But I think I'll survive without *vibing* for a few nights."

He shrugged and lay back down.

"I love that you and Brant have gotten closer," Abby said.

"So does Dee, although she won't admit it. She's been texting and giving me crap because she says I sound like you. Oh, and you'll love *this*. Remember when I found a trail of your clothes leading upstairs when you and Aiden first got together?"

Abby giggled again. "Yes, and I remember the reason *why* very explicitly."

"Well, guess what. Gail found *my* clothes leading to Brant's bedroom Saturday morning."

"Ohmygod!" Abby cracked up.

Jagger chuckled.

"I can laugh about it now, but it was mortifying."

"Nah, Gail's cool. I dig her," Jagger said.

"I like her, too, but trust me, it was embarrassing," Cait said. "She is super cool, though. Brant and I met his parents and grandparents for breakfast on his grandfather's boat this morning, and Gail was gracious enough not to bring it up. But I was so nervous thinking she might, I felt like a ticking time bomb. I finally just blurted out an apology."

"Oh, Cait, you poor thing." Abby touched her shoulder.

"I'm glad I did, actually. Roddy made a joke, which cut right through the tension. His parents told me stories about catching Brant and his brothers and sisters in compromising positions and embarrassing situations, and we ended up laughing for twenty minutes."

"I bet Brant loved that," Abby said.

"Brant had already told me about his teenage indiscretion, but the way his parents told it was much funnier. And his grandparents are the warmest, kindest people I've ever met. His grandfather told me all about what Brant was like as a kid following him around as he worked on boats. Can't you just see Brant as a little boy, asking a million questions?" She warmed all over, thinking about how fun the morning had been and how close she'd felt to his family.

"Those kinds of mornings are good for your soul," Jagger said.

"It was. I swear, it's like the universe knew I needed good people to help me through all the changes in my life. Speaking of changes, I feel bad that I haven't seen Shelley since she and Steve came in for dinner the week we opened, and she's the one who brought me to the island. I should call her and catch up."

"She knows how busy you are," Abby reassured her. "But I'm sure she'd love to hear from you. Aiden and I are seeing her this week to try to finalize our wedding plans. I'd better get back out to the kitchen and prep before we open. I'll miss you while you're at the Cape. You're coming back Thursday morning, right?"

"Yeah. I'll try to catch the first ferry."

The phone rang, and Abby said, "I'll get it. You get busy tattooing something dirty on Jagger."

Jagger chuckled as Abby answered the call, and Cait went back to tattooing.

"Sure, hold on." Abby put the call on hold. "Cait, it's Mayor Osten for you."

"Really? I wonder what he wants." Cait had met the outgoing mayor when he'd announced the winner of the Best of the Island Restaurant Competition, and he'd come into the restaurant a few times since.

Abby shrugged and sat on the edge of the desk. "I'm as curious as you are."

"I'm sorry, Jagger. Do you mind if I take it real quick?"

"Not at all. Take your time." Jagger closed his eyes again.

Cait put down her tattoo gun and took the phone. "Hello. This is Cait."

"Hi, Cait. This is Mayor Osten. How are you?"

"I'm well, thanks. And you?"

"I am fine and dandy today. Do you remember when my wife and I came into the Bistro last month and I mentioned that I was thinking about revitalizing Town Hall?"

"Yes. I remember." He'd spent a long time talking to her about the mural she'd painted in the Bistro.

"I'm ready to move on that project, and I'd like to know if you'd be interested in painting a mural inside Town Hall."

"Me?" She couldn't hide her shock. "I'm flattered, but wouldn't you rather hire someone with more experience, like Grant Silver?" Grant's paintings sold for a lot of money.

Abby mouthed, *Paint what?*

Cait held up one finger as she listened to the mayor.

"Grant is immensely talented, but the committee and I prefer your style for the revitalization project. It's fresh and youthful, and it's exactly what we're looking for. I'm not sure if you've seen the inside of the building, but it has an impressive two-story lobby. There's a walkway around the second floor, and the mural would cover the second-story wall that faces the entrance. It will be the first thing everyone who enters the building will see."

She was familiar with the impressive historical building, though she hadn't been inside. "Wow. That sounds like an enormous project."

"It is. The area for the mural is roughly twelve by twenty, and we can pay by the hour or the square foot. We've done a bit of research, and we feel thirty-five dollars per square foot is fair, which comes out to about eight thousand, four hundred dollars."

Cait's jaw dropped. "I don't know what to say."

"How about that you'd be pleased to meet with me and the committee to discuss the project? We have a few ideas for the mural. If you're interested, we'd like to talk about it with you and then give you time for your artistic muse to speak to you, and we can go from there."

Holy cow . . . "What is your timeline for the project? I'm traveling between here and the Cape. My schedule is a bit crazy right now."

"We assumed as much. We were thinking about having you start after the Bistro is closed for the season. It's an indoor project, perfectly suited for winter work. If your schedule allows for it, of course."

Her mind was running in seven different directions. She didn't even know what next *week's* schedule looked like, much less where she'd be in the winter. But now that she was thinking about it, once the Bistro closed for the season, Abby was going to travel with Aiden and do catering when they were in town. She wouldn't need Cait to work more than a few hours a month to do the accounting. Plus, this sounded like an amazing project. "I'll definitely have time over the winter."

"Great, then let's schedule a meeting with the committee to discuss the particulars. I've taken the liberty of trying to coordinate schedules on our end. How is two weeks from Wednesday at four o'clock? If that doesn't work, I have a few other times available."

Excitement bubbled up inside her. "I can make that work. Thank you."

Cait gave the mayor her cell phone number and her email address, and after they hung up, she pushed to her feet, wishing Brant were there so she could tell him. "I can't believe it! He wants me to paint a mural inside Town Hall! And he said I can do it after the Bistro is closed for the winter."

"That's fantastic!" Abby gave her another crushing hug.

Jagger bolted upright. "Congratulations."

"I can't believe it. This is *huge*. Maybe he's crazy. Is he crazy, Abby? I don't know if I have enough experience for this big of a project. I painted our mural, but that was for *us*." She paced, her nerves pinging.

"The mural you painted is gorgeous, and you have *plenty* of experience. You create elaborate lifelike tattoos, and look at the pictures you drew for me and Aiden." Cait had drawn pictures during their courtship, capturing many tender moments, and Abby had framed them and hung them up.

"I don't know. What if I mess up? I don't even like to follow other people's lines on tattoos. That's why I freehand everything. What if painting someone else's vision is too confining and I *can't* do it? He said they want me to mull over their ideas and see what I come up with, but still."

Abby took her by the shoulders. "Cait, look at me. Stop selling my sister short. This is no different, and it might be even better, than when a client tells you what they want for a tattoo. This is *your* moment. It's a *sign*. Our mother came to Silver Island to start over, and I started over here, and now it's *your* turn."

A sign. Cait liked that.

"It's pretty much the definition of kismet," Jagger added.

"Okay, you're right. I should at least consider it. I need to call Brant . . . and Tank, and I should let Dee know I'm thinking about it so she doesn't feel left out." Her thoughts stumbled as she realized she'd thought of Brant before anyone else, but she didn't have time to pick that apart. "And I need to finish Jagger's tattoo! Oh my gosh, you guys. My head is spinning."

Abby lifted Cait's hands and pulled off her gloves. "Take a deep breath, wash your hands, put on new gloves, and finish Jag's tattoo first before his shift starts. *Then* you can do anything you want. And before I forget, while you have those gloves off, mark your calendar for the last Sunday in August. I scheduled appointments with the bridal shops Daphne referred me to on the Cape, and you know I can't do that without you."

"I wouldn't miss it for the world. Sunday is perfect. I'll schedule the following Monday and Tuesday at Wicked Ink so I don't have to go back and forth in between."

"Look at you girls making all your dreams come true," Jagger said as he lay back down on the table.

Cait had dreamed of being safe for so long, when she finally had gotten to that place, all she'd hoped for was that it would last. She'd never thought in bigger terms, like about what she wanted and about her career, and certainly not about relationships.

As she sat down to finish Jagger's tattoo, anxious to share her news with Brant, she pictured his deep dimples and brilliant blue eyes and felt herself smiling. She missed him already. Maybe it *was* time to start dreaming bigger—about a life, and a future, she never before dared to imagine.

Cait was still buzzing later that evening as she packed for the Cape. Brant was taking her over again on his boat, and she'd looked forward to it all day. When she'd told him about the mural, he was so excited for her, it made the opportunity feel even more thrilling. She'd left a message for Deirdra and had shared her news with Tank, who had reiterated that she could work as many or as few hours as she wanted at Wicked Ink. She'd even called Shelley, since she was the one who had brought her to the island in the first place, but Faye had already spilled the beans.

She zipped her overnight bag and went into the living room to get her sketchbook from the table, and as she picked it up, she remembered Brant looking at her pictures. She crossed the room and studied the photograph of her with Tank, Gunner, Baz, and their cousin Justin "Maverick" Wicked. She tried to see the picture through Brant's eyes and realized why he'd been curious. Despite her smile, Tank looked like he was holding Cait against her will, which he *had* been. She'd tried to get out of the booth to escape having her picture taken, and Tank had hauled her back against him, refusing to let her go. *Get in here. You're family.* She felt a tug in her chest. Could she ever leave the safety of the life she'd built on the Cape to move to the island full-time and make a go of things there with her sisters . . . *and maybe even Brant?*

A shiver of trepidation moved through her at the thought of leaving her safe haven behind, even though she loved the life she was building on the island. She hated the uncertainty and fear of the unknown and knew it was her father's evilness still lurking, poking holes in the good-ness in her life.

She squeezed her eyes shut, pushing those thoughts away, and went back to the bedroom to put the sketchbook in her backpack. Her phone rang, and she pulled it out and saw Deirdra's name on the screen.

"I guess I know where I stand on your priority list." Cait was only joking. She knew how busy Deirdra was.

"Sorry. I've been in meetings since the ass-crack of dawn." Deirdra sounded tired. "What's the good news you wanted to talk to me about?"

Cait told her about the offer from the mayor.

"Are you freaking kidding me?" Deirdra said excitedly. "That's the best news I've heard all day! You're going to do it, right?"

"I don't know. I'm meeting with them in a couple of weeks to check it out. Abby thinks it's a sign because Ava started over here."

"The hippie must be wearing off on our starry-eyed sister," Deirdra said with a hint of distaste. She called Jagger *the hippie* and did nothing to hide her aversion to his lifestyle. "I'm really proud of you. This is a big deal."

"Thanks. Does that mean if I take on the project, you'll come to the island and see the mural?" Deirdra had too much resentment toward Ava to see the charm of the island the way Cait and Abby did. She bur-ied herself in work and had excuses at the ready not to visit. But Cait held out hope that time might heal those wounds.

"What do you think?"

"I *think* you never leave your office, and I bet you're still there." When Deirdra didn't respond, Cait knew she was still at work. "Dee, don't you worry about getting burnt out?"

"No, but I worry I might kill my boss and you guys will have to come visit me in prison."

"Then I should probably do the mural so we have bail money."

They both laughed.

"I'll come see the mural, Cait. Are things good with Brant?"

Cait sighed. "*Yes*. He's taking me to the Cape in a few minutes."

"I'm happy for you. After everything you've been through, you deserve to be with the *good one*."

"You know about that?" Cait laughed.

"Silver Island is so small, if you fart, everyone knows about it. Just remember that I'll come to the island to kick his butt if you need me to."

"Yeah, right. We both know I'd have to schedule the butt kicking with your assistant." Cait shouldered her backpack and reached for her overnight bag as Deirdra griped about the late night ahead of her. A knock sounded at her door, sending Cait's pulse racing. "Hey, Dee, I'm really sorry, but Brant's here. I've got to go. Don't work too late."

She ended the call and headed down the hall, wondering when she'd turned into one of those girls who got fluttery and dropped everything to see a guy. She hadn't even been like that when things were good with Frank. Then again, why would she have? They'd never even spent a whole night together, much less talked about anything real. How had she ever thought *that* was treating her well? Frank hadn't cared about her. She'd merely been a sidepiece to him, whereas Brant made her feel like she was his entire world. And as scary as it was, he was becoming the biggest part of hers, too. That realization sent those butterflies swarming. She dropped her bags and let those butterflies fly as she opened the door.

"Congratulations!" Brant was holding a bundle of balloons and an enormous box of chocolates in one hand, a vase full of gorgeous wildflowers in the other, and across his chest he wore the doggy sling, their pooch's adorable head peeking out of it.

Her heart skipped. "What *is* all this?"

"We're celebrating." He kissed her as he came inside. "This is a momentous day for you. I wasn't sure what you liked, so I got a little of everything." He set the vase and chocolates on the counter and let go of the balloons, and they floated to the ceiling, their long colorful ribbons dangling around them like streamers.

"Brant . . . ?" Her eyes dampened. "Thank you, but this is way too much."

He put Scrappy on the floor and set the sling on the counter, drawing Cait into his arms. "No, angel. This is just the tip of the iceberg. You're being *discovered*. Do you know how big that is?"

His belief in her brought an onslaught of happy feelings. "It's just a mural. It's not like I'm Picasso."

"You're better than Picasso. You're Cait Weatherby, artist extraordinaire."

She laughed, overwhelmed by this guy who'd waltzed into her life and for some unknown reason wanted to make it even better. "I love that you did this for me, but you really don't need to buy me things to celebrate." She grabbed his shirt, tugging his mouth closer to hers. "*This* is all I need." She went up on her toes and kissed him.

"We need more of that, but I'm still going to buy you things because I'm your guy, and I love seeing you smile." He kissed her again. "I have a little news, too. It's not nearly as exciting as yours, but some of your good fortune must have rubbed off on me."

"What do you mean?"

"I picked up a new client today, and he's got a 1928 Chris Craft Triple Cockpit. It's a sweet little antique in tragic shape, and guess who's refitting it?"

"My overzealous gift bearer?"

He leaned in for another kiss. "That's right, baby."

"*Wow.* 1928? That's incredible." She wound her arms around him. "You *do* deserve more kisses."

"Damn right I do." He took her in a deep, delicious kiss.

He deepened the kiss, backing her up against the counter, and her body caught fire. The excitement, and the hour she'd spent missing him, coalesced, bringing all of the pent-up desires she'd been trying to tamp down to the surface. They made out like they'd been apart for months instead of hours, groping and grinding, driving her out of her mind.

Brant drew back, eyes blazing. "How am I going to make it three nights without you?"

She'd been wondering the same thing, but she'd never been needy like this, so she'd been telling herself to suck it up and get over it. She pulled his mouth back to hers, reveling in the connection that had once scared her so badly but now felt like a glorious gift.

"Every time I kiss you," he said, bending to kiss her neck, "I want *more*."

"Do we have time?" She lifted her chin, giving him better access.

His eyes hit hers with the heat of a volcano. "Always."

They tore off each other's clothes between urgent kisses. He was always the giver, and she wanted to *give*, and *take*, and show him just how special he was to her. She backed *him* up against the counter, wrapping her hand around his cock. "Time for your celebratory gift." She stroked him with her hand as she sank to her knees and used her tongue to tease the broad head of his arousal. He groaned, tangling his hands in her hair.

"I love when you touch me."

She loved when he talked like that. She teased and taunted, and when his body was ripe with restraint, she took him to the back of her throat, worked him tight and slow, earning appreciative moans and eager thrusts. The pleasure on his face emboldened her, and she sucked harder, stroked faster.

"Christ, baby, you feel so good." His head tipped back, teeth gritted. "You're going to make me come." He hauled her to her feet, taking her in a series of mind-numbing kisses, and tore his mouth away. "I need to be inside you."

He grabbed his jeans and pulled out his wallet, fishing out a condom and sheathing his length.

"We're turning into sex maniacs," she said as he lifted her off her feet and set her on the counter.

"That's the best kind of maniac." He wedged himself between her legs, and with one hand behind her, pulled her to the edge, driving into her with one hard thrust. They both gasped, and as their bodies took over, pounding out a frantic rhythm, pleasure spread through her like wildfire.

"God, baby," he gritted out. "You completely unravel me."

He recaptured her mouth, devouring her with passion that built like waves, rolling, pounding, thundering between them, until the world spun. She clung to him, and he held her just as tight as sweet, brutal ecstasy crashed over them, and they both cried out. Pleasure roared through her, invading all of her senses, shattering her into a million glowing stars.

As they came down from their high, clinging together, their bodies covered with a sheen of perspiration, her name fell from his lips like a prayer, filling her with hope, happiness, and something much too decadent to name.

CHAPTER SIXTEEN

SCRAPPY SAT AT Brant's feet late Tuesday night staring up at him with sad eyes as Brant finished going through contracts at the marine equipment supply office. "I know, little buddy. I miss her, too." Cait had been gone for only one night, but that was enough to make his bed feel too empty and his cottage too quiet. He checked his phone. It was nearly ten o'clock, but there were no new messages from Cait. They'd texted earlier, and Cait had said she and Gia were working late. She had back-to-back appointments, her last one at nine, and would text him when she got off work. He worried about her working late. Even though Tank had eyes on the guy and her father hadn't tried to reach out to her, Tank's guys couldn't watch him every second. What if the asshole showed up? Worry and anger flared inside him. He was starting to get an even better understanding of the fear Cait had been living with.

He looked down at their pooch. "What do you say we get out of here and take a walk?"

Scrappy's nub of a tail wagged excitedly. He was a smart dog and already understood the words *walk*, *eat*, and *bed*. They weren't having much luck with housebreaking yet, but they'd get there.

Brant shut down the computer, threw on his sweatshirt, and locked the office. As they walked in front of the marina, he saw Archer coming toward them. The barrel-chested vintner lived on his boat at the marina and was nothing like his clean-cut twin. Jock was athletic, but Archer carried about twenty pounds more muscle, had military-short dark hair, a trim beard, and a tattoo on his neck.

Brant lifted his chin. "Hey, man. How's it going?"

"I'd be better if I weren't heading home to an empty bed." He gave Scrappy a quick pet and said, "I saw you and Cait the other night at Rock Bottom."

"Why didn't you say hello?"

Archer cocked a grin. "Y'all were holding hands and whispering and shit. I figured for as long as you'd been trying to get her to go out with you, I shouldn't interrupt."

"I appreciate that, but we are seeing each other now. You should've come by." That was a great night, and he'd give anything to be back there with her now.

"Really? Good for you. In that case, maybe I will next time. I'm taking some of the guys out fishing tomorrow evening. Want to join us?"

Fishing with his buddies sounded like the perfect distraction while Cait was away. "Yeah, sounds good. Do you mind if I bring Scrappy?"

"Nah, that's cool. But if he shits on my boat, you're cleaning it."

Brant laughed. They talked for a few more minutes; then he and Scrappy headed down to the beach. It was a warm night, and there was a cool breeze coming off the harbor. He and Scrappy walked a long way, and when he didn't hear from Cait, he debated texting her. But he didn't want to smother her. When he finally turned around to head back, she called.

"Hey, babe. Is everything okay?"

"Hi. Yeah. Sorry to call so late. I just got home, and my hands are a little sore, so I thought I'd call instead of texting."

"That's okay. I'm just walking Scrappy. I miss you, and I'd much rather hear your voice than get a text." He had a feeling that despite how much she was opening up to him, she was still protecting her heart with almost everything she had, and if she missed him and wanted to hear his voice, she was still too guarded to say it. But he wasn't going to hold back. How could her walls ever come all the way down unless she knew how he felt? "I'm sorry about your hands. If I were there, I'd give you a hand massage."

"I'm used to it. How was your day? How's Scrappy?"

"My day was great and Scrappy's lonely for you, too, but he's doing okay. How was your day? The last client must have been a doozy, huh?"

"The last one wasn't bad. I stayed late to talk with Gia. I told her about my father."

That stopped him in his tracks. "You did?"

"Yes, and about Frank, and everything I went through." She exhaled loudly, the relief in her voice evident.

"Babe, that's great. Was it hard to do?"

"At the beginning it was. But we were talking between clients this afternoon, and she said something about the night I ran out of the Salty Hog. She'd texted me that night and a few times since, and I'd texted her back, but I did what I always do. I said I was fine and not to worry about me. But today she said she felt like we were family and that she hoped I knew I could talk to her."

"She cares about you, babe."

"I know. I've known her as long as I've known Tank, and she talks to me about everything going on in her life. But you know . . ."

He sank to the sand, and Scrappy crawled into his lap. "I do, but I'm glad you talked with her. How did it go?"

"Better than I could have hoped. Gia is kind of like Wells. She's brash, but she has a serious side and a big heart, and she cares about me and Aria, and Tank and his family."

Cait told him about their conversation and shared stories about her friendships with Gia and Aria, the blonde he'd met. She'd already told him how important the Wickeds were to her, and he liked knowing Gia and Aria were special, too. He loved hearing about her life there.

"Gia said she knew I was running from something," Cait said. "She said she'd asked Tank about it a few months after I started working there, and he told her that all she needed to know was that I was safe and that was in my past."

"Tank seems to know how to handle things."

"Yeah, he's got great instincts." She told him more about her conversation with Gia, and then she surprised him by saying, "Gia asked me to tell her about when I ran away, but I didn't want to."

"That's understandable. Was she okay with that?"

"Yeah, she was. But I want to tell you, Brant."

He got choked up. "Thanks, baby. I want to know."

"I planned my escape for months before getting up the courage to do it. Every night my father had two drinks, and I was supposed to make them. I crushed up Benadryl tablets and put them in his drinks the night I ran away. After he fell asleep, I stole two thousand dollars in cash that he kept hidden in a book in his home office, and the first thing I did was dye and cut my hair in a twenty-four-hour drugstore bathroom."

She told him that her hair was naturally the color of sand, like Ava's was, and it had been long, to the middle of her back. She'd cut it above her ears like a boy's and had dyed it black. Then she'd taken a bus out of town. She told him about traveling from city to city, using fake names and being terrified every second of being caught. His heart broke, imagining her at that age, alone and fearing for her life. She said she'd connected with other teenagers at shelters for a few days here and there, but then she'd move to another town, just in case. She told him that the reason she wore sneakers all the time was so she was always ready to run and that she was trying to wear sandals more often, but that sometimes it panicked her to be without the comfort of her sneakers. That killed him, and as he learned more about those traumatic years, he discovered the depth of her strength and resilience and fell even harder for her. Every story cut deep, but when she confessed that she didn't like her smile because her father had made her fake it whenever they were in public, his heart broke anew for his beautiful girl whose fucking father had tried his best to take *everything* from her.

He looked out over the water and said, "I wish I were there with you right now."

"It's okay. You kind of are."

He knew that was as close as he'd get to an *I miss you.*

She told him how she'd taken a bus to the Cape because she'd heard about Wicked Ink, and since her father had hated that area, she thought she would be relatively safe there. She said she'd applied for a job and that Tank had hired her, but she'd found out months later that he hadn't been looking to hire anyone. He'd told her that he'd sensed she needed to be there. He'd befriended her, made sure she had a safe place to live, and had insisted on driving her to and from work. She knew he and other Dark Knights had watched over her cottage even before she'd told him the truth about her past.

"Thank God Tank was there for you."

"He's a good person, but so are you, Brant. You opened my eyes to the healing power of communication. It's not like I'm going to run around gabbing about my crappy past, but talking to the people who matter the most is making a big difference. I don't know how to explain it, but imagine if you got so used to thinking about how to frame everything you said so you wouldn't give away clues to your secrets that eventually you swallowed most of your words because it was easier than navigating around the ugly parts."

He felt a fissure form in his chest, remembering how much of an observer Cait had been when she'd first come to the island. "You explained it perfectly, angel, and I can see how that could happen."

"That's one reason I love doing tattoos. I don't really have to talk much. Nobody wants to sidetrack their tattooist. But life is better when I'm *not* doing that, and that's because of you."

"That's all you, baby. All I do is care about you. You've done the rest. You opened up to me, and I know it was probably one of the harder things you've ever had to do. But I'm so damn glad you took the leap instead of forcing me to walk away, because my life is a thousand times better with you in it."

CHAPTER SEVENTEEN

THE LATE-AFTERNOON SUN beat down on Brant's shirtless back as he pried another piece of decking off the Chris Craft he was refitting. He would move the boat inside once he was ready to take out the engine, but he preferred to work on the lot beside the shop when he could. He tossed the wood onto a pile on the ground and took off his baseball cap. He wiped the sweat from his brow and checked on Scrappy, lying in the shade by the workshop with his new favorite toy, a stuffed cat that Brant and Cait had bought for him yesterday afternoon. Not a day passed that he didn't think about how lucky he was that he'd been running the afternoon Cait had gone into the marsh after Scrappy.

He could have lost them both.

He settled his hat on his head, guzzled some water, and went back to work. As he stripped the boat down to bare bones, his thoughts returned to his raven-haired beauty who was busy shedding her own damaged layers. It had been two weeks since she'd told Gia about her past, and that night would probably always stand out in Brant's mind. He and Cait had talked for hours as he'd sat on the beach with Scrappy, too many miles away from her. Cait had done most of the talking, as if opening up to Gia had broken a dam to the words she'd been holding back for years. That night's conversation was the second most difficult one he'd ever had—the first being the night she'd told him about the abuse—and had left him aching to be closer, to have her safe in his arms. He'd gone to the Cape the following evening and had surprised her at her cottage when she'd arrived home after work. She'd shown him the sketches Ava had drawn of her when she was young, and she'd told him the heartbreaking stories behind her tattoos. They'd both been teary-eyed, and later that night, when they'd made love, he'd felt a change in the way she'd looked at and touched him. It was as if by trusting more deeply, she was slowing down to enjoy him instead of trying to get in as much as she could as fast as possible, fearing their relationship might be taken away.

He'd stayed and had lunch with her and Tank the next day, and she'd seemed happy when he and Tank had decided to keep in touch. He was glad she was comfortable with her two worlds coming together and that she'd continued opening up to him ever since, although all that opening up wasn't easy. A few days after she'd come back to the island, she'd told him that she felt like a fraud for not opening up to their friends there but that she just wasn't ready to. He'd reassured her that she didn't need to share anything about her past with anyone that she didn't want to and that their friends loved and accepted her for who she was. But he could tell she was still struggling with it, despite the fact that she hadn't brought it up again.

The rumble of his grandfather's truck pulled him from his thoughts, and he spotted the old red Chevy heading across the parking lot.

"Hey, Paps!" Brant hollered as he climbed down off the boat. His grandfather waved him over, and Brant jogged to the truck. "On your way out?"

"Nope. On my way back." He motioned to a pink box from the Sweet Barista on the seat beside him. "Thought I'd surprise your grandmother with her favorite treat, one of Keira's blueberry scones."

"Uh-oh. Did she find out about the cameras you bought or the old sea skiff you bid on?" His grandfather was always taking on new projects—some he completed, but others ended up in their shed, which his grandmother called the *project graveyard*.

His grandfather chuckled. "Neither. You know what I taught you—the day you stop treating your lady like she deserves the sun itself is the day her petals wilt. But for what it's worth, I told her about the cameras the day I brought them home."

"And the bid on the boat?"

"Let's see if I win it first." His grandfather winked and motioned toward the Chris Craft. "She looks like a diamond in the rough. What's her story?"

"She'd been passed from one neglectful owner to another before finally finding a home with a worthy owner. She's in pretty bad shape, but as you know, beneath all the rotten wood and ruined upholstery is a gorgeous gal awaiting her second chance."

"Well, she couldn't be in better hands," his grandfather said with a nod. "You've always had great vision, like your old man. I knew when you were just a tyke that you had the vision it took to bring out the best in everything and everyone around you."

"Thanks, Paps. I wouldn't be where I am today without your help."

"Sure you would have. When there's a will, there's a way, and you, son, have got a will of steel and the patience of a saint. How's Cait?"

"She's great. She's at the town hall meeting with Mayor Osten and the rejuvenation committee about the mural. She's been so nervous these last few days, she spent hours researching the history of the island, looking at dozens of pictures of murals in different small towns, and sketching ideas."

"She'll do great. I really like her, Brant, and I like the way she looks at you, like she knows how special you are. But you know what I like even more?"

"What?"

"That gal brings out the best in you. You've always been a happy guy, but there's a different light in your eyes these days. Try not to screw it up."

Brant laughed. "Thanks for the vote of confidence."

"Someone's gotta give *the good one* some tough love. I'd better go. Why don't you and Cait swing by for a late dinner tonight? Your grandmother is making lasagna."

"Sounds great. I'll run it by Cait and let you know. She loves you guys. I'm sure she'll want to go." He patted his shoulder and said, "Love you, Paps. Have a great day."

After his grandfather drove away, Brant loved up Scrappy for a few minutes, then headed up the ladder to get back to work. He wondered how Cait's meeting was going, and chuckled to himself, thinking about that morning when he'd offered to make her a peanut butter and lemon sandwich, which had earned him a dramatic eyeroll. When she'd gone back to the Cape last week, she'd called him and they'd talked until the wee hours of the morning like lovesick teenagers. They hadn't talked about anything of vital importance, but he'd loved learning little things about her, like her favorite junk food—french fries—and that she hated asparagus but loved lemons and peanut butter. Apparently she hadn't meant that she liked to eat lemons and peanut butter *together*. But he had learned that her favorite color was green because she loved the outdoors and that she'd always wished she were more athletic.

She'd gotten her wish when she'd mastered freestyle in the cove this past weekend, and he'd made her a Top Athlete medal out of tinfoil.

They'd been spending every night together, and the closer they got, the harder it was to be apart when she was at the Cape. He was taking her there tomorrow night, and he was already planning to stay. If he didn't know better, he'd think he was losing it.

But he knew better.

He'd watched Rowan and his buddies Jock and Grant fall head over heels in love with their significant others. He knew he was tumbling down that very same hill, and he had no intention of stopping.

He pulled off another piece of decking, and when he turned to toss it on the pile, he saw Cait approaching in a sexy-as-sin yellow sundress that showed off her long legs and strappy sandals, with her backpack over her shoulder. She'd worked in the morning and had gone home to get ready before her meeting. He'd seen her in a dress only once before, at the restaurant competition. She'd looked incredible then, but she looked delectable now.

He whistled.

She lowered her eyes bashfully. But she quickly met his eyes again, as if unable to resist their connection, which ran hotter than fire and deeper than the sea.

Scrappy ran to the end of his leash, barking and going up on his hind legs. Cait set down her backpack and scooped him up as Brant climbed down from the boat.

"It should be against the law for you to walk around looking that good." He leaned in and kissed her as she set Scrappy down. "How'd it go? Wait. Before you tell me, let me get one more look at you." He took her hand and stood back. "If you don't have more dresses at home, we're going shopping tonight."

She blushed, laughing. "Would you *stop?*"

"I can't stop." He kissed the back of her hand and pulled her into his arms. "Don't hate me because you're beautiful."

She rolled her eyes, but her smile didn't falter. "You're not so bad yourself." She kissed the center of his chest. "*Mm.* Your skin is hot."

"You should feel the rest of me."

"It's impossible *not* to feel the rest of you." She looked down at their bodies pressed together, and when she met his gaze, her eyes held a spark of desire. "Not that I'm complaining."

"Good, because I've made arrangements for us to be like this forever. They're going to sew us up the middle."

"You're such a goof." She laughed. "How will I paint the mural if I'm stuck to you like glue?"

"You accepted the project?" Excitement rocketed through him.

"I did, and I'm *nervous* about it."

"But you did it!" He kissed her hard and spun her around, earning more laughter, more kisses, and barks from Scrappy. "I'm so frigging proud of you! I want to hear all about it. Do you want to grab a drink or take a walk? My grandparents invited us for a late dinner if you're up to it, and if you are, then we have a couple of hours."

"Dinner with your grandparents sounds great. But I'm too nervous to do anything right now." She set down her bag and unhooked Scrappy's leash to pick him up. "Can we just sit in the sun and talk?"

"Absolutely."

They sat in the grass beside the lot, and she said, "I was so nervous when I walked into the room. There were seven people on the committee. *Seven.*"

"That sounds intimidating, but I bet you did great."

"It was kind of funny at first, because Mayor Osten introduced me to everyone and I was too nervous to remember their names. I think I had to ask some of them three times, and I was sure I'd blown it. But once we started talking about what they were looking for, I was too pumped about the project to be nervous. It turns out they aren't interested in just the history of the island. I was worried about that. They want to show the community of Silver Island with a mix of history, the changes the island has seen through the years, and the things that make it unique from other islands. I have *so* many ideas. I can't wait to get them all down on paper."

He'd never seen her that excited. "That's great. When will you start?"

"First I have to come up with the design and they need to approve it. The Bistro doesn't close for the winter until the middle of October, and Abby's wedding is the second weekend in November, so I'm thinking of starting sometime in between the two. Just getting ready, you know? Putting up scaffolding and laying it out."

"That sounds great. What will that mean for your schedule? Will you work there when you would usually work at the Bistro, and still go back and forth to the Cape?"

"I don't know. It's exhausting going back and forth. I have no idea how long the mural will take, but my guess is several weeks. It might be easier to stay here and really focus on it without breaking my creative stride." She looked down at Scrappy as she petted him. "But I'm not sure I can do that."

"Why? I thought you said Tank was okay with you working as little or as much as you wanted."

"He is. It's not because of that. The Cape is my safety net," she said softly. "I live in this safe little bubble there, and with the exception of a hot boatbuilder showing up, there are very few surprises. That's how I like it. Like I said, it's safe. But now I have my sisters and you, and the life I'm building here, and I know I'm safe when I'm here. It's not that. But . . ." She shrugged.

"Is this one of those times when you feel like you can't trust your instincts? Are you afraid you'll move here and find out it was a mistake?"

"Maybe. When I think about not having the safety of the Cape to go back to and touch base with, I get an anxious feeling rattling in my chest. I know that sounds dumb."

"No, it doesn't at all. After years of being alone and scared, you finally found a home and a family with Tank and your friends there. It's not easy to leave home or the people you love in the most ideal situations. After what you've been through, I can see how it would be unsettling and scary."

She exhaled with relief. "I'm glad you understand, because this is new for me. I've never had more than one place where I felt safe. I don't even know why I'm so worried. When I first met Abby and Dee, every time I got off the ferry back home, I felt this rush of relief, like I had been holding my breath the whole time I was here and I was finally back where I belonged, where I *knew* I would be okay. But as I got to know my sisters and everyone here, that changed. And now there's *us*, and that brings even more changes about how I feel when I go back. But the thought of not touching base at the Cape makes me anxious."

More changes. He knew she missed him, even if she couldn't say it. He looked forward to the day when she felt safe enough that those words would come freely.

"Does it have to be all or nothing?" he asked.

"What do you mean?"

"You said you feel anxious without touching base. I realize that you want to immerse yourself in the mural. I do the same thing with boats. But do you have to go back for two or three days at a time, or do you think it would help to go back for a few hours, touch base, then return so you can work on the mural the next day?"

Her brows knitted. "I don't know. I hadn't thought about that."

"Maybe you should. I can take you to the Cape anytime, and if you want me to hang out with you and your friends, I will. If you'd rather be alone with them, I'll wait at the marina until you're ready to go back. And if you don't want me to take you, that's okay, too. I've got people who work for me at the boat rental and water taxi facility. The water taxi service is open twenty-four-seven. I can always find someone to take you over."

"That's definitely something to consider. Thank you." She wrinkled her nose. "Can you tell I'm not great with change?"

"I think you're great with it. Your whole life was about change from the moment you left your father's house until you found Tank. You had a few years of stability, and then you got the letter from Shelley and your life was upended again. And look at how great you've handled it."

"Oh, *no* I haven't." She shook her head. "When I got Shelley's letter asking me to come to the island to hear the details of my *birth mother's* will, I was *floored*. I'd wondered my whole life about who I was, and then I got here and found out I had sisters, and it really threw me for a loop. I went back to the Cape feeling like I'd fallen into *The Twilight Zone*. I'd wake up in the middle of the night and look at my tickets from taking the ferry, just to be sure I hadn't dreamed it up. Those first few visits went by in a blur of excitement and fear. I worried they'd hate me and that Abby was being nice because she thought she had to be, and you know Dee didn't trust me at first. I didn't know if I could trust them or *anyone* here. But the more time I spent with Abby and Aiden, and talking with Dee on the phone after she went back to Boston, the more excited I got about being part of a real family, which brought *another* dose of fear. And then I met all of their friends, and you, and everyone welcomed me so warmly, it was what I had always wished for. And *that* scared me because I wasn't sure I could trust it."

"But look at you now, babe. You did great with all those changes."

"Yeah, I guess I did," she said with a furrowed brow. "Somehow, it all came together. I trusted my sisters, they trusted me, and I knew everything was going to be okay."

"See? It's scary, but there's nothing you can't handle, and now you've got something new and exciting to think about. A couple of weeks ago you mentioned that the Bistro was Abby's dream, and yours was art. Is this mural a dream come true for you?"

"I hate talking about me, because my answers are always weird, but I've only ever dreamed of being safe and happy. It wasn't until I got the call from Mayor Osten about the mural and Jagger said something about me and Abby making our dreams come true that I even realized I'd never had bigger dreams, and started thinking about it."

"Now's your chance, baby. Dream, and dream *big*. There's no one to stand in your way." He took her hand. "Together we'll make sure every last dream comes true, and I'm going to enjoy watching you soar."

Her gaze softened, and she looked at him the way she sometimes looked at Scrappy, with her heart on her sleeve. "Hearing you say that counts as a dream come true. I never thought I'd be in a relationship like this. I don't need big dreams. I need *this*, being with you and Scrappy, having friends and family and the chance to do something artistic that I'll enjoy."

"That's a great start." He leaned in and kissed her. "But you've got a long life ahead of you, and I have a feeling you've got many more dreams coming your way, ones that you have yet to discover. So keep thinking. What happens next with the mural?"

"I'm going to sketch my ideas, and then I'll meet with them again in a few weeks, when I have something to show them. Which reminds me, I want to show *you* something. I got a text from Grant today about doing a tattoo for him."

"Seriously? Grant never mentioned it to me."

"Yeah. I guess Jules gave him my number. He wants to get a pixie holding a lantern tattooed on his shoulder. I want to show you the design and see what you think."

She unzipped her backpack, and as she took out a sketchbook, he saw Ava's letter, still unopened. He wanted to ask about it, but she was plowing through changes and was on the cusp of a great opportunity. He had faith that she'd know when she was ready.

She opened the sketchbook, and he leaned closer, catching glimpses of incredible drawings as she turned the pages.

"Slow down, babe. I want to see these."

"They aren't very good. They're mostly just ideas I was playing with." She turned the page to a sketch of Scrappy sleeping on Brant's chest.

"Whoa. When did you do that?" He took the sketchbook to get a closer look. The details were flawless, from the scruff on Brant's cheeks and the chest hair that was growing over his attempt at a tattoo, to Scrappy's furry face and crooked mouth with two little teeth poking out. Brant had one hand on Scrappy's back, and she'd even drawn the scar on his index finger where he'd gotten stitches when he was a kid.

"Last week, when we had dinner with Abby and Aiden and then we got down and dirty on the couch, and you promptly fell asleep afterward."

He laughed. "As I recall, I put forth a tremendous amount of effort to give you *three* orgasms that night."

"Excuses, excuses." She leaned against him. "I like that picture. It's a good memory, and Scrappy was happy sleeping on you."

"I like the memory of what came *after*, when we finally made it to the bedroom." She'd gone down on him, and that had led to another wild romp. He turned the page and found a drawing of Joni wearing her scuba mask and tutu. "Babe, did you do this from memory?"

"Mm-hm."

"Amazing." The next page had a drawing of a building that looked familiar, but he couldn't place it. The front was open, and the inside looked like her work area at Wicked Ink, with a long table, a reclinable chair, counter space, and pictures on the walls. "What's this?"

"Nothing. Turn the page."

"Not yet. It doesn't look like nothing." He looked at the drawing again and recognized the slanted roof. "Is this the Daily News stand?"

"Mm-hm." She reached over to turn the page again, but he moved the pad out of her reach.

"Babe, are you thinking about opening a tattoo shop? Because I think that's a great idea."

"No, not really. I was just playing around."

The detail in the drawing made him think otherwise. "Maybe you should. The newsstand has been closed for a while. You could probably get a good deal renting it. There's only one tattoo shop on the island, and it's in Chaffee. I bet you'd make a killing."

"Or I wouldn't and I'd be broke."

"Didn't we *just* talk about dreaming big?"

"How about I worry about one big life choice at a time? Or rather, *two*. My pushy boyfriend and the mural. Now, *please* turn the page."

He turned the page and found the drawing for Grant. The pixie looked just like Jules, complete with her signature water-fountain hairdo. She was standing on her tiptoes, bent at the waist, holding a lantern in one hand and shielding her eyes with the other as she gazed into the distance. Her skirt was made of flower petals, and she had gorgeous wings with swirling designs on them. There were four lightning bugs around the lantern, their tiny black bodies illuminated in gold.

"Holy shit, angel. Grant is going to go nuts over this."

"Do you think so?"

"I know so. Grant convinced me to decorate my boat with a pixie theme for the holiday flotilla last year, and he and Jules made a pixie that looked just like this. This is incredible." He put his arm around her, pulling her closer. "When do I get *my* tattoo?"

"I think we need to put you under general anesthesia for that."

He laughed and kissed her. "Then maybe *you* can get the tattoo for me."

Her eyes turned seductive. "Maybe I already have."

"Oh, really?" He slid his hand up her leg, sending Scrappy scrambling to the grass, and kissed her neck. "I've kissed every speck of ink on your body, and I don't remember seeing a new tattoo. But you've been gone for hours. I think a full-body inspection is in order."

She smacked his hand, giggling. "Anyone can see us out here."

"I'm your body inspector. I'll tell them I have a badge."

"A *tinfoil* badge?"

He took her down to her back, kissing the giggles out of her, until she went soft beneath him. And then he kissed her longer because she was his, and he was hers, and nothing was better than that. She came away breathless and beautiful.

"You are *not* inspecting my body out here." That seductive glimmer returned, and she whispered, "Perhaps we should move this inspection indoors."

CHAPTER EIGHTEEN

CAIT SAT ON the floor of the breakfast nook in Brant's cottage sketching and stealing glances at him in his boxer briefs as he made pancakes. This had become her favorite time and place to sketch, with the early-morning sun streaming through the bay window, a cool breeze coming in through the open patio door, and her man singing into a spatula, swinging his butt and thrusting his hips to music streaming from his phone. Brant had the sexiest moves. "Rock Your Body" by Justin Timberlake came on, and he looked over, catching her staring, but she no longer looked away. They'd been together for more than a month, and she'd moved way past that embarrassment.

"Like what you see?"

"I can take it or leave it," she teased.

He laughed, shaking his head. "Toughest crowd *ever*. How's the sketch coming along?"

"I'm almost done, but you can't see it yet."

It had been almost two weeks since she'd had her meeting with the mayor and the rejuvenation committee about the mural, and she'd been sketching every free minute. Or at least, when she and Brant weren't busy with friends or getting down and dirty. Sometimes she even sketched naked when she woke up early, but that never lasted long. One look at her and Brant was all hands and mouth and delicious temptation. She also loved sketching at the marina, where she could watch him work. He was an artist in his own right, and she'd caught herself mesmerized by him many times, her sketchbook forgotten. He was as passionate about his work as he was about them *and* his family.

Scrappy walked past her and out the door. They'd finally housebroken him. Brant was so patient and loving, it was easy to imagine him with children underfoot, teaching them about boats, megaphones, and chocolate chip pancakes. She was falling hard for him, and sometimes she even daydreamed about a future together. Not that she could say all the words she felt. Many were still tethered to fears from her past. But she was getting there.

"You're looking at me that way again, Caity."

"Hm?" She blinked away her thoughts and realized she'd zoned out. She did that a lot when she thought about him. "Sorry."

He chuckled. "I'd give anything to know what you were just thinking about."

"I'll tell you, if you tell me where we're going this morning." It was Tuesday, and she wasn't scheduled to work until the afternoon. Brant had taken the morning off and told her he had a surprise for her.

"No can do, angel face. And if you keep sitting there wearing nothing but my T-shirt and those pink panties, we're not going anywhere." He turned off the stove, and as he transferred the pancakes to plates, "Adore You" by Harry Styles came on. Brant spun around and pointed the spatula at Cait, singing about walking in paradise and getting lost in her eyes.

He was so freaking cute, she could barely stand it. "What is with you and boy bands?"

"It's all in the words, baby," he said, pulling her to her feet.

Scrappy trotted in from outdoors as Brant swept Cait into his arms, singing about walking through fire and letting him adore her. Scrappy sat at the entrance to the kitchen watching Cait try to fall into step with Brant. She'd gotten better at dancing because of mornings like this, but she was still a little off and sometimes stepped on his toes by accident.

He spun her around as he had last week at the Salty Hog, when she'd gone to the Cape and he'd stayed for the first night. She hadn't made a decision about her winter schedule, but she still had time. They'd gone out with her friends to celebrate the mural and had spent the evening dancing, laughing, and kissing. It had been wonderful to replace a difficult memory with a special one. Brant was good at that. He made her bad memories feel like they'd happened in another lifetime. Most of the time, anyway. If only she could carry him around with her all the time.

When the song came to an end, he dipped her over his arm and kissed her slowly and sensually. As their lips parted, he whispered the lyrics to the unfamiliar song that was playing. It was a girl singing about being afraid to let her boyfriend know how she felt about him and a boyfriend who wouldn't give up on her.

"That's your song, baby," he said softly. "'Fight or Flight' by Cait Fairbanks. You don't need to say a word. Just never let *me* go, either." He kissed her again and swatted her butt. "Let's eat."

She was still stuck on him knowing that telling him her true feelings was hard for her.

After a delicious pancake breakfast, and an even more delectable dirty shower, they leashed Scrappy and drove into town. Cait lifted Scrappy and looked into his adorable eyes. "Where do you think Boatman is taking us, Scrap?"

Scrappy cocked his head.

"Attaboy." Brant ruffled the pup's fur. "He's been sworn to secrecy."

"Are we going to the Bistro?" she asked as he turned down the street that led to the restaurant.

"Nope." He pulled up to the curb just beyond the Sweet Barista.

"Keira's? We just ate."

"We sure did. Breakfast *and* dessert." He waggled his brows and stepped out of the truck.

He was *such* a flirty, dirty guy, and she loved it. She watched him strut around the truck wearing his bright blue baseball hat and a navy T-shirt stretched tight over his chest and biceps, and she didn't open the door. He gave her so much, she could give him that. He glanced over, flashing a deep-dimpled grin, and her heart beat a little faster.

Oh yes, this dream I'm living is plenty big enough. Some days she needed to pinch herself to believe she could be this happy.

He opened the door, and Brant took Scrappy. Then he reached for her hand, kissing her as she stepped onto the sidewalk. It was those little romantic touches that always made her breath catch. What more could she need?

As he led her down the street, the front door of the Daily News stand lifted, just like a garage door, as she'd imagined, and a tall brunette wearing a pretty blue wrap dress walked out.

"Are they reopening?" Cait asked with a pang of disappointment. "I want to peek in as we walk by." Ever since Brant had seen her drawing of the shop, she hadn't been able to stop thinking about it. Not that she could figure out how to fit anything more into her schedule, but she liked entertaining the idea of owning her own shop.

All week Brant had been bursting at the seams to share this surprise. "We're going to do better than that, babe. You can look it over for as long as you'd like."

"That would be rude," Cait whispered as they neared the building.

Charmaine Luxe, the Realtor he'd asked to show them the space, extended her hand. "Nice to see you again, Brant."

Cait looked at him curiously as he shook Charmaine's hand. "You too, Charmaine. This is my girlfriend, Cait Weatherby."

"Hi, Cait," Charmaine said. "Brant has told me wonderful things about you. I'm glad you could come out this morning."

"Thanks." Cait looked at him again, perplexed.

"I'm going to grab a coffee while you two talk," Charmaine said, giving Brant a knowing glance as she headed to the Sweet Barista.

"Thanks, Charmaine." He drew Cait into his arms.

"*What* is going on?"

"Now that you're thinking about spending more time here, I thought you might want to check this place out and see if your sketches fit."

"My sketches?" Her brows knitted, but the light in her eyes told him she was doing a happy dance inside. "I told you I was just messing around!"

"*Yeah*, I didn't really buy that. I see the way you look at this place every time we drive past."

"I like it, and I'm intrigued by how different it is and how the windows catch the late-afternoon sun, but, *Brant*. One big decision at a time, remember?" Her gaze moved to the newsstand, and she drew in a deep breath. "I don't even know what I'm doing for the winter yet."

"I know, and there's no pressure. I just wanted you to have this place in your head while you're deciding about your schedule. I talked with Tank about what it would take to open a shop, and, babe, you could *totally* do this if you wanted to. You'd be close to Abby, and the beach, and your favorite coffee shop, and it could be all yours to work as little or as much as you'd like."

She looked at the shop and then at him, and her eyes took on that dreaminess he loved so much. "I can't even tell you how I feel half the time, and you go to the ends of the earth for me." She shook her head. "I still think you've lost your marbles, but thank you!" She threw her arms around him, and he kissed her.

"You're welcome, babe. This is what couples do. We open doors and help each other find all the things that make us happy."

"What makes *you* happy?"

"*You*. The light in your eyes. Your smile. Your laugh. Your kisses. The way you get sarcastic and sassy one minute and sweet as sugar the next." He looked down at Scrappy. "And our boy. The way you love him." *The way you love me.*

"*Brant.*" She barely managed the whisper.

He pulled her closer. "Want me to keep going? Or do you want to check this place out?"

She looked at the newsstand, her smile widening to the kind of smile a kid might make on Christmas morning, and *man*, that made him happy. He gave her a quick kiss and took her hand, leading her to the entrance. "Go on, babe. Explore."

As he'd expected, she didn't run in to check it out the way other women might. She stepped inside tentatively, fidgeting with her hands as she tipped her head back and looked up. "There are skylights!"

Her gaze moved over the interior, and she didn't say a word for two or three minutes, but he could see the gears in her head churning.

She pointed to the left. "That's where I'd put a desk. A thin one, or maybe a counter all the way across with file cabinets beneath it instead of a desk. *Yeah*, that would be best. More counter space. I'd put a reclining chair here instead of where it was in the sketch." She moved around the space, pointing as she spoke. "And my worktable here. My stool would go there, and I'd need a sink."

"There's a powder room behind you. It would be easy to bring a pipe through the wall."

She spun around, eyes dancing with excitement, and opened the powder room door. "That would work." She turned again, studying the space on either side of the front door. "I could put shelves on both sides, or shelves on one and a cabinet on the other, and two chairs for people to wait right here. If I put the table here, I could put the desk over *there*..."

She moved swiftly, changing her mind about what might go where, and he could see her getting lost in the design just as she got lost in her drawings. It was a beautiful sight.

She spun again, beaming at him. "Oh, *Brant!* Thank you for doing this. I can't commit to anything right now, so I feel bad about wasting Charmaine's time. But just standing in here with you and thinking about it makes it feel like one day I might be able to!"

"That's what dreaming is all about, angel. Half the fun is thinking about it, striving for it, and making plans with the hopes that one day those dreams will come true."

"This is . . ." She looked around with awe and disbelief, then turned those gorgeous, suddenly serious eyes on him. *"No."*

"No?" *Shit, what happened?*

"The space is amazing, but it isn't the best part of what I'm feeling." She wound her arms around his neck. "What I meant to say is that *you* are unbelievable. You've opened more doors for me, literally and figuratively, than anyone ever has. You make me *want* to dream."

"Then dream, baby, because it sure looks good on you."

She was quiet for a long moment. Her fingers pressed a little harder on the back of his neck, and she licked her lips. "How does it look if I want to dream *with you?*"

His heart somersaulted. "There isn't a word big enough to describe it. I'll have to show you." He lowered his lips to hers, soaking in every ounce of her excitement and feeding it with his own.

CHAPTER NINETEEN

"ALMOST DONE?" BRANT asked for the tenth time in the last hour.

"I just need a few more minutes." Cait huddled over her sketchbook, putting the final touches on the mural she was presenting to the mayor and the committee next week.

It was late Saturday afternoon, eleven days after Brant had surprised her with a visit to the Daily News stand, and she couldn't stop thinking about the possibility of renting it and opening her own shop. She still hadn't made any decisions about her winter schedule, but she had time. They'd spent all day together mulling over the idea of opening her own shop and talking about the mural. They'd gone for a hike at the wildlife refuge, had lunch at Trista's café on Main Street, and then they'd come to the park to play fetch with Scrappy. But he'd run after the ball and then lay down in the grass with the toy between his paws. At least they'd gotten some cute pictures, and now they were sitting beneath the umbrella of a large tree.

Brant leaned closer, and she clutched the sketchbook to her chest.

He frowned. "I'm dying over here. Come on, babe. I gave you tips for wedding dress shopping with Abby tomorrow when you were nervous about it."

She gave him a deadpan look. "Telling me not to tell Abby she looked fat in any dresses and to nod a lot aren't exactly stellar tips." Deirdra was meeting Cait, Abby, and Leni on the Cape to go bridal gown shopping tomorrow. Cait was going to stay on the Cape and work at Wicked Ink Monday and Tuesday.

"At least I tried." He chuckled. "The suspense is killing me. You've been working on that drawing for three and a half weeks and you haven't shown it to me *once*."

"What if you hate it?"

"That's ridiculous. I haven't hated any of your sketches."

That was true. He'd loved them all, and when they'd gone to another barbecue with his family, he'd even raved to them about her drawings. She'd surprised him with a sketch of that evening the next day. She'd drawn his parents mooning over each other at the table and his grandma Millie leaning forward in her seat holding Tessa's hands as she'd tried to convince her that she needed to make more time for dating. She'd drawn Ford giving Randi a piggyback ride by the gardens with Scrappy chasing them and her and Brant sneaking kisses by the side of the house. Jamison, Rowan, and Joni hadn't been there, but she didn't feel right leaving them out, so she'd drawn them in a heart above the others to signify that they were always in their hearts. When she'd given the drawing to Brant, he'd gushed over it and immediately took pictures with his phone and sent them to everyone in his family. He'd since framed the drawing, and even though she'd given Abby and Aiden pictures and they'd framed them, this was different. *Better.* This was the kind of happiness that nestled into her chest.

"Okay, I'll show you," she relented. "But you have to promise that if you don't like it, or you think the committee won't like it, you'll be honest, because I can take it."

"Honest as a Boy Scout. Isn't that what Tank said?"

"You remember *everything*." That and his honesty were only two of hundreds of wonderful reasons she felt the scale tipping toward love. *Love.* Holy crap was that a scary thought. She had no experience loving a man as more than a friend. But what she felt for Brant was so big and real, he was with her even when they were apart. How could it be anything else? She tucked those feelings down deep for the umpteenth time until she was ready to face them.

She took one last look at the map of Silver Island she'd drawn for the mural, with each historical landmark called out and current scenes depicted. She'd drawn Bartholomew Silver's ship sailing in Fortune's Cove by the cliffs of Fortune's Landing, marking where he'd landed in 1601 when he'd founded the island. The *Pride* was shown off the northeast shore, with treasure hunter Zev Braden and his diving team swimming around the treasures. She'd drawn the Bra Brigaders sunbathing at Mermaid Cove, with a mermaid tail sticking out of the water, and she'd drawn children playing at the park off Main Street. Just now she'd snuck in a drawing of Scrappy with the ball between his paws. She showed elderly couples dressed in fifties-style suits and dresses holding hands as they watched fishermen unloading their daily catch at the Silver Harbor pier and a modern-day Christmas tree lighting with the community rallying in the park near Silver Monument in the center of town. The flag from Top of the Island Vineyard waved in the background. She'd included boats decorated for the holiday flotilla sailing around Rock Harbor, their lights sparkling against an evening sky, and Mayor Osten standing at a podium announcing the winner.

Brant's grandparents had told her about community breakfasts at the Seaport lighthouse, and she and Brant had attended one last weekend. She'd drawn that as well as the original seafarer's cottages that she'd fallen in love with along Seaport's main streets, which were now used as shops. Yesterday evening Brant had taken her to see Chaffee, and last night she'd drawn kids playing around the historical fountain in Chaffee's town square. She showed Silver House resort back in the day, when it was just a home, prior to all of the renovations, fishermen standing on a rickety pier, and the airport when it was established in the early 1900s, with a biplane on the runway and children wearing knickerbockers and knee-length dresses watching from behind a fence.

She couldn't help but honor Ava—the reason she'd found her sisters, Brant, and the island—and she'd drawn her as a teenager watching Olivier paint on the deck of the Bistro. She knew the mayor might not allow that picture since it was so personal, but she had to try. She showed all of the town buildings and modern-day Main Street in Silver Haven with window boxes overflowing with flowers, colorful awnings, and flags at every shop entrance. But her favorite representation of Silver Island's community spirit was the drawing of Brant and his family driving down Main Street in his grandfather's red truck when Brant and his siblings were young, all of them sitting on their knees in the back, waving to the people on the sidewalks as Roddy announced movie night with the megaphone from the driver's seat. The mayor might nix that one, too, but it was worth a shot.

With every minute of research she'd done, and every picture she'd drawn, she'd felt closer to the town and the people, as if she were becoming one of them, and she realized, she *wanted* to be.

She took a deep breath, meeting Brant's eager gaze, and handed him her heart's work.

His hand covered hers, his eyes trained on her, not the drawing. "I've watched you work on this for weeks, and before I look at it, I just want to say thank you for trusting me to be the first to see it."

Too nervous to speak, she nodded, and as he turned his attention to the drawing, she pushed to her feet and paced.

She tried not to scrutinize his every breath as he studied the drawing, but she was too anxious not to question his knitted brows and the way his jaw hung slack. "Is it too much? I know the mayor might not allow the Bistro and your family's truck because they're such personal images, but I had to try."

He held up one finger and continued studying the picture.

"I tried to keep a balance between new and old," she said anxiously as she paced. "Did I go too far in one direction? I asked the mayor about using the map as the overall premise two weeks ago, and he seemed to love the idea. But do you think it's too complicated?"

Brant shook his head and pushed to his feet. "Caity, I've lived on this island for thirty-three years, and I wouldn't have thought to put in half of this stuff. You not only captured the spirit of the island, but you showed all of the things that make up the very heart of it. I knew you were talented, but this . . ."

Her eyes welled with happy tears. "Really?"

"Really, baby. You're going to blow them away."

She squealed and threw her arms around him. He caught her with one arm, holding the sketchbook away from their bodies with the other as they kissed and laughed.

"I'm so relieved!" She took the sketchbook and looked over the drawing again. "I fell in love with the island when I was drawing it. I hope they like it." She kissed him again and then went to put the sketchbook in her backpack.

"Brant! Cait!"

She turned at the sound of Randi's voice and saw her, Tessa, Millie, and Gail approaching. Millie and Gail were wearing floppy sunhats and big movie-star-type plastic sunglasses. Scrappy barked and waggled his butt.

"Hope you guys are done making out because we're taking Cait." Randi loved up Scrappy.

"*Taking* me?" Cait looked at Brant, who was grinning like a Cheshire cat. "What's going on?"

"We're having a girls' day," Gail explained, taking her arm. "And we need to get a move on before the rain moves in."

Millie motioned toward Cait's backpack. "Tessy, get her bag, will you?"

"Got it, Gram." Tessa shouldered Cait's backpack.

"Don't look so worried, Cait. This is a rite of passage." Randi took Cait's other arm. "I promise we'll bring you back to him in one piece so you can smooch all night long."

Cait had never been kidnapped by a group of girls before. She was excited, and a little nervous. "Is this like hazing at a sorority? You're not going to make me drink too much or go streaking, are you?"

"Only if you're lucky, hon," Millie said with a wink.

The girls laughed.

"Have a blast, babe," Brant said. "We'll see you later."

As the girls led her away, she looked over her shoulder at Brant. He was holding Scrappy, and he blew her a kiss.

"That's enough ogling," Randi commanded. "It's time to put my brother and your pup out of your head for a few hours and have some fun!"

But they're my favorite kind of fun. "Putting your brother out of my head is easier said than done."

"You tell 'em, honey." Gail squeezed her arm.

"You girls could learn a little something from Cait," Millie added. "Maybe she can open your eyes to romance."

"*Gram,*" Randi and Tessa complained.

Gail and Millie giggled, and Gail said, "Let the fun begin."

CHAPTER TWENTY

"I CAN'T BELIEVE you convinced me to sit on this beach in my bra." Cait had been kidnapped for her first Bra Brigade outing. She sat on a beach chair between Abby and Deirdra—who she'd been shocked and elated to see—with her feet in the sand and her arms crossed over her stomach, surrounded by the women who had kidnapped her, along with Shelley, Faye, Leni, Jules, Daphne, Lenore, and a handful of Lenore's friends. They'd been there for about an hour, and it had taken most of that time for Cait to get comfortable.

"I'm so happy you did it!" Abby exclaimed, looking perky and adorable in a peach bra and beige shorts, with a plastic tiara on her head that had BRIDE-TO-BE across the front, which Leni had insisted she wear.

"I'm with you, Cait." Deirdra swatted at a fly, huffing as she straightened the floppy pink sunhat she'd borrowed from Lenore. She wore a sexy black silk and lace bra and an expensive-looking skirt, as if she'd come straight from work. "I came home to surprise you and Abby and *that one*"—she lowered her sunglasses and glared at Leni over them—"drags my ass out of the air-conditioning to sweat in my lingerie. My skirt will probably have a permanent sweaty butt stain." She fanned her face with her hand.

Leni scoffed. "Get over it. Better to have a sweat stain than a stick up your butt."

"I *love* these meetings of the tatas." Jules wiggled her shoulders. Her perky little boobs were nicely tucked into a pink bra that was similar to Cait's.

"Hadley calls them Mommy's Booby Parties," Daphne said.

They all laughed, and that started a conversation from the older ladies about all of the times their group had been stumbled upon and the hilarious reactions of the people doing the stumbling.

"Remember when Jamison found us on Brighton Bluffs?" Gail said. "He was fourteen and exploring there with his friends. Well, you know Jamison. He wandered off on his own, and when he saw us, he said something like, *Don't you own bathing suits?*"

"Most teenage boys gape at us or turn away red-cheeked," Lenore said.

"You can always tell when a boy has seen us sunbathing," Millie said. "They avoid us at all costs afterward."

"That's as much of a rite of passage as this is for us," Shelley added.

"Who do we think has the best bra today?" Faye pointed around the circle.

"Not me," Tessa said, looking down at her blue sports bra. "I'm all about comfort."

Faye pointed at Leni and Deirdra. "You girls remind me of Shea, spending as much on what goes under your clothes as the outfits themselves." Shea was one of Faye's daughters, and she owned the marketing and public relations firm where Leni worked.

"Aunt Faye, we have reputations to uphold. We can't very well advertise Chanel on the outside and Walmart underneath," Leni said, making everyone laugh. Like Deirdra, Leni always looked well put together, and today was no exception. Her auburn hair hung loose over her shoulders, and her forest-green lace bra brought out her eyes.

"I think Randi's bra is pretty," Daphne said.

Randi sat up straighter in her red demi bra. "Thanks, Daph. I like yours. Baby blue is a great color on you."

242

Daphne blushed. "Jock picked this one out."

"My boy has great taste." Shelley winked at Daphne.

"Okay, enough over-the-shoulder-boulder-holder talk," Lenore said from beneath an umbrella, where she sat with a number of friends. She wore a bathing suit bottom with a black wrap around her hips and a full-coverage bra like the other ladies her age were wearing. "I want the sexy vibe Cait has with all those mysterious tattoos."

"I'm going to get a tattoo as soon as Cait has some free time," Gail said.

That was news to Cait.

"She gave Jagger one a few weeks ago." Abby slid a teasing look to Deirdra. "You should have seen him lying shirtless on the table."

"Cait should have sold tickets," Tessa said. "That guy is *hot*."

"Oh, please. The *hippie?*" Deirdra looked disgusted.

"Hell yeah," Randi chimed in. "Ford hates it when we go to the Bistro, because how can you not check out a hot guy with a guitar?"

"The guy probably lives in a marijuana fog." Deirdra shook her head. "What did he say to you when you hired him, Abby?" She lowered her voice, speaking lackadaisically. "*I like to keep things loose, you know, go with the flow.*" In her regular voice, she said, "Give me a guy in a suit and tie any day."

"Just stay away from my suit-and-tie guy," Abby teased.

"I have the best of both worlds. Grant wears suits when he goes to meetings for the foundation, and then I get the artsy Grant, painting naked in the studio late at night." Jules waggled her brows. "*Yummy.* Cait's giving him a tattoo soon."

"Can I come watch?" Lenore asked, and she and her girlfriends giggled.

"*Mom,*" Shelley chided her. "That's our soon-to-be son-in-law!"

Lenore waved her hand dismissively.

"Lenore, let's get back to tattoos. I think we should all get a sexy little one," Millie said. "Maybe something to represent the Bra Brigade."

"Good idea! That way next time we go to Pytho—I mean *bingo*"—Lenore exaggerated the word *bingo*—"we'll be the cool ladies."

"We all know you go to the Pythons strip club on the Cape, Grandma," Jules said.

Lenore and Millie feigned innocence, fluttering their lashes, and said, "Who, us?" inciting more giggles from her friends.

Shelley, Faye, and Gail shook their heads.

"Cait, have you thought any more about opening your own tattoo shop?" Abby asked.

"What?" Jules exclaimed. "You're thinking about opening a shop on the island?"

"She and Brant went to check out the Daily News stand," Abby explained. "Wouldn't it be perfect?"

"Yes!" Jules said.

"You'd get a lot of foot traffic there," Leni pointed out. "You have to pass right by it to go to Sunset Beach, and it's right on the main drag. If you do it, I can help you get your name out there."

"Me too!" Daphne said. "We can get together like we did for the Bistro and brainstorm ideas."

"I love that idea!" Jules chimed in. "Mom, you can spread the word to older people."

"*Older* people? Like at the retirement home?" Shelley asked with a laugh.

"Honey, we're only as old as we feel, and I feel about twenty-eight most days," Millie said.

Lenore leaned closer. "And a hundred and five most nights after Freddy gets frisky."

"*Ugh, please.*" Randi shook her head. "Cait, if you decide to open a place, Tessa and I can help spread the word, too."

"The airport is a perfect place," Tessa added. "You get tourists as soon as they come in."

"And at the ferries." Gail pushed to the edge of her chair and said, "We can whip up flyers and make sure everyone gets them as they arrive on the island."

Overwhelmed by their support, Cait said, "That's really nice of all of you to offer, but I have a lot going on right now. I still haven't figured out my winter plans for the mural, and we just opened the Bistro. I don't want to do anything that would shortchange Abby."

"We're fully staffed," Abby pointed out.

"It would be great for you to have something of your own," Deirdra said. "And I'd imagine that the mural will earn you a reputation for your talent. By next summer, you could have more work than you can handle."

Their excitement magnified her own. "Do you really think so?"

All the women talked over each other about how big a clientele she'd probably garner, and that led to Leni and Deirdra talking about Cait expanding a business she hadn't even started yet.

"We think you should do it," Lenore said. "You'll have the full support of the Bra Brigade."

Everyone cheered.

Cait wondered if it was possible to fall in love with a group of women. "I don't know what to say, other than thank you. But there's a lot to consider. What if all these ideas don't work, and I can't make enough money to pay the rent? Then I'll be in a pickle."

"You'll make the rent," Deirdra said confidently. "You'll be on the expensive side of Silver Island and right down the road from the Silver House. Chances are, you'll get hundreds of little divas over the summer, spending Mommy and Daddy's money like water."

"That's true," Gail said. "Keira has mentioned that about the coffee shop. You do have a lot on your plate, but now is the time to take risks. When you're young and you have the energy to put into them."

"And the support of the community," Shelley said.

"But it's not *my* community," Cait pointed out.

There was a collective gasp and a multitude of "*Yes it is!*"

"You became one of us the minute we found out you were Ava's daughter," Shelley said with that maternal expression Cait had come to appreciate.

Abby put her hand on Cait's and said, "I love working with you at the Bistro, but that was my dream. I want *you* to have yours, to *live* your dream."

Cait looked around at the women who had become her friends and the ladies who acted like they were all her mothers and said, "I kind of already am."

Deirdra touched Cait's shoulder. She and Abby nodded as if they knew exactly what Cait was thinking. Knowing they probably did made Cait even more emotional.

"Look at you girls." Shelley sighed. "I miss your mama something fierce. I wish she were here with us. But I can feel her smiling down on you. This was what Ava had wanted, to have her girls come together and be happy."

Cait imagined Ava there with her friends who loved her despite her faults, and her throat thickened.

"I'm sweaty, sandy, and sitting in my bra in public," Deirdra said flatly. "As much as I like hanging out with everyone, a shower and a few margaritas might amp up my happiness factor."

Leni popped open a cooler. "I've got the margaritas. You know I'd never leave you hanging."

"You are a goddess." Deirdra peered into the cooler. "You don't have a fan hidden in there, do you?"

As the day wore on, clouds rolled in, bringing a refreshing breeze. The conversation turned to Abby's wedding, and eventually they broke off into smaller discussions, some serious, some funny, but all meaningful. When Cait had first heard about the Bra Brigade, she'd thought it sounded silly, a bunch of women sitting around in their bras. But as she sat among three generations of women, she realized this was a family, too. A family of women letting their guards down, accepting one another for who they were without exception, and taking care of each other in ways Cait had never experienced or even hoped for, because she'd never known a group of women like this existed.

"I want a picture!" Daphne jumped to her feet, telling everyone to gather around.

They all crowded together behind Daphne. Cait stood with her arms around Abby and Deirdra, with Shelley and Gail behind her, their hands on her shoulders.

Daphne yelled, "Say *Mommy's booby party!*"

As they shouted those words and Daphne took the picture, "*Ladies, put your boobs away!*" boomed from a speaker on a boat speeding into the cove.

The girls shrieked, running for their shirts and laughing hysterically. The older ladies settled into their beach chairs in their bras, as if they were the queens and everyone else had lost their minds. As Jules and Daphne strained to see who was on the boat, Cait didn't care if it was the mayor himself seeing her shirtless, because after a lifetime of longing for a mother who would love her and siblings to lean on, she'd found more than she could ever hope for. The *new* part of her, the part that was trying to build a life separate from her past, felt like she belonged with these wonderful women and deserved their friendship and support. But at the same time, she felt like a fraud, hiding so much of herself from these friends who shared so openly, and she didn't know what to do with those feelings. So for now she did what she knew best. She shoved those worries down deep, allowing happiness to rise to the surface.

Brant anchored the boat as Jock and the other guys lowered the inflatable lifeboat to the water. They were expecting storms later, but he hoped to spend a few hours on the beach with their friends before the rain hit. They loaded up the lifeboat with supplies for the bonfire and barbecue and tucked adorable Hadley in the middle of it all, surrounded by towels. Jock and Aiden held on to one side of the boat, and Wells and Grant held on to the other. Brant took up the rear, and together they swam the boat toward shore.

Brant held on to the raft, kicking his feet, eyes locked on Cait in her T-shirt and shorts, as beautiful as ever. Deirdra said something, and Cait laughed, covering her mouth, but her eyes never left his as they came to shallow water.

"Hi, Hadley!" Daphne waved.

"I at your booby party!" Hadley hollered, and everyone laughed as Jock reached for her. She shrugged away, scowling at her daddy. "*Wells* get me!"

"That's my girl," Wells said, reaching for Hadley. She threw her arms around his neck, and he carried her onto the beach.

"You've got to be kidding me." Leni glowered at him. She had dated Wells in high school and he'd two-timed her with Abby. They were still friends, but Leni had never stopped giving him hell for it. "Daph, we need to have a talk. Your little girl's taste has gone downhill."

As the rest of the guys carried the supplies to the beach and Brant dragged the lifeboat onto the sand, Wells cocked a grin and said, "Don't worry, Leni. There's plenty of me to go around."

"There wasn't plenty in high school and there's *definitely* not now." Leni stalked away.

There was a flurry of activity as the guys greeted their significant others and the other ladies, and Brant focused on the green-eyed beauty he was gathering in his arms.

"How's my girl?" He kissed her.

"Great, but *what* are you all doing here? Where's Scrappy?" She glanced at the activity on the beach.

"My grandfather's watching him. The guys and I were out fishing, and I missed you. I convinced them to make an evening of it with a bonfire and barbecue before the rain hits. Did you have fun?" He'd been a little nervous about how she'd feel about sunbathing in her bra.

"*Yes.* The Bra Brigade is *nothing* like I imagined."

"*Mother,* put your shirt *on!*" Shelley snapped at Lenore.

Lenore and the other older ladies rolled their eyes, and she crossed her arms and said, "These whippersnappers crashed *our* party. Let them look away."

"See?" Cait whispered. "I wish I could hang out with them more often."

"That's great, babe. I'm sure they'd love that, but you're not going to Pythons." He laughed and kissed her.

She wound her arms around his neck and said, "I knew you had a possessive side."

"If you were going out with the hottest girl around, you would, too." He tugged her against him, kissing her the way he'd wanted to all afternoon.

"You two want to take that to the boat?" Wells called over.

Cait buried her face in his chest.

"Sorry, babe. We'd better get the fire started." He took her hand, and as they crossed the sand, he shielded his eyes from the bra wearers and said, "Hello, ladies. I'd appreciate it if you would put your shirts on."

The ladies laughed, and the other guys vocalized their agreement. After much negotiation, the rebellious ladies finally put on their shirts.

They built a bonfire, and all the guys made up stories about the fish they'd caught, one-upping each other for the hell of it, when in reality they hadn't caught a damn thing. They cooked hot dogs and hamburgers and laughed a lot as they ate. When the temperature dropped, Brant and the guys carried the older ladies' things to their cars.

Brant hugged his mother and said, "Thanks for including Cait."

"She's a special girl, honey. I love her," his mother said.

"Good, because I'm crazy about her."

His mother patted his cheek. "Go have fun before you get rained out, and feel free to join us for dinner tomorrow when Cait's at the Cape."

"Thanks, Mom."

Brant went to join the others, and as he came through the trees, the flames of the bonfire danced in the cool evening breeze, reflecting in Cait's eyes as they followed him across the beach. He sat behind her, wrapping her in his arms and inhaling her sweet scent. He loved seeing her so relaxed, and kissed her cheek, whispering, "Remember our naked afternoon here?"

She put her arms over his, hugging them against her stomach, and shushed him over her shoulder. "Someone will hear you."

The blush on her cheeks told him she remembered it as well as he did. He kissed her again, listening to their friends chatting. Leni and Randi were sitting closest to them, talking about Randi's expedition. Jules was sitting between Grant's legs, talking with Tessa and Deirdra, and Abby was tucked against Aiden's side, the two of them talking with Daphne and Jock. Hadley was almost asleep on Jock's shoulder.

Wells grabbed a drink from the cooler and sat between Leni and Randi, putting his arms around them. "What are you girls doing later tonight?"

The girls exchanged a smirk and said, "Not you," in unison, and laughed.

A cold breeze swept off the water, and Cait snuggled against Brant. He kissed her temple and said to the group, "I can smell the rain. It's close. We should think about getting the boat back to the marina soon."

"I'm all for wrapping things up," Deirdra said. "I've had a great time, but I've got sand in places I haven't had sand in since I was a kid. Thank God Abby and Aiden chose November for their wedding. At least we'll be comfortable."

"Dee, you remember that we can get snow in November here, right?" Grant asked. "We could freeze our asses off."

"Abs and I will be in Brazil, soaking up the sun," Aiden said proudly. Everyone fell silent.

Abby's eyes widened, and she went up on her knees. "Are we going to *Brazil* for our honeymoon?"

Aiden uttered a curse.

"Oh man, you spilled the beans," Brant said.

"Oh, *Aiden!* We're going to Brazil!" Abby threw her arms around him. "I *love* you!"

Aiden's arms circled her. "Remember our first trip to Chaffee?"

"I'll never forget," Abby said dreamily. "You said it reminded you of Salvador de Bahia and that you would take me there one day, and then we went into Whimsical Things."

"And I said I love you for the very first time." Aiden brushed a kiss over her lips. "I love you, Abigail de Messiéres, and I cannot wait to marry you." As he lowered his lips to hers, all the girls *aww*ed.

Brant tightened his hold on Cait. The urge to say *That'll be us one day* was so strong, it took everything he had to hold it back. Every day it got harder to keep from telling her what he felt with every breath he took, but he didn't want to rush her. So he focused on something else. "My aunt owns Whimsical Things."

"Beverly?" Abby asked. "She was wonderful."

"She's my mom's older sister." Brant had introduced Cait to her when they had visited Chaffee, and the two had hit it off.

They talked about Chaffee, and Aiden told them all about their upcoming trip to Brazil. When the first raindrops fell from the sky, Brant kissed Cait's cheek and said, "Let's go, baby, before the sea gets rough."

There was a flurry of activity as everyone packed up and Brant put out the fire. The rain came down harder, and the wind picked up. Brant hollered, "Jock, get Hadley out of the rain. We'll get your stuff."

"Thanks, man." Jock, Hadley, and Daphne hurried toward the woods.

"We can load the coolers in my Jeep," Randi suggested.

Brant took Cait's hand. "Babe, why don't you get a ride with Randi so you don't have to deal with getting to the boat? You can pick up Scrappy, and I'll meet you at my place. My keys are on the boat, but Randi can let you in."

"Okay." Cait shouldered her bag.

As they carried supplies to the cars, Brant got a call from his father. "Hey, Dad. Can I call you back? We're trying to get everyone out of the rain."

"We need you, son," his father hollered into the phone, the wind muffling his voice. "A couple of fishermen went missing off Bellamy Island."

Shit. "I've got my boat at Mermaid Cove. I'm on my way." He ended the call. "Grant, can you guys handle this? A couple of fishermen are missing. I've got to get over there."

"*Go.* Are you taking the lifeboat? Or should I deflate it and throw it in the Jeep?" Grant said.

"Take it. It'll be faster if I swim."

Tessa jogged over. "I'm going with you in case they need a pilot."

Cait touched his hand. "Brant, this sounds dangerous."

"It's more dangerous for the guys who are missing." He hugged her tight. "I'll be fine." *I love you.* "I'll meet you at my place. Okay?" She nodded, but the worry in her eyes gutted him. "Don't worry about me, babe. There's no way in hell I'd leave you alone in this world." He kissed her again. "I really gotta go. Every second counts."

As he and Tessa ran back to the beach, Cait's voice trampled through his mind. *I was counting . . . I knew exactly how long it took. If one thing was out of place in my bedroom or if I looked the littlest bit disheveled, I'd get hurt or told how worthless I was . . .*

If anyone knew how every second counted, it was her.

CHAPTER TWENTY-ONE

BRANT WATCHED THE lights of the helicopter fading in the distance and took a deep breath, thanking the heavens above for another successful, though grueling, rescue. He was chilled to the bone and riddled with adrenaline after nearly two hours of navigating torrential swells and being battered by wind and rain, visibility nearly zero as he and a half dozen other boats searched the stormy seas for the two lost fishermen. When Brant had caught sight of a life vest just as it was swallowed by the sea, he'd flashed back to hearing Cait scream at the marsh and seeing her disappear under the water. If he'd run by a minute later, she'd have drowned. If he'd looked away when the spotlight had hit the fisherman's vest tonight, they'd have lost him. Every. Second. Mattered.

Brant didn't believe in regrets and he wasn't afraid of death, but as he'd gone into the angry sea to rescue the fisherman, tethered to the boat and thrashing in the violent waves, regret had hammered him. An honorable life didn't mean shit if the woman he loved had never heard it from his lips.

Finally back at the marina, he cut the engine and glanced at Tessa, wrapped in a blanket, elbows on knees, head in her hands. She was tough, but they'd both thought they'd hauled a dead man out of the water, devastating them for him and his family. For most people, after the gust of relief and the frantic effort to keep the man breathing came the blow of exhaustion and, on its heels, confirmation of the fragility of life. That reality brought an emotional storm with tsunami-sized waves. Tess had already succumbed to both, but for Brant, exhaustion always came last.

"How you holdin' up, Tess?"

She sat back, eyes at half-mast. "Is it weird that I want to climb into bed with Mom and Dad and be five years old again?"

"No. It'd probably be weird if you didn't. Nights like tonight make you realize how precious life is. Everyone says to live like there's no tomorrow, but you never hear love like every minute is the only one you'll ever get."

From now on, that was exactly what he planned to do.

After reporting to the search and rescue office and dropping off Tessa, Brant finally dragged his exhausted ass through his front door at nearly two o'clock in the morning.

"You're home!" Cait jumped up from the couch, rushing over to him with Scrappy at her heels. She was a sight for sore eyes in a tank top and sleeping shorts. She threw her arms around him, holding him tight. "I was worried about you guys."

He breathed her in, reveling in the warmth and comfort of the woman he knew by heart, putting all the scattered pieces of him back together. He had so much to say, but he needed to get cleaned up and clear his head first. "I'm soaked, baby."

She held him tighter. "I don't care. I'm just glad you're okay."

She tipped her face up. He could lose himself forever in her beautiful, trusting eyes. "I always keep my promises."

"I know," she whispered. "Is Tessa okay? Did you find the fishermen? Are they okay?"

"Yeah. Tessa's fine and the guys were airlifted out, but they should pull through."

"Thank goodness." She sighed with relief and took his hand. "Let's get you into a hot shower."

She led him into the bathroom and turned on the shower. He started to untie his sneakers, but she knelt before him and moved his hands.

"Let me help." She took off his sneakers and socks, and as she peeled off his wet clothes, she kissed the parts of him she bared.

Every tender touch of her lips soothed the terror of the night and the chill in his bones, driving his need to tell her how he felt deeper. He stepped into the shower and leaned his forearm on the tile. He rested his head on his arm and let the warm water beat down his back. Cait joined him in the shower, and he lifted his head.

"You don't have to move." She kissed his shoulder. "This time *I've* got *you.*"

Her sweetness wrapped around him like an embrace. She put body-wash on her hands, touching him lovingly as she bathed him, so different from their normal sexy showers. She ran her soapy hands along his neck and shoulders, kneading as she went. He'd never been cared for like this. Not once. He was overwhelmed by the tenderness of her touch, the love she was showing him. The scent of his bodywash rose with the steam as her hands moved down his back, bathing and massaging his flanks, waist, and ass. Her hands slipped between his hamstrings, and his body flamed, desire pulsing through him as she bathed his legs all the way down to his ankles.

She stepped in front of him, looking at him with so much love, he reached for her.

"I'm not done." She pressed her lips to his and continued bathing him with her love.

For a woman who couldn't talk about her feelings, she sure knew how to show them, and the more she did, the more he needed to tell her. But he let her finish washing him. Not because he was selfish, but because there was no better feeling than being loved by the woman he adored.

She kissed his body as she moved lower, washing and kissing, driving him out of his mind with love and lust. Brant gritted his teeth, his cock throbbing as she washed his legs and then began kissing a slow, torturous path up his thighs. Her hand circled his hard length, and he moaned hungrily, looking down as she swirled her tongue along the swollen head.

"Christ, baby." He buried his hands in her hair, fighting the need to take control.

She smiled up at him and lowered her mouth over his cock, working him exquisitely. He leaned back against the tile, hips thrusting as she sucked and stroked. When she licked the length of him, he didn't think, could only *feel*, as he lifted her into his arms and lowered her onto his cock. Pleasure seared through him at her tight heat, and their mouths crashed together, their bodies thrusting and grinding. He clutched her ass, backing her up against the wall for leverage, and drove into her. He'd never felt so much pleasure.

"Oh God," she panted out. *"So good."*

He reclaimed her mouth, feasting on her as their bodies banged out a frantic pace. *So good* didn't begin to describe the ecstasy of their connection, the feel of her tight heat sliding up and down his cock. *Fuck.* He came to a screeching halt and tore his mouth away, gritting out, *"Condom."*

Her eyes flew open, sending his heart into his throat.

"Sorry, angel. I got so lost in you, I wasn't thinking."

"It's okay. I wasn't either," she panted out as he turned off the water and carried her into the bedroom.

She stripped back the blanket and climbed onto the bed as he sheathed himself. When he came down over her, she pulled his mouth to hers, and their bodies came together. Their tongues tangled to the same rhythm as their hips thrusting. She made those sweet and sinful noises that lulled him deeper into her, drawing his emotions from the depths of his soul, and he breathed them into her. He pushed his hands beneath her bottom, lifting and angling, taking her deeper.

"Oh . . . Brant. Don't stop."

Her body went rigid, and her nails cut into his back. He sealed his mouth over her neck, sucking as he thrust deep, and she bowed off the bed, his name tearing from her lungs like a demand—*"Brant!"*

His hips pistoned faster as she gasped for breath, her body convulsing around him. Heat spiked down his spine, pooling in his groin. He gritted his teeth to stave off his release as she came down from hers and recaptured her mouth, quickening his actions, taking her up, up, *up*, until she shattered again, moaning and writhing, bucking uncontrollably, drawing him deeper into her.

"So beautiful," he said against her lips, and kissed her softer, thrusting slower, drawing out their lovemaking. Her hands moved along his back, and she gripped his ass, ratcheting up his arousal.

She arched beneath him, her knees opening wider. *"Ohgod, Brant . . . I'm going to . . ."*

He dipped his head beside hers, heat throbbing through his veins as he pumped faster. A stream of mewls and *Ohgods* escaped her lips, and she wrapped her legs around his waist. He pushed his hands under her ass, angling her hips until she shuddered.

"That's it, angel. Come *with* me this time."

He took her in a penetrating kiss, and they spiraled into a world of breath-stealing ecstasy. Her inner muscles clenched tight, and just fucking perfect, tidal waves of pleasure crashed over him. They clung together, their bodies ravaged with rapture until they had nothing left to give, and they collapsed to the mattress, riddled with aftershocks. He kept her close, adrift in a sea of love so vast, he didn't know where he ended and she began. He wanted *this* for the rest of his life, to love Cait, to be there when she needed him and even when she didn't. He kissed her slowly and passionately, and when she went boneless in his arms, he brushed his lips over hers.

Her eyes fluttered open, and his love poured out. "I love you, Caity."

She stilled beneath him, her eyes tearing.

"I know it's hard for you to hear, and I don't expect you to say it back. But when I was out there tonight, all I could think about was if I didn't make it back, you'd never know how much I adore you. I couldn't let another night pass without you knowing how I feel. I never felt like I was missing anything in my life, but from the moment I laid eyes on you, I knew I was wrong. Suddenly I became aware of an emptiness that needed filling."

Tears slipped down her cheeks, and he wiped them away.

"I think about you all the time, angel. Your laugh lights me up, and your smile—your gorgeous, sometimes-bashful, sometimes-sassy smile—is the most *glorious* thing I've ever seen in my entire life. Our time together has been the best of my life, and I can only hope that I bring you half as much happiness as you bring me."

"You do," she said, wiping her tears.

"Good. Then we don't have to say any more. I just wanted you to know that I love you with all that I am and all that I will ever be." He kissed her smiling lips, trying not to worry too much about the shadows in her eyes. He'd known his confession might unsettle her or rouse ghosts of her past, but he hoped that hearing it might one day bring the power to slay those ghosts. "I have to slip into the bathroom. Will you still be here when I come back?"

She laughed softly and nodded.

He went to take care of the condom, hoping he hadn't scared her off. When he returned, he climbed into bed beside her and gathered her in his arms. She still looked happy and a little troubled, but she didn't run and she didn't freak out. He kissed her forehead and whispered, "I've got you, babe."

They had nothing but time, and as she dozed off, safe and trusting in his arms, he knew that one day—a week, a year, or ten years from now—the power of their love would be stronger than the ghosts of her past.

CHAPTER TWENTY-TWO

SUNDAY AFTERNOON CAIT sat on a fancy settee between Deirdra and Leni, half listening to their conversation about the many bridal gowns Abby had already tried on and wondering if it was normal to get teary every time she saw Abby in a gown. She'd never been wedding gown shopping. In fact, she'd been to only two weddings in her entire life, Tank and Leah's and Tank's cousin Justin's, when he and Chloe got married. Cait had cried throughout each ceremony because the four of them had endured so much in their lives, she'd been happy they'd found partners who understood all their darkest pieces. At the time, she hadn't even thought about the possibility that *she'd* ever find that kind of happiness. But now, as she remembered the unfathomable love she'd seen in Brant's eyes as he'd told her he loved her, her eyes filled with tears again.

She stared at her feet, blinking her eyes dry. Her Converse looked out of place between Deirdra's wedge heels and Leni's strappy sandals. With Deirdra's fancy shorts and blouse and Leni's slacks and silk tank top, the two of them looked like they were going to tea at a country club inn. Cait had *wanted* to wear a sundress, especially after how much Brant had loved seeing her in one. But after last night, her emotions were all over the place, and she'd opted for the comfort of familiarity instead. Now she realized it was just one more thing that set her apart from her sisters and friends.

God, I'm such a mess.

"I think the A-line dresses are more elegant," Leni said. "What do you think, Cait?"

"I like them all. I don't know how she'll choose when everything looks pretty on her." Cait didn't know anything about fashion, much less wedding gowns, but Abby had tried on every style dress there was, from curve-hugging to billowing layers, and she looked gorgeous in every single one of them.

"They say brides *know* the right one when they see it," Leni said.

"You know none of this will matter anyway, right? Abby could wear a paper bag and Aiden would still think she was the most beautiful woman who's ever lived," Deirdra said.

Cait and Leni agreed as Abby came out of the dressing room in another billowy gown with a sweetheart neckline, lace overlay, and a wide satin ribbon around her waist.

"Wow!" Leni and Cait said in unison.

Abby spun around, revealing a big silk bow in the back. Cait teared up again. *Every. Damn. Time.* She'd watched Abby fall in love with Aiden so fast and easily, and now she was getting married and starting a beautiful life with him, while Cait was in love with an amazing man who somehow loved her despite all her crap, and she was still so stuck in the shackles of her past that she was unable to tell him.

"I feel like a princess in this one. What do you think, Dee?" Abby stepped onto the platform in front of the full-length mirrors.

"I like it a lot, and it does look like a princess dress," Deirdra said. "But I kind of hate that bow."

"You *hate* it?" Abby turned around and looked over her shoulder in the mirror at the back of the dress. "Why?"

"It makes your butt look big," Deirdra said.

"Dee!" Cait looked at her in shock.

"What?" Deirdra put her hand on the hip of her tan linen shorts. "She's tried on, like, *seventeen* dresses. It's time to weed some of them out."

Abby continued looking at her butt in the mirror. "Cait? Leni? What do you think about the bow?"

Leni walked behind her and crossed her arms, studying Abby's rear.

"I don't think your butt looks big," Cait said. "The dress *is* puffier than some of the others, but I like it."

"Leni?" Abby urged.

"I like it," Leni said. "But what really matters is how you feel in it. Do you want to feel like a princess?"

"I don't know!" Abby exclaimed. "I find something to love about each of the dresses."

"Well, at the end of the night, your prince is going to rip off whichever one you choose anyway. I say go with something that's easy to get out of," Deirdra said.

"Do they make tearaway dresses like they make stripper pants?" Cait teased.

The girls laughed.

"I cannot wait for our wedding night!" Abby shimmied. "We have amazing sex *all* the time, and I know that night is going to blow all the others away."

Sex was another thing Cait wished she could talk to the girls about, but girl talk was as foreign to her as saying *I love you.*

"I saved my favorite dress for last. I'll be right back." Abby gathered the train in her arms and stepped off the platform. "I appreciate your honesty, Dee. The last thing I need is to get my wedding photos back and think my butt looks big."

"Exactly." Deirdra flashed a victorious smirk.

"Off I go," Abby said in a singsong voice as she disappeared into the dressing room again.

A few minutes later, Abby returned in the most gorgeous gown Cait had ever seen. They rushed to her side as she stepped onto the platform, gushing about the A-line gown with beaded and scalloped three-quarter-length sleeves, an illusion bateau neckline over a plunging sweetheart lace bodice, and a full gathered skirt with matching scalloped lace hemline and chapel train.

"Oh, *Abby*," Cait gushed, damp-eyed again. "You look elegant."

"This is the best one yet," Deirdra said. "This dress has your spirit and Aiden's newspaper-reading class."

Abby laughed, tears welling.

"You're gorgeous, Abby," Leni said. "This is a real statement dress. It says *This is it. Our love is the real thing.*"

Even Abby's *dress* could say that. Cait tried to swallow her distress. She was thrilled for Abby and Aiden, but she was also a little jealous. She had everything she never dreamed she'd ever have right in front of her, and she couldn't grab hold of it the way Abby had.

"This is it," Abby agreed. "This is *the one!*"

They all hugged her, gushing over her and the dress.

"I can't wait to see Aiden's face when he's watching you walk down the aisle," Leni said.

Cait imagined herself in a wedding gown walking down the aisle to Brant, and a pang of longing sliced through her. Who was she kidding? She couldn't even commit to stepping outside of her safety net at the Cape, much less say she loved him. Would she ever be free of her fears, or was Brant stuck with a broken woman forever? She stepped away to get more tissues.

"Here go the waterworks again." Deirdra put her arm around Cait and said, "I bet we are going to be searching for your wedding dress next."

Her sisters' and Leni's hopeful eyes uncapped the tears she'd been holding back, and they flooded out. "I'm sorry." She ran into the dressing area to avoid making a scene.

"Cait!" Abby called after her as she ducked behind a curtain into a dressing room.

Her sisters and Leni burst through the curtain. Cait turned away from them, but her sisters flanked her, putting their arms around her, which only made her cry harder.

Leni stepped in front of her, holding out a box of tissues. "Here, honey."

"What's wrong?" Abby asked.

Cait grabbed tissues and shook her head, her throat thickening. "I'm sorry. I'm fine."

"You're *not* fine," Deirdra said. "Did you and Brant have a fight?"

Cait shook her head. "He told me he loves me—" Sobs stole her voice, and she buried her face in her hands.

Abby pulled her into her arms. "So these are *happy* tears?"

Cait shook her head again.

"I'm confused. You don't love him?" Deirdra asked. "Because that's okay. You don't have to love someone just because they love you."

Cait pushed out of Abby's arms. "I do, but I'll never be what he deserves."

"What are you talking about? You're amazing," Leni said.

"I'm *not*, Leni. I'm not like you guys. Love doesn't come easy for me like it does for all of you."

Deirdra and Leni exchanged confused glances.

"Love came easily for *Abby*," Deirdra said. "We're happy for her, and for you and Brant, but Leni and I are *anti* love for ourselves."

"She's right," Leni said. "I'm not on the marriage train."

"That's not exactly what I mean," Cait said, trying to explain as she wiped her eyes. "Knowing you're loved and that you matter affects everything we do. Abby trusted her instincts and followed her heart with Aiden, and all three of you say you love your friends *all* the time. I'm so broken, I can't even say it back to my sisters." She swiped at her tears. "But I *feel* it, and I've felt it all along."

"We know you love us," Abby said.

"I'm glad, but it's not the same as saying it." Cait grabbed more tissues. "I didn't grow up hearing those words and trusting in them like you guys did. Ava might have been awful after Olivier died, but you *knew* she and Olivier loved you. And, Leni, you have Shelley and Steve, who overflow with love for everyone around them, and you all have each other and the Silvers and the Bra Brigaders. You *know* what love looks and feels like. You *know* you can trust it."

"No one told you they loved you when you were young?" Leni asked with as much compassion as disbelief.

Cait shook her head. "My mom died when I was four, and my father was awful. He pretty much said I was unlovable."

"That *bastard.*" Leni put her arms around Cait and said, "I love you, and if you want, I'll sic my brothers on your father so he realizes how unlovable *he* is."

A knot lodged in Cait's throat. "Thanks, but I know I'm worthy of love. Therapy helped with that. It's just not easy for me. I ran away when I was sixteen, and I didn't even have *real* friends until I met Tank a few years ago. It took me *months* to believe him and his family when they said they loved me, and they're warm and wonderful like you guys."

"But I hope you know you can believe us," Abby insisted. "We *do* love you."

"And after seeing you and Brant together, it's pretty obvious that he loves you, too," Deirdra added.

"I *know.* I feel loved by all of you." Cait leaned against the wall, breathing deeply. "I know I sound crazy. It's not just saying the words. It's about doing what Abby did—grabbing hold of what I want and going after it without having a panic attack." She hated that she was worrying them. Her father had ruined so much of her life, and now she was ruining Abby's big day. "I'm sorry. I think hearing Brant say he loves me, and all of this wedding stuff, just got to me." She pushed from the wall, once again stuffing the overwhelming feelings down deep, and put on a brave face. "I'm fine, really. I'm sorry for getting all worked up over nothing."

"A guy telling you he loves you isn't nothing," Deirdra said. "If a guy said that to me, I'd probably run for the hills."

Cait was glad for the levity. "That's the thing, Dee. I don't want to run from Brant. I want to run toward him."

"Now you sound like Faye, which tells me that you're one step closer to finding a way to do just that." Abby hugged her. "You can always talk to us. That's what sisters and friends are for."

"Abby is right, Cait. We'll always make time for you," Deirdra agreed.

"So will I," Leni added. "And I just want to add that you know my mom loved Ava, and she loves you, too, Cait. Those aren't empty words. I know she's not your mother, but she's really good at listening and giving advice. If you ever want to talk with her, I'm sure she'd love to help."

There it was again, the unconditional love she craved. "Thanks, Leni. I appreciate that, but I think I've done enough talking. Abby's salesgirl is probably out there wondering why we're all holed up in here."

"Let her wonder. With the price of these dresses, they should be serving us caviar." Deirdra draped an arm around Cait, the other around Abby, and said, "I say we take care of Abby's dress and then go for dinner and drinks before Leni and I drag our butts into an Uber and go back to the airport."

"That sounds really good to me," Cait said. "Abby?"

"Dinner and drinks with all three of my besties?" Abby put her arm around Leni, linking the four of them together, and said, "Now, *that* sounds like a perfect plan."

Thankfully, Cait was able to pull herself together, and they had a great time at dinner. After Deirdra and Leni left for the airport, Cait waited with Abby for the nine o'clock ferry, wishing she was going back to see Brant instead of staying on the Cape. He'd texted her a picture of him and Scrappy earlier and had said Scrappy was spending the evening with Randi while he went out for dinner and to play pool with Aiden and some of their friends.

Abby hugged her goodbye. "Do you want me to stay with you tonight?"

"No. I'm okay. I'm so used to holding everything in, I think the reason I cracked in the bridal shop was that some part of me knows I don't have to hold it anymore. It was cathartic, but I'm sorry I ruined your afternoon."

"Don't be silly." Abby hugged her again. "I found a great dress, and I got the entire day and evening with three of my favorite people. Call me tonight if you want to talk, okay?"

"Okay. Thanks, Abby."

Cait waved as Abby boarded the ferry, then headed up to the parking lot. When she climbed into her car, another text from Brant rolled in. *Hope you're having fun. I lost ten bucks playing pool. Going in for another round. Wish you were here. Love you.*

She stared at the message, her pulse quickening as she thought about texting *I love you, too.* But that would be a coward's way out. Brant deserved to hear it from her, and didn't she deserve to say it to him? She sat back and looked at the picture of him and Scrappy. "I love you." *That wasn't so hard.* "I love you, Brant." Her heart beat faster. She clicked on his name, and her thumb hovered over the call button.

Her nerves caught fire. It wasn't like he was going to suddenly turn into a monster if she said she loved him. But saying those words was giving a promise, wasn't it? A promise to give her all to their relationship? She wanted that, too, but what if he wanted a life together on the island full-time, and she couldn't pull her shit together enough to leave her life on the Cape behind? Was she shackling *him* to her past, too? Was that fair?

She typed, *I miss you, too. Have fun*, adding a kissing emoji, which was so freaking lame, she pissed herself off. She put away her phone and headed home, but she knew she'd just overthink every little thing and stress over the thoughts in her head, so she took a detour and went to see the one person who would listen to her worries and give her straight answers.

As she drove down the wooded lane toward Tank's house, she realized it was late, and his girls were probably sleeping. She parked behind his motorcycle and texted him. *Do you have a minute to talk?*

His response came instantly. *Look up.*

She did, and she saw him walking toward her car. She swore the man had ESP. He watched her intently as she stepped out and closed the door. "Sorry to come by so late."

He towered over her in his black T-shirt and jeans. "Not a problem. You okay?"

"If I were, would I be bothering you?"

"Three years ago, *maybe*." He cracked a grin and put an arm around her. "Let's sit on the porch." As they headed up the walkway, he said, "Leah and the girls made pie. Want a piece?"

"No thanks. I went bridal gown shopping with my sisters and Leni and we had dinner together."

They sat on the porch steps, and he rested his elbows on his knees, holding one hand in the other. "Then this is a sister issue?"

"It's a *me* issue. Brant told me he loves me."

Tank nodded. "I'm not surprised. We all saw it coming. He looks at you like I look at Leah. How do you feel about him?"

"I'm crazy about him. He's *everything*, Tank. He's trustworthy and honest, patient and funny. He's smart and loving, and he accepts me and *all* of my crappy baggage."

"But . . . ?"

She sighed. "But I'm stuck. He's opened my mind and my heart more than I ever thought possible, and with him, I dream about a future I'm not sure I can ever have. It's like I've got this whole life on the island just waiting for me—Brant, my sisters, the mural, and maybe even my own tattoo shop—but when I think about packing my things and moving away from here, I panic. Why am I afraid to go for it? I know you and your family will always be here for me, so it's not that."

"If I tell you what I think, you're not going to like it."

"I figured as much. That's why I'm here. I *need* answers, Tank."

He nodded, his face solemn, serious eyes holding hers. "You can't grab hold of your future because you're still treading through the quicksand of your past. You never got closure, and without closure, your past is always hovering, sucking you in and holding you back. You know I had to face my past to be with Leah and the girls. If I hadn't done it, I'd have missed out on this incredible new life I have."

"You sound like Brant. He tried to convince me to go to the police or something, which we both know wouldn't do anything at this point but bring a hailstorm of crap down on me. I went to therapy for *two years*. I told Brant, my sisters, and Gia about my past. I even use my real last name. What *else* can I do to get closure?"

"I'm not sure I have the answer to that, but I think you need to find a way. Maybe you should do what the therapist suggested and write your father a letter to get all that shit you should have said to him years ago out of your head, and more importantly, get it out of your heart. Even if you don't send it, it might get the poison out of you."

"I forgot she suggested that." She thought about Ava's letter and felt guilty for not having read it yet. "Maybe I will."

Tank took her hand and said, "I know even thinking about your father scares the living shit out of you. But you're stronger than you think you are, and if you love Brant, then you'll figure out a way to make this happen."

She put her head on Tank's shoulder. "I love him, Tank, but I'm not sure love is enough to fix this."

"Then maybe you need to get closure for yourself and figure that out."

The door opened behind them, and Leah appeared, holding five-year-old Junie. Junie's face was buried in Leah's shoulder, her springy red curls tangled against Leah's mass of thick, curly brownish-red hair. One of Junie's hands rested on Leah's very pregnant belly. "Hey, Cait."

"Hi, Leah. Sorry to keep Tank out here so long. How are you feeling?"

"Like this baby needs to come out and meet us before I burst," she whispered in her Southern drawl. "Sorry to interrupt, but Junie's having a time of it tonight, and she just wanted a snuggle from Papa Tank."

Tank pushed to his feet and reached for Junie. "Come here, Twitch." He settled her against his shoulder.

"Hi, Cait," Junie said sleepily. "We made pie."

"I heard you and Rosie are pretty great bakers." Cait stood and patted Junie's back, earning a sleepy sigh. "Tank, I'll get out of your hair. Thanks for talking with me. I hope your baby comes soon, Leah. I can't wait to meet it."

As she headed for her car, Tank called out her name. When she turned back, he had his arm around Leah, and Junie looked like she'd already dozed off. He hugged Leah against his side, kissing her head, and said, "Figure it out, Cait. It's worth it."

CHAPTER TWENTY-THREE

BRANT WALKED INTO his cottage Sunday night, and Scrappy took off for his usual inspection on the nights when Cait was at the Cape. Their pooch scampered onto the couch, sniffing and whimpering, then darted into every room, and when he didn't find Cait, he stood at the patio doors peering outside and whining.

"She's not out there, buddy."

Brant pulled open the slider, and Scrappy ran outside to search for their girl. The silence in the cottage was deafening. He had no idea how someone as quiet as Cait could make so much noise when she wasn't even home. *Home.* Man, had that word taken on a new meaning the last month and a half. Her sketchbooks were on the tables, her sneakers by the door, and his sweatshirt that she'd claimed as her own hung over the arm of the couch. He didn't need to go into the bedroom to know that her sleeping shirt and shorts were in a pile on the floor by the bed and her favorite fuzzy slippers were on opposite sides of the room because she'd kicked them off as they'd tumbled to the mattress the night before she'd left. God help them if they ever had kids, which he hoped they would one day. They'd be known as the messy parents.

He could live with that.

Hell, he *wanted* to live with that.

That mess was progress. It was another step his girl had taken in letting go of the nightmare her father had put her through. He pulled out his phone and called Cait.

She answered on the second ring with a simple "Hi," and her sweet voice filled those empty spots inside him that her leaving always left behind.

"Hey, babe. Sorry to call so late. I hung out with Wells and Fitz for a while after the other guys took off."

"It's okay. I was out late, too. Did you have fun?"

"Yeah. We were just dicking around. How about you? How was shopping? Did Abby find a dress?"

"Abby found a beautiful dress, and we had dinner afterward. It was fun spending the day together," she said unconvincingly.

"Are you sure you enjoyed it? You don't sound very happy."

"I *am* happy. Being with them was great. I just wish I were more like them sometimes."

"Why? You're perfect as you are."

She scoffed. "Not really. When I saw Abby in those wedding dresses, so happy and excited about her life, I realized I've spent years hiding in my safe cocoon here on the Cape. I never even thought about having a real future, or falling in love, or having my own family one day. Then you and my sisters came into my life, and it's like I've been working in black and white for all these years, and suddenly there you all are, bursting with the most spectacular colors I've ever seen, and *God*, Brant, I *want* all of those things."

"Then you'll have them, babe."

"That's just it. I'm holding myself back. I'm standing in my safety net on the Cape when what I want is to leap across the ocean and into your arms. I want to grab hold of us, the mural, and maybe even open a tattoo shop, and gush to my sisters about how happy we are. But when I *think* about taking that leap, even after all these years, I feel like a marionette, and my past is clutching my strings, yanking me back to my safety zone."

"Caity, you don't need to leap. I didn't mean to push you or make you feel pressured when I told you I love you."

"You *didn't*. This isn't about you doing something unfair to me. You opened my eyes, Brant. You opened my *heart*, and I am glad you did."

He could tell she was pacing by the cadence of her voice. "You don't sound happy, angel. You sound frustrated. There's no rush. It might just take some time to trust in me enough to know that things will work out."

"Don't you see? This isn't about trusting you or anyone else. It's about trusting *myself*, trusting *my* instincts and my heart," she said vehemently. "I'm *sick* of analyzing every step before I make it. I spent my childhood holding my breath and all those middle years hiding and terrified. Then I found Tank, and he gave me a safe place where I fit in and where I was able to get therapy and learn to breathe again. And then I found *you*, Brant, and I realized I was still barely breathing, because my safety bubble is too small and too far away. I don't want that anymore. I want *you*, and you don't deserve to have my past hanging around our necks like a noose."

"What does that mean, babe? You can't change what you've been through, and I am not letting you go."

"I don't know what I mean, but I'm going to figure it out."

He fucking hated the distance between them. He had a full day of equipment inspections and their biannual meeting with their accountants for the equipment supply company tomorrow, none of which was even half as important as Cait's well-being. "Why don't I cancel tomorrow's meeting and head over there now? I don't want you to be alone tonight."

"No, don't do that. I'm fine. I really am. I'm just exhausted and angry at myself. I think I just need to try to get some sleep. I'm sure

I'll feel better tomorrow." She sighed heavily. "I'm sorry for dumping all of this on you."

"That's what I'm here for. I need to know what you're going through so I can help."

"I appreciate that, but the only person who can help with this is me. It's something I have to figure out alone."

"Alone?" *Fuck.* She'd already spent far too much of her life alone.

"It's in *my* head, Brant. Not yours. You can be the best boyfriend in the world, but until I slay my demons, I'll never have the future I want." Her voice escalated. "And if you want to be with me, you'll never have the one you deserve. You know what? I can't do this right now." She sounded pained. "Can I just call you tomorrow, please?"

"Babe . . . ?"

"I'm *sorry*. I just . . . I need to get off the phone. I'll call you tomorrow."

The line went dead.

He stared at the phone, wanting to call her back, or even better, to get Tessa to fly him to the Cape tonight. But Cait was strong, smart, and capable, and he knew her well enough to realize that she knew what she needed, even if not being there with her cut him to his core.

Cait put her phone in the charger on the table and paced, anger and grief pounding inside her. She looked around at her tidy cottage as she wore a path between the living room and kitchen. Everything was in its rightful place, the pictures perfectly aligned, throw pillows set just so. She didn't do that meticulous shit at Brant's cottage.

Her breathing came faster, anger burning in her chest. How had she ever been able to *breathe* in here, when her father's evilness was still defining where she put her things? She couldn't take it anymore! Anger roared out in a wail as she threw her arm across the table, sending her backpack, sketchbooks, and phone flying across the room. Bursting with years of pent-up rage, she ripped the cushions and pillows from the couch, the books from the shelves, and the pictures from the walls. She saw her father's face scolding her and gritted her teeth as she kicked over the coffee table and picked up the end table, hurling it across the room. She heard his voice ridiculing her, and panic stole the air from her lungs. Her body trembled and shook, her chest heaving with every painful inhalation.

She fought back with everything she had, needing to rid herself of him once and for all.

"I fucking hate you!" she seethed as she stormed into the bedroom, cursing and thrashing as she destroyed every shred of organization, from drawers to closet to bed, breaking those imaginary strings that had bound her for far too many years. She attacked the bathroom next, seeing the lunacy in her actions and feeling saner than ever.

Fury consumed her as she stomped into the kitchen, and angry tears streaked her cheeks as she cleared everything from the counter with one hard sweep of her arm. The toaster and bread box thudded to the floor. *Take that, you fucker.* Hands fisted, she looked for something else to ruin, her gaze moving over the ransacked cottage. Her breath caught in her throat at the sight of the letter from Ava among the spilled contents of her backpack. She made her way across the room, stepping on everything and not caring, and picked it up, her heart aching at the sight of Ava's handwriting. Her knees gave out, and she crumpled to the floor, trying to catch her breath. With shaky hands, she opened the envelope and withdrew the contents: a handwritten letter and a page from one of Ava's sketchbooks. She unfolded it, taking in the sketch of Ava, her skin aged with wrinkles. She was crouched on a cloud, her fingers curling over its edge as she peered down at the Bistro and Sunset Beach, where she'd drawn Abby, Deirdra, and Cait—with long sandy hair and no tattoos, as she'd looked in the pictures Karen, Cait's adoptive mother, had sent when Cait was little.

She pressed the drawing to her chest, tears sliding down her cheeks as she looked up toward the ceiling, imagining her mother smiling down on her despite the fit she'd thrown and the chaos around her. *Thank you for bringing me to them.*

She unfolded the letter with trembling hands, and something fell out. She looked down, and there on her leg was a silver and blue mermaid-tail necklace just like her adoptive mother's. Cait sat in stunned silence. It took a minute for her to get up the courage to pick it up and another minute before she could turn it over and look at the back.

Karen was engraved in cursive.

Confusion and shock sent the room spinning. Cait clutched the necklace in her fist and tried to focus on the letter.

> *My special girl,*
> *How does a mother say hello and goodbye to her daughter at the same time? I did that once on the day you were born, and it nearly killed me to let you go. You taught me what love was. I had never loved anyone or anything the way I loved you from the moment I found out I was pregnant.*

Cait inhaled a ragged breath, swiping at her tears.

> *I'm sure Shelley has filled you in on my controlling parents who made me give you up, and she's told you how I drank myself into oblivion to numb the pain of losing you. When I came to Silver Island, Olivier saved me from myself. He gave me the unconditional love I'd never had and helped me track you down. I needed to know that you were safe, and when the private investigator gave us pictures of you and your new family, as badly as I wanted to go fight for you, I knew I should leave well*

enough alone. But I couldn't bear the thought that your new mother might think I didn't want you. I had to reach out to Karen and let her know how much I loved you.

She was a godsend, and she adored you. She sent me pictures and letters every month. The mermaid-tail necklace I've included in the envelope was hers. She sent it to me in her last letter and asked that I find a way to get it to you once you were all grown up. She said her parents gave it to her the day you were adopted and that you'd always loved to play with it when she told you bedtime stories. I didn't understand why she'd sent it to me at first. But then the letters stopped coming, and I found out that she'd passed away. I'm so sorry, sweetheart. Karen loved you to the ends of the earth. I struggled when I learned that she'd died. Olivier and I talked about trying to fight for you, but you'd lost your mother, and I didn't want to cause you the pain of being taken from your father, too.

The air rushed from Cait's lungs. She could have been with Ava and her sisters for all those years? She closed her eyes, trying to tamp down the anguish eating away at her. But there was no taking the edge off all that she'd lost, that her father had stolen from her.

I'm sure you're wondering why I didn't reach out after you were an adult, but I'd lost Olivier when the girls were little, and it destroyed me. I was a mess again. I went back to drinking, and this time there was no one to save me. You didn't need that in your life. I thank God for Olivier and all he did for me, but I needed him too much. I'm not proud of my weaknesses, and I hope you can find a way to forgive me for them. I also hope that you are stronger than I ever was.

Unfortunately, life burns everyone at some point. When that happens, be strong. Don't be afraid to step into the fire and burn right back. You might go numb with fear or pain, but you'll come out stronger for having stood up for yourself. I wish I had found a way to do that when my parents made me give you up and again after I lost Olivier. When you run and hide from your fears, like I did by drinking, every step leads to new burns, until you have so many, you never fully heal. That's an awful way to live.

Learn from my mistakes, Caity. Be strong, chase your dreams, and know that from the moment you were conceived, you were wholly and truly loved.

Always your mother, Ava

Her use of *Caity* brought another onslaught of tears.

Cait looked down at the necklace in her hand, unable to believe it had been with Ava for all those years. As she put it on, her father's voice trampled through her mind. *I gave away all of her possessions. She wouldn't have wanted you to have it.*

He'd *lied* to her just to make her feel like shit. Her anger returned with a vengeance. She touched the cool silver necklace, feeling like both of her mothers were with her, empowering her to finally break free of her past. She grabbed a pad that had fallen out of her backpack, dug a pen out from under the mess on the floor, and sat with her back against the couch, writing a letter to the bastard who had raised her.

~~Dad,~~

~~Mr. Weatherby,~~

He didn't deserve a salutation.

She stared at the paper, trying to put into words what she wanted to say, but *you hurt me* was too benign, and *you destroyed me* gave him too much power. She started writing the letter, but nothing sounded right. She ripped off and crumpled page after page of weak openings. Was it even possible to put into words the trauma he'd put her through? To explain the lingering effects that caused her to be sitting in a trashed cottage?

She pressed her pen to another piece of paper, trying time and time again, until she was sick to her stomach.

There were *no* appropriate words. She could cut herself wide open and bleed out in front of him, and it still wouldn't convey the hurt he'd caused. He'd been cold back then, and she'd damn well bet he was even colder now. This time it was Brant's voice whispering in her ear. *He's a fucking coward, a goddamn bully . . . You deserve closure, and he needs to pay for what he's done.*

A letter was too easy to ignore.

She rubbed the necklace between her finger and thumb, thinking about Ava. *Learn from my mistakes . . . Step into the fire and burn right back.*

There was no way she was stepping into the fire. She was going to blow through it like a fire-breathing dragon, turning everything in her path to ash. She grabbed Ava's letter and drawing, searched the mess for her wallet and keys, and stormed out of the cottage.

CHAPTER TWENTY-FOUR

FUELED BY HER love for Brant and her sisters and the future she wanted with them, Cait had driven through the night to Connecticut and had been sitting in her car in front of the brick-and-glass building where her father worked, hyped up on coffee and fear, since the sun had come over the horizon. She'd been pummeled by flashbacks of her younger self for hours. She remembered sitting in her father's car in that very parking lot when her grandparents were out of town and she'd had no school. She could still see her father's thin lips disappearing as he bared his teeth, threatening her before getting out of the car. Sometimes he'd add a painful pinch to her side or squeeze her arm until she was near tears. But she'd known the drill. *Smile, be polite, and don't cause any trouble, or else . . .*

She remembered walking *into the offices with him, and Barbara, the bright-eyed, brunette receptionist, would greet her excitedly and offer her candy, but of course she wasn't allowed to accept it. No sweets for trouble-makers.* She remembered wanting those treats so badly, it had hurt to say *No, thank you. I just had breakfast and I'm full,* even though she usually hadn't eaten anything.

She swallowed the bile rising in her throat at the thought of facing him. She'd nearly thrown up when she'd seen the bespectacled monster arrive in his shiny sedan an hour ago, wearing an expensive suit and carrying a black briefcase. He was heavier now, his face wrinkled and jowly, but there was no mistaking Stanley Weatherby for anyone else. He reminded her of a wolf disguised as a fluffy pet rather than the vicious predator he was. Her mind screamed for her to drive back to the Cape, but she wasn't going to let him control one more minute of her life.

She'd had plenty of time to think on the long drive from the Cape, and she'd realized that Brant had known what she'd needed all along. She'd thought she'd had enough closure, but she'd only buried the hurt, turning herself into a secret keeper. Those secrets were cancerous, eating away at her, chipping away at her confidence as evilly as her father had.

She was *done*.

She was getting closure *today*, even if it killed her.

One chance. That was all she had to get this right, to say the things she needed to say. For the first time in her life, she *wanted* an audience, which meant waiting for the parking lot to fill up. She'd checked out the marked parking spaces before selecting her own and had watched his partners arrive minutes after her father had. Now the lot was nearly full.

She pocketed her driver's license, in case they didn't believe she was his daughter, and locked her wallet in the glove compartment. When she stepped from the car, she was light-headed from fear, but she forced herself to push through it. She pulled the bottom of her white tank top down over her hips and filled her lungs with the brisk morning air as she crossed the parking lot.

She entered the building, and it smelled the same as it had all those years ago, like overblown egos and dirty money, bringing a rush of anxiety. She fisted her hands, and as she stepped into the elevator, *Step into the fire* ran through her mind like a mantra. She couldn't quell the nausea as the floors ticked by. Her arm snaked across her stomach, and she rested her other elbow on her wrist. When the doors opened directly into the law offices of Wilson, Katz, Burger, and Weatherby, it took everything she had to step out of the elevator.

The receptionist looked up and said, "Good morning, welcome to Wilson, Katz, Burger, and Weatherby."

Her bright eyes hit Cait like a slap in the face, throwing her back in time. She stood frozen in place, her eyes darting to the nameplate on the desk—BARBARA WILCOX—as two men in suits walked through the lobby talking loudly. She felt like the walls were closing in and dragged air into her lungs.

"Can I help you?" Barbara asked.

Breathe. Breathe. "Yes. I'm here to see . . ." In a split second, she knew what she had to do. "I'm here to see my father, Stanley Weatherby."

Barbara's brows knitted, and then all at once, her eyes bloomed wide, and she pushed to her feet. "*Catherine?* Is it really you?"

"Yes. *Cait.* I'm *Cait.*"

Barbara hurried around the desk, her eyes damp, and hugged her. "Oh my goodness. *Look* at you. Your father searched high and low for you. We thought . . . Oh, honey, we thought the worst. Does he know you're alive?"

Her affection caused Cait's chest to constrict. Struggling to keep tears at bay, she couldn't do more than shrug.

"He'll be overjoyed to see you. Let me take you back to the conference room, where he's meeting with the partners and associates."

She ushered Cait through the offices to the glass-walled conference room. Every seat around the large conference table was taken by men and women dressed to the nines and looking at her father. Years of pent-up anger obliterated the softer emotions Barbara had stirred.

"I'll pull him out so you have privacy," Barbara offered.

"*No*" flew from Cait's lips. "Privacy is the last thing I want." She threw open the door and strode into the room.

All eyes turned to look at Cait, but hers were locked on the monster sitting at the head of the table. The hair on the back of her neck prickled, and her stomach twisted into knots.

"Barbara, what is this?" her father asked with disgust.

"*This* is your daughter," Cait said loud and firm, closing the distance between them. She had no idea where the confidence came from, but she held his ghastly stare. "You remember your daughter, don't you? The one you adopted and were supposed to care for. The one you were supposed to love and feed breakfast, lunch, and dinner. The one you locked in a room without meals." Her voice escalated, and gasps sounded from around the table as she stalked closer, her every word freeing her from his shackles. "The daughter you belittled and hurt. The daughter you told wasn't worth the air she breathed." She was vaguely aware of the people sitting near him moving their chairs farther away.

"Barbara, call security," he demanded.

Cait's eyes never wavered from his. "Yes, Barbara, *please* call security, because this man is a heinous monster who should have been arrested years ago. He's a coward and a thief who stole the memories of my mother. *You* moved me away from my friends at four years old after my mother died and refused to let me speak of her." She lowered her voice, mimicking his. *"She never loved you, you little shit. She hated the very sight of you."*

"That's *enough*," he said, rising to his feet.

Cait straightened her spine and squared her shoulders, stepping closer and staring him down. He was once terrifying, but now she saw a weak old man, a coward. Lowering her voice again, she said, *"Sit down. Troublemakers don't get to move."* She leaned closer, and he sank into his chair. "Remember those words? You ingrained them into my head on a daily basis."

"Enough," he said shakily.

"You're right. I've had *enough*. Enough living in fear. Enough being afraid to love. Enough living in the shadows of the hell you put me through."

Murmurs rose around them, and two of the men moved closer to Cait. Panic gripped her, but they stood *with* her, arms crossed, glowering at her father.

"There's no proof!" her father said anxiously. "It's her word against mine, and look at her, with all those tattoos. She's probably a drug user, strung out on dope."

Cait scoffed. "That would be convenient, wouldn't it? Let's talk about my ink, because you taught me almost *all* of the lessons that are on my body." She thrust her arm out, showing him the spiderweb. "You taught me that men spin beautiful webs for all to see, but in private, those webs bound me to your torture." She pointed to the building on her biceps that looked like their old shed in the backyard. "How many nights was I locked in that shed when I was eight?"

More gasps sounded.

"*Three*, because I had wasted three minutes of your time on the way home. When I was nine, it was eight, because I'd taken eight minutes too long in the shower." She lifted her shirt to her ribs, revealing a girl looking in a shattered mirror. "Remember this lesson? You picked me up off my feet and slammed my back against the hall mirror because I had tripped going down the stairs and cried while you were on the phone. I had cuts on my back for days. You had to take that whole week off work because you couldn't leave me with your parents. They'd ask questions."

"*Jesus*," someone said, and other sounds of shock filled the room.

Her father swallowed hard. "She's . . . she's lying!"

"I have the scars to prove it. I have the scars to prove *all* of it. Some of them you can see, but most of them aren't visible to the naked eye. Those are the ones that cut the deepest. You tried to break me, and Lord knows you almost won. But I'm not made of the same weak, pathetic fabric that you are. You taught me that people are evil and can't be trusted. Now I know better." She felt the puppetry strings breaking away with every word she said, spurring her on. "*You're* evil and *you* can't be trusted. But you're not a person. You're a monster of the worst kind. And you're right that I can't prove a damn thing in the courts." She leaned closer, and he leaned back. "But I know the truth, and you know the truth." She stood tall again, eyes trained on him. "And now every person in this room knows the monster behind the facade."

The other men and women in the room gathered around Cait, staring with disgust at her father.

Her father's eyes caught on her necklace.

"That's right—it was hers." She let that sink in. "If you *ever* come near me, I will have you arrested, and then I will go to every media outlet on the East Coast and tell them exactly what an abusive predator looks like."

She turned to leave and saw hordes of people watching them from the other side of the glass wall. A flash of embarrassment hit, and she started to lower her eyes, but she caught herself and lifted her chin. Empowered by her own courage, she allowed her smile—*my gorgeous, sometimes-bashful, sometimes-sassy smile*—to appear as she walked out of the office with Barbara and a few others calling out to her. *Are you okay? Do you want to call the police? Should we call someone for you?*

They believed her. That was everything.

Cait reassured them that she'd be fine and stepped into the elevator. As the doors closed, she knew she'd finally broken free, leaving the shackles of her painful past behind.

CHAPTER TWENTY-FIVE

"BABE, IT'S ME again. Sorry to leave so many messages, but I'm getting worried." Brant paced the hall outside the equipment supply company, leaving Cait another voicemail. "Listen, I'm sorry if I said something that upset you last night, but please just let me know you're okay. I'm heading into a meeting with the accountants, but I'll keep my phone on. I love you."

Brant ended the call. He knew Cait was always slammed at the tattoo shop, but he'd had an uneasy feeling since last night. On top of his worries, he'd already had a hell of a day. He'd left Scrappy with his grandmother and had been on a dead run between equipment inspections, handling unexpected issues with a sea crane that took hours to rectify, and now the meeting with the accountants was about to start.

He pocketed his phone as his father poked his head out of the office. "The meeting is starting, son. Did you reach her?"

"No. I left another message," he said as he headed inside.

"I'm sure she's just busy. Let's get this meeting over with."

There was nothing worse than waiting for a text and trying to focus on balance sheets and financial reports. Brant was sure he was missing half of what was said, but nobody was cursing, and he took that as a good sign. He checked his phone again, gritting his teeth at the blank screen.

It was nearly three o'clock when the meeting ended, and Brant was riddled with worry. He texted Tank on his way out of the meeting—he just needed to know she was okay.

"Did you finally hear from Cait?" his grandfather asked as they stepped outside.

"No. I'm messaging Tank and asking him to have her call me when she's done with her clients."

His father put a hand on his shoulder. "And you're pretty sure you didn't say anything she could have taken wrong last night? I told you women and men don't always speak the same language."

Brant clutched his phone. "I don't know, Dad, but we talk about everything. We don't ignore problems. It's not like her not to at least respond with a quick text between clients." His phone vibrated with a response from Tank, and as he read it, the pit of his stomach sank.

"What is it?" his father asked.

"Tank said she called him this morning and said she needed the day off. I'm calling Abby." Worry swamped him as he made the call.

"Hi, Br—"

"Abby, have you heard from Cait?"

"*No.* I've been trying to reach her since last night, and Dee said she tried her at lunchtime. She hasn't returned any of our calls or texts. Have you heard from her?"

"No. She told Tank she needed the day off. I'm heading over to the Cape. I'll touch base when I know something."

"Do you think she's out hiking? She does that when she's upset, and she was upset yesterday. She was fine by the time I left last night, but maybe she's walking off her feelings?"

"Maybe. I'll let you know what I find out." He ended the call, consumed with worry. "Abby hasn't heard from her. I'm sorry, but I've got to get over to the Cape and make sure Cait's okay."

"*Go*," his grandfather urged. "We can take care of things here." His last few words were drowned out by the sound of static and a female voice blasting through a loudspeaker.

"*Excuse me . . . Hello?*" Then softer: "Is this loud enough? Can they hear me?"

"That's Cait!" Brant spun around, spotting a water taxi in the harbor. He sprinted toward the docks.

"Attention, Silver Island residents!" Cait's voice rang out. "My name is Cait Weatherby, and I *love* Brant Remington!"

Brant bolted down the last dock, unable to believe his ears, as Cait came into view standing in the water taxi speaking into a megaphone.

"That's right, folks," she announced as people started popping up on the decks of their boats and looking over from the other docks. "I want everyone to know that I am madly and passionately in love with the kindest, most loving and patient blue-eyed dimpled-cheeked man on the planet!"

"I love you, Caity!" Brant hollered, bursting with excitement as her eyes caught on him.

"I love you, Brant! I did it! I . . . *I'm coming!*" She climbed up on the side of the boat and jumped into the water.

"*Oh shit!*" Brant dove in, swimming as fast as he could toward her—and *she* was swimming, too!

Then she was in his arms, smiling and kicking her feet, and they were kissing, and sharing *I love you*s as cheers and applause rang out around them.

"I did it! I confronted my father and everyone believed me!" Tears streaked her cheeks. "They *believed* me, Brant!"

His chest constricted. "You went to *see* him? Alone?"

"I had to. You were right. I needed closure, and he needed to pay for all he'd done. I had to leap! And I'm free! *We're* free!"

"*God*, baby. I love you." He showered her with kisses. "I was really worried. You're okay? He didn't try to hurt you?"

She shook her head. "He *can't* hurt me anymore, and I'm done living in the shadows of that pain and shame and . . . Oh, Brant! I *love* you, and I want to grab hold of the life we're building with both hands and never let go!"

Their mouths came together, and more shouts and cheers rang out. They sank beneath the surface, and he kicked his feet, propelling them back up. They laughed and kissed as they made their way toward the dock.

"I'm not sure I can swim that far," Cait said with an apologetic look. "I haven't slept since Saturday night."

"Don't worry, angel. I've got you. I've *always* got you."

CHAPTER TWENTY-SIX

SEPTEMBER SNUCK IN with cool, sunny days, brisk romantic nights, and views of a future that was clearer and brighter than Cait could have ever imagined with the man she loved wholly and completely. She hadn't just leapt with her heart after breaking away from her past. She'd jumped into a new life with both feet and hit the ground running.

And she'd never looked back.

She stood on the sidewalk, surrounded by the sugary aroma of the Sweet Barista and the comforting scent of the sea, watching Brant take down the DAILY NEWS sign from what was soon to be her new tattoo and piercing shop, Anchor and Tail. Brant smiled down at her, handsome as could be in tan shorts and a forest-green Henley, his thick hair poking out from beneath his baseball cap. It was hard to believe she'd ever been scared of walking into his safe, loving arms. He was the reason she was free from her past. He had given her the courage to stand up to her father, to move to the island, and to ease out of working at Wicked Ink so she could take out the lease on the newsstand. He'd taught her the meaning of unconditional love, and she was truly, madly, *deeply* in love with him.

She gave Scrappy a treat, thinking about how much her life had changed since she'd confronted her father last month. One of her father's business partners had contacted her the following week to let her know they'd fired the monster, and they'd offered to pay for her legal expenses if she chose to pursue charges. She'd declined because she knew the harrowing legal battle she'd face had a slim chance of a reasonable outcome, and more importantly, because she was *done* with the past and busy living her beautiful present.

Between their family and friends at the Cape and on the island, they'd had more help than they'd needed moving Cait into Brant's cottage. *Into our cottage.* She sighed inwardly. Life was so much sweeter starting and ending each day in the arms of the man she adored. Over the last month they'd enjoyed another movie night at the beach and several dinners and bonfires with friends and family. They'd gone to the Cape when Tank and Leah's son, Leo, was born, and had even gone a few times since to hang out with the Wickeds and her other friends. Brant had grown to love them as much as she did, and ever since he'd met Tank and Leah's children, he'd been gathering goodies to give them the next time they visited. But the best part of their new life together was when it was just the two of them and their spoiled little dog. Cait no longer walked into other people's homes and got jealous of the love they shared. Their life together was *built* on love, and their home radiated with it.

The icing on her new-life cake was the mural for the town hall, which had been approved, complete with the drawings of Ava watching Olivier paint at the Bistro and Brant's family announcing movie night from his grandfather's truck. Cait was set to begin working on it in November, and that made her feel even more like she belonged there, with the community that had embraced her birth mother.

"It's almost ready, angel," Brant said, drawing her back to the moment. He stood on the ladder holding the old sign.

He'd made her a gorgeous wooden sign for her shop, on which she'd painted ANCHOR AND TAIL TATTOOS AND PIERCINGS with the logo of an anchor with a mermaid tail wrapped around it, just like her and Brant's matching tattoos. Cait's was on the underside of her right wrist, and

Brant's was wherever he chose each time the Sharpie ink wore off. He was due for a new one soon.

She thought about her old tattoos, which she no longer saw as warnings but rather as markings on her journey to this wonderful life she'd found. Everyone followed their own path, and that happened to be hers. Luckily, she'd found something better than a pot of gold at the end. Or rather, at the juncture of her past and her new beginning, because she and Brant had a long, loving life ahead of them.

He flashed a sexy smile, stirring the butterflies she'd grown to treasure. She was learning that love was ever-growing, and without the weight of her past bearing down on her, it came as naturally as breathing.

"You keep looking at me like that, and we're going to end up naked in this shop instead of fixing it up." Brant winked.

They'd made love just that morning, and her body threw a little party at the thought of doing it again. She took a long, lustful look at him as he climbed down the ladder. She watched him set down the old sign and stalk toward her like a powerful lion eyeing its lioness. There was no use trying to hide her desire. His all-seeing eyes continued to notice more of her than anyone else ever had.

"You're playing a dangerous game, Weatherby." He gathered her in his arms, taking her in a long, toe-curling kiss. "Any idea where you want to hang your sign?"

"What sign?" She tugged him into a deliciously slow, scorching-hot kiss.

"Get a room." Grant's deep voice cut through their reverie.

Scrappy barked as their lips parted on a laugh, and Cait was shocked to see not only Grant, Jules, Abby, and Aiden climbing out of their vehicles armed with paintbrushes and toolboxes, but also Tank, Gunner, and Gia exiting theirs. "What are you all doing here?" she asked excitedly, and looked at Brant for an answer, but he just blew her a kiss.

"Helping!" Abby exclaimed, looking cute in cutoffs and a tank top. "After all the work you did at the Bistro, did you really think we wouldn't be here to help?"

Cait hugged her. "Thank you, but—"

"No *buts*," Aiden said as he set down a toolbox.

"Family comes first." Tank pulled Cait into a tight embrace. "Leah, Baz, and Evie wanted to be here, but Rosie wasn't feeling well, and Baz had an emergency at the vet office."

"That's okay. I can't believe you guys are here! I'm sure you have better ways to spend a day off."

"What's better than checking out hot island chicks?" Gunner said.

"Checking out hot island guys," Gia said, high-fiving Gunner.

Cait filled to the hilt with gratitude. "Seriously, Grant, Jules, I know how busy you are. Thanks for coming out."

"That's what friends are for," Grant said as he began unloading long pieces of wood from the back of his truck.

Jules set down a handful of paintbrushes and said, "Besides, with all the smooching you and Brant are doing, you'd never finish without our help."

"Hear that, Caity?" Brant pulled her into his arms again. "Sounds like an invitation for us to make out while they do the work." He dipped Cait over his arm and kissed her breathless.

"I've gotta get me an island boy." Gia sidled up to Grant as he laid a piece of wood on the ground. "Hey there, sugar. I bet you can wield a hammer."

"Hey!" Jules stomped her petite self over to Gia, her water-fountain ponytail swinging with every angry step. She was several inches shorter than Gia and quite the sight in her oversized sweatshirt and shorts as she got as close to *right* in Gia's face as she could and fumed, "That beefcake is *my* fiancé!"

"Sorry, hon." Gia held up her hands, looking like a vixen next to adorable Jules with cherry-red lipstick, a skintight low-cut shirt, and curve-hugging jeans. "I saw a hottie, and I acted on it. My bad. *Wait a second.* Water-fountain hairdo, feisty personality. You must be Jules, which means the hammer wielder is Grant. *Shit.* I'm really sorry."

"A little late, don't you think?" Cait shook her head. "Sorry, Jules." She introduced the friends who didn't know each other, filling with disbelief as Deirdra's car came down the hill. "Brant, how'd you get Dee to come?"

"I didn't." He draped his arm around her as Deirdra climbed out of her car. "She told me she had to work."

Gunner whistled. "*Hello*, gorgeous."

"Keep it in your pants, playboy." Deirdra strutted across the street in an expensive-looking blouse, skinny jeans, and high heels, hair and makeup perfectly done. "Why is everyone staring at me?"

"We just can't believe you're here!" Cait hugged her.

Deirdra lifted her brows. "Is it so weird that I came to help my sister?"

"Yes," Abby and Cait said in unison.

"You sure dressed up for a day of painting and hammering," Jules said.

"Oh no. Dee, did you finally kill your boss? Are you on the run?" Cait teased. "Because I spent the bail money on my lease. We probably need Tessa to fly you to Mexico or something."

Everyone laughed.

"Unfortunately, no," Deirdra said. "But I did take a two-month hiatus from work so I *wouldn't* kill him."

Abby's and Cait's jaws dropped.

"You took *that much* time off work?" Abby touched Deirdra's forehead, and Deirdra slapped her hand away. "Sorry! I was checking to see if you were sick."

"Just sick and tired of being told what to do," Deirdra snapped.

"Damn. I've got dibs on this firecracker tonight," Gunner said with a wink.

Deirdra scoffed. "Dream on, playboy. Do lines like that *ever* work for you?"

"I don't usually need lines." He lifted his arms and flexed, showing off his tatted, muscular physique.

Brant pulled Cait into his arms and whispered, "Remind you of someone?"

She laughed. "He's cockier than Wells and not nearly as hot as you. I can't believe you asked everyone to come help." She should be used to his surprises by now, considering that right after she'd signed the lease, he'd surprised her by having the plumber put in the sink. But she had a feeling that with Brant, she was in for a lifetime of surprises.

"I wish I could take credit, but I just mentioned we were doing it, and they offered. Jules coordinated times with a group text. My sisters and Ford wanted to come, but the team is diving today, and Tessa has flights. Face it, babe. You are loved by many." He kissed her and whispered, "But I love you the most."

"I love you, too. In fact, I love you *more*."

"Okay, lovebirds. Can we get started fixing this place up?" Deirdra said. "I've got to get off this island and back to civilization."

"You're not staying?" Abby asked.

Deirdra gave her a *get real* look.

"But she's here now," Cait said excitedly. "Before we get to work, I just want to say that I love you guys—*all* of you—and it means the world to me that you came out to help us fix this place up." In addition to newfound freedom, she'd taken hold of her emotions with both hands and run with them, and it felt fantastic to let her friends know exactly how she felt. She took Brant's hand and said, "Let's do this!"

They came up with a plan, then got to work. The sounds of power tools and laughter filled the air as they painted, built shelves, and installed countertops. Cait loved working alongside everyone from both of her worlds that she'd once thought should be kept separate and now blended together seamlessly. Brant stole kisses every chance he got and even snuck her into the powder room for a quick make-out session. But his parents stopped by with lunch, and Gail caught them when she had to use the bathroom. Cait had a feeling that wouldn't be the last time Gail caught them making out.

Hours later, Cait stood back and took it all in, still amazed that she was really opening her own shop. Several of the Bra Brigaders and some of her old clients had already scheduled appointments for tattoos, and she and Abby and the girls had brainstormed marketing ideas. They had flyers and ads ready to help spread the word once she opened the shop to customers. She was so excited, she couldn't stop smiling. And now the shop looked brand-new, with a fresh coat of paint and a stunning interior ready for the furniture she'd ordered. She listened to her friends and family laughing and giving one another a hard time as they put on the finishing touches. Brant was on the ladder again, hanging the new sign, while Aiden directed him to lift one side higher, then the other, and handed him a level. Jules was telling Gia about the holiday flotilla and trying to convince her to come to the island to see it. Tessa had come to help after work, and she was chatting with Deirdra and Abby about Abby's honeymoon as they cleaned the windows. Tank, Grant, and Gunner were deep in conversation about Grant's foundation. She'd forgotten that Gunner and Grant were both veterans and was glad they had something in common. She thought about the safe little bubble she'd lived in for too long and was thankful she'd had it when she'd needed it. But this life was so much better and included so many wonderful people, she felt gluttonous.

Scrappy barked, drawing her attention to Jagger coming down the sidewalk in his Baha hoodie and shorts, with his guitar strapped to his back and Dolly trotting happily beside him. He waved.

"Is it five already?" Cait asked. His shift started at five thirty.

"Just about." He let Dolly off her leash, and she and Scrappy went nose to nose, tails wagging. Their friends shouted hello to him, and

Cait introduced her friends from the Cape. "Wow, you really turned this place around. It looks great."

"Thanks," Cait said as Dolly ran past, making a beeline for Deirdra.

"Hey!" Deirdra snapped. She liked dogs, but for as laid-back as Dolly usually was, she got overly excited every time she saw Deirdra, and the first thing she did was put her snout in Deirdra's crotch. "Do you *mind?*" Deirdra turned away, but Dolly followed, going paws-up on her chest. "Dolly!" She tried to push the dog off, but Dolly tried to lick her face, causing everyone else to laugh and Scrappy to bark. "Come on, sweetie, *stop.*"

Abby held up her phone to take a picture.

Deirdra glowered, trying to dodge Dolly again. *"Jagger!"*

Jagger whistled and patted his leg, and Dolly trotted to his side, tongue hanging out, tail wagging excitedly. He put on her leash. "Sorry, Didi. She's just glad to see you. We all are."

"It's okay." Deirdra was smiling and brushing dirt from her clothes, but she narrowed her eyes and said, "But what did I tell you about calling me *Didi?* It sounds like a stripper."

Jagger cocked a grin. "Now, *there's* a visual."

Everyone cracked up, except Deirdra, who rolled her eyes.

"See y'all around." Jagger petted Dolly. "Come on, girl, time to go to work."

As he left, Brant climbed down the ladder and Cait reached for his hand. "Dolly is funny with Deirdra, isn't she?"

"Yeah. It's good to see Dee laugh. Look what I got for later." He held up a black Sharpie.

"We need to buy stock in Sharpie." She loved that he never let his tattoo disappear completely.

He put his arm around her, glancing at the ANCHOR AND TAIL sign. "What do you think, angel?"

She knew he was asking about all of the work they'd done, and the new sign, but as she looked at him with paint on his cheek, sawdust on his shirt, and her heart in his hands, all she could think about was that none of her new life would mean much without him by her side. "It's more wonderful than I ever imagined it could be."

"Then maybe it's time for you to start thinking about your next big dream."

That was so *him*, always thinking of her. "Look around us." Their friends chatted, checking their phones and grabbing drinks from the cooler Gail and Roddy had left. "I've been blessed many times over. It's *your* turn to dream. I know you always say you have everything you want, but there must be something that you dream about."

"There is one thing I can't stop thinking about, but I'm biding my time."

"Why? You of all people deserve to have all of your dreams come true. I think you should go for it."

"Are you sure?" He cocked a grin. "It's kind of a big one."

"I can't believe you've been holding out on me. I trust you with everything, and you can't tell me your dream?"

He drew in a deep breath and pulled the Sharpie from his pocket. "I trust you with my life. I just didn't want to rush you."

"To draw your *tattoo*?" She laughed. "I'm pretty sure I can do tha—"

Brant took her left hand in his and dropped to one knee, gazing up at her with a deep-dimpled smile.

"Caity, from the moment I saw you across the room at Rock Bottom, I was drawn to you as if we'd known each other in another life, and I knew then, just as I do now, that we're meant to brave this world together."

"Brant . . . ?" she said breathlessly.

"Baby, I love our life together, and I love you. I love the way you pour your heart into everything you do, especially me and Scrappy, and the way you look at me when you think I don't notice, and the way you're looking at me right now."

Tears welled in her eyes.

"I love your strength, Caity, and the way you get weak-kneed when we kiss. I love *you*, and I don't want to go a single day without seeing your sometimes-bashful, sometimes-sassy, *always*-beautiful smile and hearing your laughter, feeling your touch. I want it *all* with you, angel—little creative kids with your gorgeous eyes and—"

"Your dimples," she choked out through her tears.

He laughed. "Yeah. They'll mess up our cottage and probably climb into our bed at night and then pee in it."

She laughed, vaguely aware of everyone watching them.

"We'll teach them to swim in Mermaid Cove and announce duneside movies from their great-grandpa's truck."

That sounded perfect to her.

"I have a gorgeous ring that I designed and had made for you. It's hidden in my sock drawer, so I'll tell you about it." He gazed up at her, his voice thick with love. "The band has a row of white diamonds between two rows of rose gold that are twisted to look like rope, you know, because we like going out on the boat."

Tears streamed down her cheeks.

"There's a white-diamond infinity sign across the top intertwined with a rose-gold, heart-shaped rope and anchor, because our love is infinitely strong and will last forever. But for now, hopefully this will do." He drew a ring on her ring finger with the Sharpie, causing more tears to tumble down her cheeks and bringing murmurs from their friends.

"Caity, I want a lifetime of loving you so completely, our grandkids will make jokes about how we're always kissing and can't keep our hands off each other." He pushed to his feet, gazing deeply into her eyes. "Cait Weatherby, will you marry me and make my biggest dream come true?"

She looked at the beautiful man who had taught her to love and be loved, who had become her best friend and her lover and now wanted to become her husband. With a river of tears flowing down her cheeks, she said, "I have never wanted anything more than how much I want *forever* with you. Yes, Brant! Yes, I'll marry y—"

Her last word was silenced by the hard press of his lips as he lifted her off her feet and spun her around. Whoops, cheers, and Scrappy's high-pitched barks rang out, and Cait felt like the luckiest woman in the world. Who knew that by almost drowning, she'd find not only happiness but the truest, deepest love of all, right there on Silver Island, where she knew in her heart she was always meant to be.

A NOTE FROM MELISSA

Thank you for reading Cait and Brant's story. I hope you enjoyed their journey to their happily ever after, and meeting all of their friends. If this is your first Silver Harbor book, you might enjoy reading Abby and Aiden's love story, *Maybe We Will*. You can find a downloadable map of Silver Island, family trees, and series checklists for all of my books on the Reader Goodies page on my website (www.MelissaFoster.com/RG).

Each of Cait's and Brant's friends will have their own love stories, some of which are already written and can be found in my Love in Bloom big-family romance collection. Within the Love in Bloom world, you'll find several family series. If you'd like to read more about the wonderful cast of the Silver Island Steeles, Silvers, and Remingtons, you can find them in The Steeles at Silver Island series. If you're curious about Tank and his family and friends, please check out The Wickeds: Dark Knights at Bayside. And if you'd like to know more about Randi and Ford's expedition, pick up *Searching for Love*, a Braden & Montgomery novel featuring treasure hunter Zev Braden and chocolatier Carly Dylan. In *Searching for Love* you can get to know the beloved Bradens and spend time with Randi and Ford.

If you're a binge reader and prefer to start at the very beginning, the Love in Bloom big-family romance collection offers characters from all walks of life, from billionaires and cowboys to blue-collar workers, and begins with *Sisters in Love*, the first book in the Snow Sisters series.

Each of my books may be enjoyed as a stand-alone novel. Characters from each series make appearances in future books, so you never miss an engagement, wedding, or birth.

Be sure to sign up for my newsletter to keep up to date with my new releases and to receive an exclusive short story (www.MelissaFoster.com/News).

Happy reading!

Melissa Foster

ACKNOWLEDGMENTS

Unfortunately, abuse exists in too many households and often goes unnoticed by others. If you or anyone you know is suffering, I urge you to reach out to local authorities for help.

I am grateful to everyone who has shared their difficult stories with me over the years. However, any similarities to real-life individuals are merely a coincidence. I'm forever grateful for my assistants and friends, and a big thank-you goes out to Lisa Filipe for her laughter, her tears, and her incredible patience in reading the same lines five hundred times until they feel just right to me. Thank you for always having my back.

I am forever thankful for my wonderful editor Maria Gomez and the rest of the professional and talented Montlake team. My books would not shine without the editorial expertise of Kristen Weber and Penina Lopez and my capable proofreaders. Last, but never least, I am grateful to my four beautiful sons for their ongoing support and encouragement.

If you'd like to get a glimpse into my writing process and to chat with me, please join my fan club on Facebook, where I talk about our Love in Bloom stories as I write them. You never know when you'll end up in one of my books, as several members of my fan club have already discovered. I hope to see you there (www.Facebook.com/groups/MelissaFosterFans).

To keep up with sales and events, please follow me on Amazon and on my Facebook author page (www.Facebook.com/MelissaFosterAuthor).

ABOUT THE AUTHOR

Photo © 2013 Melanie Anderson

Melissa Foster is a *New York Times* and *USA Today* bestselling and award-winning author of nearly one hundred books, including the Sugar Lake series, The Steeles at Silver Island series, and the Harmony Pointe series. Her novels have been recommended by *USA Today*'s book blog, *Hagerstown* magazine, the *Patriot*, and others. She has also painted and donated several murals to the Hospital for Sick Children in Washington, DC. She enjoys discussing her books with book clubs and reader groups, and she welcomes an invitation to your event. Visit Melissa at www.melissafoster.com.